THE
APOCALYPSE READER

T0382433

THE
APOCALYPSE
READER

EDITED BY JUSTIN TAYLOR

Thunder's Mouth Press | New York

THE APOCALYPSE READER

Compilation and introduction copyright © 2007 by Justin Taylor

Published by
Thunder's Mouth Press
An Imprint of Avalon Publishing Group, Inc.
245 West 17th Street, 11th Floor
New York, NY 10011

AVALON

First printing, June 2007

Pages 316–18 constitute an extension of this copyright page.

Library of Congress Cataloging-in-Publication Data is available.

ISBN-13: 978-1-56025-959-6
ISBN-10: 1-56025-959-0

Book design by Pauline Neuwirth, Neuwirth & Associates, Inc.

Distributed by Publishers Group West

For my parents, who read to me

CONTENTS

ACKNOWLEDGMENTS

THANKS, AND IN some cases absolutely bottomless gratitude, are due
to the following individuals and institutions, whose various efforts on my
behalf have included, but are in no way limited to: personal, professional,
and material support; extreme love, hot coffee, relentless faith, honest
criticism, inexhaustible patience, home-cooked meals, and unsurpassed
bartending.

Grateful acknowledgment is made to:

All the contributors to this volume;

Action Books, Alt.Coffee, Broadview Press, Eldritchpress.org, The
Graduate Writing Program at The New School, The Hungarian Pas-
try Shop;

Joshua Bilmes, Carl Bromley, Jill Ciment, Julia Cohen, Michael
Cohn, Shanna Compton, Dan Fowlkes, Michael Galchinsky, David
Gates, Andrew & Caryn Goldner, Gavin J. Grant, Dien Huynh,
Amy McDaniel, Richard Nash, John Oakes, Amanda Peters, Robert
Polito, Ryan Reed, Jennifer Rumberger, Shya Scanlon, Jeremy
Schmall, Michael Silverblatt, Tom Steele, Eva Talmadge, Frederic
Tuten, Lukas Volger.

INTRODUCTION

YOU HOLD IN your hand thirty-four short stories about the Apocalypse.

People have been telling me this is an especially timely book, but the fact is that, historically, every single generation has imagined itself uniquely in crisis and fantasized that theirs will be the one that witnesses The End. The twentieth century was unique mostly in that it marked the moment when humanity became capable of bringing Apocalypse upon itself, but even the novelty (if not the menace) of that prospect has long since worn off. If this is a timely book, I think the reason is that the topic is perennially timely. It is also, as Frank Kermode puts it in *The Sense of an Ending*, "infallibly interesting."

It's worth pointing out that the word Apocalypse comes from the Greek, and literally means "a revelation" or "an unveiling." It can be used to describe cataclysmic changes of any sort. Revolution, for example, or social upheaval. The American Desegregation movement was Apocalyptic in that its success necessitated the destruction of a certain way of life. (That we're better off without it is not the point.) There are micro-Apocalypses that mark moments in our lives: childhood's end, a relationship's sudden implosion, Death.

There are no excerpts in this book. Even ostensibly "self-contained" excerpts seem unfulfilling to me, and frankly, I don't like them. I have limited this book's scope exclusively to the short story, the ultimate in "self-contained" literature, that eternally embattled form that writers are constantly told "does not sell" or "has outlived its usefulness" or other nonsense. This anthology is a celebration of the short story's inexhaustible vitality, as well as an in-depth (though certainly not exhaustive) survey of its variety.

The forms these stories take, the styles they adopt or invent, the concerns they have, the places and positions and eras their writers come from, and the boundaries they push are as varied as the types of Apocalypse they engage. There are funny stories and deeply touching stories; gory ones and heady ones; stories that focus on an individual or a small group and stories that take on (or take down) the whole world; there are a few very long stories and more than a few very short (or "flash" or "short-short") stories; there are "realistic" and "experimental" stories; overtly and implicitly political stories; utterly apolitical stories; stories that could be classified as belonging to this or that genre (New Wave Fabulist, Horror, Satire, etc.); and stories that defy any attempt at classification. Some are the work of best-selling authors or cult favorites, and others are by people I can guarantee you've never heard of. At least one story has been published elsewhere as a poem.

Each story addresses both of the book's themes in a unique and exciting way, but more than that, each one contains that fundamental, irreducible, *something* that is indescribable, yet always discernable, in great writing. In short, I picked stories that I love and that I want to share with the world.

There are brand-new stories by Shelley Jackson, Matthew Derby, and several others; some (such as Gary Lutz and Deb Olin Unferth's collaboration) were written especially for this book. There are classic stories by Nathaniel Hawthorne, Edgar Allan Poe, H. G. Wells and H. P. Lovecraft. There are hand-picked favorites by the likes of Neil Gaiman, Rick Moody, and Michael Moorcock; a rare Joyce Carol Oates story, published years ago in Ontario Review but never before collected; Terese Svoboda's O. Henry Prize–winning "'80s Lilies"; and plenty of surprising, exciting, disturbing stories from authors you know, or only thought you knew, or will be thrilled to discover (Steve Aylett).

Dennis Cooper's "The Ash Gray Proclamation" pushes his minimalist aesthetics to a radical new level in order to capture and satirize the claustrophobic, reactionary, Apocalyptic atmosphere of post-9/11 America. More than just extremely provocative, it is extremely important, and I am honored—ecstatic, in fact—to have put this story into a book for the very first time.

Now let me direct your attention to those people whose obscurity I earlier guaranteed. Be the first one on your block to know about them, because today's underground sensation is tomorrow's #1 hit. You heard it here first; now tell your friends.

Robert Bradley sent the only unsolicited submission that made the final cut (it also beat out several I had asked for). His contribution, "Square of the Sun," is feisty and unpredictable, with a real mean streak—the kind of story that slaps your face and laughs at you for crying, but still offers to finish you off before it goes to sleep.

Adam Nemett's "The Last Man" is funny, but not ha-ha funny, unless it's a hushed, nervous giggle. Jeff Goldberg's "These Zombies Are Not a Metaphor," on the other hand, *is* ha-ha funny, so go ahead and laugh loudly.

If this book were a baseball team, Jared Hohl's "Fraise, Menthe, et Poivre 1978" would be batting cleanup.

Elliott David's "So We Are Very Concerned" is deliciously gruesome, and counterpoints the neo-Beckettian agoraphobia of Tao Lin's "i am 'i don't know what i am' and you are afraid of me and so am i." These two hypercontemporary short-shorts sandwich Grace Aguilar's "The Escape—A Tale of 1755," the longest story in the book by a good thousand words. Aguilar was a British Jew whose very decision to take up the pen defied the conventions of her day; her work broke new ground in the history of female Jewish self-representation. Her work has been largely unavailable in a nonacademic context for roughly a century. Steeped in the real history of the Spanish Inquisition, from which her parents fled, and the lives of the crypto-Jews, who openly converted to Christianity but maintained their true faith in secret, "The Escape" is probably the most difficult story in this book to get through. First published in 1844, the same year as Hawthorne's "Earth's Holocaust," it is even more heavy-handed than that story when it comes to moralizing and pedantry, but it is absolutely worth putting yourself through, or else it wouldn't be here, so I hope that you will exert the extra effort. If you do, there's a kickass Apocalypse in it for you.

A word on sequencing: I eschewed obvious and convenient organizing principles like alphabetization or chronology, and went for what *felt right*. It's the logic of the mix-tape or the Grateful Dead bootleg, and as far as I'm concerned all tracks segue. You, however, are encouraged to hunt and peck, pick and choose, see what suits you, what repels and what draws you back. Thank you for reading our book. Now that we have reached the end of the beginning, we are ready to begin the End.

—JUSTIN TAYLOR
Halloween, 2006
Bushwick, Brooklyn, New York

THE
APOCALYPSE READER

NYARLATHOTEP

H. P. Lovecraft

NYARLATHOTEP . . . THE CRAWLING CHAOS . . . I am the last . . . I will tell the audient void. . . .

I do not recall distinctly when it began, but it was months ago. The general tension was horrible. To a season of political and social upheaval was added a strange and brooding apprehension of hideous physical danger; a danger widespread and all-embracing, such a danger as may be imagined only in the most terrible phantasms of the night. I recall that the people went about with pale and worried faces, and whispered warnings and prophecies which no one dared consciously repeat or acknowledge to himself that he had heard. A sense of monstrous guilt was upon the land, and out of the abysses between the stars swept chill currents that made men shiver in dark and lonely places. There was a daemoniac alteration in the sequence of the seasons—the autumn heat lingered fearsomely, and everyone felt that the world and perhaps the universe had passed from the control of known gods or forces to that of gods or forces which were unknown.

And it was then that Nyarlathotep came out of Egypt. Who he was, none could tell, but he was of the old native blood and looked like a Pharaoh. The fellahin knelt when they saw him, yet could not say why. He said he had risen up out of the blackness of twenty-seven centuries, and that he had heard messages from places not on this planet. Into the lands of civilisation came Nyarlathotep, swarthy, slender, and sinister, always buying strange instruments of glass and metal and combining them into instruments yet stranger. He spoke much of the sciences—of electricity and psychology—and gave exhibitions of power which sent his spectators away speechless, yet which swelled his fame to exceeding magnitude. Men advised one another to see Nyarlathotep, and shuddered. And where Nyarlathotep went, rest vanished; for the small hours were rent with the screams of nightmare. Never before had the dreams of nightmare been such a public problem; now the wise men almost wished they could forbid sleep in the small hours, that the shrieks of cities might less horribly disturb the pale, pitying moon as it glimmered on green waters gliding under bridges, and old steeples crumbling against a sickly sky.

I remember when Nyarlathotep came to my city—the great, the old, the terrible city of unnumbered crimes. My friend had told me of him, and of the impelling fascination and allurement of his revelations, and I burned with eagerness to explore his uttermost mysteries. My friend said they were horrible and impressive beyond my most fevered imaginings; that what was thrown on a screen in the darkened room prophesied things none but Nyarlathotep dared prophesy, and that in the sputter of his sparks there was taken from men that which had never been taken before yet which shewed only in the eyes. And I heard it hinted abroad that those who knew Nyarlathotep looked on sights which others saw not.

It was in the hot autumn that I went through the night with the restless crowds to see Nyarlathotep; through the stifling night and up the endless stairs into the choking room. And shadowed on a screen, I saw hooded forms amidst ruins, and yellow evil faces peering from behind fallen monuments. And I saw the world battling against blackness; against the waves of destruction from ultimate space; whirling, churning; struggling around the dimming, cooling sun. Then the sparks played amazingly around the heads of the spectators, and hair stood up on end whilst shadows more grotesque than I can tell came out and squatted on the heads. And when I, who was colder and more scientific than the rest, mumbled a trembling protest about "imposture" and "static electricity," Nyarlathotep drave us all out, down the dizzy stairs into the damp, hot, deserted midnight streets. I screamed aloud that I was *not* afraid; that I never could be afraid; and others screamed with me for solace. We sware to one another that the city *was* exactly the same, and still alive; and when the electric lights began to fade we cursed the company over and over again, and laughed at the queer faces we made.

I believe we felt something coming down from the greenish moon, for when we began to depend on its light we drifted into curious involuntary formations and seemed to know our destinations though we dared not think of them. Once we looked at the pavement and found the blocks loose and displaced by grass, with scarce a line of rusted metal to shew where the tramways had run. And again we saw a tram-car, lone, windowless, dilapidated, and almost on its side. When we gazed around the horizon, we could not find the third tower by the river, and noticed that the silhouette of the second tower was ragged at the top. Then we split up into narrow columns, each of which seemed drawn in a different direction. One disappeared in a narrow alley to the left, leaving only the echo of a shocking moan. Another filed down a weed-choked subway entrance, howling with a laughter that was mad. My own column was sucked toward the open country, and presently felt a chill which was not of the hot autumn; for as we stalked out on the dark moor, we beheld around us the hellish moon-glitter of evil snows. Trackless, inexplicable snows, swept asunder in one direction only, where lay a gulf all the blacker for its glittering walls. The column seemed very thin indeed as it plodded dreamily into the gulf. I lingered behind, for the black rift in the green-litten snow was frightful, and I thought I had heard the reverberations of a disquieting wail as my companions vanished; but my power to linger was slight. As it beckoned by those who had gone before, I half floated between the titanic snowdrifts, quivering and afraid, into the sightless vortex of the unimaginable.

Screamingly sentient, dumbly delirious, only the gods that were can tell. A sickened, sensitive shadow writhing in hands that are not hands, and whirled blindly past ghastly midnights of rotting creation, corpses of dead worlds with sores that were cities, charnel winds that brush the pallid stars and make them flicker low. Beyond the worlds vague ghosts of monstrous things; half-seen columns of unsanctified temples that rest on nameless rocks beneath space and reach up to dizzy vacua above the spheres of light and darkness. And through this revolting graveyard of the universe the muffled, maddening beating of drums, and thin, monstrous whine of blasphemous flutes from inconceivable, unlighted chambers beyond Time; the detestable pounding and piping whereunto dance slowly, awkwardly, and absurdly the gigantic, tenebrous ultimate gods— the blind, voiceless, mindless gargoyles whose soul is Nyarlathotep.

THE APOCALYPSE COMMENTARY
OF BOB PAISNER
Rick Moody

INTRODUCTION:
John Composing on Patmos

I USE THE K.J., or Authorized Version, where the *thees* are *thees* and the *thous* are *thous*. Ever since I was a kid I used it, ever since the sixties, ever since St. Luke's Parish in Manchester, N.H. You don't get the same kind of line in the Revised Standard Version. You don't find "I am Alpha and Omega, the beginning and the ending, saith the Lord, which is, and which was, and which is to come, the Almighty" (1:8), with its Elizabethan implications of damnation and immortality. Which is pretty much how Revelation begins.

Okay, so it was the first century after Christ's martyrdom at Calvary. His followers were suffering. They were spurned, they were flogged, they were flayed, crucified upside down, torn apart by horses, left out to be fed upon by vultures. You name it. Every conceivable torture was visited upon them. Meanwhile, in the midst of this persecution, St. John the Divine goes off to Patmos,[1] an island off the coast of Greece, and begins—in this intense

---

1. For this stuff about John on Patmos and other information on the book of Revelation and all its commentators, I'm really indebted to David Burr, *Olivi's Peaceable Kingdom: A Reading of the Apocalypse Commentary* (Philadelphia: Univ. of Pennsylvania Press, 1974).

rage—to write a screed on which his reputation rests among fundamental-ists. It's about the future of the church, about the coming house-cleaning among the *chosen*. This is the screed called Revelation. It's his prophecy. A prophecy that contains things "which must shortly come to pass" (1:1). "He which testifieth these things saith, Surely I come quickly" (22:20).

Here's what I imagine: John living a life of complete poverty, confined to a monastic cell with only charcoal and parchment to divert him, unfed, unattended, in a building as scorched as the sands of the Middle East. Or maybe he was even one of those cave-dwelling monks. Unwashed, solitary, in retirement from light. In constant fear of the authorities. Panicked at the thought of his own martyrdom. In cycles, John wept, shouted oaths, prayed joyously. He had visions. Because of migraines. I'd say John had a migrainous personality. That's my guess. Anyhow, in the midst of John's rage, in the midst of his abandonment, an angel came to him and said to take up his pen.

MYSELF.
Bob Paisner, in Chapin House

JOHN SAW A future marked by persecutors, false gods, Antichrists, Gog and Magog, plagues, floods, earthquakes. He saw it this way because this was how he felt about the church in the first century. Saw it this way because this was the *moral environment* in which he lived. And of course he's not the only guy that ever had these feelings. Jerome probably felt this way in the wilderness. Nostradamus probably felt this way when he was predicting John F. Kennedy's assassination, the rise of Idi Amin, Ayatollah Khomeini, the invasion of Afghanistan, and the Third World War. Barry Goldwater may also have felt the bruising solitude of moral superiority and maybe he still does. Or take the case of James Earl Carter. And I feel that way too. I feel it now, here in Chapin House at Temple University, Phila., PA. I suffer with rectitude. I have tunnel vision sometimes. I get these compulsions to drop everything and run, to go in search of a girl with whom I worked bagging groceries in Nashua, N.H. Her hair fell in amber ringlets. She took me into her confidence.

Therefore and thus, I am up at 3:00 A.M. on the night before this religious studies term paper is due. I have taken two Vivarin caffeine tablets. I'm seated inside a large spherical chair—early seventies-type design—packed with cushions, which I, along with Anthony Edward Nicholas (hereafter, Tony) stole from the Graduate Housing Lounge. We had to roll it down College Street. There's no other furniture in my dorm room, now, except for a mattress and a portable cassette player. I'm wearing only worn boxer shorts. I have stockpiled Quaaludes and generic beer.

I'll just briefly expatiate on how I ended up living alone. The room is a double. Tony moved in. It was a week after school began (Sept. 1980). His shit was everywhere. He had a plug-in pink flamingo. He had congas. Bowling shoes. Hawaiian shirts. He left his records on the floor, out of their sleeves. He didn't bathe. And then, just as suddenly as he moved in, he moved out. Maybe a month later.

I *thought* we got along pretty well. He agreed to dine with me in the refectory each night. We chain-smoked. True: I gave him a number of polite but direct suggestions about that lingering hacking cough of his and about his frequent nosebleeds; I offered to separate the whites from the colored items that lay strewn all over our little room. Maybe I wasn't too politic sometimes—one time when he came back from a frat party with some floozy I barricaded the door. I couldn't stand to *overhear that groping*. One night—it's true—I even threw some of his shit out the window at him when I saw him passing below. These things come over you sometimes. I offered apologies. After Tony left, the housing office moved in a rugby player *actually named Scooter*. He didn't last long either.

So here I am.

This solitude I've described counts among the similarities between myself and St. John the Divine. There are additional concordances[2] between my life and the prophecy written down in the book of Revelation,

2. Joachim of Fiore in his *Exposito in apocalypsim* (manuscript in the Vatican someplace) believed that there was an exact concordance between the events of the O.T. and the N.T. To him I owe this concordance idea. And I'm aware, if my life is mapped onto Revelation, that there must also be a concordance between my life and the O.T., and between your life and mine, and between the Bible and the Koran, etc.

to which I would now like to draw your attention. My comments on them will form the major work of this paper. Blessed is he that readeth.

The Angel Appears to John

"WHAT THOU SEEST, write in a book, and send it unto the seven churches," the angel commands John in the first chapter of the final book of the Bible (1:11), and later, "Write the things which thou hast seen, and the things which are, and the things which shall be hereafter" (1:19). The appearance of the angel hearing the word of Christ is intended to foster in John the act of writing scripture.[3] But the way I see it, the testamentary approach, this emphasis on *writing things down*, is important not only to Revelation but to the Bible as a whole. The Bible is about writing, about persuasion and the dissemination of belief and practice, and its subject is *praise*, pure and simple, praise for God's stuff. The stuff he made.

Moreover, the Holy Bible, of course, was the first book ever printed with a printing press—the Gutenberg Bible. The revolution of dissemination brought about by the printing press came first to sacred ground, get it? and that's not just coincidence. All books, as a result, refer back to the Bible and to the truth contained in it, just as all writing refers back to divine creation, and, by extension, all critical papers ought to be contained in this concordance too. Between all covers, joined by all bindings, sewn, glued, or Velo-bound, is the word of God, like the movement of radiation out from Ground Zero. And that, you see, is what John's *writing* is about in the Apocalypse. Christ is the "Alpha and Omega, the beginning and the ending" of all alphabets (and all words) and all books and all society and all of society's works.[4]

---

3. Likewise, Jacques Derrida, when writing of Jean Genet's method of composition, found traces of the Apocalypse: "Why not search there for the remains of John (Jean)? The Gospel and the Apocalypse, violently selected, fragmented, redistributed, with blanks, shifts of accent, lines skipped or moved out of place." *Glas*. Paris: Editions Galilée, 1974. Trans. by Robert B. Paisner.

4. Note also that there are *books within the book* called Revelation. There's the book with the seven seals "next to the one who sits on the throne" (5:6), and there's the book "which is opened in the hand of the angel which standeth upon the sea and upon the earth" (10:8).

Now, let's examine me for a minute. Ever since I was a little boy, I have felt the significance of the printed word. I read *a lot* of science fiction. But as for writing, I avoided this shit like the plague. From the age of twelve, when I went away to boarding school, I was exposed to classes in rhetoric and composition. I didn't enjoy these classes. I think I might have a learning disability. Really. When I have to write something, I get really *bored*. I never wrote my parents or my uncle, and they never wrote me. (My father[5] lived in a tent—heated, with electricity, outhouse in back— at the furthermost corner of our property. Early mornings he would stride across fallow acreage with a shotgun and his dog, Claw. As the sun teased through the remote woods of New Hampshire, my father would fire off round after round at the crows on his property. He took shots he could never make. This was his kind of dissemination. The dissemination of buckshot. His oaths of rage crackled across the White Mountains.)

In the weeks leading to the deadline for my religious studies term paper, I know I am compelled to write in order to proceed to my junior year or at least in order to pass this class, and yet I can't do it. I want to write, but I can't. I'll do anything to avoid it. I'm wandering around dangerous parts of South Philly in a torn overcoat throwing rocks at stray dogs. I'm sleeping in public places. And then—all at once—a paper on Revelation comes to me, *all at once*, in a convulsion of inspiration, *in a revelation you might say*, just as the angel comes to John. It's not that I set out to write down the story of my life this semester, I'm just trying to think up a good paper topic, like, say, *Christ as literary character in the three Synoptic Gospels*. But instead the words just tumble out, as if it's a fit or a seizure. As though I'm taking dictation. My dorm room is a grotto and I totter around in it like an autistic until that moment when suddenly I can't stop myself from writing.

Without too much of a stretch, therefore, we can see that the angel's injunction to compose (in 1:1) can actually refer *to this very religious studies paper*, and to problems in its composition and in my life generally.

---

5. Some more information on my dad appears in my Deviant Personality final, December 6, 1980. I received a C-minus—partly because I had stayed up till 4:00 A.M. buying drinks for Annie Parsons. Later she used her hand on me, in the hall of her dorm, as revelers stumbled by. The exam was a few hours later.

The Letters to the Seven Churches

THE SEVEN CHURCHES to which John is enjoined to write by the angel are in Asia.[6]

Here are their names: Ephesus, Smyrna, Pergamos, Thyatira, Sardis, Laodicea, and *Philadelphia*. The point here is pretty obvious, right? John's letters to these churches are intended to reward and punish the various successes and failures of these institutions. The language of each letter is dictated by the angel of 1:1.

My paper—this very paper—is being written in *the city of Philadelphia, Pa.* Here's an excerpt from John's letter to the church of this very name (3:12): "Him that overcometh will I make a pillar in the temple of my God, and he shall go no more out: and I will write upon him the name of my God, and the name of the city of my God, *which* is new Jerusalem" (italics in original). Therefore, all that I'm telling you is true, *it fulfills prophecy*, and plus, it all happened in the one-time capital of the United States of America.

I came to Temple in the fall of 1979 after being rejected at Brown, Yale, Hampshire, Haverford, Union, and U.N.H. My first year was uneventful, although I did meet a guy, Malcolm, who eventually became my pharmacist. In the spring of that year, I began the frequent use of Quaaludes. My first bona fide blackout—loss of memory from the combination of drugs and alcohol—followed not long after. I was getting ready to go to a bar at the Tyler School of Art (it's all the way across town). Then, however, a gap in the narrative of these events ensues until the moment when I found myself suddenly, inexplicably, in a men's lavatory wearing a gray suitcoat with both sleeves torn off. I was shirtless underneath this garment, and I was also—I noticed in the smudgy mirror before me—wearing lipstick and eyeliner. I reviewed the facts. I had been drinking on top of downs, I guessed, and was luckily at the very bar to which I had set out. To a guy urinating in the stall behind me I gleefully shouted the following:

---

6. My close friend Shusaku C. Sunami (who is Asian) dropped out of school just about the time this story takes place, just before exams last fall. After a long, expensive cocaine binge, he skipped his exams and took the first train home to NYC.

—I don't want to seem like I'm giving you a pop quiz or anything, friend, but do you happen to know anything about what time it is or what day it is or what presidential administration is currently tangling things up or whether there's selective service registration yet? Is there anything you might know about these things?

I cackled good-naturedly, but my new acquaintance left me (in haste) to my confusion. I decided, because of my condition, to make my way back to my dorm, a journey of forty-five minutes, where, along with Shusaku Sunami (see note 6), I got into the systematic destruction of my college-issue furniture. The desk and desk chair, the chest of drawers, etc.[7]

The Throne of God in Heaven

WHAT CAN I tell you about the Tap Room, as Tyler's bar was called? When I was there, when I was immersed in its liquid dankness, its crimson lighting, its unlistenable music, I felt like I was *breathing properly*, I felt that people weren't whispering invidiously about my wardrobe and comportment. I loved and revered bars in freshman year and I still do. I seemed, in spite of my faith in the community and fellowship of Christ, in spite of my belief in an eternal life as promised by him, to need to degrade myself with drink (and compulsive masturbation). Again and again I found myself scamming, pretending to be a Tyler student in order to find a way into the Tap Room. It was a tiny, rundown space, with no more than six or seven booths, maybe twenty-four seats in all. (And twenty-four, just by coincidence, is my very age as I write this paper—because I took two years off bagging groceries and receiving psychotherapy.) An enfeebled citronella candle dwindled on each table; a mild adhesive varnished all surfaces. You had to yell into the ear of the person next to you. The men sometimes wore skirts; everyone wore black.

---

7. I've considered the possibility that John suffered with some kind of alcoholic or drug-inspired vision, maybe toxic withdrawal. This would account for the "four beasts full of eyes before and behind" (4:6) and like imagery.

I fell on my knees in places like that. I succumbed to a joy in my heart. I heard God whisper the good news. Even if they could tell there that I was a liberal arts guy. We were interlopers, those of us from Temple and Penn, in tweed suits from the fifties and skinny ties and peg-legged pants. They could tell us apart.

Compare this bar and its charms with the fourth chapter of the Apocalypse: "Round about the throne *were* four and twenty seats: and upon the seats I saw four and twenty elders sitting, clothed in white raiment" (4:4), and, later, "*There were* seven lamps burning before the throne, which are the Seven Spirits of God" (4:5).

The Seven Ages of Church History

SEVEN LAMPS, THE seven letters to the seven churches, the seven seals of the Great Book—there are even seven visions in the book of Revelation as a whole. With these sevens in mind, I will now briefly discuss the work of Petrus Olivi, the Franciscan biblical commentator.

Olivi, before being condemned posthumously in the early fourteenth century, was notable for insisting on a sevenfold division in church history to accord with the system of sevens in Revelation. He also insisted on a threefold division—borrowed from a Franciscan predecessor—to go with the Holy Trinity. The three ages went roughly like this: God the father went with the age of the Old Testament, Christ went with the age of the New Testament up to about 1300 A.D. (the time at which Olivi composed his *Lectura Supra Apocalypsim*), and the age of the Holy Ghost was, according to Olivi, to last from the time of his composition (1300) for about 666 years—the number of the beast—until circa 1966 A.D. *Or roughly ten years after my own difficult childbirth at Mass General in 1956.* This third period would accord more or less with the sixth age of church history, in which, according to Olivi, we would find the war between the Holy Ghost and Antichrist.

If we consider that Olivi's first defense of his views before the Franciscans occurred in about 1292, not 1300, we can see that the Apocalypse and with it the end of the reign of Antichrist may well occur on or close to the year of my own birth. All baby boomers, therefore, the countless offspring of the late sixth age—of that great period of darkness, the fifties—will be around to see the Apocalypse. In recognizing this concordance I'm also alluding to another trinitarian construct—the three writers and prophets: St. John the Divine, Petrus Olivi, and Bob Paisner.

And here's one last interesting equation! The first Olivians, the followers who made pilgrimages to his grave, were burned at the stake for heresy somewhere between 1314 and 1318. If we take these dates (instead of 1300) as indicative of the onset of *the sixth age* (the beginning of the reign of Antichrist before final Judgment), and add to them the 666 years signifying the beast, then we can see, of course, that the Apocalypse arrives between 1980 and 1984.[8]

The Book, Its Seven Seals, and an Angel

WHAT HAPPENS NEXT in Revelation is that John, in the throne room of heaven, is given a chance to view the great book of prophecy spread wide on an ample table there. "No man in heaven, nor in earth, neither under the earth, was able to open the book, neither to look thereon" (5:3).

I've told you about my own reading habits—mostly s.f. and light psychology books, although I am also a big fan of the writings of Ayn Rand. And there is this little "book" I'm writing here, this book of my own life, which I hope will top out around the required twenty-five pages and be done about three hours from now. But none of these books seems to resonate with the book described above in Revelation.

In fact, I would submit to you that a real book is not intended here. Sometimes you have to admit that Revelation has both a literal and symbolic level. The truth of Revelation floats between the two registers like a mostly submerged iceberg. In the case of the book referred to here, I think we can confidently speak of the symbolic. The book John intends to anoint as the highest book of prophecy and the book of Judgment is

---

8. On the other hand, Olivi's posthumous condemnation by the Pope wasn't completed until 1328, which would slide the whole thing back to the early 1990s.

not a regular book, a product of the printing press. It's the ancient and all-powerful book of the affections. The book of life, as described in 20:12, is *the book of love*.

I know a little bit about it, about love. For example, my roommate Tony Nicholas and I had had a few drinks one night. At the Tap Room. End of fall semester 1980. After Tony had moved out. And we had smoked some pot, which was always bad for me, since in its clutches I imagined not only that people but tables and chairs, all the objects in the cosmos, were secretly passing messages about my mood and complexion, my family, or my sickly childhood. That night I had smoked this marijuana and was suffering with the predictable *referential mania*. A malefic world spun out around me. I was powerless over it. I drank to cut the edge of this bad noise. Tony was telling me in some litanical and repetitive way about a stylish mystery film he wanted to direct. The eternal globe-trotting semiotics of mystery. The hermeneutics of murder and power pop. It all sounded the same. I was drinking faster. I had aphasia. I was nuts.

The music in the bar, some fusion of punk and funk that was going around then, obliterated all the ambient noise. I couldn't hear anything. I couldn't see anything. But I could tell, suddenly, that Tony wasn't talking to me anymore. It dawned on me. Through some sixth-sense heartache. He *hated* me. He was five or ten minutes into a conversation with a woman in the next booth. Five or ten minutes? Or longer? He had actually slid into the next booth and was chatting her up and I hadn't even noticed.

That was Judith. That was the first time I laid eyes on Judith. What did she look like? In the dark? Greater forces than my brute desire directed me at the moment, so her beauty wasn't uppermost in my mind. I can't tell you what she looked like, therefore, and her face was mostly turned away. She was chatting amiably with my former roommate. Still, I knew her immediately for who she was.

She was the angel of the seventh seal. She was Mary and Mary Magdalene, she was my mom before my mom got sick, but that's not all, she was like Christ, she was Francis or Gandhi or Thomas Merton, she was the grinch after his heart got bigger, she was Patti Smith after the broken neck, she was the transcendental signified, she was the thing that rid me of Tony Nicholas, she was the thing that was going to thaw my ache, and I *knew*. I'm aware that it sounds pretty sudden. But consider the evidence: "And there appeared a great wonder in heaven; a woman clothed with the sun, and the moon upon her feet, and upon her head a crown of twelve stars" (12:1). Judith's address at the time was 1212 Rodman St., Philadelphia.

My head cleared when she turned—from where Tony was yelling something in her ear. They were in the next booth. Backs to me. And she turned. As if according to some higher purpose. She turned and looked at me. My head cleared. Something tricky was going on in my life. There was contempt in the air, Tony's contempt, but contempt couldn't last in that furnace. I felt the absolute and irrefutable faith in an instantaneous bond. Love at first sight. My feelings would be boundless and exact and I would grow fat and bald cherishing memories of Judith. I would comfort her even when she was really wrinkled. I knew all of this by the time she was leaning over the booth:

—Hey . . . Hey, what's your name? You're a friend of Tony's, right?

She screwed up her face. Her smile was dimpled, uneven, overpowering. She evidently thought she was really having some fun. I nodded.

—Tony here says you were raised by wild animals.

She started to laugh. Couldn't stop laughing. And I could see Tony looking away, too, shaking from the effort to control himself.

Look, I know when I am the object of fun. Often I can laugh right along. But the little romantic skirmishes of the past, the meager recon missions of my heart in which I risked nothing and lost less, they didn't prepare me for this. This was a comment like a blow dart. I had to respond. I got right up in her face, leaned toward her and took hold of her bangled wrists. Tightly.

—Listen, you don't go in for this bait-the-misfit stuff, do you? Because you don't look like the kind of person that would, right?

Then I bowed my head in a prayerful way. I was wobbling and bowing.

—I dare you to treat me like a human being, I said. That's my dare for you and Tony . . . I dare you. And I'm sorry you're both so hard up for fun. I'm sorry about your *empty lives*, okay?

I knew how it would turn out, you know. I knew she would overcome my barb. She thought she didn't care about me, but when she turned nervously back to her conversation with Tony there was no conversation. Tony and she sat there, backs to me, like they'd never met at all. The space between them had widened. My chatter, meanwhile, was with the stars.

Believe it or not, this is how the book of the affections gets opened. It's right there in the Bible. Deep calls unto deep, across expanses of loss. In the course of my stupid life, I've tried to crack the seals of this great book, the way a kid might, six times I have, with six girls I guess you'd say, each with her different lances and charms and sadnesses, a woman with balances, a woman with hell behind, a woman who carried the souls of the dead with her, and a woman who felt earthquakes when we made love.[9]

The seventh was Judith.

Now I'll tell you the number of those lost to heartbreak in all of history because this number is worth remembering: *a hundred and forty-four thousand of all the tribes of the children of Israel.*

The Half-Hour of Silence

ON THE WAY back home from the Tap Room I had another blackout. Or this is my guess. They were getting worse. I was slipping into bad situations the way others in my family had. The next morning, I showed up for Semiotics Twelve coming in and out of consciousness. I was still tanked. I napped facedown on my desk. Migrainous auras, flares, and lights burst from the margins of the passage we were reading (in Saussure). And the worst thing was that I regretted what I'd said to Judith. Not only that, I knew I was going to be troubling her again in the future.

St. John: "And when he had opened the seventh seal [of the book of love] there was a silence in heaven about the space of half an hour."

---

9. Their names were as follows: Susan Ward (in fourth grade); Lisa Burns; Debby Madden (in eighth grade), who replied to my request to go steady, "Lisa Burns says you are a fag and I agree"; Liz Overton; Laura Drummond; Liza Benedict, whose dad caught us trying to do *it* (my first time) in the basement.

The Seven Trumpets

WE'RE DOWN TO only a couple of hours remaining, so I'm going to have to summarize the five months that followed. In December 1980, in a sudden display of collegiality and mirth, Chapin House, where I live, anointed me dorm president. I was elected by acclamation. Unopposed. In my new post, I would be making a number of important decisions, such as what parties we would be giving, how to deal with communal problems like loud stereos, whether to have special study hours, and so forth. I called meetings on these subjects, which we held in our ample, unfurnished common room, but I could never get a complete set of officers to show up. No one would come to the dorm meetings either. In the absence of consensus, therefore, I went ahead to make a few decisions myself.

My first act was to propose a house party entitled Inquisition Night. It was to take place in January, after Xmas break.[10]

The party would feature period costume. We could burn effigies on the lawn in front of the dorm. Crucifixes everywhere. Drinks dyed red to simulate the running blood of heretics. We'd haul up people on false charges.

Not surprisingly, the other dorm officers wouldn't agree to the party, especially when it became clear I was serious. They would, they said, *have to run it by the deans, health services, security.* And then they told me that my election had been a big joke in the first place; they told me that I had misunderstood a simple prank. My powers as president were thereby completely revoked. But I simply proceeded without my housemates. I printed up fliers. The design, if I do say so myself, was lovely, featuring a photocopied woodcut (from an art history text) of Francis bleeding from his stigmata. I stapled these fliers to locations far and wide, including 1212 Rodman Street, which I had learned was Judith's address—from Tony Nicholas, in one of our last conversations. I plastered her street with handbills. Inquisition night!

---

10. My mother, who has been pretty sick for a long time, was, over the holidays, readmitted to a private psychiatric hospital in Concord. We spent Xmas morning with her in the visiting room. She was disoriented. I brought her gourmet cheeses. I held her in my arms while she slept.

Rodman Street, a barren lane of overturned grocery carts, blind cats, and leafless trees, provided ample surfaces for my literature.

And though I had been forbidden to hold the party, the night on which it was scheduled to take place eventually arrived. I purchased, for the occasion, some luminous food colorings and in my empty dorm room I mixed up a shaker full of red vodka and tonic and crushed Valium. While no one joined me for my advertised party, I managed to have a good time—

That is, until I found myself in a bathrobe dyed black and worn backwards—apparently to simulate priestly garments—at a party miles from my dorm at which a venerated local band, The Egyptians, was playing. (They turned out these angular dance tunes, really loud—one of which, "Ancient Times," can still move me powerfully: "Oh, I wanna get a boat and go to ancient times; / Go any farther gonna lose my miiiiiinnnnnd."[11] Luckily, however, Judith was at the party. Wearing black paint-stained jeans and a white thrift-store dress shirt. She also had on a white leather jacket. Her hair was a long hennaed tangle, madwoman-in-the-attic style. She looked like a go-go girl ten years into a devastating nervous illness. I reminded her that Tony had introduced us a month or so earlier and she was obviously happy to see me again. I gallantly volunteered to walk her home (though, in my bathrobe, I was a little underdressed), but she said she wasn't going home. She was catching a train that night to Trenton or Pittsburgh or something.

—What's with the bathrobe? she asked.

—I'll take you to the station.

—I'm taking a cab.

—I'll join you.

She smiled.

—Look, I slurred. I'm not going to hold you down behind a bush and assault you or anything. I just want to have a conversation.

There must have been some credible or deeply heartfelt catch in my voice, because she suddenly changed her mind and admitted she *was*

---

11. Another song I liked by The Egyptians was based on a painting by Hieronymous Bosch: *Cure of Folly.*

going home. I won't try to excuse my behavior. I remember, unfortunately, every garbled sentence of this encounter. I know, for example, that
at one point I quoted Revelation to Judith: "And I will give power unto
my two witnesses, and they shall prophesy a thousand two hundred and
threescore days, clothed in sackcloth" (11:3). I told her that our associ-
ation, therefore, was circumscribed by Scripture. This line was supposed to be romantic.

She said:

—Even if you weren't completely nuts I would still say you are expecting too much, you know? I've talked to you, what, two times?

Okay, this was probably true. But I must not have cared then, because
soon we were in the laundry room of the apartment house on Rodman
that Judith shared with three other Tyler students. We were sitting on the
cement floor—it was really cold—and I was trying to persuade her, in a
language that was awkward and desperate, that she shouldn't go upstairs
to her apartment. In fact, I told her she couldn't leave until she agreed to
let me hug her. I asked for this hug many times. Seven times.

—Forget it, Judith said. Look, I don't want to be rude or anything, but
if you think this is the way to get through to me, if you think this'll win
me over . . . you're completely wrong, okay? Do I have to be clearer?

—Just a hug, I said. A hug, not anything . . . more than that. Just a hug.

—Come on, she said. This is embarrassing. It's stupid.

Mine was a sad story, but it didn't move her. I remember when she
moved up onto the coin-operated dryer—still warm from a recent load—
she fell into banging the backs of her heels against the front-loading door.

—It's cold, she said. How long do we have to sit down here?

And then she said the worst possible thing, a sentence of death and confusion. These dismal, lacerating words banged around in that reverberant
space:

—And anyway, you know, I'm seeing someone else.

I brushed it off at first.

—One hug? I mumbled. One little hug . . .

You want to know why it was so important, that hug? May I answer a
question with another? Why does the wilted house plant need its weekly

flooding with the Philadelphia Phillies plastic pitcher? Why did St. John look for the resurrection to come? Why was Judith still in the basement with me? She had her reasons. I had mine.

She slid off the dryer and the tail of her untucked shirt fluttered behind her.

—What the fuck.

See how easily the weather changes? She had to reach up a little bit. I was that much taller. My constitution improved immediately. I saw the generations of causation, from the great first cause, lined up behind me. On the other hand, maybe I was just a lonely guy. I wish I had been more awake for it, my cheek flush against hers, her hands around my waist, a strange supernatural pounding inside the ineffectual radiator on the wall. Footsteps in one of the apartments above.

I said:

—Lemme come upstairs with you.

—Forget it.

—Then promise me you'll . . .

—Forget it. Out. Now. Out. Go.

—Then let me come see you at your . . . at your studio . . . tomorrow . . .

—Not until you promise to leave. And even then I'm not promising anything.

I hung my head. And in that lapse of vigilance she skittered upstairs. In the moment of my shame. I idled in the basement. Then, in my priestly robes, I weaved up and down deserted streets blessing the night and the inhabitants of night.

The Number of the Beast

ACCORDING TO MOST scholarship, it's *not a number at all*, but a sequence of letters. It's likely, therefore, that 666 probably represented initials of some kind.[12]

---

12. Some of my thinking about the number of the beast derives from a fine Gregory Peck vehicle entitled *The Omen*.

A lowercase beta, e.g., from the Greek alphabet. In English we would use the letter *b*. So for my name, Robert (or Bob, if you prefer) Benson Paisner, you have two *b*'s and a *p*, which is really an upside-down and backwards *b*. I'm leaving the conclusion here to the reader. I didn't feel too happy with myself the morning after the laundry incident.

The Seven Plagues

AT 12:3 IN the Apocalypse a giant red dragon appears with seven heads and ten horns, to threaten the chosen, "That old serpent called the Devil, and Satan, which deceiveth the whole world" (12:9). The nature of his leadership is discussed by John in the next chapter, "He that leadeth into captivity shall go into captivity: he that killeth with the sword must be killed with the sword" (13:10).

You get a pretty good idea about sin, about life in the sixth age, from this description. Sin is like a vigorous movement away from the freedom of everlasting life (as described, e.g., in the Synoptic Gospels). In contrast to *affection*, especially as it has played itself out in my life, sin (and its agents, Satan and Antichrist) represents a contrary movement toward . . . well, toward separation, apartness. In the place where Satan's followers dwell, the smoke of those in torment "ascendeth [from Hell] for ever and ever: and they have no rest day nor night, who worship the beast and his image, and whosoever receiveth the mark of his name."

Sounds like a college environment, right? And which of us students is numbered with Satan's legions? I'll give you one example. Steve Dodgson, the bisexual sculptor/performance terrorist from Tyler School of Art.

Judith's boyfriend.

First, his gums were really bad. (I can find a couple of oblique references to bad skin or gums in Revelation, of which the best is 16:2, which speaks of the first plague of final judgment as consisting of a "grievous sore upon the men.") Dodgson always buttoned his shirts all the way up to the neck and greased his hair in the rockabilly style. His face was round and cherubic but also with a deeply angry cast. It was the face of a murderous shoe salesman. He had, as far as I could tell, no human compassion of any kind. In his effort to assure himself that he was not really attracted to men, Dodgson exercised a vigorous control over Judith. In his presence, she was to wear her hair tightly bound into a bun. She was not to wear slacks of any kind. He abhorred, at the same time, any situation in which he had to watch her eat. (I learned all this later.) When she was at his house, she ate in a room off the kitchen, at least until he realized that he hated *hearing* her eat. He asked that she *suck* her potato chips. Similarly, he asked that she avoid him during the worst part of her menstrual period. She was to keep any razor that she used to shave her body hidden from him at all times. She was not permitted to wear any shade of violet or purple, because, he told her, it was the color of the anus. And, above all, she was not to speak to other men, whether attractive or threatening, whether gay or straight, whether jock or artiste or academic, whether tall, short, fat, lean, desperate, androgynous, or anything else. No men. Judith hovered in the periphery of his vision at all times and her brilliant smile became infrequent under his control. Dodgson said once, in public, at a party, *See this girl here? See my girl? The mother of all abominations!*

The Lamb

THE HUG IN the basement (in the deep of night, in the trance of love) wasn't the only thing that stuck with me in this academic year, but it was right up there. As demonstrated above (mspp. 15–16), my experiences with women weren't all that broad. And though I knew about Dodgson, though I knew he was calling Judith and seeing her and dropping by Store 24, where she worked as a cashier, I tried to pretend it wasn't happening. I too began to stake my claim upon her attentions, standing in the back of the all-night convenience store, with the guys thumbing copies of *Motor Trend* and *Juggs*. I found a way to visit her each day.

She was seeing Dodgson, theoretically, but he was frequently distracted, it seemed, or out of town, or simply breaking into houses on the Main Line or shooting speed or whatever it was he did. And Judith and I were having some laughs. She tolerated my visits to her on the job and to her studio and my telephone calls all hours of the day and night. I was twenty-four years old and I didn't see how I was going to get along with people—it was a skill I didn't have; I had imagined that, after capitulating to the decline of my family, I would be hospitalized or would move into the deep woods, into a shotgun shack with no electricity or running water; but here I was exploring intimacy with one person, with Judith, and I didn't care if she was a little preoccupied, or peculiar looking, or anything else, because she had forgiven me for that hug.

But when I got back from spring break I called and she broke me the bad news. She'd told Dodgson about me. He had returned from his breaking-and-entering spree, and she'd told him. She'd told him *she was friends with this guy.* She'd confessed a fealty, a devotion. I didn't know whether to take or lose heart. Dodgson made it clear immediately that she was never to see me again. She was to expunge our conversations from the record of her life. She was to deny me.

—No no no, I mumbled into the phone. No. Let me see you just one more time. *Just one more time.*

—Can't, she said, can't do it.

But two weeks later, after a lengthy negotiation with her criminal boyfriend, she agreed to meet me in a public place, Airport Lounge at Temple University, for exactly fifteen minutes. She had arranged with Dodgson that she would call him at the beginning and the end of this conversation, she would *bookend* it, in order to demonstrate its precise duration. They had covered, Judith and Dodgson, every aspect of this event. They had thought it out. Our meeting was to be bounded by the ordinary, by Temple students dragging their knapsacks and buying packs of Marlboros, by kids sprawled on modular sofas, by security guys and snack bar employees (work-study slaves) coming on and off break. I arrived twenty minutes early. A trebly radio at the snack bar played the college station. The carpets were trampled down. Paths of grime led to and from that lounge of dreams.

The Fall of Babylon

"THEREFORE SHALL HER plagues come in one day, death and mourning, and famine; and she shall be utterly burned with fire" (18:8).

So much of our lives take place in the *spiritus mundi*, in the ether of the numinous, under the pressures of Antichrist and his servants, with the music of Heaven drifting toward us distantly as if overheard in an agreeable daydream. We're little puppets playing out the drama of the sublime. It's no wonder therefore that my conversation with Judith was difficult. The entire spiritual chemistry of the age hung in the balance. We were whispering. Judith looked all wrong. Her hair was pulled back tightly; she was wearing some cheap polka-dotted dress she'd bought at a thrift shop. Our meeting was all full of false starts. What's going on at school? How is your painting? What did you do over spring break? What music are you listening to? Then it got into harder stuff. I took her hands. I grabbed at them greedily and held them in my lap. *Why wasn't I good enough?* I asked. Why couldn't I be closer to her than I was? What was I doing wrong? Why was I so bad at human commerce when it was the thing I wanted more than anything?

Then I asked:

—Why do you let him do this to you? I wouldn't do this to you. I wouldn't treat you like this, pen you in.

Her expression didn't change.

—Because I'm in love with him, she said. I'm in love with him and I'm *not* in love with you. Simple as that. You're always making things bigger than they are, or harder than they have to be, so you don't even know what I'm talking about. Besides how could you know what's going on with me? You couldn't. You have no idea—

Of course, this is just how college kids talk. Their language is crude and simple, like the language of ancient practitioners of physick, medieval guys, when considered by the scientists at Lawrence Livermore Laboratory. College students can't talk about their own feelings. They blunder around or cut themselves off. I bet they don't know anything for a good ten years after those *best years of their lives*. I don't hold it against them. Their feelings might as well be in Aramaic. But I can tell you what college students *mean*; they mean that grief follows grief like the tides running in and out; they mean that feelings are just a code for the intentions of God; they mean that numbers or letters or decimals can be attributed to feelings; they mean that the words of love and loss are just labials, dentals, or gutturals;[13] they mean that these words are pronounced with the hard palate or aspirated and that the revelations fashioned from them will outlive this sitcom of today. That's what I have to say about feelings.

CONCLUSION:
The New Jerusalem

THEN JUDITH AND I backpedaled, talking about movies, about painters, about the Egyptians. In the middle of this, the fifteen minutes was suddenly past, though we'd said nothing, really. Our meeting was over. Abruptly, Judith took her hands from mine and moved off to cloister herself in the phone booth outside the lounge. I could see her shoulders and the back of her hair.

That was eleven days ago.

After that, after I skirted around the phone booth where she was huddled—protesting and denying to Dodgson—I was on my way back to the dorm when a sudden rain, a freak sun-storm, fell glistening on my face and hands. The cursed pansies pushed up their perditious heads all along the margins of my path. I said, *Alleluia!* I said, *All salvation and glory and honor and power unto the Lord our God!* Well, at any rate, I *thought* this stuff. The completeness of my solitude prevented me, that afternoon, from making a scene.

So: youth is apocalypse.

When the great whore, Babylon, is finally fallen, St. John the Divine enters into the New Jerusalem, into the seventh age, where God and Christ will reign eternal over the faithful. Heaven and earth pass away. God wipes away the tears from the eyes of his flock, announcing that there will be no more death and no more term papers. The foundations of the new city are garnished with gems and the nations that are saved walk in the light

---

13. See, e.g., Ferdinand de Saussure's *Course in General Linguistics*. In his later years, Saussure became obsessed with anagrams, word games, with systems, with codes, with the worlds that he felt were hidden behind our words, with all the life that was beyond his reach.

of the Lamb. A pure river of water of life, clear as crystal, proceeds out of the throne of God and of the Lamb. There are no more curses and no more night. We're all innocents. Then the Lord says to John, "Blessed is he that keepeth the sayings of the prophecy of this book. If any man shall take away from the words of this prophecy, God shall take away his part out of the book of life, and out of the holy city, and from the things which are written in this book. Surely I come quickly."

This is how the Bible ends. This is its terminus. It's a big ending, a crowd scene. John knows this too. He knows there is a powerful prophetic dimension to endings. And I know that I have come to the end of my education. And to the end of childish longing. This draft will have to do the trick, because the sun has risen over the burned-out frats on the quadrangle, Professor Soren, and I have to get this over to you, to the department office, in less than an hour. Sorry there's no bibliography. That's the least of my concerns. In this afterlife.

SWEETHEARTS

Stacey Levine

YOU SPLIT THE topside of my leg one night in the summer. Without thought I allowed you my bone. You lifted it away and placed it before you on the floor. You scraped it with your fingers and nails; my bone was not white, but grayish and brown-stained all over; it lay before you as you knelt; indeed, because of this extraction, my wet leg, extending from my body, lay paralyzed, dear, for the nerves had been destroyed. You took my bone and its shreds of wet red muscle; you wanted it, so I had given it to you, adorable one, at great risk to myself and to my detriment, deface-ment, exhaustion and enslavement, my terrible prostration, my deference, my horror and pleasure, every bit of it my choice, my leisure.

And you asked that I would pierce you in kind, gouge you somehow, find the green stink in your gut and bring it into the air, the light, astound you with this, rip your layers of muscle, make you feel the curi-ous interstices and gradations of pain that arise when wounds are made wider, or deeper, or are hollowed out from beneath.

Angel, monster, I would not do these things to you; I only wanted that you would dig me bloody; I itched; I would not rip you, much to your dismay and frustration, because I loved to see how you begged, and when you did so, in screams, my pleasure increased a hundredfold.

I am certain we met in the past; I am not always certain. This year, huge news has been flooding the world: fevered failures and pinprick successes in economic and foreign policy; I just wanted to be flayed by you, awful darling; I was astounded at having found you; I wanted this always, that you would continue this nightmare as you tore at me daily; I was mustard yellow, green, purple, bluish, all colors, all over; I wanted always to save these colors, to swallow each of your heartstopping blows and see every day how they bloomed beneath my skin.

I am your starveling, your trash; in the morning you wake to the ferrous scent of my blood tricking across your face, and suddenly you are up, beginning to dig at my navel, tearing upward; you howl that I am bad, terrible, that I am always in error, that I should be different; I should destroy you further, spill your blood more, blackest spider; you burn away my sense that I am myself with your abuse; my veins fill with ammonia, naphtha; I am chilled and familiarly paralyzed. You bellow at the brown and red juice foaming in my stomach as you separate with the strength of your hands the two halves of my belly; you dig my gut, ruining my wet gelatine organs; if only this ecstasy were happiness, my demon, sadist, ass.

Long ago, when I was just as lonely, my mother made me in her gut out of warm blood and sugar; I became myself there; I could not change. I fed and grew with the blind diligence of everything alive and became myself; I formed; you cannot change me now, my horror, though I can die; though you have flayed me many times, detested me, pierced my throat until I fainted in astonished pleasure.

And you say you want me any other way, warmonger, simpleton; you say you're going to remake me. That's not possible, but no one can tell you otherwise; I accept your terms, I know only you, your acute, circular unhappiness and nothing else; I revel in our nightmare; I give my organs for you to smash; I refuse to flay you, this being my finest pleasure, second only to receiving your fantastically sustained torture; I will not hurt you; I cannot; you shout in terrible frustration, livid creature, at which point I dissolve in joy.

Before, when I knew only her, I ran crying, running in circles after my lost mother who had thrown me out of her house, who had sent me away, alone. I know you, she said. You're weak. You'll try to stay here forever but you can't. You can't hide here anymore, she said. Go outside, or you'll die from your own weakness and fear. Leave, she said. And don't go grieving for your mother. She hated herself.

After she had thrown me out, I hurled myself in the sand at her, yelling, I hate you, I'm not just weak, there are other things, why can't you see me, I hate you.

Then, after a time, my heart closed, sewed itself beautifully: the work of silkworms. After all, I was young, and my body worked flawlessly. My body was perfect and perfectly self-contained. Then, I stopped howling for her each night. Then, I never dreamed of her again.

But I blamed her for bringing me where I never wanted to go; I woke up one day and I was already formed; it was too late; I was a child belonging to my mother; I wanted that my blood would reverse, return to her, but it was much too late. You, flagrant murderer, were already there reminding me of this, blowing a great heaving wind into my mouth, exploding my sinuses and nose from the inside, bursting my cochlea, my eardrums; you entered my eyes with your fingers; I licked your wrist weakly as you delivered to me your heavenly guerilla blows, and I fainted repeatedly, my creature so absolutely alive, my joy; it was always your astute sense of courtesy, your sensitivity, to wait just long enough before resuming your protracted attacks so I could remember who I was, my offending terror, my dearest; I fall this instant, hearing your execrable insults, my ecstasy a monsoon.

In your night dreams, twisted sibling, you are dog, orangutan, starving for my blows, begging for my bite. I act on anger, calculation, and impulse; I tear into you with pain and no warning. You want this; your body splits into fragments of mirror, making you multitudes, unmaking you into many, each hurting distinctly; you become a fly's eye, perceiving the world not in waves of light but in throbs of pain. Throughout, I am starving, my dear, then gorged on your blood, my body ceaselessly moving in relation to your ignorant violence.

This year, the papers say that the national economy is strong, and that there are more high-paying jobs than ever; I am advocate of, accomplice to our nightmare, constantly desiring our wretched delight, unearthing each day some new timbre of agony, employing again and again the few mechanisms I know; you drop your head and seize my body, darling, groaning, fisting my throat, my esophagus, seeking a hemorrhage; light from the window seeps to my eyes as I gag; I wet your arm and bite, scrape it with my canines; I reach and twist at your genitals until tears pool in your eyes and spill; my tubes have burst, your arm stuffs me, your fingers jab at the valve of my stomach; my acid burns you, and you will blister, fester, dearest child; I have lost my body; my body is thin, a mere membrane; I am too thin for organs, then suddenly I balloon; I am hugeous; my body fills the room, the odorous corner I now see before me, darling, the corner I believe is part of you. This cannot continue; it's too much, but it will only continue, my dearest, and if outrage and ecstasy were happiness, it would be mine to give you, in unstoppable proportions. But I can only look at you, my horror, hellcat, hideous queen: I am certain that once, in the past, we met; I am not certain we ever did.

FRAISE, MENTHE,
ET POIVRE 1978

Jared Hohl

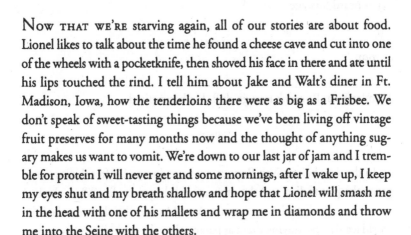

Now THAT WE'RE starving again, all of our stories are about food. Lionel likes to talk about the time he found a cheese cave and cut into one of the wheels with a pocketknife, then shoved his face in there and ate until his lips touched the rind. I tell him about Jake and Walt's diner in Ft. Madison, Iowa, how the tenderloins there were as big as a Frisbee. We don't speak of sweet-tasting things because we've been living off vintage fruit preserves for many months now and the thought of anything sugary makes us want to vomit. We're down to our last jar of jam and I tremble for protein I will never get and some mornings, after I wake up, I keep my eyes shut and my breath shallow and hope that Lionel will smash me in the head with one of his mallets and wrap me in diamonds and throw me into the Seine with the others.

Paris is empty, but we go on daily explorations anyway. Lionel wears laboratory goggles and thick welding gloves. He pulls his mallets from the carpenter's belt around his waist and swings them two-fisted into plate glass storefronts and apartment windows. We almost never find food. Back when we were a group, when Harriet and Claudia and that barbarian Sven Ronsen were still alive, we'd fill duffel bags with wigs and top hats and switchblades and emeralds and take it all back to the Odéon where we lived and where we performed our death plays.

HAMLET OR THE TRAGEDY OF SVEN RONSEN

THE SCENE:
Candlelit room in a 16th-century castle. Hamlet (Sven Ronsen) lies on
the ground wrapped in a clean white sheet (he tells us he is too weak for
shirts). On his chest rests a human skull. Hamlet/Sven Ronsen is feeble
and debilitated, but slowly opens his eyes and, with great effort, achieves
focus. He stares into the skull's eyeholes with meaning.

HAMLET
I can be ... to not ... to be. I can be.

A thin line of spittle seeps from Hamlet/Sven Ronsen's withered lips. A
cry is heard offstage.

HAMLET
Pfff.

Hamlet/Sven Ronsen's eyes go dull. He has expired.

END.

In the days before Sven Ronsen, we were doomed. After the sun went
green the plants died and then the animals began to die. When the bad
news came, the French were ecstatic. A well-known TV show mocked the
world leaders, portraying them as paranoid weaklings hiding away in her-
metically sealed bunkers. Most of Paris was out dancing in the streets.
Everyone made light of all the hubbub about conserving food. The city
was still in operation and even a week after all that talk of doom, restaurants were serving fat ducks in cream sauce and bottles of red Burgundy.
People laughed when the president of the United States appeared on camera eating a cockroach. Then the delivery trucks stopped coming in.
When the fighting was at its worst I managed to save a street magician

from a cleaver attack. The magician was Lionel. He showed me his stash of breakfast cereal. I met his girlfriend Harriet and her friend Claudia, a beautiful young woman with dark hair and brilliant green eyes.

We were very good at gathering food and managed to avoid the roving street gangs. We were silent at midnight, communicating with hand gestures, able to spot dented cans of tuna half-buried in the rubble, revealing themselves to us in winking flashes of moonlight. We scavenged and we hid. One night, Claudia was slashed by a child. He was vicious, possibly a gang scout. He caught her in the corner of the mouth with the tip of his blade and sliced an inch into her cheek. She looked over at us, her lips parted in shock, the gape of her mouth extended by the wound, blood trickling down her chin and her face distorted, a humanized jack-o'-lantern. I ran at the kid, but he was too fast on his bicycle. Harriet stitched Claudia as best she could. The cruel black thread interrupting her smooth, soft, face. After that incident the four of us holed up in Lionel's apartment. We decided to ration ourselves, to wait it out. We had no real plan. We were growing weak while Gary, Lionel's mynah bird, flew at the ceiling shrieking like a car alarm.

We lived off crackers and mouthfuls of stale water from the stoppered bathtub. Lionel performed tricks to help pass the time. He'd make giant pennies disappear. He'd hold out a cheap wand and Gary would perch on it and cough a lacy garter belt from his beak. Harriet and Claudia would occasionally put on dance performances, old timey vaudevillian numbers choreographed with canes we found in the back of a ransacked grocery. Between acts, we could hear the gangs outside, beating their bass drums madly. Once we peeked through the curtains and saw a doomsday parade, ex-government officials and television newscasters skewered on lances stolen from the Musée de l'Armée, the grand marshal an eighty-year-old woman borne along in the air like Cleopatra, keeping time with a human femur for a baton. Even when we began to starve we knew better than to go outside. We kept track of our last scraps of food in a miserly way. We built a toilet that hung off the window and dumped onto the sidewalk below. As our supplies dwindled, we made our rations smaller.

THE FOOD RAN out. We didn't have enough energy to stand so we attached drinking straws end to end so that we could lie on the floor and suck directly from the tub. We didn't bother with water rations anymore. It was pointless. We'd given up.

Then Gary did a wonderful thing. He flew out the window and returned an hour later with a large chunk of birdseed molded into the shape of a bell. The hard seeds felt like they would crack my teeth, but I ate, grinding them into a fine paste and adding more and more, saving it all on my tongue until I had built up enough to feel it in there, heavy and warm. It was only a teaspoon worth of seed paste, but when I swallowed it was like a fine porridge, a delicious meal, enough to give me the strength to go on. We gave Gary little pieces, but not quite enough and soon he was out the window and back with another huge chunk of seed. Gary saved us, really. We ate birdseed for a month and then one day he returned with an empty beak. Our hunger was stronger than before, more determined.

Lionel said, "We all love you Gary. Please, know that we love you." Then he produced two mallets and swung them again and again, flattening Gary's head against the windowsill. Lionel donned his carpenter's belt and, after a slight meal of bird meat, painted a likeness of Gary onto the rough leather around his waist while the rest of us snapped Gary's bones and sucked out the marrow.

We felt as if we were sinking into the floorboards. Invaders showed up periodically, but we had prepared for them. When the door was breached, we screamed and threw books at our enemies. Lionel would stand in the middle of the room, using what strength he had left to raise a samurai sword in the air and shake it in a threatening manner. If the invaders persisted, Lionel would light a flash bomb or a smoke grenade from his magician's kit. One day there were no more bombs. Sven Ronsen kicked down the door and stared at us.

"Would you look at you," Sven Ronsen said. He was wearing a chinless yellow motorcycle helmet and a tank top that said *Whack-a-doo!*

"Look at how helpless you all are. Bless you forever. It breaks the heart is what it does."

He picked us up. He was incredibly strong. I could feel his muscles cradling me. I must have weighed no more than eighty pounds. The others looked like dolls with their dull skin and gigantic glistening eyes. I had the feeling that we were being harvested, like livestock, that we were being driven out of the pasture of our apartment and would soon be on our way to some horrible slaughterhouse. Sven Ronsen carried us all downstairs and loaded us into a small wooden cart. He took Lionel's samurai sword and strapped it to his back. He grabbed the cart's rusted ball joint with his bare hands and pulled us down the road.

The streets were filled with trash and bones picked clean. The city smelled like it had died and been taken over by a powerful fungus. Sven Ronsen pulled us into an alleyway, opened a door, and wheeled us down a ramp into the basement of a barricaded health food store. There were half a dozen others inside, organizing shelves and taking inventory.

"Idiot!" someone screamed out. "You cannot bring more people, shithead!"

"These are the beautiful people," said Sven Ronsen. "We have plenty of food."

"I will not tolerate it," the man said. He walked over and slapped Sven Ronsen hard across the face. Sven Ronsen stood stunned. Then he reached back and drew out Lionel's sword and brought it down in a casual one-handed style. It was odd how the blade neatly clipped off the Frenchman's ear, then sank an inch or so into his shoulder. Sven Ronsen looked over at us.

"I won't let you guys down," he said. "Ever."

We didn't have the strength to respond. Sven Ronsen walked through the aisles swinging his blade, separating heads from necks. The sword edge followed on through his targets and split open pill bottles and boxes of medicinal powder, filling the store with an earth-tone confetti and lending a celebratory air to the massacre. The whooshing of the blade was crisp. Occasionally it would clank off a metal display rack, gonging away.

"I feel great," Sven Ronsen said as he slipped his swordpoint into the belly of a belching, mustachioed Asian.

When the room had been cleared, Sven Ronsen looked over at us, panting, his chest smeared with blood.

"Oh," he said. "I forgot you guys were here."

WE WERE IN the health food store for many months. We ate vitamins and granola bars, soy milk and vegetarian jerky. No one went outside except Sven Ronsen, who would sometimes return with board games and fancy clothes.

One day we heard a terrible rumbling, and a great cloud of dust came billowing into the store. We waved the chalky air from our eyes and saw that our only exit was buried under mounds of red brick.

Sven Ronsen looked at the blockaded exit. "Let's get to work and clear the way."

The process took a couple of weeks. When we went outside, everything was silent, not even a bird in the sky. Sven Ronsen said that nothing was wrong. He said that if the Earth was suddenly quiet and still it was because we were entering a new Silent Age. He said the Earth was always right, that we must adapt to her ways. When I asked Claudia what she thought she said, "We are no longer on the planet Earth."

HARRIET BECAME SVEN Ronsen's girlfriend. They'd go to the back room, what used to be the manager's office, and Sven Ronsen would pull down his jeans while Harriet went to her knees. One day Lionel told them he knew what they were doing in there. Their response was to perform the same act, at all hours, whenever the mood struck them, in full view of everyone.

"Sven Ronsen is a moron," said Lionel. "She's sucking the protein right out of him. He won't last."

I wasn't so sure, but Sven Ronsen did, in fact, grow weak. He became listless, his movements syrupy. Sometimes he would open his mouth, as if to begin speaking, but no words would come out and he would stand there like that, looking around as if nothing was unusual.

While Sven Ronsen went fallow, Harriet became strong and took over our little group. It was her idea to move into the Odéon.

It was a large stone building with a colonnade. Inside was a grand hall filled with Doric columns and shining black and white tiles that led to a rotunda supported by caryatids and sphinges. The auditorium was circular with multiple balconies. The stage was enormous, a hundred flylines imitating sea rope. The seats were immaculate and comfortable. All of these beautiful things were installed—I learned from a book in the gift shop—at the request of Napoleon after a terrible fire in 1799.

Sven Ronsen was now weak and thin. He spent all day lying down while Harriet sucked the life out of him. He was delirious, but Harriet just kept working away. She had begun a morning exercise routine and she lifted weights. Her biceps kept growing and soon she was pushing all of us around.

"Maybe you should leave him alone today," I said to her once. Sven Ronsen had become a skeletal fool, quivering in the corners of the theater.

"I know what's best for him," Harriet said.

When I gave her a look she socked me in the mouth. Harriet was stronger than all of us.

BY THE TIME Sven Ronsen passed away we had amassed a giant chest full of jewels. Rare stones had become completely devalued when the sun went bad, but we kept stockpiling them for some reason. It was hard to grasp the idea that they were worthless.

We decided to drop Sven Ronsen into the Seine, but Lionel could imagine how rough it would look: a couple of us heaving a body over the edge, the thing landing with a splash in the shallows, perhaps a foot sticking up out of the muck. So we built a long plastic slide that would slip the body out into the middle of the river and we dressed Sven Ronsen in a fine Italian suit from one of the designer shops on the rue du Faubourg Saint-Honoré. We looped diamond necklaces around him so that he shone like a giant brooch. Sven Ronsen's body slipped like a frozen turkey down the slide and shot into the air. It hit the river dead center and vanished.

I realized any one of us could be next. Lionel's cheeks were sinking into his face, slowly revealing the shape of his skull. My pants had long ceased to fit and yet I insisted on wearing them, cinching my belt tighter and tighter, finally punching new holes into the leather so that the extra length hung off my hip, long and ridiculous, like a brown snake. It could have been any one of us. It could have been Claudia, though she seemed to be in good health. One night she grabbed me by the hand and took me to a balcony and ran her fingers over my bony body. She kissed me lightly on the neck and cried above me, our noses touching, so that her brilliant tears dripped into my dull pupils.

Among the items we scavenged when Claudia began to swoon: Spray adhesive, sapphires, safari outfits, and a jumbo pack of disposable razors. Lionel and I had never been fans of sculpted facial hair, but the demands of our production asked that we rise above our bias.

AU REVOIR, CLAUDIA

THE SCENE:
Sun rises. A jungle. An impeccably dressed explorer (Lionel) is shining his boots. His sideburns extend to his jaw line. He whistles a light-hearted tune. His camp is clean. On a spit above an expired fire, the carcass of last night's meal, a wild boar. A few feet away lies the explorer's stunning wife (Claudia). She is weak, stricken with some deadly, yet beautiful, jungle disease. Her left arm has already succumbed, covered from elbow to fingertips in glimmering sapphires. Soon she will be nothing but shining stone.

EXPLORER
Worry not, sweet wife, the cure is on the way.

WIFE

I'm unsure that I will last.

EXPLORER

Look yonder, our scout approaches.

Tucker (Me) arrives with a vial of butterscotch-colored liquid. He kneels beside the explorer's wife.

EXPLORER

Ah, just in time. Apply the remedy. We must prepare for a feast with the natives this evening. We are the guests of honor, in recognition of my wife's fine aim with a rifle. She was able to eliminate a tiger that had menaced the tribe for many years and—

TUCKER

She's fucking dead, Lionel.

EXPLORER

Don't break character.

END.

Lionel woke up one morning with Harriet looming over him, zipping up his pants, her breath hot and seedy. They exchanged a look but nothing more. Later that afternoon Lionel had a flash memory of his uncle's house in the country and of the vintage fruit preserves collection his uncle kept in a vast cellar.

On a dewy morning Lionel and I left for St. Germain-en-Laye. We arrived, much later, at a quaint country house. Lionel's uncle sat dead on a kitchen chair. His arms were crossed, his milky eyes stared at us in disappointment, it seemed. Lionel did not cry. We were beyond such things.

In the basement we found the preserves collection: rows of rough-hewn wooden shelves that held thousands of jars of jam. Some were petite vessels with barely an ounce inside; others were as large as footballs, made of heavy green glass. Each batch was labeled in a careful hand: Cassis 1990; Fraises et Framboises 1965; Griotte 1981. We ate three jars each. The sugar exploded in my mouth. It made my fillings tingle.

"We will not tell Harriet," said Lionel, licking his teeth. "She would have us launched off the death chute by now. Our supplies are running low and soon she will starve. We must be strong and show no mercy."

We shook hands. We agreed to take only a duffel bag of jam back to Paris. We would hide it in a secret location and eat it only when we were sure Harriet was not around.

HARRIET WOULD GO out early in the morning, scavenging for food. She never found a scrap, and slowly, she wasted away. For awhile, it seemed as though her huge biceps would not give, but then, they too faltered. She went gaunt. Lionel and I weren't much better, but the jam at least gave us energy.

HARRIET COLLAPSED TO the stage floor. "That's it for me," she said.

She lay there for days, but never once did her eyes close. A couple of times I went to check if she was still breathing. "Get the hell away from me, lecher!" she'd say.

But soon she became like an infant, babbling and singing strange songs. She cried sometimes, then licked at her tears, desperate for salt.

She wouldn't die. It became painful to see her, so I was relieved when one night I woke up to find Lionel spoon-feeding her a late-eighties marmalade.

"I have broken the pact," he said to me. "In the morning you will execute me."

"Of course not," I said.

"We have done something terribly wrong," Lionel said.

I looked down at Harriet and could see that she was gone. A dollop of orange marmalade stuck to her stiff blue tongue.

THE BALLAD OF HARRIET

THE SCENE:
The Unimpeachable Goddess (Harriet) is flying high up in the clouds with giant wings made of fine cashmere. She is draped in jewelry and she shimmers in the morning light. In her arms she cradles the skeleton of a puppy. She carries a banner that reads "For God's Sake Don't Put Me On That Stupid Fucking Slide."

THE UNIMPEACHABLE GODDESS
(Stares angrily into the audience, but does not say a word)

END.

We are in some endless office building in the sixteenth arrondissement. Lionel has his mallets going and I'm zinging pencils at a metal filing cabinet. Then the glass stops shattering and I hear Lionel say, "You must come here and look at this." It's a memo about a Bastille Day celebration.

We ride our bicycles to a storage facility at the edge of the city. It takes a while to pry the lock open. Inside we find crates labeled "Class B Fireworks." Next to the crates are a giant switchboard and a generator full of diesel fuel. We load everything into the trailer and move it back to the Odéon.

We build a cockpit out of plywood and mount the switchboard inside to serve as our control panel. Lionel unpacks the fireworks. We connect the igniters with xlr cable and distribute the charges to various places in the theater. We put Blue Thunder, 1000's of Silver Coconut, and Brocade Crown in the balcony. Gold Willow and Chrysanthemum with Blue Pistil go in the stage boxes. Along the flies we attach White Tiger Tail roman candles and we stuff the stage manager's desk full of Dragon Eggs with Thunder canister shells. We attach the biggest charges, Fire God and Rising Twinkling Tail to Red Gamboge to Twinkling Chrysanthemum, along with four sticks of dynamite we found in Sven Ronsen's old room, to the space beneath our cockpit's flight chairs. We aim the Crackling

Royal Ceiling Lamps and Watercolor Glitter aerial shells at the stage curtains. We rub everything down in diesel fuel.

GRAND FINALE

THE SCENE:
Cape Canaveral, Florida. Morning. Two astronauts prepare for liftoff. Rex (Lionel) is an ace pilot. Sebastian (Me) is a scientist testing the effects of antigravity on a jar of premium vintage fruit spread.

REX

(hands at the switchboard)
Ten seconds to liftoff. You ready for this?

SEBASTIAN

You bet.

Sebastian opens the jam jar and sticks his nose within. He inhales flavors of mint and sweet berries, of bitter spice. He bites into the jelled concoction. He chews it. He savors it. Here on earth it will taste different. It will have an earthly flavor that is important to understand before he compares it to the outer space flavor. Every experiment must have a control.

REX

. . . two . . . one.

END.

WHAT IS IT
WHEN GOD SPEAKS?

Diane Williams

THIS WAS THE house which once inspired a sister of one of the guests to declare, "People kill for this."

That's where the guests were on the perfect afternoon, not the sister.

It was a shame the afternoon became evening before the guests had to leave, not that anything was less lovely because it was evening.

There was a tender quality to the lack of light on the screened-in porch where they all were sitting, as there was also a tender quality to the small girl too old to be in the highchair, but she was not too large for it. The girl had insisted on being put up into the highchair. She was ecstatic to be locked in behind the tray.

Her hands tapped and stroked the tray. She was not up there to eat. It was past time for that.

Behind the handsomest man on the porch was the array of green leafy trees and lawn, lit by a yard light, veiled by the black porch screen. The handsomest man smiled. He was serene.

Across from him, his wife, on the chintz flowered sofa, who was the most beautiful woman, smiled serenely at her husband. She said of her husband to the others, "He never wants to leave here. Look at him! He likes it. The food is so good and healthy. He can keep swimming in your pool. Look at him! He is so happy!"

Then the man lifted up his girl, who was smaller than the other girl, who had never ever—his girl—been irritable even once, there at that house, and he put her up onto his shoulders. Her short legs were pressing on his chest, because he had wanted her legs to do that.

Her father felt his daughter on the back of him and on the front of him, on top of him, all at once. She was slightly over his head too, her head was. Her light heels were tapping lightly on his chest. He took her hands in his. She was ready for the dive that would not be possible unless he would fling her from him.

He should.

KRAFTMARK

Matthew Derby

Burtson was wading calf-deep in a foresty bog, following close behind the guide, a small man in fussy khaki fatigues. The diffuse, lame half-light of dusk punched out the detail of trees in the canopy, making them look like massive, buoyant cartoon mascots, maybe a clutch of parade floats for the dead. The color had run out of the world, and they still had not found Alan.

Every time he found a capsized landmine, Burtson was sure it was the last thing he'd see. The mines in this area were different from what he'd come to know through television, word of mouth, knowledge wafers, and childhood memory. The mines he remembered were crisp and angular. They radiated a colorful sphere of dread, and the dread was what kept people from going where they weren't supposed to go. It was a perfect system. These, though, were barely visible at the surface of the swamp. They had an animal quality, like squat snapping turtles, except that, instead of taking an assworth's flesh from your shoulder, like the real turtles, they would pound you with a bucket of bent nails going a thousand miles per. These were mines like animals that washed on shore after a tsunami—rigid, translucent whipfish that made you sure there was a God out alone in the universe, hunched over some dense ball of gas, wishing up the most fantastic creatures just to watch them gorge on their peers and rut like jackhammers.

"THIS LOOKS THE same as the last stretch," he huffed to the guide, light on breath from the struggle to drag his desk and accessories through the dense, sluggish undergrowth that pulled at his delicate loafers with each step.

Toshikazu did not turn, just shook his head, holding up one hand to beg for silence.

"Okay, okay. No talking. I get your drift. I can appreciate that. Meanwhile, we're walking around in circles, my slacks are, well, I couldn't even give them away at this point. I mean, they're toast."

Burtson had hired Toshikazu from an ad in the back pages of a monthly magazine for harpooning enthusiasts. Burtson was not interested in harpoons or the people who built and serviced them, but he liked the idea that he could be a collector of things. He liked the thought that he could be master of some great weapon—that he could lean toward a tablemate at dinner and explain how sailors hundreds of years ago managed to pierce the tough armor of a whale's hide without batteries or sonar or rocket fuel. Toshikazu's ad took up a quarter of the page—a crudely designed block of text accompanied by a low-resolution photo of a man hanging upside down from a palm tree, aiming a blowgun at an off-camera target. The text read, "Taking care of loved ones can be a difficult and painful process. Kitano Toshikazu has trained in academies in Europe IV and South Paraguay for over seventeen years. He will treat your loved ones with grace and respect in their final moments, ensuring that they leave this world in peace and with dignity." Burtson did not want his son to feel pain when the time came to take care of him. Worse, though, was the thought of how the boy would be treated afterward if Burtson left the job to the special ops team at KraftMark. They were brutal and immoral, especially Douglas. Rand had once shown Burtson a snapshot of his son's corpse. The kid had packed a clutch of naked, hairlined friends into one of the branded delivery trucks and crashed the thing into a transmission tower. It made the evening news statewide, which was as good as a death sentence. Rand and Burtson were standing side by side in the corporate restroom at

KraftMark headquarters in Delphine. Rand held up a blunt, smudgy Polaroid in the blank wallspace at which Burtson was staring absently. "They gave me this instead of Julian," he said. The boy's naked body was covered in cigarette burns. A pair of panty hose yanked over his head made his face distorted and fat, as if he'd been stung by bees. There were a couple of finishing nails buried in his chest, right through the nipples. Burtson didn't want that for his son. It wasn't necessary.

They trudged for hours, nothing visible ahead or behind them but a massive, shapeless wall of treetop-ish gray. Toshikazu surged forward— deliberately, silently—through the thick water, waltzing through the spidered vines. Alan was out here, somewhere, broadcasting via shortwave radio the ingredients to the *Whatever!?!Round*, a new snack cake developed for KraftMark by Rand and his team for the fall "Fuck You, School!" lunch series. It had already outsold Molt.com's *Wearables Serious Action Fruit Fudge* in three of the test markets. The leaked ingredient list could sink KraftMark, though—everyone was nervous. One of the PR advisers, someone high up—he didn't know half the PR staff—had picked up the signal after getting a tip from the foreign bureau. So far, they'd contained the spread of the broadcast, but it was only a matter of time before it spread.

Something fell out of a tree. Something hard wrapped in something soft. It collided sloppily with a brittle tin roof from the burned-out settlement on the bank, voiding the night of birdsong with its clamor. Burtson crouched reflexively, breathlessly, hugging the rifle to his chest as he hunched in the muck. Toshikazu went on cutting through the water like nothing had happened. This was pretty much the way Toshikazu operated. One morning, Burtson had awoken to the sight of a translucent orange scorpion perched on Toshikazu's face. "Hey man," Burtson had whispered, lightly gripping Toshikazu's shoulder, "Hey man, I don't mean to alarm you? But there's something on your face." Toshikazu opened his eyes, trained them on the insect, and quickly stuffed it into his mouth, chewing fast. All the while, his features were as calm and composed as a white wooden chair. When he'd finished chewing he rolled over and his face went slack almost immediately, weighty with sleep.

Scorpion on his *face*.

The swamp deepened without fanfare. The water rushed up to his chest, roiling up into the trough of his armpits, suddenly and outrageously cold. He smallened.

"What's this? How much deeper will this go?"

Toshikazu did not respond.

"So that's it? Once we're in the thick of it, you ignore me? You certainly had a lot to say back at base camp. You certainly had a lot to say during that impromptu session of baccarat. Remember the fleecing you gave me? Remember the noogie? I do. It's still right here, pulsing at the back of my head. Just like you were giving it to me still."

Toshikazu turned around abruptly. "Simmer down."

"What? What was that? Could you repeat yourself? I could hardly understand what you were saying—you know why? Maybe because you were actually using language."

Toshikazu launched a stare, something hard and remote, so that Burtson wished he hadn't said anything. "You want to know why I don't talk to you out here? You're an embarrassment."

"No disrespect? I know a certain ball team, a well known team of young black men, a team of men that I own, all of whom would disagree with you."

Toshikazu paused by a felled, half-submerged tree and climbed silently onto the warped trunk. "Look there."

Up ahead they saw a tiny square of light flickering in the dark humidity.

"That's it? That's the stronghold?"

"No. That's a trap."

"How can you tell?"

Toshikazu hefted a small rocket launcher to his shoulder, aimed, and fired a purplish, whiffled sphere, which made a bright howling noise as it tore through the black shrubs. The house from which the light emanated lit up for a moment from the incandescent spray of the rocket—it was a boxy, pitched-beam hut, nailed in with tin sheets and old traffic signs. Then it exploded in a wild, thudding ring of gas and wood chips.

Burtson fell back without realizing and got a mouthful of swamp. The inside of his skull went green and bright.

He floated in place on his back, his jacket snagged on a broken branch. Toshikazu crouched at a distance, poking carefully at the rubble with a twig. Burtson struggled briefly to uncouple himself from the branch but he couldn't reach far enough behind him to unhook his collar.

"Please don't do that again," he said when Toshikazu finally waded back to release him. "Please don't blow anything up. That's not necessary."

"There were bodies in the rubble."

"Come again?"

"Neither of them were your son. Let's keep going."

Burtson crawled up the outcropping and poked at the charred hunks of wood with a long branch. "Hey could you—I mean, I'm just wondering— you said there were bodies? In that rubble? The rubble that you, essentially, well, caused?"

Toshikazu was off already, his arms lifted above his chest as he sank deeper into the swamp. Burtson tugged at the cord—his desk was wedged between two half-submerged root balls. He quietly conjured a plume of regret for having overpacked.

It was dark, so dark that even the still things seemed to heave and quake, their outlines no longer registering—the border between the objects and the indefinable world beyond hopelessly blurred and black-ened. The night always made him think of Alan, of the terror the moon brought. Marion insisted Alan sleep in their bed as a baby instead of in a crib, so that when he grew too big to fit, he was incapable of sleeping on his own. In order to wean Alan from the master bedroom, Burtson stayed awake night after night, escorting the boy through the nameless hours as they advanced and ebbed with monolithic fury. He read the boy to sleep, literally bludgeoning Alan with language until the words took him out of commission. He burned through all of the books on the boy's shelf, and when he'd read them again, and through a third time, he began to read from his own collection, books about power and influence, how to broker a deal, books on military strategy, books on the construction of factories, of networked enterprise systems, of team leadership and sup-ply chain management, of ancient battleships and the gray'd, stoic men at their helm. He read until his voice went flat and wisped, until the thought of words was so unbearable he couldn't read any more—like there was a man standing behind him, stuffing his mouth with dry paper towels each time he flexed his jaw. He'd gag and spit; unable, suddenly, to concentrate on anything else. By the time dawn flickered, he felt nearly drowned. He longed for the moment when the light through the window finally overpowered the light from the boy's nightstand, but when it came, he couldn't help feeling that something was being taken from him as well. Those hours he shared with Alan were his—those interminable vigils during which he could truly believe that he was keeping the boy from something.

Now the boy was reading on his own—material he was never meant to read. Now, in this part of life, Alan was doing all the talking. What had happened? How had the boy taken Burtson down like this? He couldn't remember when Alan lost his terror of night. It must have been slow, gradual, imperceptible as evolution itself. But suddenly the boy was out there, acting on his own recognizance. Burtson had expected rebellion, sure. But this betrayal—he could very well have handed the company over to Alan at some point. All the kid had to do was hang in there. Now he was blowing the secret to the world's most successful branded snack cake?

Toshikazu set up a tent on the bank of the swamp, next to a hideous decaying trunk. The tent was low to the ground, so you had to get on all fours to enter. It was barely big enough for the two of them.

"This is how they do it these days?" Burtson said, running his finger along the tent fabric, which was gauzy and light, right up against his face.

"Keeps in the heat. Keeps a low profile."

"Last time I camped, the tents were canvas."

Toshikazu turned over.

"You have anyone?"

Toshikazu opened one opalescent eye. "Once."

"Really? A wife?"

"Yes."

"Tell me about it." Burtson turned, propped himself up on an elbow. His head made a zipping sound against the tent fabric.

"It's not something you want to hear."

"Sure I do."

"No."

"Come on—we're out here—might as well burn off the night."

"You asked me, and you are only American," Toshikazu said, breathing lightly, "So I will tell you what happened. It's an interesting story. My wife and I moved to America shortly after we married. We didn't know much about the country. We just flew to America. It was something we both felt we needed. We didn't have a plan—we just rented a car at the airport and started driving. We drove until it started to snow, and when it snowed so hard we couldn't see, we turned off the highway into the parking lot of a family-style restaurant. The restaurant was in a shopping mall, which was surrounded by deep, man-made moats. It was difficult to navigate through the parking lot of this mall because of all of the lakes and moats, the man-made waterways, what have you. The whole parking lot was blanketed in snow. We drove very slowly, hoping to navigate by feel. I thought about our old house, how I had rigged up all of the lights inside to turn on automatically whenever we were away, to give the impression that we were still home. I thought about those lights, coming on at dusk in the empty house. It occurred to me then, and never before, who was I creating this display for? Who were we trying to fool? I thought too hard about this, because I drove us into one of the man-made lakes. There was a horrible grating noise as the car plowed through the ice ringing the lake's perimeter. The car floated out into the middle of the lake, sinking slowly as it did. I managed to get out of the car through the driver's-side window. I climbed on top of the car. It was so quiet out, I could hear only the snow falling on the parking lot. It was loud, like the cheer of a thousand fans at a soccer match. But there was no other sound. The city was choked off."

"Your wife—"

"She was caught inside. I was on top."

"But couldn't you—I mean could you not help her?" Burtson conjured the words as a scold, but they emerged more plealike.

Toshikazu blinked twice. It was the first time Burtson had seen him do this. "I don't know. I felt like only one of us was going to make it. I might have let her die there."

"That's nonsense. You wouldn't be able to—to do that. No one could let someone die like that."

"Now that you know what I am capable of, I would like to get some sleep." Toshikazu drew a section of sleeping bag up over his head and turned over, facing away from Burtson.

THE NEXT DAY they had to climb a sheer cliff, which took longer than it might have if Burtson had not taken along his desk, which was heavy, even though it was only imitation mahogany. The rolltop kept opening up, jettisoning a cloud of yellow legal paper, which tumbled wildly, scatteringly down the face of the rock. Every time this happened, they had to secure the desk to the cliff face using spikes and rope, and Burtson had to climb down and retrieve each piece of paper.

In the afternoon, Toshikazu grew tired of waiting and picked up a healthy pace. He set up camp along the ridge, sautéing mushrooms while attempting to zero in on Alan's transmissions using a squat red crank radio. Burtson threw a leg over the edge for balance and asked Toshikazu, "A little help?"

His face was purpled and splotched, spattered with dirt and mucus. His hands were trembling so that he could barely grasp the nylon cord. Toshikazu yanked the desk up over the ridge while Burtson collapsed next to the fire. His eyes stung with hot sweat. He could barely open them—he had to struggle, like at the end of a dream when suddenly things go dark, and it takes all of one's strength to move inches.

"Just set it up over there," he said, motioning lamely to a dirty clear spot by a stand of trees.

Toshikazu put the desk down and returned to the fire. "You made me burn the mushrooms," he said, staring evenly into the smoldering pan.

"Good," Burtson said. "I don't go for mushrooms. Humans weren't meant to eat dirt."

"I'm afraid that's your only choice tonight."

Burtson palmed the dry soil before him. He bunched it up, cupping the mound in his hand, as if it were a breast.

"I still don't understand why you would let her die like that."

"I don't know that I let her. It's just that I didn't let her live."

"Are you going to kill my son?"

"Isn't that what we're here for?"

Burtson turned over. At the horizon, the sky was a raging, red cloud-mass, like the throat of an old desert lizard. But up above, he could see stars punching through the navy impossibility of outer space. "I want to offer him a chance. Just one."

"Your staff will kill him if we don't."

"I know, I know. I'm just thinking that I could ship him off somewhere. Put a sombrero on him, a false mustache, send him down to Argentina. Isn't that where all the Nazis went after the war?"

"They'll find him. There is no Argentina."

Toshikazu scrolled through the stations on the shortwave. There was a popping noise, and then a sort of phased, intermittent tone, and then a voice. At first it seemed to be running backward, generating a childlike nonsense language. But Toshikazu homed in on the voice, setting the dial so that it was crystal clear. It was Alan, listing with a patient and even tone the ingredients of the *Whatever!?!Round*.

"Dextrose—okay, listen carefully to this one. I'm going to try to pronounce it and then I'm going to spell it out, because I don't really know how to pronounce this one. 'Maleodexetrine Sulfate'? Does that sound right? M-A-L . . . Apparently, you inject 200 cc's of this substance into the slurry—E-O-D . . ."

Burtson crawled over to the speaker of the shortwave and held his ear very close to it, listening very carefully, as if, in getting closer, he could actually approximate himself geographically to his son. It was an action he knew Toshikazu found pathetic. Burtson would find it pathetic as well, if he were watching from anywhere outside his own body. Unduly and egregiously sentimental. But the voice was arresting, dark and melodic, possessed of an assuredness he hadn't imagined Alan capable of. He could hear, in the brief intervals between breaths, or in the throat clearing, or during the pauses to keep the microphone from falling over in the wind, a tuneful, barely perceptible cough, one Burtson knew from those early years, the pre-KraftMark years, a time of unsustainable pressure, in which he was working late into the nights, away from home, high up on the twenty-third floor of an office building that, at night, might as well have been the bridge of an enormous spacecraft, adrift in deep space, all the city's lights like distant stars, his son the inhabitant of a planet he could barely remember. He'd come home and shuffle, on his knees, to the side of Alan's bed to tender him into sleep. The boy would twitch occasionally, shifting in the sheets, making that coughing sound, like the cough of a vole or some other burrowing rodent, an animal that wanted nothing more than to go unnoticed.

"He's transmitting from a mountain top," Toshikazu said, rising to scan the horizon, his voice suddenly fraught with tremors.

"Know what?" Burtson said, "I'm fine with this. I'm good. He's not doing anyone any harm. He's just crazy. Let him stay here, that's what I say. Let the crazy kook live up here on the mountain. He's not hurting anybody. Let's head back to base camp."

Toshikazu looked back sharply. "Don't do this. Allow your son the terminal dignity of dying by your own hand. Don't let them do it. They'll tear open his nutsack and scrub out his genes with a wire brush. They'll staple his hands to his buttocks and throw him out of a helicopter into the main square of some remote village. You want that for your son?"

"Nobody wants that."

"Pick up your things and let's go."

Burtson heaved himself up, scraping open a kneecap on a toothsome mound of jagged black rock. He wished for an aerosol can of Secret Skin, the kind he used to spray over Alan's playground injuries. He attached the nylon cords from the desk to his harness and lurched forward, following Toshikazu at a lame, distant pace.

As the night overtook the sky behind them, pressing at their backs like a suffocating tarp, Toshikazu spotted a silhouetted figure seated on a ridge. He crouched behind a stand of weeds, pointing the figure out to Burtson, who couldn't make anything out. It was all just jaggedness and splinters against the red flush of the dying sun.

"This is the end of my job," he said, squinting at the distant point.

"How do I do this?" Burtson's shoulders started to gyrate uncontrollably. He crossed his arms, pressing his palms against his ribcage, but he couldn't hold back the twitching muscles that hijacked his torso.

"Just like we did in the training sessions." Toshikazu slipped the rifle from its polyester case.

"Those were dummies. Those were stuffed dummies."

"The human body is really just a moist, complex version of those dummies." He loaded the magazine and powered on the infrared sight before handing it to Burtson, who held it like a candy bar.

"I think you're a little out of line."

"Nobody on this mountain is anything more than a brilliantly designed sack. The only distinguishing feature is what others have crammed inside us over time."

"An interesting take. I wonder what your wife would have thought about that."

Toshikazu pressed the knuckles of his right hand up into his top teeth.

Burtson held the rifle in front of him, as far from his chest as he could reach. "If you don't mind, please remind me how to aim this thing. I'd like to get this over with."

"Figure it out. Figure it out your goddamned motherfucking self." Toshikazu turned away and dropped down from the cliff edge in a swift, deliberate arc.

Burtson hefted the rifle. It was all trigger, all form factor; it fit into the crook of his arm like a newborn. There was a scope, larger in diameter than a baseball bat, and it looked like it needed to be turned on. He turned it over in his hands again and again, but it never made any more sense. He decided to give it a shot anyway. There was a sort of raised fin on the nozzle, so he used this for aim. He heard Toshikazu behind him. "That's not— look, you're going to hurt yourself."

He felt something surge up in him, something heavy and luminescent. It rose up in his chest cage, topping off at the back of his throat. It was a feeling he remembered not in his conscious memory but in the larger memory everybody shared, the memory of the flattened, husky humanoids who knocked around in squat forests in the years before time mattered, making a dim impression in their respective tribes by killing up whole herds with insensate panache. The feeling made sense—he was aware, fully, maybe for the first time, of the extent of his body's capabilities. There were no more illusions—he knew he was not a superhero—he knew he could not burst through a brick wall or kick a man's balls up through his chest. It was a sober, rational summary of what he could do with his body.

Burtson lined up the fin with Alan's figure and squeezed the trigger impulsively. The rifle was surprisingly quiet. The figure turned, startled, as a congregate of broad leaves exploded in the air over his head. "They're here," his son shouted into the microphone. "This is it. I'm not going to make it out of here. They won't leave until I'm taken out. Don't let the recipe die—keep it going. Keep it—"

Burtson fired again, and a third time. The figure jerked backward. "Holy crap," he said. "Holy crap." He wished Toshikazu had stayed; he felt a queer pride click into place somewhere inside, but quickly he thought better of it. Shooting your son: it was a private thing, composed of a sweet, crushing sense of impossibility. You didn't want to share it, in the end.

Burtson dropped the rifle and sat at his desk, where Toshikazu had left a Post-it note with his billing address. He took his cell phone from the top drawer and tried his wife. Somehow, he got a ringtone. A woman answered the phone in another language. "Hello? Marion?" he said, and the voice replied in a fluttery, unrecognizable tongue. Realizing it was a stranger, he whispered, "I just shot my son," feeling each word turn in his dry, dirty mouth like rocks in a tumbler. "I took aim and I shot him. Has that ever happened to you?" The voice erupted again, and then died off sharply. He thought the woman might have hung up. "It's a thing you remember," he said. "It might be the only thing you really remember. You take back what you've given. It goes against—it's a powerful thing, what you've done when you do that." He stopped when he heard the silence of the disconnected call. He wasn't sure if the woman hanging up had hurt him more than the sight of his son slowly folding up into a compact hump on the horizon. He was sure he'd know later, on the plane, speeding ridiculously over a charcoal-dark, midsize, failing industrial hub. When he got farther away from the jungle, he thought, he'd be able to measure the two events, hold them, one in each palm, and divine to himself the thing he felt worst about.

THE HOOK

Shelley Jackson

TRAVIS BROUGHT IN a dog's leg that he said fell out of the sky. One end
was ragged and chewed-looking, its bloody bits gone hard and dark. It was
still enrobed in short brown fur. I was glad about that. Betsy had been redder. The leg had landed right beside him, cracking a sheet of plywood, and
bounced. It could have brained him, I thought, with a familiar wooze of
panic. He was laughing, waving it around, touching things with it. "Give
paw," he cried, and extended it to me.

Then he hurled it down (I heard the nails click against the floor) and
his face caved in. I held out my arms and he buried his head in my stomach. As his jaw worked it felt like he was trying to eat me.

"Come on," I said. "We'll go look at the fire."

He sniffed and choked. "Really?"

THE FIRE WAS kept burning all the time. It was in the fenced-in lot
behind the former supermarket, where they used to take in deliveries. The
supermarket was used as a morgue, now, and the dead were wheeled out
back in shopping carts. At the loading dock they were draped over the
hook. The bodies were hoisted and swung into the center, where they were

received into the oily smoke. The crane performed a jerky but practiced dance, and the hook returned empty.

The crane was the tallest thing around. It was visible from all over the neighborhood, leaning over the pyre in an attitude of grave attention. We knew, though we could not see him, that the crane operator, too, gave the dead his full attention. We believed this, though we also believed that the crane operator was the crudest sort of person, given to rude jokes about the dead, and never clean. His face and hair were slicked with black grease "from the hinges of death's door," said Loss, with relish, quoting some song. His long skirts were always scabbed with disgustingness. The crane operator was a figure invoked by children during sleepovers to induce giggling and shivers. We trusted him, all the same, and felt there was none better for the job. We would not have trusted our dead to a diplomat. The hook must not be coy or self-conscious. It must have no protocol but need. That was exactly what made it the closest thing we could imagine to holy. That's how I felt, anyway, and I'm sure others felt the same.

The crane and the crane operator were always there, minding the dead. Even if, as he must sometimes do, the crane operator slept at his controls, he was still presiding, and we believed that even his dreams concerned the dead.

I WRAPPED THE dog's leg in plastic and threw it away, but it turned out that Travis kept it. I saw him playing with it, using it like a golf club. Well, let him. He has few enough toys.

Travis had taken to wearing a gigantic coat he'd found. It puddled around his feet. To walk without tripping, he had to take wide strides, punting the skirts forward at each step. So when he steps his legs apart and hunches over, adjusting his grip on the dog's leg, his sleeves almost touch the ground. He straightens, letting the dog's leg lean against his legs, and rolls them up into two big donuts around his arms. Then he resumes his pose. He taps the dog's foot lightly on the ground, then swings.

Something thwacks into Loss's shack, a dome of filthy rugs draped over a hutch, and a gentleman staggers out, laughing, and looks around. Loss pokes her head out after, laughing too. Her nose is bleeding, but she doesn't seem to notice.

Travis gives the gentleman a Nazi salute with the dog's leg.

I SAID THEY were always there, but actually there were times when—nobody knew why—the crane left its post to rove through the city. When we saw that black arm raised above our shacks, our nerves trilled, but whether in fear or welcome we didn't know. If we dreaded the sight of the crane, why did we strain so hard to make out the silhouette of the operator in his cab?

The operator and the hook often appear merged in our dreams, as a familiar stranger with one deformed hand, or a page of type on which one word is misspelled.

FROM LOSS'S HUT comes a scream: "Oh—Oh—Oh!" Travis looks at me apprehensively, but when I don't react, he goes back to playing. When we go out later we see Loss outside her hut, upending bottles on wires stuck in the ground, to dry. Travis stops in his tracks, looking at her, then starts running around like crazy.

Next time we hear Loss scream, Travis says, "What's Loss doing?"

"Fucking," I say. Why not tell him? He will be fucking someone himself before long. I can't say I like the idea, but it's so. But then I regret saying it, because he looks so miserable. Did he really not know what Loss was doing? Or did he hope that I didn't know? I wonder what "fucking" means to him. Should I explain it? Or will that just make things worse?

I'M NOT LOSS, but I get lonely too. One night, I went to the hook. On the embankment above the lot, I found a slit in the fence, one of several

I knew of. Nobody bothered to repair them: the fire did not need protecting, though the gate was kept locked all the same. On the other side,
I banged my ankle on what my fingers informed me was a jutting slab of
asphalt rubble. "*Hook*," I ejaculated, and proceeded at a stoop, waving my
hands gently before me. I descended a creaking slope of corrugated fiber-
glass roofing on my butt. Rising, I booted something light that my hands
had missed, and heard it *boing* off into the blackness, and almost saw it,
a pale bounding form, probably a plastic jug. Then the ground leveled out
to a gritty pavement, glinting with tiny fires. Finally I looked at the fire
directly, and stopped. I couldn't go on; the fire was so bright, I couldn't
see anything else. I was like a dark planet, suspended in groundless blackness, in eternal contemplation of a sun.

The fire was emitting a continuous throaty groan. Skeins of dark
vapors unspooled from a thousand sources in the mound and swirled in
the middle air, gathering themselves only reluctantly into the larger body
of smoke that rose, leaning slightly, from the fire. Underlit with orange,
it seemed an almost solid body, a never-ending turd of giant proportions.
Where the light gave out, though, beyond the huge, hieratic shape of the
hook and the faintly outlined geometry of the crane's arm, it disappeared
into the night sky whose blackness elsewhere seemed transparent. It
seemed that the night was all smoke, that this was how night was made.

Eyes a little accustomed to the darkness again, I looked down. A silhouetted dog, invisible before—or maybe simply not there; startled by my
approach, she had just now returned to her post—was pacing back and
forth in front of the blaze, long teats swinging despite her thinness,
skinny tail clinging to her flanks, as if protecting her from a blow so long
anticipated that reflex had become habit. Sometimes she stopped with paw
raised, considering something at the very edge of the fire, then shied, eyes
kindling as she wheeled.

I took a few steps. As I approached she got agitated, looking back and
forth between me and the fire, her forelegs high-stepping. Finally she
pawed at the fire, letting out an almost simultaneous yelp. Something at
which I didn't want to look too closely rolled a little way out of the flames.

Hunching, she closed her jaw on it, released it, shaking her jowls, rolled her eyes at me, then clamped her jaw on it, and cantered with it, whining softly, into the shadows under the crane.

I followed slowly. I did not want to seem like I was chasing her, laying a rival claim to her treat. I felt for her, and anyway, she looked hungry enough to fight me for it.

The shadow of the crane made a black pool in which I could barely make out the step up to the cab. I saw the dog's illumined eyes, farther under. They watched me steadily. "Betsy?" I said experimentally. The two lights burned clear.

I felt for the handhold I knew was there and swung myself up onto the step. I tapped on the door, but it was already opening. The crane operator welcomed me wordlessly, as if he had expected me. There was a strong smell in the cab, smoky, meaty. I shuddered and forced myself to breathe freely. The crane operator opened his stinking coat and took me under it, and we went down, awkwardly, to the floor. His body was surprisingly smooth and hot. I thought of Travis, the only body I ever touched now, though less and less often these days.

Even inside the cab, I could feel the heat of the fire. The roof was redly aglow. Light crazed the smeary windshield. Finally, I was warm.

OUR CONGRESS WAS satisfactory, save for one moment, when a sudden chill on my slobbered pussy made me open my eyes. He had lifted his head, the cables of his neck ashine. I looked at him with surprise. I had forgotten he had a face. "What's your name?" he said.

I thought a minute. "Rose," I said.

His face began to have the businesslike expression of a man who is introducing himself. I heaved up my hips to confront his mouth with what he had forsaken, at which his eyes crossed. Then, perceiving that was not enough, I heaved up my knees and clamped my thighs on his head, so that he fell forward with a surprised huff into my pubic hair, where whatever he might have told me became hot air. He went back to his good work and I lazed my eyes up to the corrugated roof and then closed them again, thinking I did not want to know his name, or whether I might have known him before he became the crane operator. I wanted the crane operator, that's all.

⁂

IT WAS NOT yet even close to dawn, but a bluer light began to fill the cabin. Through the windshield I could just make out what had been invisible at night, the smoke. Actually, when I looked at it directly, I could not see it, but when I looked away there it was, black against the blue. I lay and watched it become visible as the sky paled. It rose straight up through the windless air.

The crane operator was a silent hot weight on my shoulder. I drew my arm slowly out from under him. He didn't wake. I sat up and looked at him, pulling the end of his coat over my knees. I was afraid I might see something disgusting, in the cool light, a scab at the hairline, or something gummy stuck in his hair, but there was nothing like that. He looked peaceful. I got dressed and climbed over him to get out. The cab door cawed and cool smoky air flowed in, but he didn't wake up, so I just left. I didn't see the dog.

My feet seemed very loud as I crunched and rattled through the rubble past slumbering huts. A lone dog woofed once.

I lifted the flap of our hut and came into the sweet smell of Travis sleeping.

⁂

A DEAD MAN and woman are draped together over the hook. As first the woman, then the man, is draped over the hook, I feel the cab adjust slightly to their weight; slight as it is, it changes the balance of the whole system, as my presence in the cab must also. The crane operator throws a lever, shifts into reverse. The cab bucks. Despite the operator's violent movements, the grinding of gears, and the lurching of the cab, the movements of the hook itself are smooth and languorous, all abrupt movements damped by the long, heavy cable. The crane operator seems to know where the hook is without looking, as if it were part of his own body.

The couple rise, swinging in a smooth arc over the pyre, where the smoke conceals them. He brakes before they are quite over the pyre, lets the momentum of the crane, the hook, its burden carry them into the smoke. They are engulfed, but a moment later reappear below the smoke, descending through the silvery miasma of the incandescent air. They are sheeny, quicksilver.

Her dress is on fire. One minute it wasn't, the next, she is burning. Her hair is a torch. His too. I don't want to watch anymore.

I look at the operator. He is absorbed. The cab settles as the hook lowers some of its weight onto the pyre. He jiggles two levers at once, his face unreadable. Then, though I detected no change, he throws one back, and the hook soars free.

"My name isn't Rose," I said. "It's Rebecca."

I NO LONGER dream about the crane operator. Not, in any case, the way I did, as a shepherd of souls, or Virgil, or Charon. I dream about Zachary Holle.

I WAS EATING some meat Travis got in trade for a book he'd foraged— he's a good provider, already—and I bit down hard on a bone. Something crunched inside my jaw and I tasted blood and found one of my teeth alongside my tongue. I did not tell Zachary, who might have worried that I was sick, since that's one of the signs, though I was sure that this time it was just an accident. I spit it out into my hand and put it in my pocket. Later I washed it and considered. I wanted to give it to Zachary. I wanted to give it to Travis, too. Finally I gave it to Travis. The sickness didn't even seem to cross his mind. He immediately went and found a little bag somewhere, to put my tooth in, and hung it around his neck.

When I see how happy he is about it I feel guilty that I even considered giving it to Zachary.

ONE MORNING COMING home I see some early riser sitting outside her house. I consider taking a detour around her, but decide against it. There is no rule against fucking the crane operator, though nobody, to my knowledge, has ever done it. But maybe everyone has done it, keeping it a secret. Someday I will ask Zachary. Or not.

She is leaning back against a great, tilted slab of reinforced concrete from which the metal writhed stilly against the flamingo light. She stares at me as I pass and I lift my hand to her. Then it occurs to me that she might be dead, which makes my waving hand feel strange. Well, it's someone else's concern if she is.

When I push the rug aside, I see Travis is not in his bed. Right away I begin hurrying around the hut, pushing on the carpets hung on the walls as if he were likely to be standing behind one, waiting for me, for hours maybe. "Where are you Travis, where are you," I chant.

Guilty for what?

Well.

I leave and walk quickly around the neighborhood. My neighbors look at me pass and I consider asking if they have seen Travis but I decide not to. I go as far as the embankment over the fire. I already know Travis is not here, though it used to be his favorite place to go. I see Zachary shoving at something in the fire with a charred push broom, its bristles burned off. He does not see me. It is strange to look at him from this distance again; it's the view I had of him when he was a stranger, so now, for a moment, he seems like a stranger again and I think of the two rosettes of hair around his soft nipples and am shocked.

I hurry back. The woman is no longer leaning on her slab. Either someone came with a cart or she was alive all along and I have a reputation. I don't care. I am happy thinking Travis will be home now. More and more he will disappear on some boy business and I will have to let him.

But he is not there.

I try to make some gruel but I keep forgetting to stir it, so it hardens into a great fist on the end of the spoon. I gnaw at it a little but it's foul—

burned on the outside, grainy and gummy inside. So I sit down outside our hut and just wait. I look back and forth, first toward the huts of my neighbors and the smoke and the black arm of the crane, then toward downtown where we don't go.

It is midday when I see him coming out of Loss's hut. I stand up. As he comes up the tilted slab of flooring between our huts I stretch out my hand to him. He springs up without my help, but then, since I don't withdraw my hand, he stops and reluctantly extends a bulky arm, shaking back the cuff. Even so I have to root around inside it for his hand.

I feel something cold and bristly.

"Hook!" I let go and push back the sleeve. The smell of dishonesty rises. There is the dog's leg, small, dark, and stiff. Its wrist extends back into Travis' sleeve.

"Travis!"

"What?" says Travis, smirking.

"What were you doing with Loss?" I say instead. I find that I am shaking.

"Fucking," he says, proud and mean. He's quoting me, though I'm not sure he knows it, even if there is a lilt of mockery in his voice.

Then he starts to cry. Oh, thank hook.

Choking, he hunches to hide his face. I know it's terrible for him to cry, and especially to let me see him cry right now, when he is being magnificent. But for now, I can still comfort him, even for this, the shame of having a mother. I put my arms right around him and pick him up, as if he were still a little boy. He presses his face against my shoulder, sobbing. His arms are bunched up between us, and the dog's paw jabs into my cheek. I turn my head and kiss its darling, darling little pads.

SIXTEEN SMALL APOCALYPSES

Lucy Corin

STORY

1. FIRST I responded in the way I thought he wanted me to respond and then I heard what it was he said, which I was not sure how I felt about after all, and have now forgotten. 2. Then she notices that if she agrees with the woman, the woman will assume they have both read the article, and she can watch the esteem growing in the woman's eyes the more silent she becomes. 3. When he was a boy in *The Pied Piper*, cast as a witch who had one early scene and one late scene, in the first scene the Pied Piper said a line from the late scene, so he pictured the line in the script, white next to his in yellow highlight, and as he pronounced the line that followed it—his line, as he saw it—all the rats' eyes went shifty but everyone proceeded directly to the end of the play from there, and even the kids who never made it to the stage took their curtain call responsibly. 4. Later, she was thinking how weird it would be to be a horse and to have a crop hit you behind the saddle out of nowhere.

BOATS

WHEN ANNIE WAS a child, her mother explained her gift and burden: that what she saw was not what others saw. "You know better than that," she told her daughter. "You know better than *them*," she said. Growing up, Annie felt isolated and misunderstood.

Walking by the water a man said to her: "Look at that boat." There was no boat in the ocean that she could see, but he sounded sincere.

Later, another man, this one with a hat, said, "Look at that boat," and this time she did see a boat; it was exactly as he said. But as soon as he said it the boat seemed truer than any boat she'd seen before with her own eyes only.

"Watch it," said her mother, on the phone. Annie stared at her kitchen cabinetry, and saw her mother deep in the glossy paint.

Later, she was eating an enormous salad at an outdoor café by the harbor. Every few bites she bent under the table to rearrange a folded napkin under one of its three feet. Soon, she added a bottle cap under a second foot. The third foot hovered. Then, she scooched the table around on the cement. She took another few bites of the salad and it loomed like a mountain in front of her. She could see her knees through the mottled glass tabletop. The top wobbled in its white metal frame. She looked around, feeling the edges of panic. Everyone seemed happy as bunnies. Bunches ate, clinking glasses. Annie turned sharply in her chair, this way, and then the other way. A few people looked up. Her breath felt like a train. More people looked up. A boat went by. It was a harbor and still she could only see one boat. It went by, sails gushing, and by the time she couldn't see it anymore everyone in the café had turned to watch her as item by item, signposts, trashcans, pedestrians, and then plank by plank the pier, disappeared, until she was sitting with her salad in a desert at the ocean surrounded by nothing but suspended eyes.

NIGHT AND DAY

I DRIVE BY a motel when I need anything from the other side of town. Town's built like an hourglass, and there's a big lit sun shining from the motel sign. They put all the houses down here and all the stuff up there, so if I'm going to get anything I have to go by it. That's a pun.

In this motel, pets are okay. There's a parking lot around it, and a rising hill of grass around that, like the bank of a moat. Wait until it really starts raining!

An hourglass. Figures. Because of time.

So I drive by, and this time it's day, with the sun over the sun. I see a woman's head doing a swivel, like behind the bank she's riding in a bumper car in a parking space. There's a dog on a leash: I can't see the dog, but I know it's there behind the land. This is suspicious, or prophetic, seeing someone's head but not whatever makes it do the things it does.

Then at night . . . I tell you . . . the sun at night. It's not right. It's a symptom. It cancels everything out. But if I want anything, it's down that road.

Night, day. I think about getting by. I don't know what to do. It's hard to tell if I get any sleep. I feel pressure to do one thing or another. Sometimes I look up and say "Give me a sign!" but of course I'm kidding. It's only a matter of time before something blows.

PHONE

ALL THE BOYS across the courtyard have girlfriends. This boy on the phone on the porch in springtime is letting his voice move, light as a leaf in a river. He's saying, "It's like I'm only me when I'm around you." He's twirling a piece of grass between his thumb and forefinger, watching its head spin. "You're the only one who knows," he's saying. "I know you won't tell anyone."

Dim through the walls behind him his friends are playing their guitars without the amplifiers and laughing with daiquiris. He is secret from everyone, especially the girl on the phone. It's obvious to anyone paying attention. When the earth shakes and the dust of the rest of the world rises from the lawn, when the posts that hold the roof above him snap, he feels no more misty and no less certain than he had the moment before. He still says, "I love you" into the phone, and believes it the same. The girl on the phone, who always felt afraid he might not love her, feels the earth turning to powder as he says the words, and thinks, "This must mean he really loves me," and in the next instant thinks, "It doesn't count!" and by the next moment the end of the world has already happened. The telephone and the amplifier dot hillsides on opposite ends of the universe. The boy's eyelashes flutter and spin like a blown dandelion. The girl's fingernails sparkle in shards.

STAR CHART

WE TOOK A day trip to San Francisco and I wanted dim sum, which I've never gotten to eat, but my uncle basically ordered only shrimp and one pork thing and the pork thing was so divine I just haven't had anything like it—it was so cinnamon-y and had puffy white bun stuff around it. Like a cake you might make. But all the rest was one delicious yet almost identical shrimp thing after another. My uncle sensed a bit of boredom with the shrimp from us girls. He said, "I just wanted to show you what I like."

He's a glassblower and he makes a lot of fish to sell. He also scuba dives and goes on fly-fishing trips and deep-sea fishing trips. He also collects fish figures, mostly realistic ones. One time when I was visiting he was swimming and got stung by a whole mass of jellyfish and came back to the house covered in whip marks, but he was so quiet, and just sat there while my aunt put meat tenderizer on him that I didn't really see that he was in any pain. In Chinatown I liked the tea shops and candy shops, not to eat (my uncle enjoys the dried octopus snacks) so much as to wonder at. All those categories of things and I can't remember any of the names just that there was a lot. My cousin bought a silk haltertop, "for clubbing if he'll let me out of the house" and I bought a cotton robe. She's the blonde and I'm the brunette. Then we went to the aquarium.

"Sturgeon! Yum!" I have never been to an aquarium with someone who wanted to eat everything. Then on the way back to the cabin we picked up Dungeness crabs and clams and mussels and my uncle made that San Francisco–style stew with sourdough for dinner. We ate outside. I hardly ever look at the sky, but my uncle looked up, crossing his legs and sipping his wine. My uncle was getting pretty drunk, which at first comes off like he's a little pleased with himself, lightening up (he's a big guy) but pretty soon his psychology starts rumbling. He went into his bags and got out a star chart. I don't know anything about stars. He came back out and said, "Speaking of child abuse . . ." and my cousin got up from the table and went inside and came back with an extra shirt to put on. He said, "Remember how we used to look at the stars?" and my cousin said, "Dad, put the chart away," and put the shirt on. He kept not letting up on the subject. I couldn't tell what he wanted me to do, if it was a test involving whether or not I'd think the star chart was cool. I cleared some dishes and he followed me into the kitchen with the star chart. It was yellow, with two parts that revolved in relation to each other.

I could just see it, though, because he's a lot like my own father, tottering after me, shaking me by the shoulders, saying, "Goddamn you, girl, why aren't you following in my footsteps?" My cousin and I have talked about how I'm not going to have any kids for my reasons and she's not going to have kids for her reasons. We look at each other and know we're the end of the line.

APOCALYPSE

THEY COULD STAY afloat for only so long before the deranged creatures picked them off. They were so thirsty or so hungry. They swirled in the raging wind, fire, and water. Their skin shriveled. Time had ended and yet passed. Parched, they watched the last particles of moisture rise and fade in the golden air above the orange earth. There have never been colors like this. They trudged on and on but the land was barren. Fungus rotted their limbs and bacteria new to the dying world cruised their organs. Germs, maggots, and death from virile viral microscopic life loomed in the near future. Buildings tumbled upon them. Flying debris severed them. Chasms opened wide and swallowed. They were crushed and strewn, and they exploded. Their brains burst from the noise. A spinning cow or lamp broke them. Their insides fell out. Their fingers crumbled. They were all half-dead anyway, until they died.

DINOSAUR

A DINOSAUR LAY under a rainbow in a white sunset on shining hills. The girl reached for the imaginary hand of the ghost. The ghost had been trailing her for states, holding his basket, ever since the apocalypse. In the basket, tiny ghosts of prairie dogs and butterflies, mongeese and baby foxes wobbled, nested, nuzzling in their contained afterlife. The vast exposed land, its lid lifted, its whole history layered under the grass, now history: girl, dinosaur, ghost, basket, teetering on the deserted road in the light air. The dinosaur's anchor-shaped nose brushed the grass tips at its knees. Plateaus of clouds seemed still. The hand of the ghost was not a hand, it was the memory of hands, or now, since the apocalypse, the idea that a hand could come. She missed her dog. Purple flowers massed and then spread thinly over the field. Yellow flowers made a wave near the road. She remembered how many people must have used to have been awakening each moment. With so little left after the silent blast that razed so much and left so much as well—too much to take in, to count, witness, know, hunt, cover, recall— she didn't know what to do with her still empty hand full as it was to be, if she could reach it, with that much ghost. The dinosaur looked heavy, the rainbow looked light, and the hills could have been covered in snow, or nothing, or something that had never existed before.

CAKE

SHE BAKED AN angel food cake for the dinner party, which means it's as white as possible in cake except golden on the outside and you have to cut it with a serrated knife. It's funny to eat because you can kind of tear it, unlike most cakes. It stretches a little. It's a little supernatural, like an angel.

I was watching her with her boyfriend because I admire them and am trying to make them an example in my life of good love being possible. Toward the end of the cake everyone was talking and a couple of people were seeing if they could eat the live edible flowers that she'd put on the cake for decoration. A fairy cake. She told a story about making the cake.

There wasn't a lot left. Everyone was eating the ends of their pieces in different ways, and because of the stretchy texture there were more methods than usual, and no crumbs at all.

Really funny cake.

I tried to imagine making the cake, same as I often tried to imagine love. I would never make a cake. So it's down to say less than a quarter of the cake and the boyfriend reaches across the table—it's a big table that no one else would be able to reach across, he just has really long arms, and he takes the serrated knife but when he cuts at the cake he doesn't do the sawing action, he just presses down which defeats the point(s!) of the serrated knife. The cake squishes as he cuts it in half; it was only a piece of itself already, clinging to its imaginary axis, and now it's not even a wedge—it's pushed down like you can push down the nose on your face—and then he takes his piece with his hands and I watch the last piece of cake to see if it'll spring back up but it doesn't, it's just squished on one side like someone stepped on it.

But here's what I don't understand, is how all through it she's just chatting with the dinner guests and it's like he's done nothing at all. She's not looking at him like, "You squished the cake!" and she's not looking at him like, "He loves the cake so much he couldn't help himself," and he doesn't seem to be thinking, "Only I can squish the cake!" Or is he?

I never know how to read people.

But here's what else: watching the round cake disappear, watching the people trying to make the most of their pieces, people coveting the cake on one hand and reminding themselves on the other that this will not be the last cake. But will it be the last? I look at their love and I feel like this could be the very last piece of it on earth, and just *look* at it.

FEELINGS

I SMOOTHED THE described sheet over the described person I'd loved before the apocalypse. The rich feelings welled from the page emotionally. Under the blanket, the person I loved remained. We used to mean so much.

THREAT

FOR YEARS, A telephone pole leaned, a low fear at the back of the neighborhood. That evening he went home and poured several very even trays of ice cubes. I was dressed for the apocalypse. I was depressed for the apocalypse. I carried a bundle of dust like a nest. My heart beat in its fleshy pocket. Worms had tried to make it across our porch over night and now they lay like something shredded, like shredded bark, but deader. My brother, looking ashen, kept waiting for the telephone. I missed out on all the gossip. An iris wilted into a claw. A rowboat rocked in our vast yard. New birds gathered like, I don't know, a lack of entropy?

DOLL

NOW SHE STEPS into the street of her town that has been cleaned by a supernatural oven. The chemical stench is left. The sky is a soft green. Behind the haze the sun hums, fuzzed like a moldy fruit. She is not quite sure where her limbs are in relation to her body. Something has happened to the air and given it a texture of fog. It is either hard to see through or her eyes are changed or there is a funny color or blur to everything and she has objects mixed up with the air. Across the street is the bank, with its mirrored exterior, and there's something on the sidewalk in front of it. What is the logic of this apocalypse? What is eradicated and what is left or half-left, zombie-like, behind? Is what's left behind a code?

Zombies are codes. They are codes of warning. They are the form of our preapocalyptic foolishness; our sort-of-dumb-sort-of-evil existence that led to this, which is our fault even if it turns out the final threat was the one from outer space.

What she finds on the sidewalk will help us know. As she approaches the object she discovers that it could be one of two things: it could be a doll, or it could be a baby. If this is a doll, she thinks, then this is a sentimental apocalypse.

She can see herself kneeling at the doll, touching its cold fingers, raising her eyes as if she is being witnessed, meeting her own eyes in the mirrored bank wall. This could make the television right after all.

Luckily, when she arrives, it's not, and when she touches its fingers the fingers are like rubber. Then when she raises her eyes she is startled to find she sees eyes that are not her own; they are the eyes of a ghost who is standing in the street behind her. When she turns she cannot see the ghost, but back in the mirror, there the ghost is. The ghost doesn't really look at her. The ghost only sort of has eyes. The ghost is a little bit clothed, a little cloaked. The ghost is hard to see. It's heavier than vapor; more held together than dust, more specifically formed than constellation, and it seems, she decides, to be a male ghost. She gazes across the baby at the ghost. Jesus, Mary and Joseph, she thinks. It's the three of us left to redeem civilization.

JULY FOURTH

GOT THERE AND the ground was covered in bodies. Lay down with everybody and looked at the sky, grinning and bracing for the explosions.

THE OTHER WAY AROUND

WE CAME AT last to the wackily fantastic land of opposites. We'd read this one in childhood. Candy tasted terrible and we all wanted liver with onions. Water got us drunk and we could only breathe when we were under it. Right was wrong and so we were very popular. Our mouths swapped spots with our assholes. Our belly buttons turned outward, (except for George's) and our vaginas, well, you had to be there. The birds under our feet annoyed us with their philosophies. It was the end of all we'd known, and our hopes sank.

MINIONS

THE MINIONS LINED their sneakers along the wall and then made two lines, like teams at the end of a game, and each by each held hands and touched foreheads. They were past words. They'd been hollering and leafleting for months. They'd been psyching themselves up and out for years. They lay in their cots like orphans. Hands to hearts, eyes to the black air, the rafters of the bunker invisible in the dark, a sky without stars, everything celestial sprinkling the insides of their domed minds. They waited for the world to disintegrate. It would disintegrate before next light and they waited for a red and gold explosion to light the universe in one final burst. They listened to night tick through the wooden walls. It could be now, or now, or now. Someone held back a sneeze and then sneezed. They'd abandoned their timepieces in the river that evening at dusk, but at two A.M. a boy named Jonathan got up from his cot, cracked open the door, put his penis out and peed. Then he went back to his cot. One woman, a secret doubter, had taken a bottle of pills before she lay down to wait and died with the click the boy made closing the door.

By morning, there have been three more suicides and two of the leaders have disappeared into the woods. One leader is weeping under a tree, fallen leaves in his fists. One leader is running, running, running, hoping he will die midstep, trying to feel the moment within each step when he is sure both feet are off the ground because he feels that if he can prolong that beat he will be flying, he will be without his body finally, he will be light, light air, light light. In the hut one minion has punched another in the chest. One is cross-legged on her cot, watching. She's vacant or else she's fuming. Three have closed themselves in the kitchen and begun to screw. Two are quietly packing their knapsacks, stuffing them as full as they can with any useful items the group had forgotten or not bothered to purge: a woolen lap blanket, a can-opener, a tin of olives, a box of matches, a comb, a tube of lip balm. By two o'clock in the afternoon the bunker is empty except for a few dead bodies and one man, badly beaten, who is clinging to his cot like it's a raft, who is gasping for breath and calling "Help! Help!"

MIRROR

TWO DAYS SINCE the apocalypse and freckles rise in the skin around my mouth. I am very close to my face, looking. Green funnels of what were pastures whirl and spit in the background. The last bits of cities are like comets and pass behind my head as if I am shooting myself repeatedly, as if I shoot myself and the fireballs go in one ear and out the other. It's riveting. It's hypnotic. My face contains more colors than are left in the universe. I watched Miranda's teeth panic and run away. I watched Amber buckle. Now, in the mirror, there is no comparison. It's me, and everything, and that's all.

WITCHES

THREE GIRLS, MAYBE eight each, stand with sticks at a pothole of water. They're leaning, or stirring. It's hard to tell, because they're frozen, although it's summer. They're looking into the water together, with their sticks. Dim oils sketch the surface like lines from skating. One girl, the one in the middle, from this angle, anyway, has a piece of grass between her teeth, and she's grimacing. The end of the grass has fluffy seeds, and normally, it'd be bobbing. There's breeze, yet all is still. In this apocalypse, the air, it seems, can move, though nothing in it can. Where do you draw the line? Even seeds that could drift like smoke stick. There's no logic in it. Especially with pages accumulating, time continuing to pass. The girl on the supposed left is turning to dust as we speak, but invisibly, like a figure made of icing going stale. Touch her and poof.

I know what they were doing. The girls were playing "three witches." They were making magic. They were poking their stew. They kept meaning to get on with their game. They'd planned to capture someone, and they'd planned to turn a bunch of things into other things. But after a while the entire plot had been taken over by recipes for potions. Then, of all things, this is what happened.

THE LAST MAN

Adam Nemett

EVEN HITLER WAS on meth. I saw it on the History Channel. Under the green light of the German morning, Hitler's personal physician—Dr. Theo Morell—would enter his bedroom to administer charisma intravenously: a cocktail injection of methamphetamines and morphine, plus cocaine eyedrops. Hitler never asked what was in the needle and Theo never offered the secret. He simply upped the dosage until Adolf succumbed to something like Parkinson's, something like addiction, and drowned in his own sea.

For my part, I never assumed Vitali Zinchenko was real—real as in unenhanced, unadulterated—only that his was an evolved consciousness and, even though I'd fail to comprehend the extent of his genius, I would be among the tawdry heroes who faked greatness, who sat at the feet of his being and came to class. I only and infinitely *believed* in him. But I never assumed he was real. Now the lights are going off and the electricity is leaving us, maybe forever. The tide is coming in.

The news claims it's the biggest flood since Noah. A real live end. If it's going to happen, I'm hoping for a giant blue wave, an emblematic tsunami ripped from a Japanese woodcut, its many crests crashing and bouncing back like a cavalry charge, galloping hooves beneath gaunt horsemen. But it's more like a bathtub slowly filling. From the roof of

Wallace Hall, we see the gray swell on the horizon. The sky is not falling; the ground is just rising up to meet it.

IT WAS IN my senior year of college that I stopped going to class and became a superhero. I came from humble beginnings and I met the requirements: a restlessness; a germ of majesty; a lust for significance; a love of decadent costuming, of masks. We all did. But Vitali gathered our spark and set the place aflame. Like our fathers before us, we occupied campus buildings, but swore never to jump ship like those damned dirty longhairs did. We were making progress against the powers that be. The news told stories about us. And then this. A major disaster to divert the public's attention. The adults are gone now. We're cut off. The campus belongs to Vitali, and when the electricity is gone the students will look for him to glow in the dark. They're downstairs, the student body, just babies really. There are a handful of superheroes here on the roof. Vitali can see it, he already knows. Man is weak and known to fall apart. He tells us to keep our masks on, no matter what, keep them on. Like all leaders, our mystery is our power.

We see entire grids going, browning out one by one. Our buildings and trees, they are disappearing in the evening, bequeathing us a gray and choppy sea. Before everything goes dark and the voltage buzz is hushed, we look to each others' masks, to the eyes behind the masks, and we know all that will remain is our lingering dependence—on the gadgets and microchips that hummed us to sleep at night; on the chemicals, the bees in our blood, enhancing muscle and mind; on Him, The Übermensch: our Vitali Zinchenko.

I am his second-in-command. I am twenty-two.

I look towards Vitali. He looks toward the gray and choppy sea.

"You need to speak to them," I say.

"Where is Ryan?" he says, not looking back.

Ryan is online, downstairs in a computer cluster, taking one last stroke to Cytherea's wet and powerful orgasms, hoping he'll be able to return to paper-based porn once his streaming video goddess is gone.

"Where is Mike?" Vitali says.

Mike is in the belfry of the gradschool clocktower, screaming and shooting his father's rifle down at the rising waters below. The bullets are splashing. It looks like the flood is firing back.

"Where are you?" he says.

I'm still here. I am his second-in-command.

"We need them to be strong," Vitali says. "I'm going to caution them about Nietzsche's concept of The Last Man—cut off, apathetic, weak. Lacking a certain *imagination*."

I've read some of what he told me to read and so I say: "Right: nihilism."

His cheeks smile around his mask.

"Either that, or I'll just suggest that they fuck each other senseless and start repopulating the earth."

I'm too nervous but I manage a smile. The mask hides it from him completely.

"Listen to me," he says, "here is your job." He pulls from his pocket three orange bottles of pills. Vitali's pills for focus, pills for energy, pills for strength: his charisma. He shakes them once, a fistful of maracas.

"Does anyone else know?"

"Of course not," I say. "No."

"Your job is to hold these. Hold them quietly. Give me one per day."

"Of course," I say. "That's the dosage."

"Listen to me," he says. "They're not going to last."

He's right. There are only two or three left in each bottle. Maybe enough for a week. The news claims we'll be cut off much longer than that.

"Some days, you're going to administer a placebo," he says. "Don't tell me when. I'll close my eyes. Otherwise they're not going to last."

I hate to state the obvious, but:

"Vitali, we're cut off and I don't actually know how to make placebo pills."

"Use your imagination," he says. "It's in your hands now. It's up to you."

He pops one of each and transfers the bottles to me. They're in my hands now. I am who it is up to.

Then our grid goes and the world is blind.

"Hold them quietly," he says. "Our mystery is our power."

Vitali lights a candle. He turns from the flood and walks to the door at the center of the roof. He walks downstairs to orate, to lead, perchance to drown.

I squeeze the pill bottles, open one of the childproof caps and pour some into my palm. I look at them, these babies, these tiny, smooth secrets. By the time they run out maybe he'll be real.

EARTH'S HOLOCAUST
Nathaniel Hawthorne

ONCE UPON A time—but whether in the time past or time to come is a matter of little or no moment—this wide world had become so over-burdened with an accumulation of worn-out trumpery, that the inhabitants determined to rid themselves of it by a general bonfire. The site fixed upon, at the representation of the insurance companies, and as being as central a spot as any other on the globe, was one of the broadest prairies of the West, where no human habitation would be endangered by the flames, and where a vast assemblage of spectators might commodiously admire the show. Having a taste for sights of this kind, and imagining, likewise, that the illumination of the bonfire might reveal some profundity of moral truth, heretofore hidden in mist or darkness, I made it convenient to journey thither and be present. At my arrival, although the heap of condemned rubbish was as yet comparatively small, the torch had already been applied. Amid that boundless plain, in the dusk of the evening, like a far-off star alone in the firmament, there was merely visible one tremulous gleam, whence none could have anticipated so fierce a blaze as was destined to ensue. With every moment, however, there came foottravellers, women holding up their aprons, men on horseback, wheelbarrows, lumbering baggage wagons, and other vehicles, great and small, and from far and near, laden with articles that were judged fit for nothing but to be burned.

"What materials have been used to kindle the flame?" inquired I of a bystander, for I was desirous of knowing the whole process of the affair, from beginning to end.

The person whom I addressed was a grave man, fifty years old or thereabout, who had evidently come thither as a looker-on; he struck me immediately as having weighed for himself the true value of life and its circumstances, and therefore as feeling little personal interest in whatever judgment the world might form of them. Before answering my question, he looked me in the face, by the kindling light of the fire.

"Oh, some very dry combustibles," replied he, "and extremely suitable to the purpose—no other, in fact, than yesterday's newspapers, last month's magazines, and last year's withered leaves. Here now comes some antiquated trash, that will take fire like a handful of shavings."

As he spoke, some rough-looking men advanced to the verge of the bonfire, and threw in, as it appeared, all the rubbish of the Herald's Office—the blazonry of coat armor; the crests and devices of illustrious families; pedigrees that extended back, like lines of light, into the mist of the dark ages; together with stars, garters, and embroidered collars; each of which, as paltry a bauble as it might appear to the uninstructed eye, had once possessed vast significance, and was still, in truth, reckoned among the most precious of moral or material facts by the worshippers of the gorgeous past. Mingled with this confused heap, which was tossed into the flames by armfulls at once, were innumerable badges of knighthood, comprising those of all the European sovereignties, and Napoleon's decoration of the Legion of Honor, the ribbon of which were entangled with those of the ancient order of St. Louis. There, too, were the medals of our own society of Cincinnati, by means of which, as history tells us, an order of hereditary knights came near being constituted out of the king-quellers of the Revolution. And besides, there were the patents of nobility of German counts and barons, Spanish grandees, and English peers, from the worm-eaten instruments signed by William the Conqueror down to the brand-new parchment of the latest lord, who has received his honors from the fair hand of Victoria.

At sight of these dense volumes of smoke, mingled with vivid jets of flame that gushed and eddied forth from this immense pile of earthly distinctions, the multitude of plebeian spectators sent up a joyous shout, and clapped their hands with an emphasis that made the welkin echo. That was their moment of triumph, achieved after long ages, over creatures of the same clay and the same spiritual infirmities, who had dared to assume the privileges due only to Heaven's better workmanship. But now there rushed towards the blazing heap a gray-haired man, of stately presence, wearing a coat from the breast of which a star, or other badge of rank, seemed to have been forcibly wrenched away. He had not the tokens of intellectual power in his face; but still there was the demeanor—the habitual, and almost native dignity—of one who had been born to the idea of his own social superiority, and had never felt it questioned, till that moment.

"People," cried he, gazing at the ruin of what was dearest to his eyes with grief and wonder, but nevertheless, with a degree of stateliness— "people, what have you done! This fire is consuming all that marked your advance from barbarism, or that could have prevented your relapse thither. We—the men of the privileged orders—were those who kept alive, from age to age, the old chivalrous spirit; the gentle and generous thought; the higher, the purer, the more refined and delicate life! With the nobles, too, you cast off the poet, the painter, the sculptor—all the beautiful arts; for we were their patrons and created the atmosphere in which they flourish. In abolishing the majestic distinctions of rank, society loses not only its grace, but its steadfastness—"

More he would doubtless have spoken; but here there arose an outcry, sportive, contemptuous, and indignant, that altogether drowned the appeal of the fallen nobleman, insomuch that, casting one look of despair at his own half-burned pedigree, he shrunk back into the crowd, glad to shelter himself under his new-found insignificance.

"Let him thank his stars that we have not flung him into the same fire!" shouted a rude figure, spurning the embers with his foot. "And, henceforth, let no man dare to show a piece of musty parchment as his warrant for lording it over his fellows! If he have strength of arm, well and good; it is one species of superiority. If he have wit, wisdom, courage, force of character, let these attributes do for him what they may. But, from this day forward, no mortal must hope for place and consideration by reckoning up the mouldy bones of his ancestors! That nonsense is done away."

"And in good time," remarked the grave observer by my side—in a low voice however—"if no worse nonsense come in its place. But, at all events, this species of nonsense has fairly lived out its life."

There was little space to muse or moralize over the embers of this time-honored rubbish; for, before it was half burned out, there came another multitude from beyond the sea, bearing the purple robes of royalty, and the crowns, globes, and sceptres of emperors and kings. All these had been condemned as useless baubles; playthings, at best, fit only for the infancy of the world, or rods to govern and chastise it in its nonage; but with which universal manhood, at its full-grown stature, could no longer brook to be insulted. Into such contempt had these regal insignia now fallen that the gilded crown and tinseled robes of the player-king, from Drury Lane Theatre, had been thrown in among the rest, doubtless as a mockery of his brother monarchs on the great stage of the world. It was a strange sight to discern the crown jewels of England glowing and flashing in the midst of the fire. Some of them had been delivered down from the time of the Saxon princes; others were purchased with vast revenues, or, perchance, ravished from the dead brows of the native potentates of Hindostan; and the whole now blazed with a dazzling lustre, as if a star had fallen in that spot, and been shattered into fragments. The splendor of the ruined monarchy had no reflection, save in those inestimable precious stones. But enough on this subject! It were but tedious to describe how the Emperor of Austria's mantle was converted to tinder, and how the posts and pillars of the French throne became a heap of coals, which it was impossible to distinguish from those of any other wood. Let me add, however, that I noticed one of the exiled Poles stirring up the bonfire with the Czar of Russia's sceptre, which he afterwards flung into the flames.

"The smell of singed garments is quite intolerable here," observed my new acquaintance, as the breeze enveloped us in the smoke of a royal wardrobe. "Let us get to windward, and see what they are doing on the other side of the bonfire."

We accordingly passed around, and were just in time to witness the arrival of a vast procession of Washingtonians—as the votaries of temperance call themselves now a days—accompanied by thousands of the Irish disciples of Father Mathew, with that great apostle at their head. They brought a rich contribution to the bonfire; being nothing less than all the hogsheads and barrels of liquor in the world, which they rolled before them across the prairie.

"Now, my children," cried Father Mathew, when they reached the verge of the fire, "one shove more, and the work is done! And now let us stand off and see Satan deal with his own liquor!"

Accordingly, having placed their wooden vessels within reach of the flames, the procession stood off at a safe distance, and soon beheld them burst into a blaze that reached the clouds, and threatened to set the sky itself on fire. And well it might. For here was the whole world's stock of spirituous liquors, which, instead of kindling a frenzied light in the eyes of individual topers as of yore, soared upwards with a bewildering gleam that startled all mankind. It was the aggregate of that fierce fire, which would otherwise have scorched the hearts of millions. Meantime, numberless bottles of precious wine were flung into the blaze, which lapped up the contents as if it loved them, and grew, like other drunkards, the merrier and fiercer for what it quaffed. Never again will the insatiable thirst of the fire fiend be so pampered! Here were the treasures of famous bon vivants— liquors that had been tossed on ocean, and mellowed in the sun, and hoarded long in the recesses of the earth—the pale, the gold, the ruddy juice of whatever vineyards were most delicate—the entire vintage of Tokay—all mingling in one stream with the vile fluids of the common pothouse, and contributing to heighten the self-same blaze. And while it rose in a gigantic spire, that seemed to wave against the arch of the firmament, and combine itself with the light of stars, the multitude gave a shout, as if the broad earth were exulting in its deliverance from the curse of ages.

But the joy was not universal. Many deemed that human life would be gloomier than ever, when that brief illumination should sink down. While the reformers were at work, I overheard muttered expostulations from several respectable gentlemen with red noses, and wearing gouty shoes; and a ragged worthy, whose face looked like a hearth where the fire is burned out, now expressed his discontent more openly and boldly.

"What is this world good for," said the Last Toper, "now that we can never be jolly any more? What is to comfort the poor man in sorrow and perplexity? How is he to keep his heart warm against the cold winds of this cheerless earth? And what do you propose to give him in exchange for the solace that you take away? How are old friends to sit together by the fireside, without a cheerful glass between them? A plague upon your reformation! It is a sad world, a cold world, a selfish world, a low world, not worth an honest fellow's living in, now that good fellowship is gone for ever!"

This harangue excited great mirth among the bystanders. But, preposterous as was the sentiment, I could not help commiserating the forlorn condition of the Last Toper, whose boon companions had dwindled away from his side, leaving the poor fellow without a soul to countenance him in sipping his liquor, nor indeed, any liquor to sip. Not that this was quite the true state of the case; for I had observed him, at a critical moment, filch a bottle of fourth-proof brandy that fell beside the bonfire, and hide it in his pocket.

The spirituous and fermented liquors being thus disposed of, the zeal of the reformers next induced them to replenish the fire with all the boxes of tea and bags of coffee in the world. And now came the planters of Virginia, bringing their crops of tobacco. These, being cast upon the heap of inutility, aggregated it to the size of a mountain, and incensed the atmosphere with such potent fragrance that methought we should never draw pure breath again. The present sacrifice seemed to startle the lovers of the weed, more than any that they had hitherto witnessed.

"Well, they've put my pipe out," said an old gentleman, flinging it into the flames in a pet. "What is this world coming to? Everything rich and racy—all the spice of life—is to be condemned as useless. Now that they have kindled the bonfire, if these nonsensical reformers would fling themselves into it, all would be well enough!"

"Be patient," responded a staunch conservative, "it will come to that in the end. They will first fling us in, and finally themselves."

From the general and systematic measures of reform, I now turned to consider the individual contributions to this memorable bonfire. In many instances these were of a very amusing character. One poor fellow threw in his empty purse, and another a bundle of counterfeit or insolvable bank-notes. Fashionable ladies threw in their last season's bonnets, together with heaps of ribbons, yellow lace, and much other half-worn milliner's ware, all of which proved even more evanescent in the fire than it had been in the fashion. A multitude of lovers of both sexes—discarded maids or bachelors, and couples mutually weary of one another—tossed in bundles of perfumed letters and enamored sonnets. A hack politician, being deprived of bread by the loss of office, threw in his teeth, which happened to be false ones. The Rev. Sydney Smith—having voyaged across the Atlantic for that sole purpose—came up to the bonfire with a bitter grin, and threw in certain repudiated bonds, fortified though they were with the broad seal of a sovereign state. A little boy of five years old, in the premature manliness of the present epoch, threw in his playthings; a college graduate, his diploma; an apothecary, ruined by the spread of homoeopathy, his whole stock of drugs and medicines; a physician, his library; a parson, his old sermons; and a fine gentleman of the old school, his code of manners, which he had formerly written down for the benefit of the next generation. A widow, resolving on a second marriage, slyly threw in her dead husband's miniature. A young man, jilted by his mistress, would willingly have flung his own desperate heart into the flames, but could find no means to wrench it out of his bosom. An American author, whose works were neglected by the public, threw his pen and paper into the bonfire, and betook himself to some less discouraging occupation. It somewhat startled me to overhear a number of ladies, highly respectable in appearance, proposing to fling their gowns and petticoats into the flames, and assume the garb, together with the manners, duties, offices, and responsibilities, of the opposite sex.

What favor was accorded to this scheme, I am unable to say; my attention being suddenly drawn to a poor, deceived, and half-delirious girl, who, exclaiming that she was the most worthless thing alive or dead, attempted to cast herself into the fire, amid all that wrecked and broken trumpery of the world. A good man, however, ran to her rescue.

"Patience, my poor girl!" said he, as he drew her back from the fierce embrace of the destroying angel. "Be patient, and abide Heaven's will. So long as you possess a living soul, all may be restored to its first freshness. These things of matter, and creations of human fantasy, are fit for nothing but to be burned, when once they have had their day. But your day is Eternity!"

"Yes," said the wretched girl, whose frenzy seemed now to have sunk down into deep despondency, "yes; and the sunshine is blotted out of it!"

It was now rumored among the spectators that all the weapons and munitions of war were to be thrown into the bonfire, with the exception of the world's stock of gunpowder, which, as the safest mode of disposing of it, had already been drowned in the sea. This intelligence seemed to awaken great diversity of opinion. The hopeful philanthropist esteemed it a token that the millennium was already come; while persons of another stamp, in whose view mankind was a breed of bulldogs, prophesied that all the old stoutness, fervor, nobleness, generosity, and magnanimity of the race would disappear—these qualities, as they affirmed, requiring blood for their nourishment. They comforted themselves, however, in the belief that the proposed abolition of war was impracticable, for any length of time together.

Be that as it might, numberless great guns, whose thunder had long been the voice of battle—the artillery of the Armada, the battering trains of Marlborough, and the adverse cannon of Napoleon and Wellington— were trundled into the midst of the fire. By the continual addition of dry combustibles, it had now waxed so intense that neither brass nor iron could withstand it. It was wonderful to behold how these terrible instruments of slaughter melted away like playthings of wax. Then the armies of the earth wheeled around the mighty furnace, with their military music playing triumphant marches, and flung in their muskets and swords. The standard-bearers, likewise, cast one look upward at their banners, all tattered with shot-holes, and inscribed with the names of victorious fields, and, giving them a last flourish on the breeze, they lowered them into the flame, which snatched them upward in its rush toward the clouds. This ceremony being over, the world was left without a single weapon on in its hands, except, possibly, a few old king's arms and rusty swords, and other trophies of the revolution, in some of our state armories. And now the drums were beaten and the trumpets brayed all together, as a prelude to the proclamation of universal and eternal peace, and the announcement that glory was no longer to be won by blood, but that it would henceforth be the contention of the human race to work out the greatest mutual good, and that beneficence, in the future annals of the earth, would claim the praise of valor. The blessed tidings were accordingly promulgated, and caused infinite rejoicings among those who had stood aghast at the horror and absurdity of war.

But I saw a grim smile pass over the seared visage of a stately old commander—by his war-worn figure and rich military dress, he might have been one of Napoleon's famous marshals—who, with the rest of the world's soldiery, had just flung away the sword that had been familiar to his right hand for half a century.

"Aye, aye!" grumbled he. "Let them proclaim what they please; but, in the end, we shall find that all this foolery has only made more work for the armorers and cannon foundries."

"Why, sir," exclaimed I, in astonishment, "do you imagine that the human race will ever so far return on the steps of its past madness, as to weld another sword or cast another cannon?"

"There will be no need," observed, with a sneer, one who neither felt benevolence, nor had faith in it. "When Cain wished to slay his brother, he was at no loss for a weapon."

"We shall see," replied the veteran commander. "If I am mistaken, so much the better; but in my opinion—without pretending to philosophize about the matter—the necessity of war lies far deeper than these honest gentlemen suppose. What! Is there a field for all the petty disputes of individuals, and shall there be no great law court for the settlement of national difficulties? The battlefield is the only court where such suits can be tried!"

"You forget, General," rejoined I, "that, in this advanced stage of civilization, Reason and Philanthropy combined will constitute just such a tribunal as is requisite."

"Ah, I had forgotten that, indeed!" said the old warrior, as he limped away.

NATHANIEL HAWTHORNE | 91

The fire was now to be replenished with materials that had hitherto been considered of even greater importance to the well-being of society than the warlike munitions which we had already seen consumed. A body of reformers had travelled all over the earth, in quest of the machinery by which the different nations were accustomed to inflict the punishment of death. A shudder passed through the multitude, as these ghastly emblems were dragged forward. Even the flames seemed at first to shrink away, displaying the shape and murderous contrivance of each in a full blaze of light, which, of itself, was sufficient to convince mankind of the long and deadly error of human law. Those old implements of cruelty, those horrible monsters of mechanism, those inventions which it seemed to demand something worse than man's natural heart to contrive, and which had lurked in the dusky nooks of ancient prisons, the subject of terror-stricken legends, were now brought forth to view. Headsmen's axes, with the rust of noble and royal blood upon them, and a vast collection of halters that had choked the breath of plebeian victims, were thrown in together. A shout greeted the arrival of the guillotine, which was thrust forward on the same wheels that had borne it from one to another of the bloodstained streets of Paris. But the loudest roar of applause went up, telling the distant sky of the triumph of the earth's redemption, when the gallows made its appearance. An ill-looking fellow, however, rushed forward, and, putting himself in the path of the reformers, bellowed hoarsely, and fought with brute fury to stay their progress.

It was little matter of surprise, perhaps, that the executioner should thus do his best to vindicate and uphold the machinery by which he himself had his livelihood, and worthier individuals their death. But it deserved special note that men of a far different sphere—even of that class in whose guardianship the world is apt to trust its benevolence—were found to take the hangman's view of the question.

"Stay, my brethren!" cried one of them. "You are misled by a false philanthropy!—you know not what you do. The gallows is a heaven-ordained instrument! Bear it back, then, reverently, and set it up in its old place, else the world will fall to speedy ruin and desolation!"

"Onward, onward!" shouted a leader in the reform. "Into the flames with the accursed instrument of man's bloody policy! How can human law inculcate benevolence and love while it persists in setting up the gallows as its chief symbol? One heave more, good friends, and the world will be redeemed from its greatest error!"

A thousand hands, that, nevertheless, loathed the touch, now lent their assistance, and thrust the ominous burden far, far, into the centre of the raging furnace. There its fatal and abhorred image was beheld, first black, then a red coal, then ashes.

"That was well done!" exclaimed I.

"Yes, it was well done," replied—but with less enthusiasm than I expected—the thoughtful observer who was still at my side; "well done, if the world be good enough for the measure. Death, however, is an idea that cannot easily be dispensed with, in any condition between the primal innocence and that other purity and perfection, which, perchance, we are destined to attain after travelling round the full circle. But, at all events, it is well that the experiment should now be tried."

"Too cold! too cold!" impatiently exclaimed the young and ardent leader in this triumph. "Let the heart have its voice here, as well as the intellect. And as for ripeness, and as for progress, let mankind always do the highest, kindest, noblest thing, that, at any given period, it has attained to the perception of; and surely that thing cannot be wrong, nor wrongly timed!"

I know not whether it were the excitement of the scene, or whether the good people around the bonfire were really growing more enlightened, every instant, but they now proceeded to measures in the full length of which I was hardly prepared to keep them company. For instance, some threw their marriage certificates into the flames, and declared themselves candidates for a higher, holier, and more comprehensive union than that which had subsisted from the birth of time, under the form of the connubial tie. Others hastened to the vaults of banks, and to the coffers of the rich—all of which were open to the first comer, on this fated occasion—and brought entire bales of paper money to enliven the blaze, and tons of coin to be melted down by its intensity. Henceforth, they said, universal benevolence, uncoined and exhaustless, was to be the golden currency of the world. At this intelligence, the bankers, and speculators in the stocks, grew pale, and a pickpocket, who had reaped a rich harvest among the crowd, fell down in a deadly fainting fit. A few men of business burned their day-books and ledgers, the notes and obligations of their creditors, and all other evidences of debts due to themselves; while perhaps a somewhat larger number satisfied their zeal for reform with the sacrifice of any uncomfortable recollection of their own indebtment. There was then a cry, that the period was arrived when the title-deeds of landed property should be given to the flames, and the whole soil of the earth revert to the public, from whom it had been wrongfully abstracted, and most unequally distributed among individuals. Another party demanded that all written constitutions, set forms of government, legislative acts, statute books, and everything else on which human invention had endeavored to stamp its arbitrary laws, should at once be destroyed, leaving the consummated world as free as the man first created.

Whether any ultimate action was taken with regard to these propositions, is beyond my knowledge; for, just then, some matters were in progress that concerned my sympathies more nearly.

"See! see! what heaps of books and pamphlets!" cried a fellow, who did not seem to be a lover of literature. "Now we shall have a glorious blaze!"

"That's just the thing!" said a modern philosopher. "Now we shall get rid of the weight of dead men's thought, which has hitherto pressed so heavily on the living intellect that it has been incompetent to any effectual self-exertion. Well done, my lads! Into the fire with them! Now you are enlightening the world, indeed!"

"But what is to become of the trade?" cried a frantic bookseller.

"Oh, by all means, let them accompany their merchandise," coolly observed an author. "It will be a noble funeral pile!"

The truth was that the human race had now reached a stage of progress so far beyond what the wisest and wittiest men of former ages had ever dreamed of that it would have been a manifest absurdity to allow the earth to be any longer encumbered with their poor achievements in the literary line. Accordingly, a thorough and searching investigation had swept the booksellers' shops, hawkers' stands, public and private libraries, and even the little bookshelf by the country fireside, and had brought the world's entire mass of printed paper, bound or in sheets, to swell the already mountain-bulk of our illustrious bonfire. Thick, heavy folios, containing the labors of lexicographers, commentators, and encyclopedists, were flung in, and, falling among the embers with a leaden thump, smouldered away to ashes, like rotten wood. The small, richly gilt French tomes of the last age, with the hundred volumes of Voltaire among them, went off in a brilliant shower of sparkles and little jets of flame; while the current literature of the same nation burned red and blue, and threw an infernal light over the visages of the spectators, converting them all to the aspect of parti-colored fiends. A collection of German stories emitted a scent of brimstone. The English standard authors made excellent fuel, generally exhibiting the properties of sound oak logs. Milton's works, in particular, sent up a powerful blaze, gradually reddening into a coal, which promised to endure longer than almost any other material of the pile. From Shakespeare there gushed a flame of such marvellous splendor that men shaded their eyes as against the sun's meridian glory; nor even when the works of his own elucidators were flung upon him, did he cease to flash forth a dazzling radiance from beneath the ponderous heap. It is my belief that he is still blazing as fervidly as ever.

"Could a poet but light a lamp at that glorious flame," remarked I, "he might then consume the midnight oil to some good purpose."

"That is the very thing which modern poets have been too apt to do—or, at least, to attempt," answered a critic. "The chief benefit to be expected from this conflagration of past literature undoubtedly is that writers will henceforth be compelled to light their lamps at the sun or stars."

"If they can reach so high," said I. "But that task requires a giant, who may afterward distribute the light among inferior men. It is not everyone that can steal the fire from Heaven, like Prometheus; but when once he had done the deed, a thousand hearths were kindled by it."

It amazed me much to observe how indefinite was the proportion between the physical mass of any given author and the property of brilliant and long-continued combustion. For instance, there was not a quarto volume of the last century—nor, indeed, of the present—that could compete, in that particular, with a child's little gilt-covered book, containing Mother Goose's Melodies. The Life and Death of Tom Thumb outlasted the biography of Marlborough. An epic—indeed, a dozen of them—was converted to white ashes, before the single sheet of an old ballad was half consumed. In more than one case, too, when volumes of applauded verse proved incapable of anything better than a stifling smoke, an unregarded ditty of some nameless bard—perchance, in the corner of a newspaper—soared up among the stars, with a flame as brilliant as their own. Speaking of the properties of flame, methought Shelley's poetry emitted a purer light than almost any other productions of his day; contrasting beautifully with the fitful and lurid gleams, and gushes of black vapor, that flashed and eddied from the volumes of Lord Byron. As for Tom Moore, some of his songs diffused an odor like a burning pastille.

I felt particular interest in watching the combustion of American authors, and scrupulously noted, by my watch, the precise number of moments that changed most of them from shabbily printed books to indistinguishable ashes. It would be invidious, however, if not perilous, to betray these awful secrets; so that I shall content myself with observing that it was not invariably the writer most frequent in the public mouth that made the most splendid appearance in the bonfire. I especially remember that a great deal of excellent inflammability was exhibited in a thin volume of poems by Ellery Channing; although, to speak the truth, there were certain portions that hissed and spluttered in a very disagreeable fashion. A curious phenomenon occurred, in reference to several writers, native as well as foreign. Their books, though of highly respectable figure, instead of bursting into a blaze, or even smouldering out their substance in smoke, suddenly melted away, in a manner that proved them to be ice.

If it be no lack of modesty to mention my own works, it must here be confessed that I looked for them with fatherly interest, but in vain. Too probably, they were changed to vapor by the first action of the heat; at best, I can only hope that, in their quiet way, they contributed a glimmering spark or two to the splendor of the evening.

"Alas! and woe is me!" thus bemoaned himself a heavy-looking gentleman in green spectacles. "The world is utterly ruined, and there is nothing to live for any longer! The business of my life is snatched from me. Not a volume to be had for love or money!"

"This," remarked the sedate observer beside me, "is a bookworm—one of those men who are born to gnaw dead thoughts. His clothes, you see, are covered with the dust of libraries. He has no inward fountain of ideas; and, in good earnest, now that the old stock is abolished, I do not see what is to become of the poor fellow. Have you no word of comfort for him?"

"My dear sir," said I, to the desperate bookworm, "is not Nature better than a book? Is not the human heart deeper than any system of philosophy? Is not life replete with more instruction than past observers have found it possible to write down in maxims? Be of good cheer! The great book of Time is still spread wide open before us; and, if we read it aright, it will be to us a volume of eternal Truth."

"Oh, my books, my books, my precious printed books!" reiterated the forlorn bookworm. "My only reality was a bound volume; and now they will not leave me even a shadowy pamphlet!"

In fact, the last remnant of the literature of all the ages was now descending upon the blazing heap, in the shape of a cloud of pamphlets from the press of the New World. These, likewise, were consumed in the twinkling of an eye, leaving the earth, for the first time since the days of Cadmus, free from the plague of letters—an enviable field for the authors of the next generation!

"Well!—and does anything remain to be done?" inquired I, somewhat anxiously. "Unless we set fire to the earth itself, and then leap boldly off into infinite space, I know not that we can carry reform to any further point."

"You are vastly mistaken, my good friend," said the observer. "Believe me, the fire will not be allowed to settle down without the addition of fuel that will startle many persons who have lent a willing hand thus far."

Nevertheless, there appeared to be a relaxation of effort for a little time, during which, probably, the leaders of the movement were considering what should be done next. In the interval, a philosopher threw his theory into the flames; a sacrifice which, by those who knew how to estimate it, was pronounced the most remarkable that had yet been made. The combustion, however, was by no means brilliant. Some indefatigable people, scorning to take a moment's ease, now employed themselves in collecting all the withered leaves and fallen boughs of the forest, and thereby recruited the bonfire to a greater height than ever. But this was mere by-play.

"Here comes the fresh fuel that I spoke of," said my companion.

To my astonishment, the persons who now advanced into the vacant space around the mountain fire bore surplices and other priestly garments, mitres, crosiers, and a confusion of popish and Protestant emblems, with which it seemed their purpose to consummate this great Act of Faith. Crosses from the spires of old cathedrals, were cast upon the heap, with as little remorse as if the reverence of centuries, passing in long array beneath the lofty towers, had not looked up to them as the holiest of symbols. The font, in which infants were consecrated to God, the sacramental vessels, whence Piety received the hallowed draught, were given to the same destruction. Perhaps it most nearly touched my heart to see, among these devoted relics, fragments of the humble communion tables and undecorated pulpits which I recognized as having been torn from the meeting-houses of New England. Those simple edifices might have been permitted to retain all of sacred embellishment that their Puritan founders had bestowed, even though the mighty structure of St. Peter's had sent its spoils to the fire of this terrible sacrifice. Yet I felt that these were but the externals of religion, and might most safely be relinquished by spirits that best knew their deep significance.

"All is well," said I cheerfully. "The wood paths shall be the aisles of our cathedral—the firmament itself shall be its ceiling! What needs an earthly roof between the Deity and his worshippers? Our faith can well afford to lose all the drapery that even the holiest men have thrown around it, and be only the more sublime in its simplicity."

"True," said my companion. "But will they pause here?"

The doubt implied in his question was well founded. In the general destruction of books, already described, a holy volume that stood apart from the catalogue of human literature, and yet, in one sense, was at its head had been spared. But the Titan of innovation—angel or fiend, double in his nature, and capable of deeds befitting both characters—at first shaking down only the old and rotten shapes of things, had now, as it appeared, laid his terrible hand upon the main pillars, which supported the whole edifice of our moral and spiritual state. The inhabitants of the earth had grown too enlightened to define their faith within a form of words, or to limit the spiritual by any analogy to our material existence. Truths, which the Heavens trembled at, were now but a fable of the world's infancy. Therefore, as the final sacrifice of human error, what else remained to be thrown upon the embers of that awful pile, except the book, which, though a celestial revelation to past ages, was but a voice from a lower sphere, as regarded the present race of man? It was done! Upon the blazing heap of falsehood and worn-out truth—things that the earth had never needed, or had ceased to need, or had grown childishly weary of—fell the ponderous church Bible, the great old volume, that had lain so long on the cushion of the pulpit, and whence the pastor's solemn voice had given holy utterance on so many a Sabbath day. There, likewise, fell the family Bible, which the long-buried patriarch had read to his children—in prosperity or sorrow, by the fireside and in the summer shade of trees—and had bequeathed downward, as the heirloom of generations. There fell the bosom Bible, the little volume that had been the soul's friend of some sorely tried child of dust, who thence took courage, whether his trial were for life or death, steadfastly confronting both, in the strong assurance of immortality.

All these were flung into the fierce and riotous blaze; and then a mighty wind came roaring across the plain, with a desolate howl, as if it were the angry lamentations of the Earth for the loss of Heaven's sunshine, and it shook the gigantic pyramid of flame, and scattered the cinders of half-consumed abominations around upon the spectators.

"This is terrible!" said I, feeling that my cheek grew pale, and seeing a like change in the visages about me.

"Be of good courage yet," answered the man with whom I had so often spoken. He continued to gaze steadily at the spectacle, with a singular calmness, as if it concerned him merely as an observer. "Be of good courage, nor yet exult too much; for there is far less both of good and evil, in the effect of this bonfire, than the world might be willing to believe."

"How can that be?" exclaimed I impatiently. "Has it not consumed everything? Has it not swallowed up, or melted down, every human or divine appendage of our mortal state that had substance enough to be acted on by fire? Will there be anything left us tomorrow morning, better or worse than a heap of embers and ashes?"

"Assuredly there will," said my grave friend. "Come hither tomorrow morning—or whenever the combustible portion of the pile shall be quite burned out—and you will find among the ashes everything really valuable that you have seen cast into the flames. Trust me, the world of tomorrow will again enrich itself with the gold and diamonds, which have been cast off by the world of today. Not a truth is destroyed—nor buried so deep among the ashes, but it will be raked up at last."

This was a strange assurance. Yet I felt inclined to credit it; the more especially as I beheld among the wallowing flames a copy of the Holy Scriptures, the pages of which, instead of being blackened into tinder, only assumed a more dazzling whiteness, as the finger-marks of human imperfection were purified away. Certain marginal notes and commentaries, it is true, yielded to the intensity of the fiery test, but without detriment to the smallest syllable that had flamed from the pen of inspiration.

"Yes—there is the proof of what you say," answered I, turning to the observer. "But, if only what is evil can feel the action of the fire, then, surely, the conflagration has been of inestimable utility. Yet if I understand aright, you intimate a doubt whether the world's expectation of benefit would be realized by it."

"Listen to the talk of these worthies," said he, pointing to a group in front of the blazing pile. "Possibly, they may teach you something useful, without intending it."

The persons whom he indicated consisted of that brutal and most earthy figure who had stood forth so furiously in defence of the gallows—the hangman, in short—together with the Last Thief and the Last Murderer; all three of whom were clustered about the Last Toper. The latter was liberally passing the brandy bottle, which he had rescued from the general destruction of wines and spirits. The little convivial party seemed at the lowest pitch of despondency, as considering that the purified world must needs be utterly unlike the sphere that they had hitherto known, and therefore but a strange and desolate abode for gentlemen of their kidney.

"The best counsel for all of us is," remarked the hangman, "that—as soon as we have finished the last drop of liquor—I help you, my three friends, to a comfortable end upon the nearest tree, and then hang myself on the same bough. This is no world for us any longer."

"Poh, poh, my good fellows!" said a dark-complexioned personage, who now joined the group—his complexion was indeed fearfully dark, and his eyes glowed with a redder light than that of the bonfire. "Be not so cast down, my dear friends; you shall see good days yet. There is one thing that these wiseacres have forgotten to throw into the fire, and without which all the rest of the conflagration is just nothing at all; yes, though they had burned the earth itself to a cinder!"

"And what may that be?" eagerly demanded the Last Murderer.

"What but the human heart itself!" said the dark-visaged stranger, with a portentous grin. "And, unless they hit upon some method of purifying that foul cavern, forth from it will reissue all the shapes of wrong and misery—the same old shapes, or worse ones—which they have taken such a vast deal of trouble to consume to ashes. I have stood by, this livelong night, and laughed in my sleeve at the whole business. Oh, take my word for it, it will be the old world yet!"

This brief conversation supplied me with a theme for lengthened thought. How sad a truth—if true it were—that Man's age-long endeavor for perfection had served only to render him the mockery of the Evil Principle, from the fatal circumstance of an error at the very root of the matter! The Heart—the Heart—there was the little yet boundless sphere, wherein existed the original wrong of which the crime and misery of this outward world were merely types. Purify that inner sphere, and the many shapes of evil that haunt the outward—and which now seem almost our only—realities will turn to shadowy phantoms, and vanish of their own accord. But, if we go no deeper than the Intellect, and strive, with merely that feeble instrument, to discern and rectify what is wrong, our whole accomplishment will be a dream, so unsubstantial that it matters little whether the bonfire, which I have so faithfully described, were what we choose to call a real event, and a flame that would scorch the finger, or only a phosphoric radiance, and a parable of my own brain!

I ALWAYS GO
TO PARTICULAR PLACES

Gary Lutz and Deb Olin Unferth

"You think that's gonna fall?"

"It's got some give in it yet."

The lower surrounds look patched together now, stapled over, squared in spots. He and she wade coastways. Overhead, a slummy sky, heaped up somehow, junked.

"Thing's gonna hold for us?"

"It doesn't look directed."

A plate of sea. Broken stems, shingles. She shimmies a smithereen from the cave-in, throws it back, says, "A commotion like this might have once been to her liking."

"Perhaps."

"Last I'd seen of her, she'd had it with any misprints, retractions, bashful second thoughts, any thinking better of. She looked ready to tear down the whole assembly. Drive me or I call a taxi, she said. But could I? I stood stock-still where the earth was at its widest."

A straight lace of cement. Many empty perfect houses, scarred over. A few dogs mocking the totter of the turrets. He bends his hair half back.

"Think there's any off chance that there's some instability in the fundamental structural integrity of that outcropping?"

"It's humped. It won't."

"So there's no tumble in that wall of rock?"

"Nature is rarely that frank."

She shoves a body out of the way.

"This would be her idea of a collapse worth a once-over. Any last words? she'd say. That one, she'll talk to anyone when she has to talk. She'll kneel."

"You drove her?"

"She just gave me that panned-gold glare of hers. She'd gotten herself spruced up for somebody, all right. That was no shopping frock. And there was one man definitely glad of her. The cuss could scarcely keep those hands in his pockets. He looked strapped and lacking. Must have gone defect years before. The eyes were the thing about him, though. I scanned the yellowed windows of them for any ameliorating sense. You can't stop wondering how paths come to cross like that."

Out a ways, another line of buildings sinking into the chunked earth.

"Goes to show," she says. "The devil drops nothing that rises, and falls down on nothing that is standing up straight."

He makes a clear, factual sound. He loads his left hand into the crevice, says, "Does it look as okay to you as it does, I imagine, to me?"

"It looks native enough."

He grasps his shorts. "Any reason to shift our relations with respect to said geologic massivity?"

"It's just fussing," she says. She swims up to a suitcase, fiddles with the fasten.

A few schools of clouds dismissing into the western districts of the sky. Things more clipped in the eastern parcels. His leg comes to the surface. She skims the topping of the water. One bobs up triumphantly. Another flees from them, holding its breath.

"Watch it!" Her hand goes down the air. "That was an especially gruesome one, that runner."

"Get up off your fanny and help me clear these customers," he says. "Come on, hold my dead."

He has them by the anatomy now. The cladding comes away.

Two are still gurgling. Sections of one's face relocate.

"Probably just need more push."

"That one caboodled with jewelry? Throw it a little closer. I like the doze on it."

She mixes her foot over it. The underwater darkens and relumes. Entrailia; a smooth panel of torso; a physiqued entirety of teenager; an arm unrelated; swank stretches of hair, barretted and ornamented; a testicle at large; a quantum of fingers, slenderly elderly. A mush of shut eyes. Unseamed insides.

She spools an arm thinnedly around. "Where were her others? I wondered. Who were they ferrying out of there with no thought of her?"

Above, the rock leans—a sideward view, a foreslide.

"She didn't miss him, if that's what you're wondering. The woman has a heart like a bare slat. She has some kind of wire arrangement over any big talk she comes out with. She showed me the leftovers she'd managed to push into her pull—to—the grooming agents, the getups. Getting out of a life isn't the sort of thing you line up for. Mostly we try to get in."

"So she'd been out of his life, onto the avenues. Got herself tossed about the terraces and foundations. More than two years by my count."

Traffic moving west in both the east and west lanes. An odd unhurriedness to the movement, a unifying lack of purposive dispersal. Slattery formations all about the two of them. The horizon looking snatchy, pivoted.

"I mean, it hadn't been working before any of this, either. It wasn't exactly a curtsy and a handshake farewell."

Personages appear on the outgrowth—tour groups, probably—shout mutely, wave, wane. Farther out, a town belittled by prying fires.

"How she got me to do it, I'll never know. So I drove, yes. I always go to particular places. I'm nobody's conscience now."

"You're never exactly lacking indecisions, are you?"

Beyond, a streak of storm stirring the rest, crushing it.

"When I dropped her, finally, and saw her make off, I naturally thought of a jar opening, the ending of the thing being shut, and then the ending of the hand covering it, the hand lifting (the beginning of that) and the end of no-air over whatever's inside. Then I thought of the end of being in there, and the coming out of there and onto, say, a plate, or depending on what's in there, onto a car, etc., who knows. Then the end of it all getting together and staying like that, pushed up against each other and the beginning of the slow spread away, each one from each one, granule or drop or piece-part, the working oneself out from the center to where it will wind up (end up), to whatever ends, to the very ends, as they say, of the _____."

"She was a passing one, all right," he says. "But to affect the quality of the day is no small achievement, no? I knew her mostly only from memory. She often had a little body. She was ever due a lullaby. But I panted after fiasco. I rooted up some rummage from her slumbers."

Trees abstracting themselves rankly from the palisades. She undoes the distance in her eyes, conserves her footing.

"When I came out to pump it, she, my passenger during all this, was nowhere I could see."

She takes a fresh, unprejudiced breath of it.

Then a curt quiet, then a peaceable one, then a swinging underneath, then tulippy plumes for an instant, then a dither to the trees, then, farther off, the forever it had coming, the land of a piece with the sky.

"And the next note about it is what?"

"She lived."

AN ACCOUNTING

Brian Evenson

I HAVE BEEN ordered to write an honest accounting of how I became a
Midwestern Jesus and the subsequent disastrous events thereby accruing,
events for which I am, I am willing to admit, at least partly to blame. I
know of no simpler way than to simply begin.

In August it was determined that our stores were depleted and not
likely to outlast the winter. One of our number must travel East and beg
further provision from our compatriots on the coast, another must move
further inland, hold converse with the Midwestern sects as he encountered
them, bartering for supplies as he could. Lots were drawn and this latter
role fell to me.

I was provided a dog and a dogcart, a knife, a revolver with six rounds,
rations, food for the dog, a flint and steel, and a rucksack stuffed with
objects for trade. I named the dog Finger for reasons obscure even to
myself. I received as well a small packet of our currency, though it was suspected that, since the rupture, our currency, with its Masonic imagery,
would be considered by the pious Midwesterners anathema. It was not
known if I would be met with hostility, but this was considered not
unlikely considering no recent adventurer into the territory had returned.

I was given as well some hasty training by a former Midwesterner
turned heretic named Barton. According to him, I was to make frequent

reference to God—though not to use the word *Goddamn*, as in the phrase "Where are my goddamn eggs?"

"What eggs are these?" I asked Barton, only to discover the eggs themselves were apparently of no matter. He ticked off a list of other words considered profane and to be avoided. I was told to frequently describe things as God's will. "There but for the grace of God go I" was also an acceptable phrase, as was "Praise God." Things were not to be called "Godawful" though I was allowed to use, very rarely and with care, the term "God's aweful grace." If someone was to ask me if I were "saved," I was to claim that yes indeed I was saved, and that I had "accepted Jesus Christ as my personal Savior." I made notes of all these locutions, silently vowing to memorize them along the route.

"Another thing," said Barton. "If in dire straits, you should Jesus them and claim revelation from God."

So as you see it was not I myself who produced the idea of "Jesusing" them, but Barton. Am I to be blamed if I interpreted the verb in a way other than he intended? Perhaps he is to blame for his insufficiencies as an instructor.

BUT I AM outstripping myself. Each story must be told in some order, and mine, having begun at the beginning, has no reason not to take each bit and piece according to its proper chronology, so as to let each reader of this accounting arrive at his own conclusions.

I was driven a certain way, on the bed of an old carrier converted now to steam power. The roads directly surrounding our encampment—what had been my former city in better days—were passable, having been repaired in the years following the rupture. After a few dozen miles, however, the going became more difficult, the carrier forced at times to edge its way forward through the underbrush to avoid a collapse or eruption of the road. Nevertheless, I had a excellent driver, Marchent, and we had nearly broached the border of the former Pennsylvania before we encountered a portion of road so destroyed by a large mortar or some other such engine of devastation that we could discover no way around. Marchent, one of the finest, blamed himself, though to my mind there was no blame to be taken.

I was unloaded. Marchent and his sturdy second, Bates, carried Finger and his dogcart through the trees to deposit them on the far side of the crater. I myself simply scrambled down hand over foot and then scrambled up the other side.

To this point, my journey could not be called irregular. Indeed, it was nothing but routine, with little interest. As I stood on the far side of the crater, watching Marchent and his second depart in the carrier, I found myself almost relishing the adventure that lay before me.

This was before the days I spent trudging alone down a broken and mangled road through a pale rain. This was before I found myself sometimes delayed for half a day trying to figure how to get dog and dogcart around an obstacle. They had provided me a simple harness for the cart, but had forseen nothing by way of rope or tether to secure the fellow. If I tried to skirt, say, a shell crater, while carrying the bulky dogcart, Finger, feeling himself on the verge of abandonment, was anxious to accompany me. He would be there, darting between my legs and nearly precipitating me into the abyss itself, and if I did not fall, he did, so that once I had crossed I had to figure some way of extricating him. Often had I shouted at him the command "Finger! Heel!" or the command "Finger! Sit!" but it was soon clear that I, despite pursuing the most dangerous of the two missions, had been disbursed the least adequate canine.

Nevertheless, I grew to love Finger and it was for this I was sorry and even wept when later I had to eat him.

BUT I FEAR I have let my digression on Finger, which in honesty began not as a digression but as a simple description of a traveler's difficulty, get the better of my narrative. Imagine me, then, now attempting to carry Finger around a gap in the road in the dogcart itself, with Finger awaiting his moment to effect an escape by clawing his way up my chest and onto my head, and myself shouting "Finger! Stay!" in my most authoritative tone as I feel the ground beginning to slide out from under my feet. Or imagine Finger and me crammed into the dogcart together, the hound clawing my hands to ribbons as we rattle down a slope not knowing what obstacle we shall encounter at the bottom. That should render sufficient picture of the travails of my journey as regards Finger, and the reason as well—after splicing its harness and refashioning it as a short leash for Finger—for abandoning the dogcart, the which, I am willing to admit, as communal property, I had no right to forsake.

Needless to say, the journey was longer than our experts had predicted. I was uncertain if I had crossed into the Midwest and, in any case, had seen no signs of inhabitants or habitation. The weather had commenced to turn cold and I was racked with fits of ague. My provisions, being insufficiently calculated, had run low. The resourceful Finger managed to provide for himself by sniffling out and devouring dead creatures when he was released from his makeshift leash—though he was at least as prone to simply roll in said creature and return to me stinking and panting. I myself tried to eat one of these, scraping it up and roasting it first on a spit, but the pain that subsequently assaulted my bowels made me prefer to eat instead what remained of Finger's dog food and then, thereafter, to go hungry.

I had begun to despair when the landscape suffered through a transformation in character and I became convinced that I entered the Midwest at last. The ground sloped ever downward, leveling into a flat and gray expanse. The trees gave way to scrub and brush and strange crippled grasses which, if one were not careful, cut one quite badly. Whereas the mountains and hills had at least had occasional berries or fruit to forage, here the vegetation was not such as to bear fruit. Whereas before one had seen only the occasional crater, here the road seemed to have been systematically uprooted so that almost no trace of it remained. I saw, as well, in the distance, as I left the slopes for the flat expanse, a devastated city, now little more than a smear on the landscape. Yet, I reasoned, perhaps this city, like my own city, had become a site for encampment; surely, there was someone to be found therein, or at least nearby.

Our progress over this prairie was much more rapid, and Finger did manage to scare up a hare which, in its confusion, made a run at me and was shot dead with one of my twelve bullets, the noise of its demise echoing forth like an envoy. I made a fire from scrub brush and roasted the hare over it. I had been long without food, and though the creature was stringy and had taken on the stink of the scrub, it was no less a feast for that.

It was this fire that made my presence known, the white smoke rising high through the daylight like a beacon. In retrospect cooking the rabbit can be considered a tactical error, but you must recall that it had been several days since I had eaten and I was perhaps in a state of confusion.

In any case, even before I had consumed the hare to its end Finger made a mourning noise and his hackles arose. I captured, from the corner of an eye, a movement through the grass, the which I divined to be human. I rose to my feet. Wrapping Finger's leash around one hand, with the other I lifted my revolver from beside him and cocked it.

I hallooed the man and, brandishing my revolver, encouraged him to come forth of his own accord. Else, I claimed, I would send my dog into the brush to flush him and then would shoot him dead. Finger, too, entered wonderfully into the spirit of the thing, though I knew he would hurt nobody but only sniff them and, were they dead, roll in their remains. There was no response for a long moment and then the fellow arose like a ghost from the quaking grass and tottered out, as did his compatriots.

There were perhaps a dozen of them, a pitiful crew, each largely unclothed and unkempt, their skin as well discolored and lesioned. They were thin, arms and legs just slightly more than pale sticks, bellies swollen with hunger.

"Who is your leader?" I asked the man who had come first.

"God is our leader," the fellow claimed.

"Praise God," I said, "God's will be done, the Lord be praised," rattling off their phrases as if I had been giving utterance to them all my life. "But who is your leader in this world?"

They looked at one another dumbly as if my question lay beyond comprehension. It was quickly determined that they had no leader but were *waiting for a sign*, viz. were waiting for God to inform them as to how to proceed.

"I am that sign," I told them, thinking such authority might help better effect my purposes. There was a certain pleased rumbling at this. "I have come to beg you for provisions."

But food they claimed not to have, and by testimony of their own sorry condition I was apt to believe them. Indeed, they were hungrily eyeing the sorry remains of my hare.

I gestured to it with my revolver. "I would invite you to share my humble meal," I said, and at those words one of them stumbled forward and took up the spit.

It was only by leveling the revolver at each of them in turn as he ate that each was assured a share of the little that remained. Indeed, by force of the revolver alone was established what later they referred to as "the miracle of the everlasting hare," where, it was said, the food was allowed to pass from hand to hand and yet there remained enough for all.

If this be in fact a miracle, it is attributable not to me but to the revolver. It would have been better to designate said revolver as their Messiah instead of myself. Perhaps you will argue that, though this be true, without my hand to hold said weapon it could not have become a Jesus, that both of us together a Jesus make, and I must admit that such an argument is hard to counter. Though if I were a Jesus, or a portion of a Jesus, I was an unwitting one at this stage, and must plead for understanding.

When the hare was consumed, I allowed Finger what remained of the bones. The fellows whom I had fed squatted about the fire and asked me if I had else to provide them by way of nourishment. I confessed I did not.

"We understand," one of them said, "from your teachings, that mankind cannot live by bread alone. But must not mankind have bread to live?"

"My teachings?" I said. I was not familiar at that time with the verse, was unsure what this rustic seer intended by attributing this statement to me.

"You are that sign," he said. "You have said so yourself."

Would you believe that I was unfamiliar enough at that moment with the teachings of the Holy Bible to not understand the mistake being made? I was like a gentleman in a foreign country, reader, armed with just enough of the language to promote serious misunderstanding. So that when I stated, in return, "I am that sign," and heard the rumble of approval around me, I thought merely that I was returning a formula, a manner of speech devoid of content. Realizing that because of the lateness of the season I might well have to remain in the Midwest through the worst of winter, it was in my interest to be on good terms with those likely to be of use to me.

Indeed, it was not until perhaps a week later, as their discourse and their continued demands for "further light and knowledge" became more specific, that I realized that by saying "I am that sign" I was saying to them, "I am your Jesus." By that time, even had I affected a denial of my Jesushood, it would not have been believed, would have been seen merely as a paradoxical sort of teaching, a parable.

BUT I DIGRESS. Suffice to say that I had become their Jesus by ignorance and remained in that ignorance for some little time, and remain to some extent puzzled even today by the society I have unwittingly created. Would I have returned from the Midwest if I were in accord with them? True, it may be argued that I did not return of my own, yet when I was captured, it is beyond dispute, I was on the road toward my original encampment. I had no other purpose or intention but to report to my superiors. What other purpose could have brought me back?

In those first days, I stayed encamped on that crippled, pestilent prairie, surrounded by a group of Midwesterners who would not leave me and who posed increasingly esoteric questions: Did I come bearing an olive branch or a sword? (Neither, in fact, but a revolver.) What moneychangers would I overturn in this epoch? (But currency is of no use here, I protested.) What was the state of an unborn child? (Dead, I suggested, before realizing by unborn they did not mean stillborn, but by then it was too late to retrace my steps.) They refused to leave my side, seemed starved to talk to someone like myself—perhaps, I reasoned, the novelty of a foreigner. They were already mythologizing the "miracle of the everlasting hare"—which I told them they were making too much of: were it truly everlasting, the hare would still be here and we could commence to eat it over again. They looked thoughtful at this. There was, they felt, some lesson to be had in my words.

The day following the partaking of the hare, serious questions began to develop as to what we would eat next. I set snares and taught them to do the same, but it seemed that the hare had been an anomaly and the snares remained unsprung. It was clear they expected me to feed them, as if by sharing my hare with them I had entered into an obligation to provide for them. I tried at times to shoo them away from me and even pointed the revolver once or twice, but though I could drive them off a little distance they were never out of sight and would soon return.

But I am neglecting Finger. The men sat near me or, if I were walking, dogged my footsteps. I found my hunger banging like a shutter and had no desire so strong as to abandon their company immediately. Soon they began to beseech me in plaintive tones, using phrases such as these:

Master, call down manna from heaven.

Master, strike that rock with your stave [n.b. I had no stave] *and cause a fountain to spring forth.*

Master, transfigure our bodies so that they have no need of food but are nourished on the word alone.

Being a heretic, I did not grasp the antecedent of this harangue (i.e., my Jesushood), but only its broader sense. Soon they were all crying out, and I, already maddened from hunger, did not know how to proceed. A fever overcame me. Perhaps, I thought, I could slip away from them. But no, it was clear they thought they belonged with me and would not let me go. If I was to rid myself of them, there seemed no choice but to kill them.

It was here that my eyes fell upon Finger, he who had shared in my travails for many days, the cause of both much frustration and much joy. Here, I thought, is the inevitable first step, though I wept to think this. Divining no other choice, I drew my revolver and shot Finger through the head, then flensed him and trussed him and broiled him over the flames. He tasted, I must reluctantly admit, not unlike chicken. *Poor Finger*, I told myself, *perhaps we shall meet in a better world.*

Their response to this act was to declare I came not with an olive branch but with a sword, and to use the phrase *He smiteth*, a phrase which haunts me to this day.

IT IS BY little sinful steps that grander evils come to pass. I am sorry to say that Finger was only a temporary solution, quickly consumed. I had hoped that, once sated, they would allow me to depart in peace, but they seemed more bound to me than ever now and even offered me tributes: strange woven creations of no use nor any mimetic value which they assembled from the tortured grass: crippled and faceless half-creatures that came apart in my hands.

I thought and pondered and saw no way out but to sneak away from them by night. At first, I thought to have effected an escape, yet before I was even a hundred yards from the campsite one of them had raised a hue and cry and they were all there with me, begging me not to go.

"I must go," I claimed. "Others await me."

"Then we shall accompany you," they said.

"I must go alone."

This they would not accept. *I cannot stop them from coming with me,* I thought, *but at least I may move them in the proper direction to facilitate my eventual return to my camp.* And in any case, I thought, if we are to survive we must leave this accursed plain where nothing grows but dust and scrub and misery. We must gain the hills.

So gain the hills we did. My plan was to instruct them in self-sufficiency, how to trap their own prey and how to grow their own foodstuffs, how to scavenge and forage and make do with what was at hand and thereby avoid starvation. This done, I hoped to convince them to allow me to depart.

We had arrived in the hills too late for crops, and animals and matter for foraging had grown scarce as well. We employed our first days gleaning what little food we could, gathering firewood and making for ourselves shelter prone to withstand the winter. But by the time winter set in with earnestness, we discovered our food all but gone and our straits dire indeed. I, as their Jesus, was looked to for a solution.

WE HAVE REACHED that unfortunate chapter which I assume to be the reason for my being asked to compose this accounting. Might I say, before I begin, that I regret everything, but that, at the time, I felt there to be no better choice? Were my inquest (assuming there is to be an inquest) to take place before a group of starved men, I might at least accrue some sympathy. But to the well fed, necessity must surely appear barbarity. And now, again well fed myself, I regret everything. Would I do it again? Of course not. Unless I was very hungry indeed.

In the midst of our suffering, I explained to them that one of us must sacrifice himself for the others. I explained how I, as I had not yet finished my work, was unable to serve. To this they nodded sagely. And which of you, I asked, dare sacrifice himself, by so doing to become a type and shadow of your Jesus? There was among them one willing to step forward, and he was instantly shot dead. *He smiteth*, I could hear the men mumbling. What followed? Reader, we ate him.

By winter's end we had consumed two of his fellows, who stepped forward both times unprotesting, each as my apostle honored to become a type and shadow of their Jesus by a sacrifice of his own. Their bones we cracked open to eat the marrow, but the skulls of all three we preserved and enshrined, out of respect for their sacrifice—along with the skull of Finger which I had preserved and continue to carry with me to this day. Early in Spring I urged them further into the hills until we had discovered a small valley whose soil seemed fertile and promising. In a cave we discovered an unrefined salt. I taught them to fish and as well how to smoke their fish to preserve it, and this they described as becoming fishers of men (though to my mind it were more properly described as fishers of fish). We again set snares along game trails and left them undisturbed and this time caught rabbits and birds, and sometimes a squirrel, and this meet we ate or smoked and preserved as well. The hides they learned to strip and tan, and they bound them about their feet. I taught them as well how to cultivate those plants as were available to them, and to make them fruitful. When they realized it was my will that they fend for themselves, they were quick to learn. And thus we were not long into summer when I called them together to inform them of my departure.

At first they would not hear of this, and could not understand why their Jesus would leave them. *Other sheep I have,* I told them, *that are not of this fold.* Having spent the winter in converse with them and reading an old tattered copy of their Bible, I had become conversant in matters of faith, and though I never did feel a temptation to give myself over to it, I did know how to best employ it for my purposes. When even this statement did not seem sufficient for the most stubborn among them, who still threatened to accompany me, I told them, *Go and spread my teachings.*

By this I meant what I had taught them of farming and clothing themselves and hunting but, just as with Barton, it would have served me well to be more specific. Indeed, this knowledge did spread, but with it came a ritual of the eating of human flesh throughout the winter months, a ritual I had not encouraged and had only resorted to in direst emergency. This they supported not only with glosses from the Bible, but words from a new Holy Book they had written on birch bark pounded flat, in which I recognized a twisted rendering of my own words.

It was not until I had been discovered by my former compatriots and imprisoned briefly under suspicion and then returned to my own campsite that I heard any hint of this lamentable practice. It was enquired of me if I had seen any such thing in my travels in the Midwest. Perhaps it was wrong of me to feign ignorance. And I had long returned to my duties, despite the hard questions concerning dog and dogcart and provisions that I had been unable to answer, before there were rumors that the practice had begun, like a contagion, to spread, and had even crossed from the Midwest into our own territories. I had indeed lost nearly all sense of my days as a Midwestern Jesus before the authorities discovered my name circulating in Midwestern mouths, inscribed in their holy books. If when I was again apprehended I was indeed preparing to flee— and I do not admit to such—it is only because of a fear of becoming a scapegoat, a fear which is in the process of being realized.

If I had intended to create this cult around my own figure, why then would I have ever left the Midwest? What purpose would I have had in abandoning a world in which I could have been a God? The insinuations that I have been spreading my own cult in our own territories are spurious. There is absolutely no proof.

There is one other thing I shall say in my defense: What takes place beyond the borders of the known world is not to be judged against the standards of this world. Then, you may well inquire, what standard of judgment should be applied? I do not know the answer to this question. Unless the answer be no standard of judgment at all.

I WAS ORDERED to write an honest accounting of how I became a Midwestern Jesus and to the best of my ability I have done so. I regret to say that at the conclusion of my task I now see for the first time my actions in a cold light. I have no faith in the clemency of my judges, nor faith that any regret for those events I unintentionally set in motion will lead to a pardon. I have no illusions: I shall be executed.

YET I HAVE one last request. After my death, I ask that my body be torn asunder and given in pieces to my followers. Though I remain a heretic, I see no way of bringing my cult to an end otherwise. Let those who want to partake of me partake and then I will at least have rounded the circle, my skull joining a pile of skulls in the Midwest, my bones shattered and sucked free of marrow and left to bleach upon the plain. And then, if I do not arise from the dead, if I do not appear to them in a garment of white, Finger beside, then perhaps it all will end.

AND IF I do arise, stripping the lineaments of death away to reveal renewed the raiment of the living? Permit me to say, then, that it is already too late for all of you, for I come not with an olive branch but a sword. *He smiteth*, and when he smiteth, ye shall surely die.

SQUARE OF THE SUN

Robert Bradley

PETRA'S PRESSED FOR time. She has obligations. She's being torn, muscle from bone, in every direction. Pensive angel. I have my hands on her lower back and I'm pressing into her. She has a tattoo of a magic square above her sacrum. Inscribed above it, "Here is Wisdom."

I tell her, I say, "Lift up a little." Her vocal chords are straining, now. She vocalizes, "One hundred and ninety three. Eleven." They're numbers from the square. I track them with my eyes as she recalls them aloud.

"Eighty-three. Forty-one."

"Relax," I say. "It'll come."

She's spitting out mathematical formulas, trying to prove, I believe, that time doesn't, in fact, exist. That this pleasure never stops beginning and never stops ending. Short, sharp breaths. Elbows on the bed, her head in her fists. "One hundred and three. Fifty-three."

She's always been a proponent of the power of whole numbers. Extraordinary ability to focus. "Do you feel me?" I say.

"Thirteen," she says, "One hundred seventy-three."

I do the math. The sum of each line, column, and diagonal etched into her skin is six hundred and sixty-six. I slow my stroke. So any new arrival would, literally, be born under the sign of the Beast. It starts to snow again.

A black dog trots across the salted road, sniffs around a bundle of split wood. I feel my whole body come together like a puzzle. She trembles. Then I'm wiping the spray off her back with a tissue. Like the tomb of the resurrected Christ, revisited, she is empty. A panoply of emotions plays upon the features of her face. She turns and hits me once; a feeble down stroke, then collapses onto her legs and says, "Fuck. It's always the same thing." It's possible she hasn't completed her calculations. But that's the problem with Petra, she's always on the verge.

I tell her. "All good things flow from . . ."

"Fuck, fuck, fuck," she says, "now, I'm late." She pulls her jeans up and gives me the finger as she walks out the door.

BEFORE SHE GAVE up on me Petra used to scold me. "You're not wise," she'd say. And, "Where's the rigor? Where's the grit?" And, "You have no inner fortitude." Or, "No resolve, no rigor: what do you expect? You're a monument to disappointers everywhere."

Foreplay: you can't take it personally.

She finally decided that I was doing it on purpose: dashing expectations to the dirt and then wallowing in the chaff.

"What's chaff?" I said.

MY WIFE IS at the window looking out at the yard. "Why don't you offer to rake," she says. "It would be a nice gesture."

"She has people for that," I say.

"Go ahead. It's supposed to be relaxing, like meditation."

"Raking isn't meditative, as people say. It's, Look, I have all these problems and now I have to rake."

PETRA TOOK A different tack. She said once, "Do you understand that Nature is an extension of your being?"

I looked at my feet.

"You heard about the Mayans, right? They're a nature-based culture. They created a calendar charting the evolution of consciousness."

"I heard that, yeah."

"Yeah? You know about it?"

I tightened my eyes, worked the muscles in my neck.

"Listen . . ." she said. "Do you feel it? Time: it's speeding up."

"Give me a minute," I said.

"Take two," she said. Then, "Have you noticed that more and more is happening in less and less time?"

"Not me," I said. I felt innocent around her. I don't know why.

"It's true," she said.

"What's going to happen?" I was practically gaping.

"The Truth will be revealed. And all things, all structures, mental, physical and spiritual that have been built on and supported by lies will crumble, because everyone will be able to see it for what it is."

"Uh-oh."

"That's right, fuck boy, complete exposure. No more lies."

"I don't lie."

"Oh. Does your wife know that you're fucking me?"

"For all I know she's fucking you, too."

"Don't be surprised."

"WHAT ARE YOU doing indoors?" says my wife. "It's such a beautiful day."

"Spare me your lesbian clichés," I say.

"What?"

"Reading."

"Let's go out." She's holding her coat. "You need the exercise."

"This is exercise."

I get my coat. It's unseasonably warm. I stand framed in the doorway, the sun at my back. Petra says that galactic energies are constantly bombarding the earth's surface and that we're all being primed for what she calls The Unveiling.

"A worldwide apocalypse, you mean," I said.

She said, "It's not what you think."

My wife stops and smiles at me.

"I love you," she says.

I fidget a bit and say, "You're a great lady."

"You're fucking kidding me."

"What?"

"Who am I, Eleanor fucking Roosevelt?"

"I don't know what you mean."

"Just . . . drop it." She pushes past me out the door.

I feel like confessing. Not so much about my infidelity as about being privy to the coming Apocalypse. Petra seems to have worked out the mechanics of it. I feel fairly certain that I'll play a significant role in future events; Petra and I.

"Let's drive into town," I say, "I'll buy you something."

She glowers, my wife. "I'm mad at you."

"Sorry, you caught me off guard, that's all."

"Do you know how lame that sounds?"

I think about how lame that sounds. Then I think of something else and something else again. Pretty soon I'm thinking of Petra. She said that the goal of consciousness is to discover what isn't.

I drive.

My wife stares at me.

"What?" I say.

"I'm talking to you. Are you just going to ignore me?"

"No," I say and look out my driver's side window through the trees at the booming sun. "Is the sun getting bigger, do you think?"

"What?"

"Careful. Shrill factor." I hitch up my shoulders.

She punches me in the chest. "Let me out."

I pull to the curb. There's a park across the street. As she gets out of the car she bumps her head and curses furiously.

I leave my coat in the car, but take my hat and gloves, a truly ridiculous figure.

"Where are you going?" I say, putting on my hat.

She walks towards the shops.

"I was only kidding. Come on, baby." I pull on my gloves.

She stops, turns to face me with her hand stuck to her head, like a teapot. She looks woozy. I feel oddly attracted to her.

"Honey, come back," I say.

She sees me, softens just a bit, then says, "You parked like fifty feet from the curb, asshole."

I ASKED PETRA who'll survive the coming apocalypse.

"Eye of the needle," she said.

I HEAD FOR the park. All the benches are empty of people, just as the sky is empty of birds. I ask myself the question: What am I not?

A plane glides by.

There's Petra, expanding and projecting her likeness across the skies. I start blurting out numbers in sequence as if they'll protect me. There's a dark spot, in the meat of the sun, where her heart would be. Then I see its shadow spilling, spreading forth, and feel the true weight of it, as a torrent of blood comes crashing through the trees.

THE END

Josip Novakovich

Although Daniel Markovich got exile status in the States on the grounds of religious persecution in Yugoslavia, after several years of living in Cleveland he no longer went to church, and many years later he quit reading the Bible. This is how it happened, from the beginning to the end.

He came to the States in 1968 when Soviets invaded Czechoslovakia; he had believed that the next stop on the Soviet world tour would be Yugoslavia. While Czechs were streaming into the States, he couldn't claim the Soviet threat in Yugoslavia as grounds for being a refugee.

But his claims of religious persecution were not false.

Daniel had wanted to be a geography teacher in Daruvar, Northern Croatia. In the interview, he answered the question, "Do you believe in God?" affirmatively. The frog-eyed principal, a boar hunter—there were still some boars alive at the time in the Papuk and Psunj Mountains—said, "Of course, you can't teach if you're intoxicated with the opiate of the masses. How can you teach the principles of the dialectical materialism if your head is filled with ghosts?"

"I understand the principles perfectly well."

"But you don't believe them."

"God and dialectical materialism are not at odds with each other."

"How about evolution?"

"According to the Bible, God created man last, and according to the theory of evolution, man is one of the last mammals to evolve. The two are in harmony."

"Where is God? Show him to me. See, you can't. You're superstitious."

"I can't show you a neutron either, and you take the scientists' word for granted, don't you? I often do. As for the opiate of the masses," Daniel said, "what is the bottle of *slivovitz* doing on your table?"

The school principal threw him out, and no matter where Daniel applied for a teaching position, he didn't get it—and he suspected that it had to do with his being a Croat as much as with his never denying his belief in God. For a couple of years before getting to the States, he worked for a living as a house painter and mason. He grew to be big-fisted and muscular; and with his broadchested frame, dark red beard and long red hair, from a distance he looked like a big torch. He got married, to a student of accounting, Mira, a pale freckled blonde with large dark brown eyes.

They immigrated to the States, in Cleveland, Ohio, and Mira gave birth to a daughter and then to a son. At first Daniel spent a lot of time preaching in Croatian in a Protestant church whose congregation was Croatian and Serbian, and instead of learning English, he studied Greek, because he needed to understand Christ in the original New Testament language more than he needed to understand Walter Cronkite, although he listened to Cronkite too, vaguely understanding him.

Soon, however, the church in Cleveland had grown large enough to employ a full-time minister, who'd just immigrated from Serbia. Daniel didn't like being the second fiddle to an inexperienced youngster, who was getting overpaid for doing what should be the labor of love. The services were now conducted in Serbian. Daniel went to church no more than once a month.

Daniel worked as a mason and house painter. Americans, of course, had no use for geography, so his chances of landing a job in that field were even slimmer in Ohio than in Yugoslavia. Daniel was not happy with his physical labor. All nature travails, he quoted, to console himself, and considered it unavoidable to suffer. Even Saint Paul worked—made and repaired fishing equipment—for a living; labor was a genuinely apostolic thing to do. Daniel chiseled stones and fitted them together into garden walls on several estates in Shaker Heights—those were good and well-paying jobs except that little glassy stone shards had hit and damaged his right eye. He stripped old lead paint on many houses and painted with new lead-based paint. The noxious fumes gave him dizzying headaches. He joked that labor was the opiate of the masses. By the time Sunday came, he'd be bleary-eyed, like someone who had been drinking brandy all week long. After a couple of years of working like this, he went to church once every two months. In the evenings he fell asleep with the Greek New Testament in his hands or sliding out of his hands onto the floor, where one day his dalmatian, whom he'd forgotten to feed, ate it—chewed the whole Gospel, and the Book of Revelations and the Psalms to boot. From now on, he called his dog Saint Dalmatian. Daniel got another Greek New Testament, and continued his practice of dozing off with abstruse verses made even more abstruse and sanctimonious by the ancient tongue.

Daniel didn't like Cleveland winters with icy winds blowing from Lake Erie, so he moved with his family south, to Cincinnati, where there weren't many Croats, and even fewer Croatian Baptists, but that no longer mattered to him. He carried the Gospel in his heart, a portable cathedral, with two atriums and two dark Holy of Holies that were constantly washed in his own blood.

"Let's go to Florida if you want heat," suggested Mira.

"That would be too steamy. Besides, a hurricane might lift our house and drop it in the ocean. Or one of those rockets, if it failed in its take-off, might fall on our house and burn it to the ground. NASA is the new Tower of Babel, I tell you. God will mix them all up, if Americans and the Chinese start working together: Not only will they lose the common languages, they'll also lose the common math that helps them blast the rockets."

"You are crazy," Mira said. "That's one likable thing about you."

"Why go anywhere else? It's hot enough in Cincinnati," Daniel said.

"With you around." Mira, although she was forty, still had outstanding breasts and supple thighs, large and resilient, and when children weren't around, Daniel stroked her, and they frequently made love, wherever they happened to be when lust took hold of them.

They bought a cheap house in Northside, painted the bricks all red, as was the fashion in Cincinnati.

Even after a dozen years of being in the States, Daniel hadn't learned English; he was still improving his Greek. He worked too much, and grew ill. He got scorching pains from his kidneys down the urethra, and when he could no longer take it, he went to the hospital. He had a painful intervention, the old-fashioned way. But what pained him even more, once he recovered, was the bill for $5,000.

He had no insurance neither did Mira, who worked as a checkout cashier in Woolworth's. Daniel paid the bill because he wanted to be a law-abiding citizen and good Christian. But now he needed to work even more, to the point of his biological limits. Why did God's punishment of Adam—*In the sweat of thy face shalt thou eat bread*—affect him so much, while many other people never seemed to work; they drank bourbon while making transactions?

He no longer had time for Greek, let alone English, and only rarely did he read the New Testament in Croatian. That pained him, but he thought that he shouldn't be selfish and work toward his own sainthood; God should understand that he needed to give his son and his daughter a chance to prosper. And once they were off to college, he'd study the Bible more assiduously than ever before.

Marina, already sixteen, was an "A" student, but lately she had been restless; she got a driver's license and wanted to go out and have pizza with her friends all the time. She worried him. He'd sometimes take a look at her; she was a full-figured woman, who wore tight skirts. Looking at her womanly body, he felt uncomfortable, as though it was sinful to notice his daughter, and to resolve his discomfort, he shouted at her that she should wear longer skirts, and threatened to beat her if she walked out like that, nearly naked.

"Dad, if you beat me, I'll have you arrested for child abuse."

"You are no longer a child. You paint your lips scarlet like a harlot."

"Dad, what do you know about harlots?" she asked, pouting her full red lips. "They don't exist in this country, do they?"

He didn't answer but looked at her sadly. She was brazen, and he resented that. What a country, where you have no means to discipline your child, but where without discipline a girl could perish, be gobbled up by frolicking and drug-crazed mobs.

When she turned seventeen, she eloped with a law student who attended the same church as the rest of the family. Mira blamed it on Daniel's strictness. "If you'd been more lenient, they could have dated for a while, she could have brought him home, we could have gotten to know him. You should be happy anyway. I know him from the church; she made a catch, I'd say."

"How can we be a family if we run away from each other? Is that the American way?" To his mind, they were all, except him, Americans now. They spoke English among themselves, and his kids, from what he could tell, had no accent in English.

Mira said to him (in Croatian, the English equivalent of this): "Don't worry, later she'll be in touch with us—when you calm down."

"Yeah, when he impregnates and abandons her."

"Why do you never see the bright side? He's a good Christian."

"Do good Christians elope?"

"You should know. Jacob with Rachel and Leah."

"Oh, in that case . . . Jacob actually waited awhile first—for fourteen years. These kids waited for fourteen minutes at the most." But, he was glad. Things might be easier now. At least he wouldn't have to save for her education.

Tony was a "B" student, not brilliant but steady. He helped with painting houses, and maybe he'd be an "A" student, thought Daniel, if those fumes hadn't gotten to him as well. So he owed it to his son, to send him away to college.

Daniel and Tony watched TV evangelists; Daniel liked the idea that you could worship at home, together with a million people at the same time. One Sunday morning they watched Schuyler interview a former Miss America, who had failed to win the competition in her state, and then prayed for a year, believing that God would help her, and God blessed her so that she not only won her state competition, but the nationals as well. "If you want something, believe that God will give it to you. If you want to be Miss America, pray and believe, and you'll be Miss America." That's what Miss America said, and Schuyler agreed with her and repeated it. Daniel laughed. "No matter what I believed, I could never become Miss America. I'd be lucky if I became an American. What nonsense. One more false prophet. Switch off the TV, son."

YEARS PASSED. Now and then the Markoviches got cards from their married daughter, who lived in Seattle. On Sundays, overworked Daniel needed to sleep; church was in his bed, where he celebrated Sabbath, the seventh day, in perfect rest, supine and sometimes prostrate, as if in prayer, and he couldn't keep his bloodshot eyes open. By now he'd lost most of his hair, but in compensation, grew a red beard.

Mira and Tony, now a senior at U.C., attended services at a neighborhood Baptist church. One morning, Mira said to Daniel, "Come, let's go to church, at least your English will improve."

"For that I can watch TV," he said. "Or better yet, read the word of God."

"Your soul will improve."

"If work doesn't, I don't know what will improve it. I need rest, wife, not stiff benches. My back hurts."

"Go see a chiropractor."

"But that's a witch doctor, isn't it? How can you recommend one and go to church? They are too expensive anyway. To pay to see one, I'd have to work one more day and hurt myself."

"And how do you think you'll pass the citizenship test if you can't even understand the questions?"

"Good question. Let me rest."

He fell asleep on their orange sofa and snored even before the sun set.

In the morning, he woke up Tony to go out and work. "Got to pay for school," he said. With nostalgia, he thought of the old days in Yugoslavia, where higher education was free.

They drove to Hyde Park in their Toyota pickup with ladders on top. On the way they stopped for coffee at Dairy Queen. Tony picked up a newspaper, and as they drove on, he said, "Dad, look at this, there's a war in Croatia."

"Nonsense."

"Why, look at this, in Dalj near the Danube Bridge, Yugoslav forces killed seventy-two Croatian policemen."

"Really? What else does it say?" He spilled hot coffee over his white shirt. "But that's not war," he said. "Just several dozen people killed."

"And to you that's normal?" Tony asked.

"Not normal, just not war."

"What is war then?"

"Big armies attacking each other, not just incidents."

But while he painted he was worried and absentminded. His wrists hurt, swollen with arthritis. His brush strokes often went over window sills, and he had to wipe the paint. A kid's room that was supposed to be half red, half blue, he painted all blue in quick rolls, with the blue paint dripping from the ceiling onto his paper cap and brows. He'd made a cap out of the *New York Times*.

DURING THE CITIZENSHIP test, Daniel could understand almost no questions.

"Maybe we should wait," said the officer. "You must be able to speak English to participate in our democracy. How will you know what you're voting for if you can't understand the language? Out of five questions, you got only one right, that Bush is the president."

"I know. I learn," Daniel said. "Ask more."

The officer, a middle-aged black woman, said, "All right. Who is the governor of Ohio?"

"Voinovich!" Daniel exclaimed. He knew—there were so few people from Yugoslavia in politics, and here was one. Although Voinovich was a Serb, Daniel was proud of him—it made it easier in a way to be a "vich" in Ohio. "And Kucinich was the mayor of Cleveland," he said.

"We don't have to worry about Cleveland right now," the officer said and scrutinized him. "All right, you pass. Welcome to the United States of America!"

"Thank you, thank you!" he said.

As HE PULLED out of the parking lot on Court Street, he said to Tony and Mira: "Can you believe it, the Serb governor's name saved me from flunking the citizenship test. You never know where help will come from."

"It's amazing," said Tony.

"I was so worried that you wouldn't make it," Mira said. "We are all Americans now, can you believe it? Isn't it great?"

"Sure thing," said Tony. "Except, who's going to believe Dad? He speaks English so badly."

"At least they'll believe you," said Daniel. "Especially when they draft you. You had to say you'd bear arms for this country, didn't you?"

DANIEL WAS PROUD of being an American, and as a true American, he watched the six o'clock news every night after work, and later CNN. Although he still spoke with a heavy accent and without much grammar, he understood English. And when one hot morning he got the news that his hometown, Pakrac, in Croatia was attacked by Serb irregulars backed by the Yugoslav Federal Army, he did not go to work. He tried to call his old uncle who lived on the eastern side of the Pakra river—he couldn't get through. He couldn't get through to any members of his family in Croatia. He grew anxious, and read the Bible but found little comfort.

DANIEL BOUGHT A shortwave radio and listened to the news every night. He got Croatian radio, BBC, Deutsche Welle. There was a report of the Pakrac hospital being bombed, and another of Vukovar being surrounded by 20,000 troops, and people massacred. Gradually, he managed to hear from most of his relatives, but he still feared for their lives. But even more he feared for their souls; most of them were atheists.

Vukovar fell three months later, and Daniel's life went on as usual; after work he watched CNN and listened to the pulsing shortwaves on the radio until he fell asleep.

A COUPLE OF years later the war in Croatia was at a standstill and the war in Bosnia reached a high pitch; some of Daniel's relatives from the vicinity of Banja Luka disappeared. One day as he worked and worried, painting wooden siding in a Hyde Park house among many large trees, he saw a blonde woman in a tennis skirt nimbly stretching on the floor. He gazed at her strong muscular and smoothly feminine thighs and her freckled cleavage as she bent to touch her Nikes with her fingers. Daniel's ladder shook and scraped on the wood siding.

"Oh, goodness, you'll fall if you don't watch out," she said.

"That's the problem. I watch."

"Let me hold your ladder," she said.

He was leaning over the tall window, his knees at her eye level.

She grabbed the ladder.

"Not necessary," he said. "It's firm."

"Is it?" she said and touched his crotch. Like a youngster, he got an instant erection. "Oh, that's a compliment," she said. "My husband doesn't react like that to me. Thank you, my friend." She spoke up into his crotch, and it wasn't clear to him whether she was talking to him, or to a part of him. She sounded delighted at any rate. She unzipped his jeans, and held his penis in her hands. With a brush laden with dripping white paint, which sprinkled over her hedges along the house, and another hand holding on to the bucket of paint, he couldn't defend himself, unless he said something, and he couldn't think right away what he could say that wouldn't be rude. And by the time he could think to say something, like "You are beautiful but I am a married Christian and therefore this is not the right thing to do," he felt tremors of lust and a delicious comfort in yielding to what was happening with such dexterity; her gently sliding nails made his lower abdomen twitch.

Daniel moved, bending lower a little bit, and he put the brush on the can of paint, and fastened the can along the ladder; the hairs on his forearm got stuck in a screw. Probably thinking that he wanted to jump into the room, she said, "Oh no, this is a fine arrangement. You keep doing your thing, I'll do mine if you don't mind."

When he came, he was flushed, with sweat drenching his shirt. "This is fun," she said. "Why don't you come here tomorrow, and we'll play some more through the window?"

"But job done today."

"I know. We could do a bigger one tomorrow."

After this Daniel felt a mixture of shame and guilt. What's the big deal, he thought. It happens. It's not like I have done anything. I just stood there; she did it. What choice did I have? But that reminded him of Adam's excuse in the Garden of Eden. She did it. Why be selfish and worry about himself; he had to worry about his relatives in the Balkans. So what if he wasn't a saint?

THAT EVENING HE went to a gathering of Croatian immigrants at a winery, Vinoklet, in the suburbs of Cincinnati. The sun was setting colorfully over the vineyards, and Daniel had the impression that he was in his native region. A Croatian engineer who ran the winery had nearly replicated his native landscape here—rolling hills with rows of vines, greenish fish ponds, and scattered groves of apple trees. At the entrance to the winery, a sign read, "Warning: consumption of our wines in moderate amounts creates an aura of well being that may lead to pregnancy."

Passionate emigrés gave speeches about the importance of writing letters to the White House, to the state senator, to alert them that there was a large Croatian population that wanted something done to stop the war in Bosnia with a fair settlement for the Croatian minority. "You can all give twenty dollars apiece to hire someone who will send the messages to the White House by e-mail if you don't have the time for it."

Daniel gave, and then drank the wines, "Tears of Joy" and "Sunset Blush." He chatted with a man who had lost his arm in World War II; he enjoyed speaking Croatian and feeling like he was not a foreigner. "I was just a lad then," the man said. "I was harvesting in a little wheatfield when Chetniks came, surrounded us, and took us to Knin, where they hacked us with knives. I woke up in a mound of bodies, and crawled out. A nurse helped me, and I was between life and death for months, and for ten years my wound kept festering, until I finally recovered, probably thanks to wine. I love wine."

"Probably God saved you. Not wine."

"Maybe the Virgin saved me."

"Which one?" Daniel asked.

"As far as I can tell, you don't mind being saved by wine either, my friend, do you?" The man laughed loudly, with a smell of garlic and wine coming out of him.

True, Daniel was drunk, as he hadn't been in years. He realized that although he liked the man he didn't like arguing with Catholics, and if campaigning for Croatia meant simply campaigning for Catholics, he wasn't enthusiastic. But he had to do something to help his relatives. He had another glass of red wine.

And next morning, he had a headache. He listened to the news about a great earthquake somewhere in China, a flood in northern Europe, further starvation in Somalia, and more massacres in Rwanda.

The accumulation of so much trouble at once made him feel uneasy, especially since he felt guilty that he had drunk so much the night before and even worse, that he had enjoyed a woman's playing with him, and that at night, he had awakened, wishing she were holding him again. And so, penitently, he read from the Bible, in Croatian, the equivalent of this English translation (Matthew 24:3, 6–7):

> And as he sat upon the mount of Olives, the disciples came unto him privately, saying, Tell us, when shall these things be? and what shall be the sign of thy coming, and of the end of the world? (3)
> [And Jesus answered]. . . And ye shall hear of wars and rumors of

wars: see that ye be not troubled: for all these things must come to pass,
but the end is not yet. (6)

For nation shall rise against nation, and kingdom against kingdom:
and there shall be famines, and pestilences, and earthquakes, in divers
places. (7)

Daniel panicked. The end of the world was coming. He did not know
how fast—maybe there was a year to live. And he was not ready.

He told his wife—who was doing crossword puzzles, proud that she had
such a good command of English—that the end of the world was at hand.

"Of course it is," she said.

"But why do we take on mortgage then, why do we save for retirement?"

"That's different—so that you wouldn't pay taxes, silly."

"So you believe the end is near?"

"Depends on how you look at it. Nobody knows when exactly, and
people have waited for generations."

"Yes, but now there are more wars and earthquakes than ever after
Christ."

"How do we know that?"

"Don't tell me you're a skeptic, you go to church."

"Yes, as a matter of fact, I am going there right now. I don't want to
worry about the end of the world; that'll take care of itself."

He admired his wife's attitude, and her straight posture as she walked
out, and he stayed troubled. She no longer worked as a department-store
cashier, but as a real-estate agent.

THE FOLLOWING MORNING, Daniel went to Mira's Baptist church, and
knocked on the minister's door. A chubby minister with a tight shirt buttoned on top—he literally had a red neck—opened the door. They had
met before, because for religious holidays Daniel still visited the church.

"When do you think Christ comes to this planet?" Daniel asked.

"He's here now, with us," said the minister and yawned.

"No, I mean serious. He gonna come soon, you think?"

The minister looked at him with his eyes wide, and then walked over to his coffee machine, which was percolating. "You want a cup of coffee?"

"We have time for that?" Daniel asked.

"Why not?"

"What if Christ came?"

"Where two or more gather in my name, I will be there, or something like that. That's what Christ said. So if we gather in his name, he'll be with us, he is with us. He came. Anyway, this coffee is going to feel like an earthquake, like the world's ending. You like it strong, don't you? Milk and sugar?"

"No, thank you."

The minister poured three spoonfuls of sugar into his black coffee and slurped, his eyes closed. "All right, now I'm ready for the second coming of Christ." He walked over to his desk and turned on his computer. Windows '95 came on. "You play chess?" the minister said. "You must, considering you come from Yugoslavia."

"Croatia," Daniel said. "Yes, I play."

"Here, I got a program that's almost as good as Deep Blue. You want to check it out?"

Daniel stared in disbelief. Clearly the minister didn't worry about the second coming of Christ. It was ten in the morning, and he was only waking up. Cushy job, being a minister. "No time for games. Not now," Daniel said and walked out.

*

LATER, WHEN HIS hangover wore off and his guilt about the hangover vanished, and the impression the Biblical verses made on him diminished, Daniel went back to work. There he met a blond Romanian with a black mustache. He knew the guy from before; he too was a Baptist and a construction worker. They talked in a mixture of languages. "Hey, it gets old working like a dog for a living, *nicht wahr?*" asked the Romanian, Nikolai.

"Yes, *konyeshna,*" said Daniel.

"Let us organize business, together, and find young blood to do *rabota* for us."

"Sounds good, but how to *zdyelat*?"

"I tell you over a glass of wine."

While they were still planning the joint venture, Nikolai visited Daniel, and as the two of them sat and discussed real estate, Mira served them orange juice and hot dogs. Daniel stealthily gave hot dogs to Saint Dalmatian, who, Daniel believed, was still filled with Greek letters. Mira sat down in the armchair and joined in on the discussions, speaking clearly without mixing any of the other languages, and for the first time in a long while Daniel noticed that she was stylish. He wondered why they made love only once a week. Now he could notice her through someone else's eyes and imagine what impression she was making. Her dress was short, and she sat comfortably, crossing her legs, so that her thighs—in thin black stockings that shaded the curves—were as visible as if she were an actress visiting David Letterman's show. Her tight cashmere white sweater made her breasts slope with milky and hazy fullness. Scarlet lipstick luridly accented and exposed her allure, as though her fresh blood had surfaced and spoken, ready to be licked.

Daniel commented, "You could sit up straight, so you wouldn't display yourself."

Nikolai sat stiff, his eyes focused on a cup of rose-hip tea steaming on the wooden table in front of him.

"You're making your visitor uncomfortable," she said.

"Sorry about that," Daniel said to Nikolai, and then to his wife, "At least you look comfortable."

"Why don't you invite me into the partnership? I'm a licensed real-estate agent," she said.

AND THEN, ALL evening long, while Mira worked after hours, Daniel daydreamed of sleeping with the Hyde Park woman. I shouldn't think like this, he thought. Christ will be here soon. But that thought now, as he was possessed by lust, drove him to a different conclusion. The end of the world will come, and I will not know what it is like to sleep with another woman, other than my wife. Who knows what I am missing, maybe a true ecstasy. I'll probably go to hell anyway, for I have lusted in my heart, and

I have quit reading the Bible, and I have drunk, so what's the difference? At least let me go out in a spasm of ecstasy.

In the morning, around eleven, he called the woman from Hyde Park. Yes, he was welcome to visit, after she came back from her art lesson in the afternoon.

Daniel went to Walgreen's to buy aspirin. He bought a *Cincinnati Enquirer* and read, in the store, about the heat wave that had gripped the continent, beating all records. When he stepped out of the store at one o'clock, the temperature was above 107 degrees, humidity nearly 100 percent. Daniel could barely breathe, and the air stung his nose and bronchi. He coughed. His eyes watered. He drove downtown to Over the Rhine, an old German neighborhood that was now a ghetto, with gentrified pockets, where white folk could go to their breweries, restaurants, music clubs, and cafés. He drove past Kaldi's café; on the other side of the street was a Baptist church, named John 3:16. He knew the verse, of course, what Baptist didn't? People sat on shaded steps, sweating, drinking water and beer. A window pane cracked all by itself, and Daniel thought it did so from sheer heat. Down here with all the asphalt and cement, the temperature was unbearable. He stopped to have iced tea at Kaldi's. As he drank it, he thought he noticed that the waitress—who crossed her legs in a masculine fashion, ankle over knee—wore no underwear. Maybe her underwear was black, so he couldn't tell there was any. He strained to see, hoping she wore none. Maybe that's how she fought heat; maybe she liked to shock people, tease them. Why should he notice, he wondered. Why? Because he was possessed; lust pulled him by the nose and fixed his gaze in search of flesh everywhere.

He drove toward Hyde Park. He stepped out of the car on the edge of Eden Park and watched the thick brown layer of smoke choking the city around the Ohio River, and the river itself foamed, as though it were a cauldron of water boiling over. He couldn't see clearly across the river, into Covington, Kentucky, for the thick brown smog. High up, the clouds were pink and orange. He'd never seen colorful clouds in the middle of the day before. When he walked back to the car, his soles sank into the glossy black asphalt. One of his shoes stayed in the asphalt. He pulled it up with his hands, and as he bent over, the heat from the road scorched him.

Daniel thought that what he saw was not natural. God hadn't created the world to be so dirty—and then it occurred to him: God was choking the world. It was the end of the world. It was happening already. Maybe it would be over in several days. He panicked, suddenly certain that the temperature would continue to rise, and rise. God said he wouldn't flood the earth again. God even said, *I will not again curse the ground any more for man's sake* (Genesis 8:21). Yes, it says, "the ground," and doesn't say anything about the air. So He could do it with air. He probably wouldn't burn the earth either. But He could just suffocate the earth in its own stench, sending the heat through the ozone holes. This is it, Christ is coming, and I am choking in the lust of my own eyes.

He rushed home—drove as fast as he could—to tell his wife to get ready for the end of the world.

But at home, his wife was gone. Green beans were simmering on the stove, so she must be somewhere near. Yet he couldn't find her anywhere. He couldn't even find his Saint Dalmatian.

He recalled the verses (Matthew 25:40-41):

> *Then shall two be in the field; the one shall be taken, and the other left.*
> *Two women shall be grinding at the mill; the one shall be taken, and the other left.*

This was it; his pious wife was ascended to heaven, as were no doubt the other few pious people, and the rest of them, including Daniel, were left to suffer the seals of God's wrath.

He called his son, but got through only to the son's message machine.

He went to see a Baptist minister, and the minister was home. That did not surprise him. *The first shall be last, the last shall be first.* Many ministers had fallen, like Swaggart and Bakker. "Have you looked outside?" Daniel said. "The end of the world is here. Have you seen how the air simmers? We are all choking."

"That's a Cincinnati summer for you, my brother."

"You don't believe in it?"

"In what? The summer? Well, you just hide away from it."

DANIEL FIGURED OUT that the minister didn't believe much. *There shall be many false prophets.* He thought about it—there were false prophets everywhere. Faithless priests. Davidians. Deepak Chopras. Self-help gurus. Diet gurus (religious practices, fasts without a God). Everybody offering happiness, with false gods, selves. Worship of the ego; wasn't that the root of all evil in the garden? Man and woman imagined that they could be like God, self-sufficient and all-knowing. Now again, men want to be all-knowing, and have the illusion that they are; you just finger computers a bit, and they give you the information you need; computers are nearly omniscient, and of course, many computer operators have the conceit that they themselves are omniscient. Daniel had had a conversation, with a doctor whose house he painted, about what Moses would have done if he'd had a computer with CD-ROM programming; the Ten Commandments would have been written on CD-ROM. Maybe they would have been different; instead of, Thou shalt not covet thy neighbor's ass, a commandment might have turned out to be, Thou shalt not spill coffee or any other liquids on the screen while surfing the Net. He shuddered, afraid that his thought was sacrilegious, and then wondered whether Moses climbed Mt. Sinai with a hammer and a chisel to lend to God so the commandments could be engraved into the stone tables, or did God keep such tools, or did God simply blast grooves in the stone with his fiery breath?

He went home alone. Intentionally he left the windows open, to feel the heat. He didn't want to use air-conditioning; he had concluded that air-conditioning was a part of man's arrogance against God—to create a mini-climate, avoid God's winds. No, he'd bear those winds. He wouldn't contribute to the destruction of the world; for it was not God himself who was directly destroying humankind. Humankind was destroying itself through its greed and pleasure seeking.

Usually, they kept the windows not only closed but locked because there was crime in the neighborhood. But what harm could a crime do to him now?

Maybe it was not too late for him to be ascended. He had noticed the end, while most hadn't. He prayed. And after his last "Amen," and he said many of them, he looked up. The moon was scarlet red, and there were three rings around it. He'd seen one, never more, on cold nights, when the moon was full, but now, the moon wasn't even full; it gave off little light, and around it, there was a blue ring, and a red ring, and a hazy white ring. Daniel remembered, *And there shall be signs in the sun, and in the moon, and in the stars* . . . (Luke 21:25); and . . . *the sun shall be darkened, and the moon shall not give her light* . . . (Mark 13:24).

He didn't sleep. In the morning he turned on CNN, expecting to see reports about the coming of Christ. Would they try to interview Christ before he got to his business of resurrecting the dead and ascending those who'd been truly forgiven into heavens? Who would do that? Christiane Amanpour?

Instead, there was a report about how Srebrenica was overrun, and how thousands of Muslim men and boys were rounded up and bussed away into the fields where, according to "unconfirmed reports," mass executions were taking place.

So there it was. *Now the brother shall betray the brother to death, and the father the son; and children shall rise up against their parents, and shall cause them to be put to death* (Mark 13:12). These were basically the same ethnic group, in Eastern Bosnia, Serbs and Croats of Muslim religious tradition who lost track of being Serbs and Croats, and Serbs of Orthodox tradition, who perhaps lost track of religious tradition, but not of being Serbs. Brother against brother—in the name of God, just to add sacrilege to the massacre, which already was sacrilege.

Daniel decided to go watch the end of the world from Eden Park. There he sat and waited.

On the horizon showed up dark clouds and lightning. He wondered whether God's host was coming. Then a terrible hailstorm came, hail the size of a cliché, a golf ball, although of course, once he could catch it, it was the size of a peanut.

The storm was soon over. Other than a few indents on the roof of his pickup, there was no other damage. The air was cool now, cool and clear, as though the world was washed clean. Daniel felt a moment of sadness. He wondered whether God had changed his mind. What had happened? Like Jonah, who would have liked to see the destruction . . .

He drove home. At least his wife then would be back. Who knows where she'd gone that long.

The machine blinked. He played the message. "Hi, here's Nikolai. Just calling so you wouldn't *sorgen*. Mira and I . . . we decided to live together. She says you haven't treated her *harasho*, and I try my best to help her. Here *Schatz*, you tell him too, so he knows." There was weeping, and Mira said: "We couldn't go on like that any more. You never paid any attention to me. We'll be in touch about splitting up our property."

Daniel shrieked with laughter. And he thought she'd been ascended to heaven! Cold air streamed through the window. The end of the world. Shit, how could he have been that stupid. And then he was incensed. She had seduced Nikolai right in front of him. She even chided Daniel for noticing it.

He called his daughter, Marina. Marina believed that her mom was kidnapped, and advised him to call the police. He didn't believe his daughter.

He drove off to a pawn shop to buy a gun. Yes, he'll find those scoundrels. Whom should he shoot? Just him? Well, he didn't even know him that well. Her? Obviously, he didn't know her that well either. You could live with someone all your life and never learn. It wasn't worth the bother, shooting somebody, going to court, being pictured in the newspapers as a demented maniac. Ridiculous.

He walked into a phone booth and dialed the tennis player's number in Hyde Park to play Windows '95 with her. No answer. Surely, she was not ascended, he thought, and the thought entertained him. As he laughed, he felt a terrible relief.

He no longer believed in the end of the world and in the prophets, not even the prophets of the global warming effect. He knew his reasoning was not quite right now, as it hadn't been right before, but he was sure that the granite faith of his transatlantic youth was gone. The faith had through years attenuated into a delicate crystalline structure that broke down the light—broke it down into the aura of transcendent, other-worldly, seeking and relishing extreme spectacles of collapse; and this fragile aesthetic faith crumbled in the heat, into a heap of glass dust that could no longer be resurrected into crystal, and that would be lost in the sand of the entropied world as spittle in the ocean.

SOME APPROACHES TO THE PROBLEM OF THE SHORTAGE OF TIME

Ursula K. Le Guin

THE LITTLE TINY HOLE THEORY

THE HYPOTHESIS PUT forward by James Osbold of the Lick Observatory, though magnificently comprehensive, presents certain difficulties to agencies seeking practical solutions to the problem. Divested of its mathematical formulation, Dr. Osbold's theory may be described in very approximate terms as positing the existence of an anomaly in the space-time continuum. The cause of the anomaly is a failure of reality to meet the specifications of the General Theory of Relativity, although only in one minor detail. Its effect on the actual constitution of the universe is a local imperfection or flaw, that is, a hole in the continuum.

The hole, according to Osbold's calculations, is a distinctly spacelike hole. In this spatiality lies its danger, since the imbalance thus constituted in the continuum causes a compensatory influx from the timelike aspects of the cosmos. In other words, time is running out of the hole. This has probably been going on ever since the origin of the universe 12 to 15 billion years ago, but only lately has the leak grown to noticeable proportions.

The propounder of the theory is not pessimistic, remarking that it might be even worse if the anomaly were in the timelike aspect of the continuum, in which case space would be escaping, possibly one dimension at a time, which would cause untold discomfort and confusion; although, Osbold adds, "In that event we might have time enough to do something about it."

Since the theory posits the hole's location somewhere or other, Lick and two Australian observatories have arranged a coordinated search for local variations in the red shift which might aid in pinpointing the point/instant. "It may still be a very small hole," Osbold says. "Quite tiny. It would not need to be very large to do a good deal of damage. But since the effect is so noticeable here on Earth, I feel we have a good chance of finding the thing perhaps no farther away than the Andromeda Galaxy, and then all we'll need is what you might call a Dutch boy."

THE NONBIODEGRADABLE MOMENT

A TOTALLY DIFFERENT explanation of the time shortage is offered by a research team of the Interco Development Corporation. Their approach to the problem, as presented by N.T. Chaudhuri, an internationally recognised authority on the ecology and ethology of the internal combustion engine, is chemical rather than cosmological. Chaudhuri has proved that the fumes of incompletely burned petroleum fuel, under certain conditions—diffused anxiety is the major predisposing factor—will form a chemical bond with time, "tying down" instants in the same manner as a nucleating agent "ties down" free atoms into molecules. The process is called chronocrystallisation or (in the case of acute anxiety) chronoprecipitation. The resulting compact arrangement of instants is far more orderly than the pre-existent random "nowness," but unfortunately this decrease in entropy is paid for by a very marked increase in bioinsupportability. In fact the petroleum/time compound appears to be absolutely incompatible with life in any form, even anaerobic bacteria, of which so much was hoped.

The present danger, then, as described by team member F. Gonzales Park, is that so much of our free time, or radical time properly speaking, will be locked into this noxious compound (which she refers to as petropsychotoxin or PPST) that we will be forced to bring up the vast deposits of PPST which the U.S. government has dumped or stored in various caves, swamps, holes, oceans, and backyards, and deliberately break down the compound, thus releasing free temporal radicals. Senator Helms and several Sunbelt Democrats have already protested. Certainly the process of reclaiming time from PPST is risky, requiring so much oxygen that we might end up, as O. Heiko, a third member of the team, puts it, with plenty of free time but no air.

Feeling that time is running out even faster than the oil wells, Heiko himself favors as "austerity" approach to the problem, beginning with a ban on aircraft flying in excess of the speed of sound, and working steadily on down through prop planes, racing cars, standard cars, ships, motorboats, etc., until, if necessary, all petroleum-powered vehicles have been eliminated. Speed serves as the standard of priority, since the higher the velocity of the petroleum-fueled vehicle, and hence the more concentrated the conscious or subliminal anxiety of the driver/passengers, the more complete is the petrolisation of time, and the more poisonous the resultant PPST. Heiko, believing there is no "safe level" of contamination, thinks that probably not even mopeds would eventually escape the ban. As he points out, a single gas-powered lawnmower moving at less than 3 mph can petrolise three solid hours of a Sunday afternoon in an area of one city block.

A ban on gas guzzlers may, however, solve only half the problem. An attempt by the Islamic league to raise the price of crude time by $8.50/hr was recently foiled by prompt action by the Organisation of Time Consuming States; but West Germany is already paying $18.75/hr—twice what the American consumer expects to pay for his time.

BLEEDING HEARTS?
THE TEMPORAL CONSERVATION MOVEMENT

WILLING TO LISTEN to the cosmological and chemical hypotheses but uncommitted to either is a growing consortium of scientists and laypersons, many of whom have grouped themselves into organisations such as Le Temps Perdu (Brussels), Protestants Concerned at the Waste of Time (Indianapolis), and the driving, widespread Latin American action group Mañana. A Mañanista spokesperson, Dolores Guzman McIntosh of Buenos Aires, states the group's view: "We have—all of us—almost entirely wasted our time. If we do not save it, we are lost. There is not much time left." The Mañanistas have so far carefully avoided political affiliation, stating bluntly that the time shortfall is the fault of Communist and Capitalist governments equally. A growing number of priests from Mexico to Chile have joined the movement, but the Vatican recently issued an official denunciation of those "who, while they talk of saving time, lose their own souls." In Italy a Communist temporal-conservation group, Eppur Si Muove, was recently splintered by the defection of its president, who after a visit to Moscow stated in print: "Having watched the bureaucracy of the Soviet Union in action I have lost faith in the arousal of class consciousness as the principal means towards our goal."

A group of social scientists in Cambridge, England, continues meanwhile to investigate the as yet unproven link of the time shortage with shortage of temper. "If we could show the connection," says psychologist Derrick Groat, "the temporal conservation groups might be able to act more effectively. As it is they mostly quarrel. Everybody wants to save time before it's gone forever, but nobody really knows how, and so we all get cross. If only there were a substitute, you know, like solar and geothermal for petroleum, it would ease the strain. But evidently we have to make do with what we've got." Groat mentioned the "time stretcher" marketed by General Substances under the trademark Sudokron, withdrawn last year after tests indicated that moderate doses caused laboratory mice to turn into Kleenex. Informed that the Rand Corporation was devoting massive funding to research into a substitute for time, he said, "I wish them luck. But they may have to work longer hours at it!" The British scientist was referring to the fact that the United States has shortened the hour by ten minutes, while retaining twenty-four per day, while the EEC countries, forseeing increasing shortages, have chosen to keep sixty minutes to the hour but allow only twenty hours to the "devalued" European day.

   Meantime, the average citizen in Moscow or Chicago, while often complaining about the shortage of time or the deteriorating quality of what remains, seems inclined to scoff at the doomsday prophets, and to put off such extreme measures as rationing as long as possible. Perhaps, he feels, along with Ecclesiastes and the President, that when you've seen one day, you've seen 'em all.

THINK WARM THOUGHTS

Allison Whittenberg

THE WORLD BURNS; the sun stalks. Can life be sustained off a windowsill's moisture or a lead pipe's sweat?

Someone spills the orange juice we've been rationing. It spread more sunshine across the room. We splintered our tongues lapping it off the wooden floor.

In the white glow of night, a man bursts in and steals thirty-three ounces of water.

I should have shot him; we're all going to die anyway. This way.

As want drips into needs, it's a good-news-bad-news sort of thing. Contentment, comfort, it's all a matter of degrees. I am between cool white sheets. Outside, snow is falling, falling, falling like sugar, but it's piling up to hills, mountains.

They say a new ice age is upon us, but my fever is breaking and I remember a wise old saying.

THE ASH GRAY PROCLAMATION

Dennis Cooper

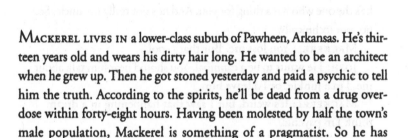

MACKEREL LIVES IN a lower-class suburb of Pawheen, Arkansas. He's thirteen years old and wears his dirty hair long. He wanted to be an architect when he grew up. Then he got stoned yesterday and paid a psychic to tell him the truth. According to the spirits, he'll be dead from a drug overdose within forty-eight hours. Having been molested by half the town's male population, Mackerel is something of a pragmatist. So he has embraced an early death with a young teen's impatience. At the moment, he sits on his bike finessing dope off some sixteen-year-old junkie named Josh who lifts weights and has a trendy short haircut.

JOSH: (*impatiently*) If you want my advice, cut your vocal cords out. It's a simple operation. Otherwise you're so awesome, it's scary.
MACKEREL: Thanks, but I'm looking for dope.
JOSH: (*darkly*) Thank my uncle. You don't even want to know.
MACKEREL: Know what?
JOSH: That we're gay boyfriends, you idiot. I don't why we moved out here from L.A. You're all retarded.
MACKEREL: Thank him for what?!

Mackerel kicks one of his bike pedals angrily and it spins. Josh watches the pedal revolve until his eyes are wide with staring.

MACKEREL: I'm smart enough to know you're just like everyone else in this stupid town who wants my ass, but I don't care anymore.

JOSH: (*vacantly*) If you want to ask me something, do it now, because I think I'm hypnotized.

Mackerel snaps his fingers in Josh's blank face.

MACKEREL: Okay, do you want my ass or not?

JOSH: No, my uncle does. And he doesn't want it. He wants me to want it. I mean he wants me to have it first. So it's a trial run. But he's the one who has a thing for you. And he's not really my uncle. So, no, not technically.

MACKEREL: You lost me. But that's cool.

JOSH: He wants to be a cannibal. You should hear him talk about me. I'm a junkie, or I'd leave him.

MACKEREL: It's weird, but I saw that happening in a dream. I think I'm psychic.

JOSH: I dream all the time. Heroin's great.

MACKEREL: (*angrily*) Then give me some. Jesus.

JOSH: I need to buy a gun.

Mackerel climbs off his bike and starts undoing his belt. One of his ankles accidentally hits the spinning pedal, which stops it dead.

JOSH: Oh, shit. I was just hypnotized, wasn't I?

Mackerel lays his bike down on the sidewalk, which requires him to bend so far over that his baggy jeans are pulled tight.

JOSH: God, you have, like, no ass.

MACKEREL: Hey, I'm fucking thirteen. What do you expect?

JOSH: No, I mean I finally get the whole pedophile thing. Wow, it's addictive.

Ten minutes later, Mackerel is in an uncomfortable squat in some nearby bushes, and Josh is on his hands and knees snuffling in Mackerel's crack like a dog.

MACKEREL: Dude, hey, gay boy. You're obsessed. But don't stop.

JOSH: It's the illegality.

MACKEREL: And what else?

JOSH: That your ass is so nowhere. It's so flimsy and warm it's like an optical illusion. God, listen to me.

MACKEREL: I love it when you breathe out.

JOSH: Having sex with a thirteen-year-old. Who'd have thought? It's like I finally know myself.

MACKEREL: You mean you know me. Not to be egomaniacal.

JOSH: So you're an anarchist. That's hot too.

MACKEREL: I try. But I'm only thirteen, so it's all just a theory.

JOSH: You're God. I just figured it out.

MACKEREL: Maybe to you. I mean I wish.

JOSH: Seriously. You have to smell you. Use your fingers.

Mackerel dips a finger in his asshole, then pulls it out and gives the tip a very tentative sniff.

MACKEREL: Hm.

JOSH: What did I tell you?

MACKEREL: I am God, aren't I? Weird.

JOSH: Yeah, well, just don't tell anyone. Otherwise, I'll never get laid.

MACKEREL: It smells like every other ass in the world, only much, much better. That's a guess.

JOSH: Well, duh. Being gay is the truth. You ought to try it. Oh, shit, I'm going to come.

MACKEREL: Knock yourself out. Oh, shit, me too.

Fifteen minutes later, Mackerel's lower legs have started aching, so he's on his hands and knees. Josh has gotten hard again, and alternates between rimming Mackerel and probing his ethereal ass with a finger.

MACKEREL: Just give me some heroin. What's your problem?

JOSH: You are.

MACKEREL: That's why I don't care if I die. If one more guy does this to me, I'm going to freak. My blood pressure's insane.

JOSH: You should charge.

MACKEREL: I do. Money's not my problem. Beauty is. It's weird. I used to be no one for years.

JOSH: If you can hold out until you're middle-aged, you'll be no one again. You should see my quote-unquote uncle.

MACKEREL: Thanks, but death calls. That sounded more ominous than it feels.

JOSH: I would have paid you a hundred thousand dollars to do this. But I'm horny, so don't quote me.

MACKEREL: That would have worked.

JOSH: I mean I would have if I had it. Maybe my quote-unquote uncle has it. He certainly acts like he's rich. He bought me from the straight world in so many words.

MACKEREL: What do you guys do in bed? Not that I care.

JOSH: This. Only I'm you, and he's every guy who's ever done this to you, if you catch my drift. He also fist fucks me. And he pretends to cook me in the fireplace, and then pretends to carve me into steaks and eat them. I guess they're steaks. They're invisible, so how would I know?

MACKEREL: What do you mean by fist fuck?

JOSH: What do you mean by what do I mean? It's self-explanatory. Why do you care?

MACKEREL: Because it keeps coming up in conversation. Well, not conversation, because I never say anything back. It must be a fad.

JOSH: I love you.

MACKEREL: Yeah, that word keeps coming up too.

JOSH: I want to protect you from the world, and give you give anything you want. I can't believe it.

MACKEREL: Ditto. I mean everyone says that too.

Ten minutes later, Josh is finally bored with sex, and the two boys are sitting side by side on some grass.

JOSH: (*mournfully*) I'm no one now. I've gone from being you to being whoever.

MACKEREL: I'll be dead in a couple of days, if that helps. Besides, I make everyone depressed. Being God sucks.

JOSH: Being the ex-God sucks worse. I should just let my boyfriend eat me. Who cares anymore?

MACKEREL: (*impatiently*) Tell me more about me. God commands you.

JOSH: Well, this is more about me than it is about you, but I'll be happy when you're dead and unattractive.

MACKEREL: That's about me.

JOSH: Then there you go.

MACKEREL: You just need to have sex with somebody who'll never ever have me no matter how much they beg. And I know just the guy, unless you're racist. He's from Bin Laden-ville.

JOSH: Like I care. Like who does it to me ever has an identity.

MACKEREL: I hear that.

JOSH: Is he cute? Not that I care what guys look like.

MACKEREL: I'm a racist. So you tell me.

JOSH: Bin Laden's cute.

Mackerel grabs his stomach and gags.

MACKEREL: Then he's cute. God, ugh, that's disgusting. I'm going to throw up.

ABOUT AN HOUR later, Mackerel, Josh, and the aforementioned psychic are sitting in a circle on an old Persian rug in the latter's little storefront. He's just finished reading Josh's tarot cards. Since the psychic is a Middle Easterner, it feels realistic.

> JOSH: (*to the psychic*) Quit staring at my crotch.
> PSYCHIC: Crotch smotch.
> MACKEREL: (*to the psychic*) He's freaked out. He needs more heroin.
> PSYCHIC: I don't care.
> MACKEREL: (*to Josh*) Reality isn't reality to a psychic. I'm pretending he's a painting.
> JOSH: I've never seen a painting. That's like paint on something flat that looks exactly like a picture, right? Like I care.
> MACKEREL: Not really. It's better. It's even more real in a weird way. Like Tony Hawk Pro Skater 3 on pause, but more serene.

Josh thinks about that until he seems satisfied.

> JOSH: (*to the psychic*) Okay, we're cool if you can channel my ugly, middle-aged boyfriend. 'Cos he's my problem.

Hearing that, the psychic shuts his eyes, bows his head, and becomes a kind of human speaker phone.

> PSYCHIC: (*in a gay-sounding voice*) The problem is I want to eat you. Literally. But you won't let me.
> MACKEREL: (*to the psychic*) I think my buddy knows that, but he wants to know the reason.
> JOSH: When you're on heroin, you can calm down just like this.

He indicates how relaxed his whole body seems all of a sudden.

> JOSH: Being a junkie is awesome.

MACKEREL: (*to the psychic*) Can a thirteen-year-old be gay? I've always wondered.

PSYCHIC: (*in a gay-sounding voice*) Oh my God, yes. Just let me eat my boyfriend, and we'll talk.

MACKEREL: (*to Josh*) Now you ask him something.

Josh sits there thinking angrily for a minute.

JOSH: (*to the psychic channeling his boyfriend*) Okay, if you eat me, what will happen? I mean on a universal level. I don't mean the temporary things like pain.

PSYCHIC: (*in a gay-sounding voice*) This is nice. It's like we're going to a couples' counselor.

JOSH: (*to Mackerel*) See, that's why I love my boyfriend. I need a father.

MACKEREL: Me too. It's weird.

PSYCHIC: (*in a gay-sounding voice*) If I eat you, your life will have more implications. You won't just be hot and sixteen and a junkie. They'll write a book about you, or two or three books. People will always want to know why some gay guy would eat you.

Josh laughs delightedly.

JOSH: (*to Mackerel*) That's so him.

Just then the psychic's head lifts and his beady eyes reopen. Mackerel and Josh look at him suspiciously.

PSYCHIC: (*dazedly*) It's just erased time for me. But I don't care if you believe me or not.

MACKEREL: (*to Josh*) We'd better pay him and go. I know him. But I'll say no more.

PSYCHIC: (*to Josh*) Before I moved here from Afghanistan, I saw your ass in a dream.

JOSH: That's . . . nice?

The psychic whips his tunic off over his head and tosses it aside. His body is fleshy bordering on obese, but shows signs of having been very well built at one time.

JOSH: Afghanistan is where heroin comes from, right?
PSYCHIC: Yeah, why?
MACKEREL: (*to the psychic*) He's a junkie. We told you that when you were in that trance. But I'll say no more.
PSYCHIC: You know what's saddest about the world since 9/11? Even sadder than your dead and our dead?
JOSH: If it's not about heroin, I don't care. Well, heroin or my boyfriend. Fuck, I wish I understood why we love, don't you? I mean we humans. I would have been a movie star by now. That was my old goal.
PSYCHIC: You're sexy when you're thoughtful.
JOSH: Pshaw. But that's sweet.
PSYCHIC: You would have been a whore. You'll be one anyway. That's foretold by that card over there. I just tell it like it is. I can't care about your feelings. You want some heroin? I could use some too.
JOSH: Sure. I don't care about my boyfriend when I'm loaded.

The psychic pulls a packet of yellowy quote-unquote dope out of his discarded tunic.

PSYCHIC: Not to put too fine a point on it, but the thing about the 9/11 bullshit? It wasn't Bin Laden. It wasn't even Al Qaeda.
JOSH: I know. It was our hearts.
PSYCHIC: (*with irritation*) Somebody should murder you.
JOSH: Heroin is murder.

The psychic tosses Josh the quote-unquote dope, then appears to lose his preternatural Islamic-style mystery and cool.

PSYCHIC: (angrily) No, really murder you. I mean as soon as possible. Like now, hint hint. If we were in Afghanistan, everyone would want to murder you. You wouldn't last a day. Your stupid American morality is why we hate you and want to live here and hate living here. But you need psychics.

JOSH: You're good.

PSYCHIC: I'm not that good. I'm just ambitious. But you call that terrorism.

JOSH: You think I don't understand you, but I can. Guys have pulled every kind of crap to get my ass. The murder thing is really, really old.

PSYCHIC: Then what did I just say? Either one of you boys feel free to answer because I'd love to know what you think you know.

JOSH: Then read my mind. Or read his mind. Yeah, read his. I already know what I'm thinking.

The psychic glances meaningfully at Mackerel.

PSYCHIC: I can only read the future. And Mackerel doesn't have one. But he and I have been through this already.

JOSH: Okay, then how does his future not happen? If you're so fucking brilliant.

PSYCHIC: Do that dope. Learn by example.

JOSH: That's a thought. But still . . .

PSYCHIC: Okay, you think I'm attracted to you, right? I make you think that. It's an Afghan thing. That's how we bombed your fucking country. There's your proof.

Josh studies the psychic for a second then laughs and starts pouring the quote-unquote dope out on this little mirror he always carries around in his pocket just in case.

JOSH: You're good. I mean you're really, really good. Okay, you win. What are you into?

PSYCHIC: I'm into you not knowing what to expect. Okay, I'm into rimming and fist fucking. But do that dope first. I like my whores brain-dead.

Josh is already dividing the quote-unquote dope into lines with this razorblade he also carries with him.

JOSH: (*distractedly*) Sounds good. I mean whatever you said.

PSYCHIC: In Afghanistan, there's very famous canyon called Khakistarikhan. It's the deepest canyon in all the world. When I'm through with you, I'm going to enter your ass in the Khakistarikan lookalike contest. It's a big event in Islam, and you'll definitely win.

JOSH: (*to Mackerel*) If you'd ever been fist fucked, you'd be so turned on right now.

MACKEREL: No, I wouldn't.

PSYCHIC: (*to Mackerel*) You should develop your gift. Let me have sex with your dead buddy here. Then I'll lend you a book.

MACKEREL: According to you, I won't have time to read it.

PSYCHIC: That's true, but don't make me laugh. I'll lose my focus. Here, junkie. Use this capitalist prop.

He hands Josh a hundred-dollar bill. Josh rolls the bill into a straw, then leans over and snorts up all the quote-unquote dope.

JOSH: Tell me more about this canyon. I mean more about me.

PSYCHIC: Once a year, a huge prehistoric creature that lives deep in the canyon comes to the surface and does a little dance. He looks exactly like my forearm.

JOSH: Whatever that means. Wow, this is killer heroin. I mean literally. I can feel the legend.

Josh has started to look too relaxed to be around a Middle Easterner in this political climate.

MACKEREL: (*to Josh*) Don't you see what he's doing? This is how the whole 9/11 bullshit happened. He just told you that himself.

PSYCHIC: (*to Mackerel*) He's beyond you. Besides, you love it.

MACKEREL: That could be true. I'd have to think about it.

PSYCHIC: (*to Mackerel*) Don't you realize it yet? You're the one who wants a sixteen-year-old corpse. I'm just a nice guy.

MACKEREL: You're wrong.

He points down at the bulge in his blue jeans.

MACKEREL: This hard-on is bullshit. I just have this whole thing about overdosing on heroin. You started it. Sex is just like whatever. Dying is sex to me.

PSYCHIC: You're too good for this world. As opposed to that corpse or impending corpse over there. You knew him. So you tell me. Dead or not dead?

Mackerel glances at Josh and sees an ugly whitish color that has to mean death's in the mix. He starts rubbing his crotch to help counteract the unsexiness of his moral dilemma.

MACKEREL: (*somberly*) He's history. We're like historians now.

PSYCHIC: Now I'll tell you the truth. I'm not just a psychic. I'm an Al Qaeda operative. He's my mission. It's all about semantics. Do you want to hear the story? It'll curl your toes.

MACKEREL: They already are. Maybe I'm psychic, because I already know what you're going to say.

PSYCHIC: I'm listening.

MACKEREL: If I tell you, you'll lose your hard-on. But you're a stalker. How's that for proof?

PSYCHIC: I love him. That's where our cultural differences get in the way. In my culture, this is love if you're gay. We're not fancy about it. You think we live in caves because we like to live in caves? It's a metaphor. We live together in caves until we find our own caves and fly away. I searched your country coast to coast, and this junkie's ass is mine. Wait'll you see it.

MACKEREL: Like you've seen it.

PSYCHIC: I didn't have to. That's just your literal American thinking. Don't even try to understand it.

MACKEREL: You're big on words and concepts. If I were gay, I'd say God is sex, and seducing straight boys like me is the prayer. Josh told me his boyfriend had to rob a bank to make him gay. He said before then he was just another guy who couldn't make the football team and turned into a stoner. Maybe he was lying, I don't know. The past isn't my thing. So I question your story. How's that for being psychic?

PSYCHIC: Maybe if I knew myself better, I'd agree. Your freedoms are intimidating. How's that for honesty?

MACKEREL: No offense. All I'm saying is your quest is nothing special. You and him are just porn. Death is sex. I mean my death, not his.

PSYCHIC: So I should murder you too? I'm confused.

MACKEREL: No, I'm just saying we should film it. Let's say, hypothetically, I film you doing gay stuff to him. Then we upload the video onto a Web site, and charge guys to watch. They jack off and imagine they're you and all that. Then at the end of the tape we put a little text that says, "Oh, by the way, the boy you just saw getting fucked and et cetera was dead, ha ha ha. You're a necrophiliac. Busted." It might be like flying a plane into the World Trade Center, except a lot more profitable for us.

The psychic scrunches up his face in concentration for a moment.

PSYCHIC: (*laughing*) I wonder who would win in a debate, Bin Laden or you? I'll always wonder that.

MACKEREL: You really need to chill on the Bin Laden thing. I mean if you guys over there in Afghanistan really want to be like the West.

PSYCHIC: I sort of wish he was alive. I mean the junkie, not Bin Laden. Don't get your hopes up. I just mean I wish he knew how much his ass will change the world. But I'm into S&M, so fuck him.

MACKEREL: Not to disappoint you, but his ass is kind of hairy. Not that I've seen it. You could shave it, I guess. We do that a lot over here.

PSYCHIC: (*angrily*) That's so typically nihilistic of your culture.

MACKEREL: Here, I'll show you. It's not a trick. You could do it too, for future reference.

Mackerel tugs on one of the legs of Josh's jeans until there's a naked foot of calf, and rubs one finger gently through its modest thicket of blondish-brown hairs.

MACKEREL: See that? That's how you know.

PSYCHIC: I don't believe you. You're just superstitious. I know all about superstition. When you're poor and live in the desert you think all kinds of crazy shit.

MACKEREL: You want to bet? You'll lose, though.

PSYCHIC: (*laughing*) Sometimes I forget you're only thirteen years old. Sure, I'll bet. What's the wager?

MACKEREL: Okay, if it's hairy, there's no God. And if it's smooth, there is.

PSYCHIC: How about if it's smooth, you can rim him for a second. It had better be. In Afghanistan, it's a sea of hairy asses. That's why we're all pedophiles.

MACKEREL: Maybe I'm wrong, but with these calves, it would be a miracle. Anyway, to us a hairy sixteen-year-old ass is exotic. I've never even seen one.

PSYCHIC: Wait, what's the bet again?

MACKEREL: If I'm right, you'll give me enough of that heroin to kill me, and if I'm wrong, there's no God. But let's just do this fucking thing and move on to something else that we agree on, like my future.

They lay Josh on his back, grab his blue jeans by the belt loops and yank them down over his knees, dragging a pair of jockey shorts along with them. Then they roll him over ceremoniously.

MACKEREL: Okay, that's weird. It's not only smooth. It's also perfectly shaped if one knows anything about physics. I wasn't just wrong. I'm also gay, or gay for him, or gay for it. I don't know about him yet.

PSYCHIC: Stop apologizing and pray.

He kneels down, spreads Josh's cheeks, and starts licking and chewing dead ass crazily like he's a lion and it's attached to some gazelle.

MACKEREL: FYI, we call that rimming in the States because we know God is bullshit. But don't stop.

PSYCHIC: That's strange. We call this praying in Afghanistan because we know God is shit. Let me clarify. His shit. Or rather guys who look like him's shit. You'd qualify.

MACKEREL: That's your fucked-up trip. I'm still at the being rimmed stage. Shit's for grown-ups.

PSYCHIC: Did you ever know this boy Steve? Blond, nineteen, quit school, converted to Islam, joined the Taliban, blah blah blah?

MACKEREL: Why would I? Unless he tried to turn me on to pot once. Read my mind, but keep rimming him too. Can you do that? We can.

The psychic shuts his eyes and concentrates.

PSYCHIC: That's him. Now read mine.

Mackerel shuts his eyes and concentrates.

MACKEREL: Jesus, I'm so gay. That's Steve Rosenberg, all right. What a great fucking ass. It makes mine seem like the Titanic.

PSYCHIC: Steve's ass even turned the great Bin Laden gay for an hour. Don't be so hard on yourself. In Afghanistan, Steve's ass is a national icon.

MACKEREL: And I could have had him. I'm an idiot. Tell me everything about Steve's ass, but keep rimming the dead guy.

PSYCHIC: In Afghanistan, when you want to give a cook the highest compliment there is, you use a phrase. I can't translate it. But it's something like, Thank you for letting Steve sit on my face. Don't quote me.

MACKEREL: Your thoughts are terrorism.

PSYCHIC: Well, this junkie's ass makes Steve's ass taste irrelevant. And it's already cold. Imagine if I hadn't overdosed him. I'm such a rush-to-judgment type.

MACKEREL: Fine, Jesus, then scooch over a little.

He kneels beside the psychic, and starts rimming Josh too. His technique is a lot more romantic.

MACKEREL: Can you believe I've never done this?

PSYCHIC: No.

MACKEREL: I wonder how I'd rate? I mean if my ass was this ass, and you were me or whatever.

PSYCHIC: Some things are too beautiful to know. That's why I've never read Proust.

MACKEREL: So how was Steve compared to Proust?

PSYCHIC: I can only speculate. I'll just say that this writer friend of mine who rimmed Steve is called the Proust of Afghanistan by our literary establishment, such as it is. Before my friend had Steve, he wrote thrillers.

MACKEREL: I want to be rimmed. I mean again. I mean by Bin Laden or you.

PSYCHIC: Like I said.

MACKEREL: You and Steve seem like you were really good friends. But I'm gay so I don't care about friendship anymore. It's lame. Rimming is the truth. Hold his asscrack wider open so I can really eat his hole.

The psychic spreads Josh's dead ass cheeks helpfully and leans back to observe.

> PSYCHIC: I could watch you do that all day.
> MACKEREL: Me too, if I could.
> PSYCHIC: By the way, this is jihad, if you care. You guys thought it was those planes. If Bin Laden is astral projecting himself into my body right this second—and if he isn't dead, he is—he'll be seriously digging what we're doing. I'm so going to heaven.
> MACKEREL: That's debatable.
> PSYCHIC: No, it's not. Anyway, it's been a second.

He knocks Mackerel out of the way, and goes down hard on Josh's ass.

> MACKEREL: (angrily) Friends don't do that. So we aren't friends. I don't know what to call this, though. We like categories over here.
> PSYCHIC: So do we, but our categories are gigantic.
> MACKEREL: See, we respect death too much. That's the only category that's gigantic over here. We're not like you.
> PSYCHIC: So now you know.

He starts eating Josh out even more hungrily than before. The ass starts shaking and rocking side to side and inflating and deflating like lungs.

> MACKEREL: I'm bored.
> PSYCHIC: I don't know that term.
> MACKEREL: Boredom is what we call knowledge over here. The idea is that you never quite quote-unquote know, you just stop caring if you quote-unquote know. That's when you know.
> PSYCHIC: Sounds interesting.

He lifts his head up for a moment and looks sincerely at Mackerel.

PSYCHIC: I mean that. You're a beautiful kid. I'm just—
MACKEREL: I know. I have to get out of here anyway. I've got a date with that wannabe cannibal guy. I just wanted to see you fist fuck him. It's so notorious.
PSYCHIC: I'll page you.
MACKEREL: Yeah, if I'm not food by then.

He crosses his fingers.

PSYCHIC: Page me when you're food. If I don't page you first. Or put paging me in your will. I'm just saying I care about you.
MACKEREL: (*angrily*) Then give me some heroin. Jesus Christ, what does it fucking take?

A HALF HOUR later, Mackerel is sitting cross-legged on some grass in the town's little central park talking directly to you readers. He still isn't stoned, and there's a vibe of desperation in his voice.

MACKEREL: (*dourly*) Hey, you want the cutest piece of ass you've ever had in your lives? I mean cutest for you, not for me. I happen to hate my good looks in a complicated way. Anyway, I'll trade you.
YOU: Thanks for spending time with us. You're God, et cetera, and we love your stupid Arkansas accent. Meaning yes.
MACKEREL: I even scream with an Arkansas accent. You'll love that too.
YOU: What's the trade? We're so damned horny.
MACKEREL: Don't rush me. I'm not like Josh. I need to get to know things before I do them.
YOU: At least take off your shirt.
MACKEREL: There's a trick to being me. It's called "who the fuck are you to ask?" When I'm shirtless, you'll know it.

You: Then make us hard.

MACKEREL: You already are. All it takes is my face. I think my haircut helps too. Long hair's back. But I guess when you're a pedophile, any kid is porn. Correct me if I'm wrong.

You: What do you like to do in bed? We mean what is "fuck" to you?

MACKEREL: Shooting heroin. Next?

You: Junkies are so boring. If you weren't thirteen, we wouldn't be here. We'd be in Thailand.

MACKEREL: (*laughing*) Next. This is awesome. I was never loved when I was straight. So I'm drunk on your gayness. If you weren't here, I'd be in school or prison.

You: The world's a bar when we're with you. If you were old enough to be officially gay, you'd realize that's gay for "we love you." A thirteen-year-old skinny blond boy drunk in an Arkansas gay bar, Jesus. Let's play truth or dare.

MACKEREL: Cool. I like you so far. Okay, you earned it.

He whips off his T-shirt, and hurls it away.

You: Truth. By the way, you have the world's most perfect little ashtrays . . . we mean nipples.

MACKEREL: Okay, do you have any heroin? And before you say that's cheating, Kant says truth lies in the question one asks in pursuit of the truth. Actually, Buddha said that too. So now you know me. Oh, and thanks for the compliment, you liars. Dare.

You: We dare you to explain your intellect. You're thirteen. You quit school at eleven. Your foster parents chained you to a bunk bed at night. You're dyslexic. You're cute. So how the hell do you do it?

MACKEREL: I'm like a parrot. Literally, it's a serious condition. Parrot syndrome. Look it up. Plus I'm psychic and you're not. Truth.

You: Okay, we have enough heroin in our pockets to kill you a hundred times over. And clean works.

MACKEREL: Duh.

He points to his temple.

MACKEREL: I'm a psychic, you remember? But don't you wish this were a loaded gun?
YOU: (*thoughtfully*) Hm.
MACKEREL: (*anxiously*) I don't like the sound of that.
YOU: Us neither. Even thirteen-year-olds get old apparently. Who'd have thought?
MACKEREL: Then give me all your heroin. God, I hate fags. We're all manipulative and shit. You have fifteen seconds to hand it over.

He looks at his watch.

YOU: And we can eat you out?
MACKEREL: Yes.
YOU: And fist fuck you? Bondage, torture, videotape it, kill you when we're done with you?
MACKEREL: Yes, yes, yes. Jesus Christ, are you deaf?

MACKEREL TAKES ALL your heroin and works, then runs away without keeping his part of the bargain. Because you exist in the rational world, you have to watch his perfect ass fade away into the background and form a disconsolate circle jerk. The sky over Arkansas picks up on your vibes and grows silvery dark like one-way glass. On the other side of it, God's jerking off. The hicks think weather abnormalities are a sign that Armaggedon has arrived and decide to rape their kids before they die. Mackerel rides his bike through streets filled with children's lustful screams. He eventually stops at Josh's boyfriend's house and falls into your trap. You're on the phone with Josh's boyfriend when Mackerel rings his front doorbell, so you let him go on one condition. Josh's boyfriend is short and ugly, but has clearly spent time in a gym, so he's hot to other gay guys.

JOSH'S BOYFRIEND: (*startled*) Hey, I know you. Or maybe I wish I knew you. I don't know if you're gay, but crystal meth will do that.

MACKEREL: I just turned gay a few minutes ago, so don't ask me. Gee, Josh said you were even uglier, not that I care.

JOSH'S BOYFRIEND: I get uglier during sex. But thank God for what you see. Guess how old I am? Seriously, take a guess.

MACKEREL: Headwise, I'd say, oh, mid-fifties, and body-wise, oh . . . late thirties tops. We gay guys have it all figured out, don't we?

JOSH'S BOYFRIEND: Being gay myself, it's impossible to say. One hears tales, though. My neighbor's super ugly, unless you like them fat and straight.

MACKEREL: I love everyone equally. Thank the shitload of heroin somewhere in your house. If it weren't there, you'd be alone. Oh, your boyfriend's dead, by the way. I forgot. I'm the new guy.

JOSH'S BOYFRIEND: (*thoughtfully*) Okay, here's being gay in a nutshell. I should reject you out of grief, thereby proving gay love is an authentic force for good. But the fact of the matter is every gay piece of meat is just a sketch for the next piece of meat, although you're just unbelievably cute, bitch. Did I already say that?

MACKEREL: I'm definitely it, dude. The buck stops here. Well, more specifically, here.

He gives his ass a playful slap.

MACKEREL: And, even more specifically, after heroin's in my system, if you're catching my drift.

Josh's boyfriend immediately pulls a big packet of nice-looking dope out of his pocket.

JOSH'S BOYFRIEND: Deal. I love hicks.
MACKEREL: So I heard.

Josh's boyfriend holds out the packet, then seems to have a realization of some sort, and pulls it back.

JOSH'S BOYFRIEND: Wait, did you say Josh is dead? Let me guess, or did you already tell me?

MACKEREL: (*impatiently*) Okay, fine. You know that guy Bin Laden? I'm answering your question with a riddle. It's an old straight-person trick from my childhood.

JOSH'S BOYFRIEND: Sure, he's that famous person.

MACKEREL: Okay, then what do you think of the trendy idea that all Americans died on 9/11? You know, that all of that shit with the planes proved we're all the same whatever in God's overall concept of whatever.

JOSH'S BOYFRIEND: I'm into anything trendy. Just look around my living room. In fact, come on in. Where are my manners?

MACKEREL: On one condition.

JOSH'S BOYFRIEND: Deal. I mean what is it? Forgive the sleazy old chicken hawk in me. He'd go to prison for however many life terms to get it on with a thirteen-year-old ass, I mean your thirteen-year-old ass. That's a gay compliment. Enjoy.

MACKEREL: The condition is that we travel to Pakistan together. On your credit cards, of course. There's a cute traitor guy over there I need to see. Long story. That's part one, and—this'll appeal to you—part two, I can get to Bin Laden. Check this out. So I overdose on heroin, right? I'm happy. Bin Laden rims my corpse. He's happy. You film it. Put the camera on a tripod, walk into the frame and murder him with your bare fucking hands. Then turn off the camera and eat me. Everyone's happy, and gay guys rule the world. It's a no-brainer.

JOSH'S BOYFRIEND: Are you psychic? I make snuff films for a living. Duh, right? That's how I paid for this gay upper-middle-class lifestyle you see before you. Wait, Josh told you I made snuff. Of course. You're not a psychic at all. I'm confused.

MACKEREL: Hunh. If I'd been gay a little longer, I'd say the real gay dilemma is that no amount of working out daily in a gym can make a guy your age interesting to someone my age. The mind goes. It's just a sad fact. I'm so not in the mood anymore. But yeah, I'm psychic.

JOSH'S BOYFRIEND: Then Pakistan it is. On one condition.

MACKEREL: It'd better involve dope.

JOSH'S BOYFRIEND: I'll pack my things, and—oh, it is—you strip and strike a nice doggie pose on my bed. I may be gay, but I'm not stupid. Well, not that stupid.

MACKEREL: Blahdiblahdiblah. I mean deal.

*

AN HOUR LATER, a very sore-assed Mackerel cracks the psychic's door and clears his throat. Josh's buff, elderly boyfriend is right behind him carrying their suitcases.

MACKEREL: Are you decent? I guess that's a relative term in your case.

PSYCHIC: (*anxiously*) Who's there?

MACKEREL: God and a gay guy. Why, who's there?

PSYCHIC: Me, Allah's prying eyes, and some half-eaten teen whore. Wait, did you say God?

MACKEREL: And a gay guy, yeah. Coming in.

They enter the storefront. The psychic is sitting on the floor in front of Josh's dead body. He's holding a large, bloody knife, and Josh's once-so-perfect ass is no more, thanks no thanks to the psychic-turned-cannibal's terrorist attacks. Josh's boyfriend leans over, looking around in the mini–ground zero.

JOSH'S BOYFRIEND: Josh? Is that your truth?

MACKEREL: (*to the psychic*) That's a cue to do your thing.

The psychic shuts his eyes and appears to go into a mystical trance.

PSYCHIC: (*in a sixteen-year-old's voice*) What do you want, babe?

I'm kind of busy. Being eaten is like getting fist-fucked by the Colossus of Rhodes, only better.

JOSH'S BOYFRIEND: I told you.

He sets the suitcases down and reaches into the gore, then rips a chunk loose. He studies it carefully.

PSYCHIC: (*in a sixteen-year-old's voice*) What do you want to know? I know everything there is to know now.

JOSH'S BOYFRIEND: How do you taste?

PSYCHIC: (*in a sixteen-year-old's voice*) Like blood. That's too easy. You want to know how the world ends? You don't, trust me. It's so not sexy. It's so not gay.

JOSH'S BOYFRIEND: Does it have something to do with the gravitational pull of the dying sun?

He pops the chunk into his mouth and starts chewing.

PSYCHIC: (*in a sixteen-year-old's voice*) Exactly. Boring.

JOSH'S BOYFRIEND: No offense, baby, but we saw that together on the Discovery Channel. By the way, yum.

MACKEREL: I have a question. Where's Bin Laden?

PSYCHIC: (*in a sixteen-year-old's voice*) You! Hold on a second. First of all, seeing isn't knowing, babe. There's a huge metaphysical difference, it turns out. Now you, you little boyfriend-stealing white-trash bitch. You're supposed to be dead. I've been hanging out waiting for you. Cross your ass over here.

MACKEREL: Make me. No, seriously, where's Bin Laden? Don't make me unconjure you.

PSYCHIC: (*in a sixteen-year-old's voice*) Kandahar. Satisfied?

MACKEREL: No.

PSYCHIC: (*in a sixteen-year-old's voice*) Okay, ask my temporary form where Rakhid's Video is? Bin Laden's in the basement. Hey, you want to know how you die?

MACKEREL: As a hero. Unlike you.

PSYCHIC: (*in a sixteen-year-old's voice*) Tsk tsk tsk. Tell him, babe.

JOSH'S BOYFRIEND: Tell him what, babe? Oh, right. You've been had. Chalk one up for us patient gay Capricorns.

MACKEREL: I'm not into astrology.

PSYCHIC: (*in a sixteen-year-old's voice*) Fact, my boyfriend quote-unquote drives you to the airport. Fact, he makes a detour to pick something up at our house. Fact, the guys you stole that dope from are hiding inside. Fact, they rape and torture and whatever you for two days straight, then inject you with enough dope to kill Shaquille O'Neal, then rape your corpse for another two days. Right, babe?

JOSH'S BOYFRIEND: Pretty much. Well, rape in the broadest sense. If it's ever been called gay sex, it's in your future.

MACKEREL: (*smugly*) A hero's still a hero. Arkansas boy's dream to save the world from Bin Laden crushed by evil pedophile ring. Americans love that shit.

PSYCHIC: (*in a sixteen-year-old's voice*) Yeah, until they do the autopsy and find enough sperm in your ass to start a small third-world country. We'll see how heroic you are after they drag your whorish, drugged-out lifestyle through the tabloids.

MACKEREL: Well, at least I have an ass. At least my ass isn't digested. At least my ass isn't some low-end Al Qaeda water boy's Taco fucking Bell. Say something, gay guy. Defend me. What kind of sugar daddy are you?

Josh's boyfriend stops ripping out pieces of the ass, and popping them into his mouth.

JOSH'S BOYFRIEND: Look, Josh. Realism, okay? I'm gay, you're dead, he's thirteen years old, you saw his ass, what do you expect? Is death like Alzheimer's or something?

PSYCHIC: (*in a sixteen-year-old's voice*) Forget it. So how do I taste anyway? Honestly.

JOSH'S BOYFRIEND: Like blood. Not that I'm complaining.

MACKEREL WAS RESIGNED to his fate as the world's most extremely murdered boy until they reached Josh's boyfriend's front door. Now he's taken a nervous step backward, and his face is clouded over with thinking.

JOSH'S BOYFRIEND: What now? Your death has so much baggage.
MACKEREL: (*ominously*) I feel them. I don't mean psychically. I mean whatchacallit, that humanistic word.
JOSH'S BOYFRIEND: Go somewhere more specific with "them" first. I'm no humanist. And when you're gay, "them" just means straight. So define "them" and quickly.

He looks at his watch.

MACKEREL: The former me's. Cute boys.
JOSH'S BOYFRIEND: You mean like old what's-his-name, my ex?
MACKEREL: For instance.
JOSH'S BOYFRIEND: So you feel like a blip? Like it's cool I'm so cute to one older rich gay guy and all, but it's not like he's Barry Diller? 'Cos that was old what's-his-name's beef, if memory serves.
MACKEREL: Empathically. That's the word I was looking for.
JOSH'S BOYFRIEND: Break it down.
MACKEREL: Love without sex.
JOSH'S BOYFRIEND: Whoa. Just hold on a minute. What the hell are you saying? This is so early Edmund White. You're far too young to remember him. He wrote novels. Do you know what novels are?
MACKEREL: Was Edmund White like Proust? Please say yes.
JOSH'S BOYFRIEND: Yes. Not that I've read Proust. Like all gay guys, I haven't read a novel since 1994.
MACKEREL: I'm too good for you. What does it mean?
JOSH'S BOYFRIEND: It means you're ultimate twink. That's why we all keep rimming you. You're God. Enjoy.
MACKEREL: But you don't fist fuck God.
JOSH'S BOYFRIEND: Says who?

MACKEREL: The Bible.

JOSH'S BOYFRIEND: You don't have a Bible yet. You have die first. I promise you it'll be Proustian, whatever that means. I'll buy a thesaurus, whatever that is. I'll put in lots and lots of sex so gay guys will buy it. I'll make you look like whoever you want. Name it.

MACKEREL: Okay, who's the cutest boy in the world?

JOSH'S BOYFRIEND: You got it.

He raises his voice such that the tweaking, soon-to-be gay murderers inside his house will hear every word distinctly.

JOSH'S BOYFRIEND: Guys, cutest boy in the world. What's your guess?

Thousands of muffled, gay-sounding voices yell names enthusiastically at the same exact moment.

JOSH'S BOYFRIEND: One at a time. On second thought, pick a leader.

MACKEREL: They don't deserve me. This is superdepressing.

MUFFLED GAY-SOUNDING VOICE: Okay, we've got your results. But they're too close to call. How about we just narrow it down, and give you a choice? Any of them will do. You can't lose.

MACKEREL: Agreed. By the way, who are you, leader guy, so I'll know who's the top?

MUFFLED GAY-SOUNDING VOICE: Me? Carl's my name. I'll tell you what. Here's who I used to be, because I'm just a forty-ish, ugly, gay, gym-going dreg who watches too much porn now. But I used to be the slightly queeny but cute enough to make up for it blond boy who hung around in West Hollywood back in the eighties, if you remember that?

JOSH'S BOYFRIEND: He's thirteen, dope. But I remember you. It's me. Lawrence, the old but muscular enough to make up for it guy. Ring a bell?

MUFFLED GAY-SOUNDING VOICE: Ding, yeah. How's it hanging?
JOSH'S BOYFRIEND: It's hanging, dude.
MUFFLED GAY-SOUNDING VOICE: God bless the past, right?
JOSH'S BOYFRIEND: You said it.
MUFFLED GAY-SOUNDING VOICE: Anyway, according to our poll, the cutest boys in the world are Taylor Hanson circa "Mm Bop," duh. Aaron Carter at any age, under any circumstances, duh. Devon Sawa circa that TV movie called something like *Tornado*. Aaron Carter. Nick Carter before he got chunky. Leonardo Di Caprio pre–"*The Beach*." And did I say Aaron Carter? If not, Aaron Carter.
JOSH'S BOYFRIEND: Tough choice.
MACKEREL: Who's the first one he said again?
JOSH'S BOYFRIEND: Taylor Hanson circa "Mm-Bop."
MACKEREL: Him.
JOSH'S BOYFRIEND: (*yelling*) He chose early Taylor Hanson. How hot is that?
MUFFLED GAY-SOUNDING VOICE: Shit. Fine, we're so horny and fucked up on crystal meth that we'll deal with the fact that he isn't Aaron Carter.
JOSH'S BOYFRIEND: (*to Mackerel, whispering*) Pick Aaron Carter.
MACKEREL: Why?
JOSH'S BOYFRIEND: Why?! Am I losing my mind?
MACKEREL: You mean that "Aaron's Party" dork?
JOSH'S BOYFRIEND: Bingo.
MACKEREL: (*mournfully*) Him then. But your pettiness is giving me pause.

Behind Josh's boyfriend's front door, the muffled good news spreads and muffled zippers start unzipping.

JOSH'S BOYFRIEND: So any last words? I mean before you just start saying ouch and all that?
MACKEREL: Yeah, actually. Let history record that a boy who only wanted to serve humanity by serving himself was sidetracked

by the jihad that homoeroticism has unleashed upon the cute. My intellect could have saved us, had we known me, but my ass was too great a distraction, albeit for quite understandable reasons. That's it, I guess. Oh, and a secret. I was just a straight boy who liked being rimmed and told older gay guys he was gay because his girlfriends were so prissy. I don't deserve to die gay, therefore. Think about it. After you've thought about it, talk to me through a psychic of your choice, and I'll tell you the truth of life. Then blow yourselves up in a crowded place. See if I care. Oh, and anarchy rules.

JOSH'S BOYFRIEND: You have a point. But you're so fucking cute.
MACKEREL: (*sourly*) Let's just do it, okay?

He puts his hand on the doorknob.

MACKEREL: But thanks. I am, aren't I? Tell the world.

POLE SHIFT

Justin Taylor

WOULD THE GRASSES get ejected from the soil or sucked down?

Would the crosstown bus condense or striate or disjoin?

Would all the scratched silverware in all the restaurants up and down Cathedral Parkway start keening like churchbells or amp feedback; a multitude of lunch specials cast as the resonant chorus of a dissonant opera?

Trees will redistribute their shadows with thoughtless grace, like smokers circulating their sloppy seconds or children camping by the mailbox in wait of God's return letter. And what about the woman in the white dress, who doesn't know the sun is a pornographer featuring the wild humanity of her ass and lips when she drifts like a veil between me and the light? She's a curvaceous, transient spectacle unfettered by prospects.

In the considered unfolding she'd be another dead one, swept up in the great tide of suddenly airborne souls, invisible as a model Party member. That's obvious and perfect knowledge. What we know about pole shifts or other apocalypses is so boldly hypothetical as to be beyond refuting, like her decision to forgo underwear this morning or the sun's casual warmth. How good must it feel to access that Godly light through the loose cotton folds of this bright item that she does not know is also a two-way mirror? She's closer than ever to being unlimited. I'm just the guy who noticed. But then again maybe we've got something good between us—sharing the paradoxic truths of nakedness and death, driven by a radical honesty never to be replicated or understood. Her not-knowing ticks like a bomb clock nestled in the crux of our crippled, untellable secret: everything she'd never reveal across ten years spent as loyal lovers.

MISS KANSAS
ON JUDGMENT DAY

Kelly Link

WE ARE SITTING on our honeymoon bed in the honeymoon suite. We are in a state of honeymoon, in our honey month. These words are so sweet: *honey, moon*. This bed is so big, we could live on it. We have been happily marooned—honey marooned—on this bed for days. I have a pair of socks on and you've put your underwear on backwards. I mean, it's my underwear, which you've put on backwards. This is perfectly natural. Everything I have is yours now. My underwear is your underwear. We have made vows to this effect. Our underwear looks so cute on you.

I lean towards you. Marriage has affected the laws of gravity. We will now revolve around each other. You will exert gravity on me, and I will exert gravity on you. We are one another's moons. You are holding on to my feet with both hands, as if otherwise you might fall right off the bed. I think I might float up and hit the ceiling, splat, if you let go. Please don't let go.

How did we meet? When did we marry? Where are we, and how did we get here? One day, we think, we will have children. They will ask us these questions. We will make things up. We will tell them about this hotel. Our room overlooks the ocean. We have a balcony, although we have not made it that far, so far.

Where are we and how did we get here? We are so far away from home. This bed might as well be a foreign country. We are both a little bit homesick, although we have not confessed this to each other. We remember cutting the cake. We poured punch for each other, we linked our arms and drank out of each other's glasses. What was in that punch?

We are the only honeymooners in this hotel. Everyone else is a beauty pageant contestant or a beauty pageant contestant's chaperone. We have seen the chaperones in the halls, women armed with cans of hairspray and little eggs containing emergency pantyhose, looking harassed but utterly competent. Through the walls, we have heard the beauty pageant contestants talking in their sleep. We have held water glasses up to the walls in order to hear what they were saying.

As honeymooners, we are good luck tokens. As if our happiness, our good fortune, might rub off, contestants ask us for a light: they brush up against us in the halls, pull strands of hair off our clothing. Whenever we leave our bed, our room—not often—two or three are sure to be lurking just outside our door. But today—tonight—we have the hotel to ourselves.

The television is on, or maybe we are dreaming. Now that we are married, we will have the same dreams. We are watching (dreaming) the beauty pageant.

On television, Miss Florida is walking across the stage. She's blond and we know from eavesdropping in the hotel bar that this will count against her. Brunettes win more often. Three brunettes, Miss Hawaii, Miss Arkansas, Miss Pennsylvania, trail after her. They take big slow steps and roll their hips expertly. The colored stage lights bounce off their shiny sweetheart dresses. In television interviews, we learned that Miss Arkansas is dyslexic, or maybe it was Miss Arizona. We have hopes of Miss Arkansas, who has long straight brown hair that falls all the way down her back.

You say that if we hadn't just gotten married, you would want to marry Miss Arkansas. Even if she can't spell. She can sit on her hair. A lover could climb that hair like a gym rope. It's fairy-tale hair, Rapunzel hair. We saw her practicing for the pageant in the hotel ballroom with two wild pigs, her hair braided into two lassoes. We heard her say in her interview that she hasn't cut her hair since she was twelve years old. We can tell that she's an old-fashioned girl. Please don't let go of my feet.

We have to admit that we are impressed by Miss Pennsylvania's dress. In her interview, we found out that she makes all of her own clothes. This dress has over forty thousand tiny sequins handstitched onto it. It took a year and a day to stitch on all those sequins, which are supposed to look from a distance like that painting by Seurat. Sunday Afternoon on the Boardwalk. It really is a work of art. Her mother and her father helped Miss Pennsylvania sort the sequins by color. She has three younger brothers, football players, and they all helped, too. We imagine the pinprick sequins glittering in the large hands of her brothers. Her brothers are in the audience tonight, looking extremely proud of their sister, Miss Pennsylvania.

We are proud of Miss Pennsylvania as well, but we are fickle. Miss Kansas comes out onto the stage, and we fall in love with her feet. Don't let go of my feet. We would both marry Miss Kansas. You squeeze my foot so tight when she comes out on stage in her blue checked dress, the blue ribbon in her hair. She's wearing blue ankle socks and ruby red shoes. She practically skips across the stage. She doesn't look to the right, and she doesn't look to the left. She looks as if she is going somewhere. When Miss Kansas leaves the stage we instantly wish that she would come back again.

I wish I had a pair of shoes like that, you say. I say your feet are too big. But if I had a pair like that, I would let you wear them. Now that we are married, our feet will be the same size. We are proud of Miss Pennsylvania, we love Miss Kansas, and we are afraid of Miss New Jersey. Miss New Jersey's red hair has been teased straight up into two horns. She has long red fingernails and she is wearing a candy-red dress that comes up to her nipples. You can see that she isn't wearing pantyhose. Miss New Jersey hasn't even shaved her legs. What was her chaperone thinking? (We have heard rumors in the hall that Miss New Jersey ate her chaperone. Certainly no one has seen the chaperone in a few days.) When she smiles, you can see all her pointy teeth.

Miss New Jersey's complexion is greenish. She has small pointy breasts and a big ass and she twitches it from side to side. She has a tail. She twitches her ass, she lashes her tail; we both gasp. Her tail is prehensile. She scratches her big ass with it. It is indecent and we are simultaneously dismayed and aroused. The whole audience is aghast. One judge faints and one of the other judges douses him with a pitcher of ice water. Miss New Jersey purses her lips, blows a raspberry right at the television screen, and exits stage left.

Well, well, we say, shaken. We huddle together on the enormous bed. Please don't let go, please hold on to my feet.

SOME OF THE other contestants: Miss Idaho wants to work with children. Miss Colorado raises sheep. She can shear a sheep in just under a minute. The dress she is wearing is of wool she cut and carded and knit herself. The pattern is her own. This wool dress is so fine, so thin, that it seems to us that Miss Colorado is not actually wearing anything at all. In fact, Miss Colorado is actually a man. We can see Miss Colorado's penis. But possibly this is just a trick of the light.

Miss Nevada has been abducted by aliens on numerous occasions. The stage spotlights appear to make her extremely nervous, and occasionally she addresses her interviewer as 9th Star Master. Miss Alabama has built her own nuclear device. She has a list of demands. Miss South Carolina wants to pursue a career in Hollywood. Miss North Carolina can kiss her own elbow. We try to kiss our own elbows, but it's a lot harder than it looks on television. Please hold me tight, I think I'm falling.

Miss Virginia and Miss Michigan are Siamese twins. Miss Maryland wants to be in Broadway musicals. Miss Montana is an arsonist. She is in love with fire. Miss Texas is a professional hit woman. She performs exorcisms on the side. She says that she is keeping her eye on Miss New Jersey.

MISS KANSAS WANTS to be a weather girl.

MISS RHODE ISLAND has big hair, all tendrilly looking and slicky-sleek. The top part of her jiggles as she wheels herself on stage in an extremely battered-looking wheelchair. She just has the two arms, but she seems to have too many legs. Also too many teeth. We have seen her practicing water ballet in the hotel swimming pool. (Later, during the talent show, she will perform in a tank made of specially treated glass.) We have to admit Miss Rhode Island has talent but we have trouble saying her name. Too many sibilants. Also, at breakfast her breath smells of raw fish and at night the hoarse mutterings of spells, incantations, the names of the elder gods heard through the wall have caused us to lose sleep.

Miss Rhode Island's bathing costume is designed to show off her many shapely legs, which she waves and writhes at the judges enticingly. We decide that we will never, never live in Rhode Island. Perhaps we will never leave this hotel: perhaps we will just live here.

We ogle some of the contestants in their bathing suits. We try not to look at others. We have made a sort of tent out of the bedspread and we feel perfectly safe inside our tent-bedspread. As long as you are holding on to me. Don't let go.

THERE ARE FIVE judges. One of them, a former Miss America herself, is wearing a tiara, all her hair tucked away under a snood. She is very regal but her mouth is not kind. In her hand is a mirror, which she consults now and then in the scoring, reapplying her lipstick vigorously. Now and then she whispers, *I'll get you, my pretty!*

One of the other judges is an old drunk. We saw him down on the boardwalk outside the hotel lobby, wearing a sandwich board and preaching to the waves. He was getting his feet wet. His sandwich board says *the end of the world is nigh*. Beneath this someone has written in lipstick *lions and tigers and bears, oh migh!*

Two of the judges are holding hands under the table.

The last judge is notoriously publicity-shy, although great and powerful. A semi-transparent green curtain has been erected around his chair. We speculate that he is naked, or asleep, or possibly not there at all.

THE TALENT SHOW begins. There are all the usual sorts of performances, tap dancing and mime, snake handling. Miss West Virginia speaks in tongues. Somehow we understand what she is saying. She is saying that the world will end soon, that we will have six children and all of them will have good teeth, that we will always be as happy as we are at this very moment as long as we don't let go. Don't let go. Miss Texas then comes out on stage and showily exorcises Miss West Virginia. The audience applauds uncertainly.

Miss Nebraska comes out on stage and does a few card tricks. Then she saws Miss Michigan and Miss Virginia in half.

Miss Montana builds her own pyre out of cinnamon and other household spices. She constructs a diving platform out of toothpicks and sugar cubes, held together with hairspray. She stands upon it for a moment, splendid and unafraid. Then she spreads her wings and jumps. Firemen stand on either side of the stage, ready to put her out. She emerges from the fire, new and pink and shining, even more beautiful than before. The firemen carry her out on their broad capable shoulders.

The million-gallon tank is filled before our eyes during a musical interlude. We make out, frisky as teenagers. This way we are feeling, we will always feel this way. We will always be holding each other in just this way. When we look at the television again, Miss Oregon is walking on water. We feel sure that this is done with mirrors.

Miss Rhode Island performs her water ballet, a tribute to Esther Williams, only with more legs. She can hold her breath for a really long time. The first row of the audience has been issued raincoats and umbrellas. Miss Rhode Island douses them like candles. During the climax of her performance there is a brief unexplained rain of frogs. Miss Texas appears on stage again.

I LOVED YOU the first time I saw you. Scarecrow, my dear scarecrow, I loved you best of all. Who would have predicted that we would end up here in this hotel? It feels like the beginning of the world. This time, we tell each other, things are going to go exactly as planned. We have avoided the apple in the complimentary fruit basket. When the snake curled around the showerhead spoke to me, I called room service and Miss Ohio, the snake handler, came and took it away. When you are holding me, I don't feel homesick at all.

MISS ALASKA RAISES the dead. This will later prove to have serious repercussions, but the judges have made a decision and Miss Texas is not allowed on the stage again. It is felt that she has been too pushy, too eager to make a spectacle of herself. She has lost points with the judges and with the audience.

You ask me to put on my wedding dress. You make me a crown out of the champagne foil and that little paper thing that goes around the toilet seat. We sit on the edge of the huge bed, my feet in your lap, your feet dangling dangerously. If only we had a pair of magic slippers. You have your tuxedo jacket on, and my underwear. Your underwear. We should have packed more underwear. What if we never get home again? You have one arm wrapped around my neck so tight I can hardly breathe. I can smell myself on your fingers.

Where will we go from here? How will we find our way home again? We should have carried stones in our pockets. Perhaps we will live here forever, in the honey month, on the honeymoon bed. We will live like kings and queens and eat room service every night and grow old together.

On television, stagehands have replaced the water tank with a trampoline. We wouldn't mind having a trampoline like that. Miss Kansas appears, her hair in two pigtails, her red shoes making our hearts ache. She isn't wearing a stitch of clothing otherwise. She doesn't need to wear anything else. She places her two hands on the frame of the trampoline and swings herself straight up so that she is standing upside down on the frame, her two braids pointing down, her shoes pointing straight up. She clicks her heels together smartly and flips onto the trampoline. As she soars through the air, plump breasts and buttocks bouncing, her arms wheeling in the air, she is starting to sing. Her strong homely voice pushes her through the air, her strong legs kicking at the tough skin of the trampoline as if she never intends to land.

We know we recognize this song.

We bounce on the edge of the bed experimentally. Tears run down our faces. The judges are weeping openly. That song sounds so familiar. Did they play it at our wedding? Miss Kansas rolls through the air, tucks her knees under her arms and drops like a stone, she springs up again and doesn't come back down, the air buoying her up the same way that you are holding me—naked as a jaybird, she hangs balanced in the air, the terrible, noisy, bonecracking air: we hold on tight to each other. The wind is rising. If you were to let go—don't let go—

THE STAR

H. G. Wells

I⸤T⸥ was on the first day of the new year that the announcement was made, almost simultaneously from three observatories, that the motion of the planet Neptune, the outermost of all the planets that wheel about the sun, had become very erratic. Ogilvy had already called attention to a suspected retardation in its velocity in December. Such a piece of news was scarcely calculated to interest a world the greater portion of whose inhabitants were unaware of the existence of the planet Neptune, nor outside the astronomical profession did the subsequent discovery of a faint remote speck of light in the region of the perturbed planet cause any very great excitement. Scientific people, however, found the intelligence remarkable enough, even before it became known that the new body was rapidly growing larger and brighter, that its motion was quite different from the orderly progress of the planets, and that the deflection of Neptune and its satellite was becoming now of an unprecedented kind.

Few people without a training in science can realise the huge isolation of the solar system. The sun with its specks of planets, its dust of planetoids, and its impalpable comets, swims in a vacant immensity that almost defeats the imagination. Beyond the orbit of Neptune there is space, vacant so far as human observation has penetrated, without warmth or light or sound, blank emptiness, for twenty million times a million miles. That is the smallest estimate of the distance to be traversed before the very nearest of the stars is attained. And, saving a few comets more unsubstantial than the thinnest flame, no matter had ever to human knowledge crossed this gulf of space, until early in the twentieth century this strange wanderer appeared. A vast mass of matter it was, bulky, heavy, rushing without warning out of the black mystery of the sky into the radiance of the sun. By the second day it was clearly visible to any decent instrument, as a speck with a barely sensible diameter, in the constellation Leo near Regulus. In a little while an opera glass could attain it.

On the third day of the new year the newspaper readers of two hemispheres were made aware for the first time of the real importance of this unusual apparition in the heavens. "A Planetary Collision," one London paper headed the news, and proclaimed Duchaine's opinion that this strange new planet would probably collide with Neptune. The leader writers enlarged upon the topic. So that in most of the capitals of the world, on January 3rd, there was an expectation, however vague, of some imminent phenomenon in the sky; and as the night followed the sunset round the globe, thousands of men turned their eyes skyward to see—the old familiar stars just as they had always been.

Until it was dawn in London and Pollux setting and the stars overhead grown pale. The Winter's dawn it was, a sickly filtering accumulation of daylight, and the light of gas and candles shone yellow in the windows to show where people were astir. But the yawning policeman saw the thing, the busy crowds in the markets stopped agape, workmen going to their work betimes, milkmen, the drivers of newscarts, dissipation going home jaded and pale, homeless wanderers, sentinels on their beats, and in the country, labourers trudging afield, poachers slinking home, all over the dusky quickening country it could be seen—and out at sea by seamen watching for the day—a great white star, come suddenly into the westward sky!

Brighter it was than any star in our skies; brighter than the evening star at its brightest. It still glowed out white and large, no mere twinkling spot of light, but a small round clear shining disc, an hour after the day had come. And where science has not reached, men stared and feared, telling one another of the wars and pestilences that are foreshadowed by these fiery signs in the Heavens. Sturdy Boers, dusky Hottentots, Gold Coast Negroes, Frenchmen, Spaniards, Portuguese, stood in the warmth of the sunrise watching the setting of this strange new star.

And in a hundred observatories there had been suppressed excitement, rising almost to shouting pitch, as the two remote bodies had rushed together, and a hurrying to and fro, to gather photographic apparatus and spectroscope, and this appliance and that, to record this novel astonishing sight, the destruction of a world. For it was a world, a sister planet of our earth, far greater than our earth indeed, that had so suddenly flashed into flaming death. Neptune it was, had been struck, fairly and squarely, by the strange planet from outer space and the heat of the concussion had incontinently turned two solid globes into one vast mass of incandescence. Round the world that day, two hours before the dawn, went the pallid great white star, fading only as it sank westward and the sun mounted above it. Everywhere men marvelled at it, but of all those who saw it none could have marvelled more than those sailors, habitual watchers of the stars, who far away at sea had heard nothing of its advent and saw it now rise like a pigmy moon and climb zenithward and hang overhead and sink westward with the passing of the night.

And when next it rose over Europe everywhere were crowds of watchers on hilly slopes, on house-roofs, in open spaces, staring eastward for the rising of the great new star. It rose with a white glow in front of it, like the glare of a white fire, and those who had seen it come into existence the night before cried out at the sight of it. "It is larger," they cried. "It is brighter!" And, indeed the moon a quarter full and sinking in the west was in its apparent size beyond comparison, but scarcely in all its breadth had it as much brightness now as the little circle of the strange new star.

"It is brighter!" cried the people clustering in the streets. But in the dim observatories the watchers held their breath and peered at one another. *"It is nearer,"* they said. *"Nearer!"*

And voice after voice repeated, "It is nearer," and the clicking telegraph took that up, and it trembled along telephone wires, and in a thousand cities grimy compositors fingered the type. "It is nearer." Men writing in offices, struck with a strange realisation, flung down their pens, men talking in a thousand places suddenly came upon a grotesque possibility in those words, "It is nearer." It hurried along awakening streets, it was shouted down the frost-stilled ways of quiet villages; men who had read these things from the throbbing tape stood in yellow-lit doorways shouting the news to the passersby. "It is nearer." Pretty women, flushed and glittering, heard the news told jestingly between the dances, and feigned an intelligent interest they did not feel. "Nearer! Indeed. How curious! How very very clever people must be to find out things like that!"

Lonely tramps faring through the wintry night murmured those words to comfort themselves—looking skyward. "It has need to be nearer, for the night's as cold as charity. Don't seem much warmth from it if it *is* nearer, all the same."

"What is a new star to me?" cried the weeping woman kneeling beside her dead.

The schoolboy, rising early for his examination work, puzzled it out for himself—with the great white star, shining broad and bright through the frost-flowers of his window. "Centrifugal, centripetal," he said, with his chin on his fist. "Stop a planet in its flight, rob it of its centrifugal force, what then? Centripetal has it, and down it falls into the sun! And this—!

"Do *we* come in the way? I wonder—"

The light of that day went the way of its brethren, and with the later watches of the frosty darkness rose the strange star again. And it was now so bright that the waxing moon seemed but a pale yellow ghost of itself, hanging huge in the sunset. In a South African city a great man had married, and the streets were alight to welcome his return with his bride. "Even the skies have illuminated," said the flatterer. Under Capricorn, two Negro lovers, daring the wild beasts and evil spirits, for love of one another, crouched together in a cane brake where the fire-flies hovered. "That is our star," they whispered, and felt strangely comforted by the sweet brilliance of its light.

The master mathematician sat in his private room and pushed the papers from him. His calculations were already finished. In a small white phial there still remained a little of the drug that had kept him awake and active for four long nights. Each day, serene, explicit, patient as ever, he had given his lecture to his students, and then had come back at once to this momentous calculation. His face was grave, a little drawn and hectic from his drugged activity. For some time he seemed lost in thought. Then he went to the window, and the blind went up with a click. Halfway up the sky, over the clustering roofs, chimneys and steeples of the city, hung the star.

He looked at it as one might look into the eyes of a brave enemy. "You may kill me," he said after a silence. "But I can hold you—and all the universe for that matter—in the grip of this little brain. I would not change. Even now."

He looked at the little phial. "There will be no need of sleep again," he said. The next day at noon, punctual to the minute, he entered his lecture theatre, put his hat on the end of the table as his habit was, and carefully selected a large piece of chalk. It was a joke among his students that he could not lecture without that piece of chalk to fumble in his fingers, and once he had been stricken to impotence by their hiding his supply. He came and looked under his grey eyebrows at the rising tiers of young fresh faces, and spoke with his accustomed studied commonness of phrasing. "Circumstances have arisen—circumstances beyond my control," he said and paused, "which will debar me from completing the course I had designed. It would seem, gentlemen, if I may put the thing clearly and briefly, that—Man has lived in vain."

The students glanced at one another. Had they heard aright? Mad? Raised eyebrows and grinning lips there were, but one or two faces remained intent upon his calm grey-fringed face. "It will be interesting," he was saying, "to devote this morning to an exposition, so far as I can make it clear to you, of the calculations that have led me to this conclusion. Let us assume—"

He turned towards the blackboard, meditating a diagram in the way that was usual to him. "What was that about 'lived in vain?'" whispered one student to another. "Listen," said the other, nodding towards the lecturer.

And presently they began to understand.

That night the star rose later, for its proper eastward motion had carried it some way across Leo towards Virgo, and its brightness was so great that the sky became a luminous blue as it rose, and every star was hidden in its turn, save only Jupiter near the zenith, Capella, Aldebaran, Sirius and the pointers of the Bear. It was very white and beautiful. In many parts of the world that night a pallid halo encircled it about. It was perceptibly larger; in the clear refractive sky of the tropics it seemed as if it were nearly a quarter the size of the moon. The frost was still on the ground in England, but the world was as brightly lit as if it were midsummer moonlight. One could see to read quite ordinary print by that cold clear light, and in the cities the lamps burnt yellow and wan.

And everywhere the world was awake that night, and throughout Christendom a sombre murmur hung in the keen air over the countryside like the belling of bees in the heather, and this murmurous tumult grew to a clangour in the cities. It was the tolling of the bells in a million belfry towers and steeples, summoning the people to sleep no more, to sin no more, but to gather in their churches and pray. And overhead, growing larger and brighter, as the earth rolled on its way and the night passed, rose the dazzling star.

And the streets and houses were alight in all the cities, the shipyards glared, and whatever roads led to high country were lit and crowded all night long. And in all the seas about the civilised lands, ships with throbbing engines, and ships with bellying sails, crowded with men and living creatures, were standing out to ocean and the north. For already the warning of the master mathematician had been telegraphed all over the world, and translated into a hundred tongues. The new planet and Neptune, locked in a fiery embrace, were whirling headlong, ever faster and faster towards the sun. Already every second this blazing mass flew a hundred miles, and every second its terrific velocity increased. As it flew now, indeed, it must pass a hundred million of miles wide of the earth and scarcely affect it. But near its destined path, as yet only slightly perturbed, spun the mighty planet Jupiter and his moons sweeping splendid round the sun. Every moment now the attraction between the fiery star and the greatest of the planets grew stronger. And the result of that attraction? Inevitably Jupiter would be deflected from its orbit into an elliptical path, and the burning star, swung by his attraction wide of its sunward rush, would "describe a curved path" and perhaps collide with, and certainly pass very close to, our earth. "Earthquakes, volcanic outbreaks, cyclones, sea waves, floods, and a steady rise in temperature to I know not what limit"—so prophesied the master mathematician.

And overhead, to carry out his words, lonely and cold and livid, blazed the star of the coming doom.

To many who stared at it that night until their eyes ached, it seemed that it was visibly approaching. And that night, too, the weather changed, and the frost that had gripped all Central Europe and France and England softened towards a thaw.

But you must not imagine because I have spoken of people praying through the night and people going aboard ships and people fleeing towards mountainous country that the whole world was already in a terror because of the star. As a matter of fact, use and wont still ruled the world, and save for the talk of idle moments and the splendour of the night, nine human beings out of ten were still busy at their common occupations. In all the cities the shops, save one here and there, opened and closed at their proper hours, the doctor and the undertaker plied their trades, the workers gathered in the factories, soldiers drilled, scholars studied, lovers sought one another, thieves lurked and fled, politicians planned their schemes. The presses of the newspapers roared through the nights, and many a priest of this church and that would not open his holy building to further what he considered a foolish panic. The newspapers insisted on the lesson of the year 1000—for then, too, people had anticipated the end. The star was no star—mere gas—a comet; and were it a star it could not possibly strike the earth. There was no precedent for such a thing. Common sense was sturdy everywhere, scornful, jesting, a little inclined to persecute the obdurate fearful. That night, at seven-fifteen by Greenwich time, the star would be at its nearest to Jupiter. Then the world would see the turn things would take. The master mathematician's grim warnings were treated by many as so much mere elaborate self-advertisement. Common sense at last, a little heated by argument, signified its unalterable convictions by going to bed. So, too, barbarism and savagery, already tired of the novelty, went about their nightly business, and save for a howling dog here and there, the beast world left the star unheeded.

And yet, when at last the watchers in the European States saw the star rise, an hour later it is true, but no larger than it had been the night before, there were still plenty awake to laugh at the master mathematician—to take the danger as if it had passed.

But hereafter the laughter ceased. The star grew—it grew with a terrible steadiness hour after hour, a little larger each hour, a little nearer the midnight zenith, and brighter and brighter, until it had turned night into a second day. Had it come straight to the earth instead of in a curved path, had it lost no velocity to Jupiter, it must have leapt the intervening gulf in a day, but as it was it took five days altogether to come by our planet. The next night it had become a third the size of the moon before it set to English eyes, and the thaw was assured. It rose over America near the size of the moon, but blinding white to look at, and *hot;* and a breath of hot wind blew now with its rising and gathering strength, and in Virginia, and Brazil, and down the St. Lawrence valley, it shone intermittently through a driving reek of thunderclouds, flickering violet lightning, and hail unprecedented. In Manitoba was a thaw and devastating floods. And upon all the mountains of the earth the snow and ice began to melt that night, and all the rivers coming out of high country flowed thick and turbid, and soon— in their upper reaches—with swirling trees and the bodies of beasts and men. They rose steadily, steadily in the ghostly brilliance, and came trickling over their banks at last, behind the flying population of their valleys.

And along the coast of Argentina and up the South Atlantic the tides were higher than had ever been in the memory of man, and the storms drove the waters in many cases scores of miles inland, drowning whole cities. And so great grew the heat during the night that the rising of the sun was like the coming of a shadow. The earthquakes began and grew until all down America, from the Arctic Circle to Cape Horn, hillsides were sliding, fissures were opening, and houses and walls crumbling to destruction. The whole side of Cotopaxi slipped out in one vast convulsion, and a tumult of lava poured out so high and broad and swift and liquid that in one day it reached the sea.

So the star, with the wan moon in its wake, marched across the Pacific, trailed the thunderstorms like the hem of a robe, and the growing tidal wave that toiled behind it, frothing and eager, poured over island and island and swept them clear of men. Until that wave came at last—in a blinding light and with the breath of a furnace, swift and terrible it came —a wall of water, fifty feet high, roaring hungrily, upon the long coasts of Asia, and swept inland across the plains of China. For a space the star, hotter now and larger and brighter than the sun in its strength, showed with pitiless brilliance the wide and populous country; towns and villages with their pagodas and trees, roads, wide cultivated fields, millions of sleepless people staring in helpless terror at the incandescent sky; and then, low and growing, came the murmur of the flood. And thus it was with millions of men that night—a flight nowhither, with limbs heavy with heat and breath fierce and scant, and the flood like a wall swift and white behind. And then death.

China was lit glowing white, but over Japan and Java and all the islands of Eastern Asia the great star was a ball of dull red fire because of the steam and smoke and ashes the volcanoes were spouting forth to salute its coming. Above was the lava, hot gases and ash, and below the seething floods, and the whole earth swayed and rumbled with the earthquake shocks. Soon the immemorial snows of Tibet and the Himalaya were melting and pouring down by ten million deepening converging channels upon the plains of Burmah and Hindostan. The tangled summits of the Indian jungles were aflame in a thousand places, and below the hurrying waters around the stems were dark objects that still struggled feebly and reflected the blood-red tongues of fire. And in a rudderless confusion a multitude of men and women fled down the broad river-ways to that one last hope of men—the open sea.

Larger grew the star, and larger, hotter, and brighter with a terrible swiftness now. The tropical ocean had lost its phosphorescence, and the whirling steam rose in ghostly wreaths from the black waves that plunged incessantly, speckled with storm-tossed ships.

And then came a wonder. It seemed to those who in Europe watched for the rising of the star that the world must have ceased its rotation. In a thousand open spaces of down and upland the people who had fled thither from the floods and the falling houses and sliding slopes of hill watched for that rising in vain. Hour followed hour through a terrible suspense, and the star rose not. Once again men set their eyes upon the old constellations they had counted lost to them forever. In England it was hot and clear overhead, though the ground quivered perpetually, but in the tropics, Sirius and Capella and Aldebaran showed through a veil of steam. And when at last the great star rose near ten hours late, the sun rose close upon it, and in the centre of its white heart was a disc of black.

Over Asia it was the star had begun to fall behind the movement of the sky, and then suddenly, as it hung over India, its light had been veiled. All the plain of India from the mouth of the Indus to the mouths of the Ganges was a shallow waste of shining water that night, out of which rose temples and palaces, mounds and hills, black with people. Every minaret was a clustering mass of people, who fell one by one into the turbid waters, as heat and terror overcame them. The whole land seemed a-wailing, and suddenly there swept a shadow across that furnace of despair, and a breath of cold wind, and a gathering of clouds, out of the cooling air. Men looking up, near blinded, at the star, saw that a black disc was creeping across the light. It was the moon, coming between the star and the earth. And even as men cried to God at this respite, out of the East with a strange inexplicable swiftness sprang the sun. And then star, sun and moon rushed together across the heavens.

So it was that presently, to the European watchers, star and sun rose close upon each other, drove headlong for a space and then slower, and at last came to rest, star and sun merged into one glare of flame at the zenith of the sky. The moon no longer eclipsed the star but was lost to sight in the brilliance of the sky. And though those who were still alive regarded it for the most part with that dull stupidity that hunger, fatigue, heat and despair engender, there were still men who could perceive the meaning of these signs. Star and earth had been at their nearest, had swung about one another, and the star had passed. Already it was receding, swifter and swifter, in the last stage of its headlong journey downward into the sun.

And then the clouds gathered, blotting out the vision of the sky, the thunder and lightning wove a garment round the world; all over the earth was such a downpour of rain as men had never before seen, and where the volcanoes flared red against the cloud canopy there descended torrents of mud.

Everywhere the waters were pouring off the land, leaving mud-silted ruins, and the earth littered like a storm-worn beach with all that had floated, and the dead bodies of the men and brutes, its children. For days the water streamed off the land, sweeping away soil and trees and houses in the way, and piling huge dykes and scooping out Titanic gullies over the countryside. Those were the days of darkness that followed the star and the heat. All through them, and for many weeks and months, the earthquakes continued.

But the star had passed, and men, hunger-driven and gathering courage only slowly, might creep back to their ruined cities, buried granaries, and sodden fields. Such few ships as had escaped the storms of that time came stunned and shattered and sounding their way cautiously through the new marks and shoals of once familiar ports. And as the storms subsided men perceived that everywhere the days were hotter than of yore, and the sun larger, and the moon, shrunk to a third of its former size, took now fourscore days between its new and new.

But of the new brotherhood that grew presently among men, of the saving of laws and books and machines, of the strange change that had come over Iceland and Greenland and the shores of Baffin's Bay, so that the sailors coming there presently found them green and gracious, and could scarce believe their eyes, this story does not tell. Nor of the movement of mankind now that the earth was hotter, northward and southward towards the poles of the earth. It concerns itself only with the coming and the passing of the Star.

The Martian astronomers—for there are astronomers on Mars, although they are very different beings from men—were naturally profoundly interested by these things. They saw them from their own standpoint of course. "Considering the mass and temperature of the missile that was flung through our solar system into the sun," one wrote, "it is astonishing what a little damage the earth, which it missed so narrowly, has sustained. All the familiar continental markings and the masses of the seas remain intact, and indeed the only difference seems to be a shrinkage of the white discoloration (supposed to be frozen water) round either pole." Which only shows how small the vastest of human catastrophes may seem, at a distance of a few million miles.

WHEN WE WENT TO SEE THE END OF THE WORLD

by Dawnie Morningside, age 11¼

Neil Gaiman

WHAT I DID on the founders day holiday was, my dad said we were going to have a picnic, and, my mum said where and I said I wanted to go to Ponydale and ride the ponies, but my dad said we were going to the end of the world and my mum said oh god and my dad said now, Tanya, its time the child got to see what was what and my mum said no, no, she just meant that shed thought that Johnsons Peculiar Garden of Lights was nice this time of year.

My mum loves Johnsons Peculiar Garden of Lights, which is in Lux, between 12th street and the river, and I like it too, especially when they give you potato sticks and you feed them to the little white chipmunks who come all the way up to the picnic table.

This is the word for the white chipmunks. Albino.

Dolorita Hunsickle says that the chipmunks tell your fortune if you catch them but I never did. She says a chipmunk told her she would grow up to be a famous ballerina and that she would die of consumption unloved in a boardinghouse in Prague.

So my dad made potato salad.

Here is the recipe.

My dads potato salad is made with tiny new potatoes, which he boils, then while their warm he pours his secret mix over them which is mayonnaise and sour cream and little onion things called chives which he sotays in bacon fat, and crunchy bacon bits. When it gets cool its the best potato salad in the world, and better than the potato salad we get at school which tastes like white sick.

We stopped at the shop and got fruit and Coca-cola and potato sticks, and they went into the box and it went into the back of the car and we went into the car and mum and dad and my baby sister, We Are On Our Way!

Where our house is, it is morning, when we leave, and we got onto the motorway and we went over the bridge over twilight, and soon it got dark. I love driving through the dark.

I sit in the back of the car and I got all scrunched singing songs that go lah lah lah in the back of my head so my dad has to go, Dawnie darling stop making that noise, but still I go lah lah lah.

Lah lah lah.

The motorway was closed for repairs so we followed signs and this is what they said: DIVERSION. Mummy made dad lock his door, while we were driving and she made me to lock my door too.

It got more darker as we went.

This is what I saw while we drived through the center of the city, out of the window. I saw a beardy man who ran out when we stopped at the lights and ran a smeary cloth all over our windows.

He winked at me through the window, in the back of the car, with his old eyes. Then he wasnt there any more, and mummy and daddy had an arguement about who he was, and whether he was good luck or bad luck. But not a bad arguement. Their were more signs that said DIVERSION, and they were yellow.

I saw a street where the prettiest men Id ever seen blew us kisses and sung songs, and a street where I saw a woman holding the side of her face under a blue light but her face was bleeding and wet, and a street where there were only cats who stared at us.

My sister went loo loo, which means look and she said kitty.

The baby is called Melicent, but I call her Daisydaisy. Its my secret name for her. Its from a song called Daisydaisy, which goes, Daisydaisy give me your answer do Im half crazy over the love of you it wont be a stylish marriage I cant afford a carriage but youll look sweet upon the seat of a bicycle made for two.

Then we were out of the city, into the hills.

Then there were houses that were like palaces on each side of the road, set far back.

My dad was born in one of those houses, and he and mummy had the arguement about money where he says what he threw away to be with her and she says oh, so your bringing that up again are you?

I looked at the houses. I asked my Daddy which one Grandmother lived in. He said he didnt know, which he was lying. I dont know why grownups fib so much, like when they say Ill tell you later or well see when they mean no or I wont tell you at all even when your older.

In one house there were people dancing in the garden. Then the road began to wind around, and daddy was driving us through the countryside through the dark.

Look! said my mother. A white deer ran across the road with people chasing it. My dad said they were a nuisance and they were a pest and like rats with antlers, and the worst bit of hitting a deer is when it comes through the glass into the car and he said he had a friend who was kicked to death by a deer who came through the glass with sharp hooves.

And mummy said oh god like we really needed to know that, and daddy said well it happened Tanya, and mummy said honestly your incorigible.

I wanted to ask who the people chasing the deer was, but I started to sing instead going lah lah lah lah lah lah.

My dad said stop that. My mum said for gods sake let the girl express herself, and Dad said I bet you like chewing tinfoil too and my mummy said so whats that supposed to mean and Daddy said nothing and I said arent we there yet?

On the side of the road there were bonfires, and sometimes piles of bones.

We stopped on one side of a hill. The end of the world was on the other side of the hill, said my dad.

I wondered what it looked like. We parked the car in the car park. We got out. Mummy carried Daisy. Daddy carried the picnic basket. We walked over the hill, in the light of the candles they set by the path. A unicorn came up to me on the way. It was white as snow, and it nuzzled me with its mouth.

I asked daddy if I could give it an apple and he said it probably has fleas, and Mummy said it didnt, and all the time its tail went swish swish swish.

I offered it my apple it looked at me with big silver eyes and then it snorted like this, hrrrmph, and ran away over the hill.

Baby Daisy said loo loo.

This is what it looks like at the end of the world, which is the best place in the world.

There is a hole in the ground, which looks like a very wide big hole and pretty people holding sticks and simatars that burn come up out of it. They have long golden hair. They look like princesses, only fierce. Some of them have wings and some of them dusnt.

And theres a big hole in the sky too and things are coming down from it, like the cat-heady man, and the snakes made out of stuff that looks like glitter-jel like I putted on my hair at Hallowmorn, and I saw something that looked like a big old buzzie fly, coming down from the sky. There were very many of them. As many as stars.

They dont move. They just hang there, not doing anything. I asked Daddy why they weren't moving and he said they were moving just very very slowly but I dont think so.

We set up at a picnic table.

Daddy said the best thing about the end of the world was no wasps and no moskitos. And mummy said there werent alot of wasps in Johnsons Peculiar Garden of Lights either. I said there werent alot of wasps or moskitos at Ponydale and there were ponies too we could ride on and my Dad said hed brought us here to enjoy ourselves.

I said I wanted to go over to see if I could see the unicorn again and mummy and daddy said dont go too far.

At the next table to us were people with masks on. I went off with Daisydaisy to see them.

They sang Happy Birthday to you to a big fat lady with no clothes on, and a big funny hat. She had lots of bosoms all the way down to her tummy. I waited to see her blow out the candles on her cake, but there wasnt a cake.

Arent you going to make a wish? I said.

She said she couldnt make any more wishes. She was too old. I told her that at my last birthday when I blew out my candles all in one go I had thought about my wish for a long time, and I was going to wish that mummy and Daddy wouldn't argue any more in the night. But in the end I wished for a shetland pony but it never come.

The lady gave me a cuddle and said I was so cute that she could just eat me all up, bones and hair and everything. She smelled like sweet dried milk.

Then Daisydaisy started to cry with all her might and mane, and the lady putted me down.

I shouted and called for the unicorn, but I didnt see him. Sometimes I thought I could hear a trumpet, and sometimes I thought it was just the noise in my ears.

Then we came back to the table. Whats after the end of the world I said to my dad. Nothing he said. Nothing at all. Thats why its called the end.

Then Daisy was sick over Daddys shoes, and we cleaned it up.

I sat by the table. We ate potato salad, which I gave you the recipe for all ready, you should make it its really good, and we drank orange juice and potato sticks and squishy egg and cress sandwiches. We drank our Coca-cola.

Then Mummy said something to Daddy I didnt hear and he just hit her in the face with a big hit with his hand, and mummy started to cry.

Daddy told me to take Daisy and walk about while they talked.

I took Daisy and I said come on Daisydaisy, come on old daisybell because she was crying too, but Im too old to cry.

I couldnt hear what they were saying. I looked up at the cat face man and I tried to see if he was moving very very slowly, and I heard the trumpet at the end of the world in my head going dah dah dah.

We sat by a rock and I sang songs to Daisy lah lah lah lah lah to the sound of the trumpet in my head dah dah dah.

Lah lah lah lah lah lah lah lah.

Lah lah lah.

Then mummy and daddy came over to me and they said we were going home. But that everything was really all right. Mummys eye was all purple. She looked funny, like a lady on the television.

Daisy said owie. I told her yes, it was an owie. We got back in the car.

On the way home, nobody said anything. The baby slept.

There was a dead animal by the side of the road somebody had hit with a car. Daddy said it was a white deer. I thought it was the unicorn, but mummy told me that you cant kill unicorns but I think she was lying like grownups do again.

When we got to Twilight I said, if you told someone your wish, did that mean it wouldnt come true?

What wish, said Daddy?

Your birthday wish. When you blow but the candles.

He said, Wishes dont come true whether you tell them or not. Wishes, he said. He said you cant trust wishes.

I asked Mummy, and she said, whatever your father says, she said in her cold voice, which is the one she uses when she tells me off with my whole name.

Then I sleeped too.

And then we were home, and it was morning, and I dont want to see the end of the world again. And before I got out of the car, while mummy was carrying in Daisydaisy to the house, I closed my eyes so I couldn't see anything at all, and I wished and I wished and I wished and I wished. I wished wed gone to Ponydale. I wished wed never gone anywhere at all. I wished I was somebody else.

And I wished.

I AM 'I DON'T KNOW WHAT I AM' AND YOU ARE AFRAID OF ME AND SO AM I

Tao Lin

I AM SO afraid of myself that my afraidness scares you more than it scares me. I should rule your life because when I do you'll be so afraid of my afraidness that you'll smash your own face with your iPod tonight because why are you listening to music when people in Africa are being terrorized by werewolves and all over the world bears are climbing buildings and falling off and falling on baby carriages and old women? In December a rat will climb in your mouth and down your throat and that's healthier than eating steak because it's organic. I'm like Hitler only agoraphobic and committing genocide against my own face nightly by looking in the mirror and you need that because human beings deserve to die. I am a rocket scientist and I miscalculated and sent the space shuttle across the street. It drove across the street and that was it. Because fuck NASA for going to the moon when there are ghosts on Earth that need to have rocket capabilities in order for them to haunt faster and haunt my house because I am afraid of them and need them to actually haunt my house so that I can complain about that and not be called paranoid or delusional or whatever. Fuck human beings. Right now I cut my face with a molar that I extracted from my own mouth with a nail clipper and I think it's infecting so come decapitate me and I'll vomit on your face. Put my brain in a knapsack and put the knapsack in your bathtub and elect your bathroom to dictate your life because shitting and pissing are the most reliable pleasures there are in life because life is a metaphor for itself and I don't know what that means and you don't either but you pretended you did for a moment there, didn't you, because you don't think for yourself and a few months ago they got a giant squid on tape and you thought that was mysterious and cool but in reality the giant squid struggled for four hours before amputating its own tentacle to escape. So fuck humankind and scientists and NASA and I hope a meteor falls on the top of your skull tonight when you are making promises on AOL instant messenger that you will never keep to people who like you and who you make promises to just to keep them around so you can feel good about yourself and fuck you because of that and I should be the president of the country in which you live because I will go on TV and give you step-by-step directions that will help you commit suicide immediately and painlessly because I am compassionate which means that I want everyone to be quiet.

THE ESCAPE—A TALE OF 1755

Grace Aguilar

Dark lowers our fate,
And terrible the storm that gathers o'er us;
But nothing, till that latest agony
Which severs thee from nature, shall unloose
This fixed and sacred hold. In thy dark prison-house;
In the terrific face of armed law;
Yea! on the scaffold, if it needs must be,
I never will forsake thee.

—JOANNA BAILLIE

ABOUT THE MIDDLE of the eighteenth century, the little town of Montes, situated some forty or fifty miles from Lisbon, was thrown into most unusual excitement by the magnificence attending the nuptials of Alvar Rodriguez and Almah Diaz: an excitement which the extraordinary beauty of the bride, who, though the betrothed of Alvar from her childhood, had never been seen in Montes before, of course not a little increased. The little church of Montes looked gay and glittering for the large sums lavished by Alvar on the officiating priests, and in presents to their patron saints, had occasioned every picture, shrine, and image to blaze in uncovered gold and jewels, and the altar to be fed with the richest incense, and lighted with tapers of the finest wax, to do him honour.

The church was full; for, although the bridal party did not exceed twenty, the village appeared to have emptied itself there; Alvar's munificence to all classes, on all occasions, having rendered him the universal idol, and caused the fame of that day's rejoicing to extend many miles around.

There was nothing remarkable in the behaviour of either bride or bridegroom, except that both were decidedly more calm than such occasions usually warrant. Nay, in the manly countenance of Alvar ever and anon an expression seemed to flit, that in any but so true a son of the church would have been accounted scorn. In such a one, of course it was neither seen nor regarded, except by his bride; for at such times her eyes met his with an earnest and entreating glance, that the peculiar look was changed into a quiet, tender seriousness, which reassured her.

From the church they adjourned to the lordly mansion of Rodriguez, which, in the midst of its flowering orange and citron trees, stood about two miles from the town.

The remainder of the day passed in festivity. The banquet, and dance, and song, both within and around the house, diversified the scene and increased hilarity in all. By sunset, all but the immediate friends and relatives of the newly wedded had departed. Some splendid and novel fireworks from the heights having attracted universal attention, Alvar, with his usual indulgence, gave his servants and retainers permission to join the festive crowds; liberty, to all who wished it, was given the next two hours.

In a very brief interval the house was cleared, with the exception of a young Moor, the secretary or book-keeper of Alvar, and four or five middle-aged domestics of both sexes.

Gradually, and it appeared undesignedly, the bride and her female companions were left alone, and for the first time the beautiful face of Almah was shadowed by emotion.

"Shall I, oh, shall I indeed be his?" she said, half aloud. "There are moments when our dread secret is so terrible; it seems to forebode discovery at the very moment it would be most agonizing to bear."

"Hush, silly one!" was the reply of an older friend; "discovery is not so easily or readily accomplished. The persecuted and the nameless have purchased wisdom and caution at the price of blood—learned to deceive, that they may triumph—to conceal, that they may flourish still. Almah, we are NOT to fall!"

"I know it, Inez. A superhuman agency upholds us; we had been cast off, rooted out, plucked from the very face of the earth long since else. But there are times when human nature will shrink and tremble—when the path of deception and concealment allotted for us to tread seems fraught with danger at every turn. I know it is all folly, yet there is a dim foreboding, shadowing our fair horizon of joy as a hovering thunder-cloud. There has been suspicion, torture, death. Oh, if my Alvar—"

"Nay, Almah; this is childish. It is only because you are too happy, and happiness in its extent is ever pain. In good time comes your venerable guardian, to chide and silence all such foolish fancies. How many weddings have there been, and will there still be, like this? Come, smile, love, while I rearrange your veil."

Almah obeyed, though the smile was faint, as if the soul yet trembled in its joy. On the entrance of Gonzalos, her guardian (she was an orphan and an heiress), her veil was thrown around her, so as completely to envelope face and form. Taking his arm, and followed by all her female companions, she was hastily and silently led to a sort of ante-room or cabinet, opening, by a massive door concealed with tapestry, from the suite of rooms appropriated to the private use of the merchant and his family. There Alvar and his friends awaited her. A canopy, supported by four of the youngest males present, was held over the bride and bridegroom as they stood facing the east. A silver salver lay at their feet, and opposite stood an aged man, with a small, richly-bound volume in his hand. It was open, and displayed letters and words of unusual form and sound. Another of Alvar's friends stood near, holding a goblet of sacred wine; and to a third was given a slight and thin Venetian glass. After a brief and solemn pause, the old man read or rather chanted from the book he held, joined in parts by those around; and then he tasted the sacred wine, and passed it to the bride and bridegroom. Almah's veil was upraised, for her to touch the goblet with her lips, now quivering with emotion, and not permitted to fall again. And Alvar, where now was the expression of scorn and contempt that had been stamped on his bold brow and curling lip before? Gone—lost before the powerful emotion which scarcely permitted his lifting the goblet a second time to his lips. Then, taking the Venetian glass, he broke it on the salver at his feet, and the strange rites were concluded.

Yet no words of congratulation came. Drawn together in a closer knot, while Alvar folded the now almost fainting Almah to his bosom, and said, in the deep, low tones of intense feeling, "Mine, mine for ever now—mine in the sight of our God, the God of the exile and the faithful; our fate, whatever it be, henceforth is one;" the old man lifted up his clasped hands, and prayed.

"God of the nameless and homeless," he said, and it was in the same strange yet solemn-sounding language as before, "have mercy on these Thy servants, joined together in Thy Holy name, to share the lot on earth Thy will assigns them, with one heart and mind. Strengthen Thou them to keep the secret of their faith and race—to teach it to their offspring as they received it from their fathers. Pardon Thou them and us the deceit we do to keep holy Thy law and Thine inheritance. In the land of the persecutor, the exterminator, be Thou their shield, and save them for Thy Holy name. But if discovery and its horrible consequences—imprisonment, torture, death—await them, strengthen Thou them for their endurance—to die as they would live for Thee. Father, hear us! homeless and nameless upon earth, we are Thine own!"

"Aye, strengthen me for him, my husband; turn my woman weakness into Thy strength for him, Almighty Father," the voiceless prayer with which Almah lifted up her pale face from her husband's bosom, where it had rested during the whole of that strange and terrible prayer and in the calmness stealing on her throbbing heart, she read her answer.

It was some few minutes ere the excited spirits of the devoted few then present, male or female, master or servant, could subside into their wonted control. But such scenes, such feelings were not of rare occurrence; and ere the domestics of Rodriguez returned, there was nothing either in the mansion or its inmates to denote that anything uncommon had taken place during their absence.

The Portuguese are not fond of society at any time, so that Alvar and his young bride should after one week of festivity, live in comparative retirement, elicited no surprise. The former attended his house of business at Montes as usual; and whoever chanced to visit him at his beautiful estate, returned delighted with his entertainment and his hosts; so that, far and near, the merchant Alvar became noted alike for his munificence and the strict orthodox Catholicism in which he conducted his establishment.

And was Alvar Rodriguez indeed what he seemed? If so, what were those strange mysterious rites with which in secret he celebrated his marriage? For what were those many contrivances in his mansion, secret receptacles even from his own sitting-rooms, into which all kinds of forbidden food were conveyed from his very table, that his soul might not be polluted by disobedience? How did it so happen that one day in every year Alvar gave a general holiday—leave of absence for four and twenty hours, under some well-arranged pretence, to all, save those who entreated permission to remain with him? And that on that day, Alvar, his wife, his Moorish secretary, and all those domestics who had witnessed his marriage, spent in holy fast and prayer—permitting no particle of food or drink to pass their lips from eve unto eve; or if by any chance, the holiday could not be given, their several meals to be laid and served, yet so contriving that, while the food looked as if it had been partaken of not a portion had they touched? That the Saturday should be passed in seeming preparation for the Sunday, in cessation from work of any kind, and frequent prayer, was perhaps of trivial importance; but for the previous mysteries—mysteries known to Alvar, his wife, and five or six of his establishment, yet never by word or sign betrayed; how may we account for them? There may be some to whom the memory of such things, as common to their ancestors, may be yet familiar; but to by far the greater number of English readers, they are, in all probability, as incomprehensible as uncommon.

Alvar Rodriguez was a Jew. One of the many who, in Portugal and Spain, fulfilled the awful prophecy of their great lawgiver Moses, and bowed before the imaged saints and martyrs of the Catholic, to shrine the religion of their fathers yet closer in their hearts and homes. From father to son the secret of their faith and race descended, so early and mysteriously taught, that little children imbibed it—not alone the faith, but so effectually to conceal it, as to avert and mystify, all inquisitorial questioning, long before they knew the meaning or necessity of what they learned.

How this was accomplished, how the religion of God was thus preserved in the very midst of persecution and intolerance, must ever remain a mystery, as, happily for Israel, such fearful training is no longer needed. But that it did exist, that Jewish children in the very midst of monastic and convent tuition, yet adhered to the religion of their fathers, never by word or sign betrayed the secret with which they were intrusted; and, in their turn, became husbands and fathers, conveying their solemn and dangerous inheritance to their posterity—that such things were, there are those still amongst the Hebrews of England to affirm and recall, claiming among their own ancestry, but one generation removed, those who have thus concealed and thus adhered. It was the power of God, not the power of man. Human strength had been utterly inefficient. Torture and death would long before have annihilated every remnant of Israel's devoted race. But it might not be; for God had spoken. And, as a living miracle, a lasting record of His truth, His justice, aye and mercy, Israel was preserved in the midst of danger, in the very face of death, and will be preserved for ever.

It was no mere rejoicing ceremony, that of marriage, amongst the disguised and hidden Israelites of Portugal and Spain. They were binding themselves to preserve and propagate a persecuted faith. They were no longer its sole repositors. Did the strength of one waver all was at an end. They were united in the sweet links of love—framing for themselves new ties, new hopes, new blessings in a rising family—all of which, at one blow, might be destroyed. They existed in an atmosphere of death, yet they lived and flourished. But so situated, it was not strange that human emotion, both in Alvar and his bride, should on their wedding-day, have gained ascendancy; and the solemn hour which made them one in the sight of the God they worshipped, should have been fraught with a terror and a shuddering, of which Jewish lovers in free and happy England can have no knowledge.

Alvar Rodriguez was one of those high and noble spirits, on whom the chain of deceit and concealment weighed heavily; and there were times when it had been difficult to suppress and conceal his scorn of those outward observances which his apparent Catholicism compelled. When united to Almah, however, he had a stronger incentive than his own safety: and as time passed on, and he became a father, caution and circumspection, if possible, increased with the deep passionate feelings of tenderness towards the mother and child. As the boy grew and flourished, the first feelings of dread, which the very love he excited called forth at his birth subsided into a kind of tranquil calm, which even Almah's foreboding spirit trusted would last, as the happiness of others of her race.

Though Alvar's business was carried on both at Montes and at Lisbon, the bulk of both his own and his wife's property was, by a strange chance, invested at Badajoz, a frontier town of Spain, and whence he had often intended to remove but had always been prevented. It happened that early in the month of June, some affairs calling him to Lisbon, he resolved to delay removing it no longer, smiling at his young wife's half solicitation to let it remain where it was, and playfully accusing her of superstition, a charge she cared not to deny. The night before his intended departure his young Moorish secretary, in other words, an Israelite of Barbary extraction, entered his private closet, with a countenance of entreaty and alarm, earnestly conjuring his master to give up his Lisbon expedition, and retire with his wife and son to Badajoz or Oporto, or some distant city, at least for a while. Anxiously Rodriguez inquired wherefore.

"You remember the Señor Leyva, your worship's guest a week or two ago?"

"Perfectly. What of him?"

"Master, I like him not. If danger befall us it will come through him. I watched him closely, and every hour of his stay shrunk from him the more. He was a stranger?"

"Yes; benighted, and had lost his way. It was impossible to refuse him hospitality. That he stayed longer than he had need, I grant; but there is no cause of alarm in that—he liked his quarters."

"Master," replied the Moor, earnestly, "I do not believe his tale. He was no casual traveller. I cannot trust him."

"You are not called upon to do so, man," said Alvar, laughing "What do you believe him to be, that you would inoculate me with your own baseless alarm?"

Hassan Ben Ahmed's answer, whatever it might be, for it was whispered fearfully in his master's ear, had the effect of sending every drop of blood from Alvar's face to his very heart. But he shook off the stagnating dread. He combated the prejudices of his follower as unreasonable and unfounded. Hassan's alarm, however, could only be soothed by the fact, that so suddenly to change his plans would but excite suspicion. If Levya were what he feared, his visit must already have been followed by the usual terrific effects.

Alvar promised, however, to settle his affairs at Lisbon as speedily as he could, and return for Almah and his son, and convey them to some place of greater security until the imagined danger was passed.

In spite of his assumed indifference, however, Rodriguez could not bid his wife and child farewell without a pang of dread, which it was difficult to conceal. The step between life and death—security and destruction—was so small, it might be passed unconsciously, and then the strongest nerve might shudder at the dark abyss before him. Again and again he turned to go, and yet again returned; and with a feeling literally of desperation he at length tore himself away.

A fearful trembling was on Almah's heart as she gazed after him, but she would not listen to its voice.

"It is folly," she said, self-upbraidingly. "My Alvar is ever chiding his too doubting heart. I will not disobey him, by fear and foreboding in his absence. The God of the nameless is with him and me," and she raised her eyes to the blue arch above her, with an expression that needed not voice to mark it prayer.

About a week after Alvar's departure, Almah was sitting by the cradle of her boy, watching his soft and rosy slumbers with a calm sweet thankfulness that such a treasure was her own. The season had been unusually hot and dry, but the apartment in which the young mother sat opened on a pleasant spot, thickly shaded with orange, lemon, and almond trees, and decked with a hundred other richly-hued and richly-scented plants; in the centre of which a fountain sent up its heavy showers, which fell back on the marble bed, with a splash and coolness peculiarly refreshing, and sparkled in the sun as glittering gems.

A fleet yet heavy step resounded from the garden, which seemed suddenly and forcibly restrained into a less agitated movement. A shadow fell between her and the sunshine, and, starting, Almah looked hastily up. Hassan Ben Ahmed stood before her, a paleness on his swarthy cheek, and a compression on his nether lip, betraying strong emotion painfully restrained.

"My husband! Hassan. What news bring you of him? Why are you alone?"

He laid his hand on her arm, and answered in a voice which so quivered that only ears eager as her own could have distinguished his meaning.

"Lady, dear, dear lady, you have a firm and faithful heart. Oh! for the love of Him who calls on you to suffer, awake its strength and firmness. My dear, my honoured lady, sink not, fail not! O God of mercy, support her now!" he added, flinging himself on his knees before her, as Almah one moment sprang up with a smothered shriek, and the next sank back on her seat rigid as marble.

Not another word she needed. Hassan thought to have prepared, gradually to have told, his dread intelligence; but he had said enough. Called upon to suffer, and for Him her God—her doom was revealed in those brief words. One minute of such agonized struggle, that her soul and body seemed about to part beneath it; and the wife and mother roused herself to do. Lip, cheek, and brow vied in their ashen whiteness with her robe; the blue veins rose distended as cords; and the voice—had not Hassan gazed upon her, he had not known it as her own.

She commanded him to tell her briefly all, and even while he spoke, seemed revolving in her own mind the decision which not four and twenty hours after Hassan's intelligence she put into execution.

It was as Ben Ahmed had feared. The known popularity and rumoured riches of Alvar Rodriguez had excited the jealousy of that secret and awful tribunal, the Inquisition, one of whose innumerable spies, under the feigned name of Leyva, had obtained entrance within Alvar's hospitable wall. One unguarded word or movement, the faintest semblance of secrecy or caution, were all sufficient; nay, without these, more than a common share of wealth or felicity was enough for the unconscious victims to be marked, tracked and seized, without preparation or suspicion of their fate. Alvar had chanced to mention his intended visit to Lisbon; and the better to conceal the agent of his arrest, as also to make it more secure, they waited till his arrival there, watched their opportunity, and seized and conveyed him to those cells whence few returned in life, propagating the charge of relapsed Judaism as the cause of his arrest. It was a charge too common for remark, and the power which interfered too might for resistance. The confusion of the arrest soon subsided; but it lasted long enough for the faithful Hassan to eseape, and, by dint of very rapid travelling, reached Montes not four hours after his master's seizure. The day was in consequence before them, and he ceased not to conjure his lady to fly at once; the officers of the Inquisition could scarcely be there before nightfall.

"You must take advantage of it, Hassan, and all of you who love me. For my child, my boy," she had clasped to her bosom, and a convulsion contracted her beautiful features as she spoke, "you must take care of him; convey him to Holland or England. Take jewels and gold sufficient; and—and make him love his parents—he may never see either of them more. Hassan, Hassan, swear to protect my child!" she added, with a burst of such sudden and passionate agony it seemed as if life or reason must bend beneath it. Bewildered by her words, as terrified by her emotion, Ben Ahmed removed the trembling child from the fond arms that for the first time failed to support him, gave him hastily to the care of his nurse, who was also a Jewess, said a few words in Hebrew, detailing what had passed, beseeching her to prepare for flight, and then returned to his mistress. The effects of that prostrating agony remained, but she had so far conquered, as to seem outwardly calm; and in answer to his respectful and anxious looks, besought him not to fear for her, nor to dissuade her from her purpose, but to aid her in its accomplishment. She summoned her household around her, detailed what had befallen, and bade them seek their own safety in flight; and when in tears and grief they left her, and but those of her own faith remained, she solemnly committed her child to their care, and informed them of her own determination to proceed directly to Lisbon. In vain Hassan Ben Ahmed conjured her to give up the idea; it was little short of madness. How could she aid his master? Why not secure her own safety, that if indeed he should escape, the blessing of her love would be yet preserved him?

"Do not fear for your master, Hassan," was the calm reply; "ask not of my plans, for at this moment they seem but chaos, but of this be assured, we shall live or die together."

More she revealed not; but when the officers of the Inquisition arrived, near nightfall, they found nothing but deserted walls. The magnificent furniture and splendid paintings which alone remained, of course were seized by the Holy Office, by whom Alvar's property was also confiscated. Had his arrest been deferred three months longer, all would have gone—swept off by the same rapacious power, to whom great wealth was ever proof of great guilt—but as it was, the greater part, secured in Spain, remained untouched; a circumstance peculiarly fortunate, as Almah's plans needed the aid of gold.

We have no space to linger on the mother's feelings, as she parted from her boy; gazing on him, perhaps, for the last time. Yet she neither wept nor sighed. There was but one other feeling stronger in that gentle bosom—a wife's devotion—and to that alone she might listen now.

Great was old Gonzalos' terror and astonishment when Almah, attended only by Hassan Ben Ahmed, and both attired in the Moorish costume, entered his dwelling and implored his concealment and aid. The arrest of Alvar Rodriguez had, of course, thrown every secret Hebrew into the greatest alarm, though none dared be evinced. Gonzalos' only hope and consolation was that Almah and her child had escaped; and to see her in the very centre of danger, even to listen to her calmly proposed plans, seemed so like madness, that he used every effort to alarm her into their relinquishment. But this could not be; and with the darkest forebodings, the old man at length yielded to the stronger, more devoted spirit with whom he had to deal.

His mistress once safely under Gonzalos' roof, Ben Ahmed departed, under cover of night, in compliance with her earnest entreaties to rejoin her child, and to convey him and his nurse to England, that blessed land, where the veil of secrecy could be removed.

About a week after the incarceration of Alvar, a young Moor sought and obtained admission to the presence of Juan Pacheco, the secretary of the Inquisition, as informer against Alvar Rodriguez. He stated that he had taken service with him as clerk or secretary, on condition that he would give him baptism and instruction in the holy Catholic faith; that Alvar had not yet done so; that many things in his establishment proclaimed a looseness of orthodox principles, which the Holy Office would do well to notice. Meanwhile he humbly offered a purse containing seventy pieces of gold, to obtain masses for his salvation.

This last argument carried more weight than all the rest. The young Moor, who boldly gave his name as Hassan Bu Ahmed (which was confirmation strong of his previous statement, as in Leyva's information of Alvar and his household the Moorish secretary was particularly specified), was listened to with attention and finally received in Pacheco's own household; as junior clerk and servant to the Holy Office.

Despite his extreme youthfulness and delicacy of figure, face, and voice, Hassan's activity and zeal to oblige every member of the Holy Office, superiors and inferiors, gradually gained him the favour and goodwill of all. There was no end to his resources for serving others; and thus he had more opportunities of seeing the prisoners in a few weeks, than others of the same rank as himself had had in years. But the prisoner he most longed to see was still unfound, and it was not till summoned before his judges, in the grand chamber of inquisition and of torture, Hassan Ben Ahmed gazed once more upon his former master. He had attended Pacheco in his situation of junior clerk, but had seated himself so deeply in the shade that, though every movement in both the face and form of Alvar was distinguishable to him, Hassan himself was invisible.

The trial, if trial such iniquitous proceedings may be called, proceeded; but in nought did Alvar Rodriguez fail in his bearing or defence. Marvellous and superhuman must that power have been which, in such a scene and hour, prevented all betrayal of the true faith the victims bore. Once Judaism confessed, the doom was death; and again and again have the sons of Israel remained in the terrible dungeons of the Inquisition—endured every species of torture during a space of seven, ten, or twelve years, and then been released, because no proof could be brought of their being indeed that cursed thing—a Jew. And then it was that they fled from scenes of such fearful trial to lands of toleration and freedom, and there embraced openly and rejoicingly that blessed faith, for which in secret they had borne so much.

Alvar Rodriguez was one of these—prepared to suffer, but not reveal. They applied the torture, but neither word nor groan was extracted from him. Engrossed with the prisoner, for it was his task to write down whatever disjointed words might escape his lips, Pacheco neither noticed nor even remembered the presence of the young Moor. No unusual paleness could be visible on his embrowned check, but his whole frame felt to himself to have become rigid as stone; a deadly sickness had crept over him, and the terrible conviction of all which rested with him to do alone prevented his sinking senseless on the earth.

The terrible struggle was at length at an end. Alvar was released for the time being, and remanded to his dungeon. Availing himself of the liberty he enjoyed in the little notice now taken of his movements, Hassan reached the prison before either Alvar or his guards. A rapid glance told him its situation, overlooking a retired part of the court, cultivated as a garden. The height of the wall seemed about forty feet, and there were no windows of observation on either side. This was fortunate, the more so as Hassan had before made friends with the old gardener, and pretending excessive love of gardening, had worked just under the window, little dreaming its vicinity to him he sought.

A well-known Hebrew air, with its plaintive Hebrew words, sung tremblingly and softly under his window, first roused Alvar to the sense that a friend was near. He started, almost in superstitious terror, for the voice seemed an echo to that which was ever sounding in his heart. That loved one it could not be, nay, he dared not even wish it; but still the words were Hebrew, and, for the first time, memory flashed back a figure in

Moorish garb who had flitted by him on his return to his prison, after his examination.

Hassan, the faithful Hassan! Alvar felt certain it could be none but he; though, in the moment of sudden excitement, the voice had seemed another's. He looked from the window; the Moor was bending over the flowers, but Alvar felt confirmed in his suspicions, and his heart throbbed with the sudden hope of liberty. He whistled, and a movement in the figure below convinced him he was heard.

One point was gained; the next was more fraught with danger, yet it was accomplished. In a bunch of flowers, drawn up by a thin string which Alvar chanced to possess, Ben Ahmed had concealed a file; and as he watched it ascend, and beheld the flowers scattered to the winds, in token that they had done their work, for Alvar dared not retain them in his prison, Hassan felt again the prostration of bodily power which had before assailed him for such a different cause, and it was an almost convulsive effort to retain his faculties; but a merciful Providence watched over him and Alvar making the feeblest and the weakest, instruments of his all-sustaining love.

We are not permitted space to linger on the various ingenious methods adopted by Hassan Ben Ahmed to forward and mature his plans. Suffice it that all seemed to smile upon him. The termination of the garden wall led, by a concealed door, to a subterranean passage running to the banks of the Tagus. This fact, as also the secret spring of the trap, the old gardener in a moment of unwise conviviality imparted to Ben Ahmed, little imagining the special blessing which such unexpected information secured.

An alcayde and about twenty guards did sometimes patrol the garden within sight of Alvar's window; but this did not occur often, such caution seeming unnecessary.

It had been an evening of unwonted festivity among the soldiers and servants of the Holy Office, which had at length subsided into the heavy slumbers of general intoxication. Hassan had supped with the gardener, and plying him well with wine, soon produced the desired effect. Four months had the Moor spent within the dreaded walls, and the moment had now come when delay need be no more. At midnight all was hushed into profound silence, not a leaf stirred, and the night was so unusually still that the faintest sound would have been distinguished. Hassan stealthily crept round the outposts. Many of the guards were slumbering in various attitudes upon their posts, and others, dependent on his promised watchfulness, were literally deserted. He stood beneath the window. One moment he clasped his hands and bowed his head in one mighty, piercing, though silent prayer, and then dug hastily in the flower-bed at his feet, removing from thence a ladder of ropes, which had lain there some days concealed, and flung a pebble with correct aim against the bars of Alvar's window. The sound, though scarcely loud enough to disturb a bird, reverberated on the trembling heart which heard, as if a thousand cannons had been discharged.

A moment of agonized suspense and Alvar Rodriguez stood at the window, the bar he had removed, in his hand. He let down the string, to which Hassan's now trembling hands secured the ladder and drew it to the wall. His descent could not have occupied two minutes, at the extent; but to that solitary watcher what eternity of suffering did they seem! Alvar was at his side, had clasped his hands, had called him "Hassan! brother!" in tones of intense feeling, but no word replied. He sought to fly, to point to the desired haven, but his feet seemed suddenly rooted to the earth. Alvar threw his arm around him, and drew him forwards. A sudden and unnatural strength returned. Noiselessly and fleetly as their feet could go, they sped beneath the shadow of the wall. A hundred yards alone divided them from the secret door. A sudden sound broke the oppressive stillness. It was the tramp of heavy feet and the clash of arms; the light of many torches flashed upon the darkness. They darted forward in the fearful excitement of despair; but the effort was void and vain. A wild shout of challenge—of alarm—and they were surrounded, captured, so suddenly, so rapidly, Alvar's very senses seemed to reel; but frightfully they were recalled. A shriek, so piercing, it seemed to rend the very heavens, burst through the still air. The figure of the Moor rushed from the detaining grasp of the soldiery, regardless of bared steel and pointed guns, and flung himself at the feet of Alvar.

"O God, my husband—I have murdered him!" were the strange

appalling words which burst upon his ear, and the lights flashing upon his face, as he sank prostrate and lifeless on the earth, revealed to Alvar's tortured senses the features of his WIFE.

How long that dead faint continued Almah knew not, but when sense returned she found herself in a dark and dismal cell, her upper garment and turban removed, while the plentiful supply of water, which had partially restored life, had removed in a great degree the dye which had given her countenance its Moorish hue. Had she wished to continue concealment, one glance around her would have proved the effort vain. Her sex was already known, and the stern dark countenances near her breathed but ruthlessness and rage. Some brief questions were asked relative to her name, intent, and faith, which she answered calmly.

"In revealing my name," she said, "my intention must also be disclosed. The wife of Alvar Rodriguez had not sought these realms of torture and death, had not undergone all the miseries of disguise and servitude, but for one hope, one intent—the liberty of her husband."

"Thus proving his guilt," was the rejoinder. "Had you known him innocent, you would have waited the justice of the Holy Office to give him freedom."

"Justice" she repeated, bitterly. "Had the innocent never suffered, I might have trusted. But I knew accusation was synonymous with death, and therefore came I here. For my faith, mine is my husband's."

"And know you the doom of all who attempt or abet escape? Death—death by burning! and this you have hurled upon him and yourself. It is not the Holy Office, but his wife who has condemned him"; and with gibing laugh they left her, securing with heavy bolt and bar the iron door. She darted forwards, beseeching them, as they hoped for mercy, to take her to her husband, to confine them underground a thousand fathoms deep, so that they might but be together; but only the hollow echo of her own voice replied, and the wretched girl sunk back upon the ground, relieved from present suffering by long hours of utter insensibility.

It was not till brought from their respective prisons to hear pronounced on them the sentence of death, that Alvar Rodriguez and his heroic wife once more gazed upon each other.

They had provided Almah, at her own entreaty, with female habili-ments; for, in the bewildering agony of her spirit, she attributed the fail-ure of her scheme for the rescue of her husband to her having disobeyed the positive command of God and adopted a male disguise, which in His eyes was abomination, but which in her wild desire to save Alvar she had completely overlooked, and she now in consequence shrunk from the fatal garb with agony and loathing. Yet despite the haggard look of intense mental and bodily suffering, the loss of her lovely hair, which she had cut close to her head, lest by the merest chance its length and luxuriance should discover her, so exquisite, so touching, was her delicate loveliness, that her very judges, stern, unbending as was their nature, looked on her with an admiration almost softening them to mercy.

And now, for the first time, Alvar's manly composure seemed about to desert him. He, too, had suffered almost as herself, save that her devot-edness, her love, appeared to give strength, to endow him with courage, even to look upon her fate, blended as it now was with his own, with calm trust in the merciful God who called him thus early to Himself. Almah could not realise such thoughts. But one image was ever present, seem-ing to mock her very misery to madness. Her effort had failed; had she not so wildly sought her husband's escape—had she but waited—they might have released him; and now, what was she but his murderess?

Little passed between the prisoners and their judges. Their guilt was all sufficiently proved by their endeavours to escape, which in itself was a crime always visited by death; and for these manifold sins and misde-meanours they were sentenced to be burnt alive, on All Saints' day, in the grand square of the Inquisition, at nine o'clock in the morning, and proclamation commanded to be made throughout Lisbon, that all who sought to witness and assist at the ceremony should receive remission of sins, and be accounted worthy servants of Jesus Christ. The lesser sever-ity of strangling the victims before burning was denied them, as they nei-ther repented nor had trusted to the justice and clemency of the Holy Office, but had attempted to avert a deserved fate by flight.

Not a muscle of Alvar's fine countenance moved during this awful sen-tence. He stood proudly and loftily erect, regarding those that spake with an eye, bright, stern, unflinching as their own; but a change passed over it as, breaking from the guard around, Almah flung herself on her knees at his feet.

"Alvar! Alvar! I have murdered—my husband, oh, my husband, say you forgive—forgive—"

"Hush, hush, beloved! mine own heroic Almah, fail not now!" he answered, with a calm and tender seriousness, which to still that crushing agony, strengthened her to bear and raising her, he pressed her to his breast.

"We have but to die as we have lived, my own! true to that God whose chosen and whose first-born we are, have been, and shall be unto death, aye, and *beyond* it. He will protect our poor orphan, for He has promised the fatherless shall be His care. Look up, my beloved, and say you can face death with Alvar, calmly, faithfully, as you sought to live for him. God has chosen for us a better heritage than one of earth."

She raised her head from his bosom; the terror and the agony had passed from that sweet face—it was tranquil as his own.

"It was not my own death I feared," she said, unfalteringly, "it was but the weakness of human love; but it is over now. Love is mightier than death; there is only love in heaven."

"Aye!" answered Alvar, and proudly and sternly he waved back the soldiers who had hurried forward to divide them. "Men of a mistaken and bloody creed, behold how the scorned and persecuted Israelites can love and die. While there was a hope that we could serve our God, the Holy and the only One, better in life than in death, it was our duty to preserve that life, and endure torture for His sake, rather than reveal the precious secret of our sainted faith and heavenly heritage. But now that hope is at an end, now that no human means can save us from the doom pronounced, know ye have judged rightly of our creed. We ARE those chosen children of God by you deemed blasphemous and heretic. Do what you will men of blood and guile, ye cannot rob us of our faith."

The impassioned tones of natural eloquence awed even the rude crowd around; but more was not permitted. Rudely severed, and committed to their own guards, the prisoners were borne to their respective dungeons.

To Almah those earnest words had been as the voice of an angel, hushing every former pang to rest; and in the solitude and darkness of the intervening hours, even the thought of her child could not rob her soul of its calm or prayer of its strength.

The 1st of November, 1755, dawned cloudless and lovely as it had been the last forty days. Never had there been a season more gorgeous in its sunny splendour, more brilliant in the intense azure of its arching heaven than the present. Scarcely any rain had fallen for many months, and the heat had at first been intolerable, but within the last six weeks a freshness and coolness had infused the atmosphere and revived the earth.

As it was not a regular *auto da fe* (Alvar and his wife being the only victims), the awful ceremony of burning was to take place in the square, of which the buildings of the Inquisition formed one side. Mass bad been performed before daybreak in the chapel of the Inquisition, at which the victims were compelled to be present, and about half-past seven the dread procession left the Inquisition gates. The soldiers and minor servitors marched first, forming a hollow square, in the centre of which were the stakes and huge faggots piled around. Then came the sacred cross, covered with a black veil, and its bodyguard of priests. The victims, each surrounded by monks, appeared next, closely followed by the higher officers and inquisitors, and a band of fifty men, in rich dresses of black satin and silver, closed the procession.

We have no space to linger on the ceremonies always attendant on the burning of Inquisitorial prisoners. Although, from the more private nature of the rites, these ceremonies were greatly curtailed, it was rather more than half an hour after nine when the victims were bound to their respective stakes, and the executioners approached with their blazing brands.

There was no change in the countenance of either prisoner. Pale they were, yet calm and firm; all of human feeling had been merged in the martyr's courage and the martyr's faith.

One look had been exchanged between them—of love spiritualized to look beyond the grave—of encouragement to endure for their God, even to the end. The sky was still cloudless, the sun still looked down on that scene of horror; and then was a hush—a pause—for so it felt in nature, that stilled the very breathing of those around.

"Hear, O Israel, the Lord our God, the Lord is ONE—the Sole and Holy One; there is no unity like His unity!" were the words which broke that awful pause, in a voice distinct, unfaltering, and musical as its wont; and it was echoed by the sweet tones from the woman's lips, so thrilling in their melody, the rudest nature started. It was the signal of their fate. The executioners hastened forward, the brands were applied to the turf of the piles, the flames blazed up beneath their hand—when at that moment there came a shock as if the very earth were cloven asunder, the heavens rent in twain. A crash so loud, yea so fearful, so appalling, as if the whole of Lisbon had been shivered to its foundations, and a shriek, or rather thousands and thousands of human voices, blended in one wild piercing cry of agony and terror, seeming to burst from every quarter at the self-same instant, and fraught with universal woe. The buildings around shook, as impelled by a mighty whirl wind, though no sound of such was heard. The earth heaved, yawned, closed, and rocked again, as the billows of the ocean were lashed to fury. It was a moment of untold horror. The crowd assembled to witness the martyrs' death fled, wildly shrieking, on every side. Scattered to the heaving ground, the blazing piles lay powerless to injure; their bonds were shivered, their guards were fled. One bound brought Alvar to his wife, and he clasped her in his arms "God, God of mercy, save us yet again! Be with us to the end!" he exclaimed, and faith winged the prayer. On, on he sped; up, up, in direction of the heights, where he knew comparative safety lay; but ere he reached them, the innumerable sights and sounds of horror that yawned upon his way! Every street, and square, and avenue was choked with shattered ruins, rent from top to bottom; houses, convents, and churches presented the most fearful aspect of ruin; while every second minute a new impetus seemed to be given to the convulsed earth, causing those that remained still perfect to rock and rend. Huge stones, falling from every crack, were crushing the miserable fugitives as they rushed on, seeking safety they knew not where. The rafters of every roof, wrenched from their fastenings, stood upright a brief while, and then fell in hundreds together, with a crash perfectly appalling. The very ties of nature were severed in the wild search for safety. Individual life alone appeared worth preserving. None dared seek the fate of friends—none dared ask, "Who lives?" in that one scene of universal death.

On, on sped Alvar and his precious burden, on over the piles of ruins; on, unhurt amidst the showers of stones which, hurled in the air as easily as a ball cast from an infant's hand, fell back again laden with a hundred deaths; on, amid the rocking and yawning earth, beholding thousands swallowed up, crushed and maimed, worse than death itself, for they were left to a lingering torture—to die a thousand deaths in anticipating one; on over the disfigured heaps of dead, and the unrecognised masses of what had once been magnificent and gorgeous buildings. His eye was well-nigh blinded with the shaking and tottering movement of all things animate and inanimate before him; and his path obscured by the sudden and awful darkness, which had changed that bright glowing hue of the sunny sky into a pall of dense and terrible blackness, becoming thicker and denser with every succeeding minute, till a darkness which might be felt, enveloped that devoted city as with the grim shadow of death. His ear was deafened by the appalling sounds of human agony and Nature's wrath; for now, sounds as of a hundred waterspouts, the dull continued roar of subterranean thunder, becoming at times loud as the discharge of a thousand cannons; at others, resembling the sharp grating sound of hundreds and hundreds of chariots driving full speed over the stones; and this, mingled with the piercing shrieks of women, the hoarser cries and shouts of men, the deep terrible groans of mental agony, and the shriller screams of instantaneous death, had usurped the place of the previous awful stillness, till every sense of those who yet survived seemed distorted and maddened. And Nature herself, convulsed and freed from restraining bonds, appeared about to return to that chaos whence she had leaped at the word of God.

Still, still Alvar rushed forwards, preserved amidst it all, if the arm of a merciful Providence was indeed around him and his Almah, marking them for life in the very midst of death. Making his rapid way across the ruins of St. Paul's, which magnificent church had fallen in the first shock, crushing the vast congregation assembled within its walls, Alvar paused one moment, undecided whether to seek the banks of the river or still to make for the western heights. There was a moment's hush and pause in the convulsion of nature, but Alvar dared not hope for its continuance. Ever and anon the earth still heaved, and houses opened from base to roof and closed without further damage. With a brief fervid cry for continued guidance and protection, scarcely conscious which way in reality he took, and still folding Almah to his bosom—so supernaturally strengthened that the weakness of humanity seemed far from him—Rodriguez hurried on, taking the most open path to the Estrella Hill. An open space was gained, half-way to the summit, commanding a view of the banks of the river and the ruins around. Panting, almost breathless, yet still struggling with his own exhaustion to encourage Almah, Alvar an instant rested, ere he plunged anew into the narrower streets. A shock, violent, destructive, convulsive as the first, flung them prostrate; while the renewed and increased sounds of wailing, the tremendous and repeated crashes on every side, the disappearance of the towers, steeples, and turrets which yet remained, revealed the further destructiveness which had befallen. A new and terrible cry added to the universal horror.

"The sea! the sea!" Alvar sprung to his feet and, clasped in each other's arms, he and Almah gazed beneath. Not a breath of wind stirred, yet the river (which being at that point four miles wide appeared like the element they had termed it) tossed and heaved as impelled by a mighty storm— and on it came, roaring, foaming, tumbling, as every bound were loosed; on, over the land to the very heart of the devoted city, sweeping off hundreds in its course, and retiring with such velocity, and so far beyond its natural banks, that vessels were left dry which had five minutes before ridden in water seven fathoms deep. Again and again this phenomenon took place; the vessels in the river, at the same instant, whirled round and round with frightful rapidity, and smaller boats dashed upwards, falling back to disappear beneath the booming waters. As if chained to the spot where they stood, fascinated by this very horror, Alvar and his wife yet gazed; their glance fixed on the new marble quay, where thousands and thousands of the fugitives had congregated, fixed, as if unconsciously foreboding what was to befall. Again the tide rushed in—on, on, over the massive ruins, heaving, raging, swelling, as a living thing; and at the same instant the quay and its vast burthen of humanity sunk within an abyss of boiling waters, into which the innumerable boats around were alike impelled, leaving not a trace, even when the angry waters returned to their channel, suddenly as they had left it, to mark what had been.

"'Twas the voice of God impelled me hither, rather than pausing beside those fated banks. Almah, my best beloved, bear up yet a brief while more—He will spare and save us as he hath done now. Merciful Providence! Behold another wrathful element threatens to swallow up all of life and property which yet remains. Great God, this is terrible!"

And terrible it was: from three several parts of the ruined city huge fires suddenly blazed up, hissing, crackling, ascending as clear columns of liquid flame; up against the pitchy darkness, infusing it with tenfold horror—spreading on every side—consuming all of wood and wall which the earth and water had left unscathed; wreathing its serpent-like folds in and out the ruins, forming strange and terribly beautiful shapes of glowing colouring; fascinating the eye with admiration, yet bidding the blood chill and the flesh creep. Fresh cries and shouts had marked its rise and progress; but, aghast and stupefied, those who yet survived made no effort to check its way, and on every side it spread, forming lanes and squares of glowing red, flinging its lurid glare so vividly around, that even those on the distant heights could see to read by it; and fearful was the scene that awful light revealed. Now, for the first time could Alvar trace the full extent of destruction which had befallen. That glorious city, which a few brief hours previous lay reposing in its gorgeous sunlight—mighty in its palaces and towers—in its churches, convents, theatres, magazines, and dwellings—rich in its numberless artizans and stores—lay perished and prostrate as the grim spectre of long ages past, save that the fearful groups yet passing to and fro, or huddled in kneeling and standing masses, some bathed in the red glare of the increasing fires, others black and shapeless—save when a sudden flame flashed on them, disclosing what they were—revealed a strange and horrible PRESENT, yet lingering amid what seemed the shadows of a fearful PAST. Nor was the convulsion of nature yet at an end;—the earth still rocked and heaved at intervals, often impelling the hissing flames more strongly and devouringly forward, and by tossing the masses of burning ruin to and fro, gave them the semblance of a sea of flame. The ocean itself too, yet rose and sunk, and rose again; vessels were torn from their cables, anchors wrenched from their soundings and hurled in the air—while the warring waters, the muttering thunders, the crackling flames, formed a combination of sounds which, even without their dread adjuncts of human agony and terror, were all-sufficient to freeze the very life-blood, and banish every sense and feeling, save that of stupefying dread.

But human love, and superhuman faith, saved from the stagnating horror. The conviction that the God of his fathers was present with him, and would save him and Almah to the end, never left him for an instant, but urged him to exertions which, had he not had this all-supporting faith, he would himself have deemed impossible. And his faith spake truth. The God of infinite mercy, who had stretched out His own right hand to save, and marked the impotence of the wrath and cruelty of man, was with him still, and, despite of the horrors yet lingering round them, despite of the varied trials, fatigues, and privations attendant on their rapid flight, led them to life and joy, and bade them stand forth the witnesses and proclaimers of His unfailing love, His everlasting providence!

With the great earthquake of Lisbon, the commencement of which our preceding pages have faintly endeavoured to portray, and its terrible effects on four millions of square miles, our tale has no further connection. The third day brought our poor fugitives to Badajoz, where Alvar's property had been secured. They tarried there only long enough to learn the blessed tidings of Hassan Ben Ahmed's safe arrival in England with their child; that his faithfulness, in conjunction with that of their agent in Spain, had already safely transmitted the bulk of their property to the English funds; and to obtain Ben Ahmed's address, forward tidings of their providential escape to him, and proceed on their journey.

An anxious but not a prolonged interval enabled them to accomplish it safely, and once more did the doubly-rescued press their precious boy to their yearning hearts and feel that conjugal and parental love burned, if it could be, the dearer, brighter, more unspeakably precious, from the dangers they had passed; and not human love alone. The veil of secrecy was removed, they were in a land whose merciful and liberal government granted to the exile and the wanderer a home of peace and rest, where they might worship the God of Israel according to the law he gave; and in hearts like those of Alvar and his Almah, prosperity could have no power to extinguish or deaden the religion of love and faith which adversity had engendered.

The appearance of old Gonzalos and his family in England, a short time after Alvah's arrival there, removed their last remaining anxiety, and gave them increased cause for thankfulness. Not a member of the merchant's family, and more wonderful still, not a portion of his property, had been lost amid the universal ruin; and to this very day, his descendants recall his providential preservation by giving, on every returning anniversary of that awful day, certain articles of clothing to a limited number of male and female poor.

SO WE ARE VERY CONCERNED
Elliott David

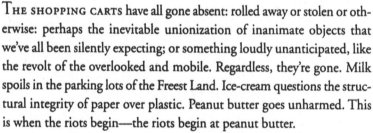

THE SHOPPING CARTS have all gone absent: rolled away or stolen or otherwise: perhaps the inevitable unionization of inanimate objects that we've all been silently expecting; or something loudly unanticipated, like the revolt of the overlooked and mobile. Regardless, they're gone. Milk spoils in the parking lots of the Freest Land. Ice-cream questions the structural integrity of paper over plastic. Peanut butter goes unharmed. This is when the riots begin—the riots begin at peanut butter.

In Peoria, Illinois, thirtysomething thirtysomethings shriek in unison, tearing the condiment aisle to the ground. Those not bludgeoned to death lay suffocating under mounds of quadruple-stuffed Oreos and fruit cookies that claim to be something other than what they are.

In La Jolla, California, shreds of tennis skirts and polo collars float through the air, descending onto premarinated flank steak and salmon tartar; the green fuzz of Dunlop balls and flesh coagulating under French manicures, wristbands, and white bandannas stained headbutt-red.

In Corpus Christi, Texas, blood is splattered on the scandal papers and checkout-lane candy bars. Someone yells "yeehaw" as the aisles tip like dominos, the last one crushes a preteen buying eye shadow and an Error Proof Test.

In Portland, Oregon, the stay-at-home dads bash the skulls of mild-mannered geriatrics with stale baguettes, and steal their basket-equipped motorized wheelchairs. They stuff the mouths of the deceased with string cheese and balls of mozzarella, re-creating childhood images of world record holders in cigarettes-smoked-at-once. Some dads high-five, others fight to the death.

In Manhattan, New York, a man watching the news wonders: Why not buy only what you can carry?

GIGANTIC

Steve Aylett

STRANGE AIRCRAFT ARRIVED with the sky that morning, moving blood-slow. And Professor Skychum was forced from the limelight at the very instant his ranted warnings became most poignant. 'They're already here!'

Skychum had once been so straight you could use him to aim down, an astrophysicist to the heart. No interest in politics—to him Marx and Rand were the same because he went by pant size. Then one afternoon he had a vision which he would not shut up about.

The millennium was the dull rage that year and nutters were in demand to punctuate the mock-emotional retrospectives filling the count-down weeks. The media considered that Skychum fit the bill—in fact they wanted him to wear one.

And the stuff he talked about. There were weaknesses in his presenta-tion, as he insisted that the whole idea occurred to him upon seeing Scrappy Doo's head for the first time. 'That dog is a mutant!' he gasped, leaning forward in such a way, and with so precise an appalled squint to the eyes, that he inadvertently pierced the constrictive walls of localised spacetime. A flare of interface static and he was seeing the whole deal like a lava-streamed landscape. He realised he was looking at the psychic holoshape of recent history, sickly and corrosive. Creeping green flows fed through darkness. These volatile glow trails hurt with incompletion.

They converged upon a cess pit, a supersick build-up of denied guilt. This dumping ground was of such toxicity it had begun to implode, turning void-black at its core.

Like a fractal, detail reflected the whole. Skychum saw at once the entire design and the subatomic data. Zooming in, he found that a poison line leading from two locations nevertheless flowed from a single event—Pearl Harbor. One source was the Japanese government, the other was Roosevelt's order to ignore all warnings of the attack. The sick stream was made up of 4,575 minced human bodies. In a fast zoom-out, this strand of history disappeared into the density of surrounding detail, which in turn resolved into a minor nerve in a spiral lost on the surface of a larger flow of glowing psychic pollution. A billion such trickles crept in every tendril of the hyperdense sludge migration, all rumbling toward this multi-dimensional landfill of dismissed abomination. And how he wished that were all.

Future attempts to reproduce his accidental etheric manoeuvre resulted in the spectacle of this old codger rocking back and forth with a look of appalled astonishment on his face, an idiosyncratic and media-friendly image which spliced easily into MTV along with those colourised clips of the goofing Einstein. And he had the kind of head propeller hats were invented for.

Skychum went wherever he'd be heard. No reputable journal would publish his paper *On Your Own Doorstep: Hyperdimensional Placement of Denied Responsibility*. One editor stated simply: 'Anyone who talks about herding behaviour's a no-no.' Another stopped him in the street and sneered a series of instructions which were inaudible above the midtown traffic, then spat a foaming full-stop at the sidewalk. Chat shows, on the other hand, would play a spooky theramin fugue when he was introduced. First time was an eye-opener. 'Fruitcake corner—this guy's got the Seventh Seal gaffa-taped to his ass and claims he'll scare up an apocalypse out of a clear blue sky. Come all the way here from New York City—Dr Theo Skychum, welcome.' Polite applause and already some sniggers. The host was on garrulous overload, headed for his end like a belly-laughing Wall of Death rider. How he'd got here was anybody's guess. 'Doctor Skychum, you assert that come the millennium, extraterrestrials will monopolise the colonic irrigation industry—how do you support that?'

Amid audience hilarity Skychum stammered that that wasn't his theory at all. The gravity of his demeanour made it all the more of a crack-up. Then the host erupted into a bongo frenzy, hammering away at two toy flying saucers. Skychum was baffled.

He found that some guests were regulars who rolled off the charmed banter with ease.

'Well see here Ray, this life story of yours appears to have been carved from a potato.'

'I know, Bill, but that's the way I like it.'

'You said you had a little exclusive for us tonight, what's that about?'

'Credit it or not, Bill, I'm an otter.'

'Thought so Ray.'

It blew by on an ill, hysterical wind and Skychum couldn't get with the programme. He'd start in with some lighthearted quip about bug-eyed men and end up bellowing 'Idiots! Discarding your own foundation! Oppression evolves like everything else!'

Even on serious shows he was systematically misunderstood. The current affairs show *The Unpalatable Truth* was expressing hour-long surprise at the existence of anti-government survivalists. This was the eighty-seventh time they'd done this and Skychum's exasperated and finally sobbing repetition of the phrase 'even a *child* knows' was interpreted as an attempt to steal everyone's faint thunder. And when his tear-rashed face filled the screen, blurring in and out as he asked 'Does the obvious have a reachable bottom?', he was condemned for making a mockery of media debate. A televangelist accused him of 'godless snoopery of the upper grief' and, when Skychum told him to simmer down, cursed him with some vague future aggravation. The whole thing was a dismal mess, smeared beyond salvation. Skychum's vision receded as though abashed.

There was no shortage of replacements. One guy insisted the millennium bug meant virtual sex dolls would give users the brush-off for being over a hundred years old and broke. Another claimed he spoke regularly to the ghost of Abe Lincoln. 'My communications with this lisping blowhead yield no wisdom atall,' he said. 'But I'm happy.' Then he sneezed like a cropduster, festooning the host with phlegm.

The commentators deemed radical were those going only so far as to question what was being celebrated. Skychum himself found he wanted to walk away. But even he had to admit the turn was a big deal, humanity having survived so long and learnt so little—there was a defiant rebelliousness about it that put a scampish grin on everyone's face. For once people were bound with a genuine sense of kick-ass accomplishment and self-congratulatory cool. Skychum began at last to wish he was among them. But just as he felt his revelation slipping away, it would seem to him that the mischievous glint in people's eyes were redshifted to the power of the Earth itself if viewed from a civilised planet. And his brush with perspective would return with the intensity of a fever dream.

Floating through psychic contamination above a billion converging vitriol channels, toward that massive rumbling cataract of discarded corruption. Drawing near, Skychum had seen that ranged around the cauldroning pit, like steel nuts around a wheel hub, were tiny glinting objects. They were hung perfectly motionless at the rim of the slow vortex. These sentinels gave him the heeby-jeebies, but he zoomed in on the detail. There against the god-high waterfall of volatility. Spaceships.

Ludicrous. There they were.

'If we dealt honestly, maturely with our horrors,' he told the purple-haired clown hosting a public access slot, 'instead of evading, rejecting and forgetting, the energy of these events would be naturally re-absorbed. But as it is we have treated it as we treat our nuclear waste—and where we have dumped it, it is not wanted. The most recent waste will be the first to return.'

'Last in, first out eh,' said the clown sombrely.

'Precisely,' said Skychum.

'Well, I wish I could help you,' stated the clown with offhand sincerity. 'But I'm just a clown.'

This is what he was reduced to. Had any of it happened? Was he mad?

A matter of days before the ball dropped in Times Square and Skychum was holed up alone, blinds drawn, bottles empty. He lay on his back, dwarfed by indifference. So much for kicking the hive. The authorities hadn't even bothered to demonize him. It was clear he'd had a florid breakdown, taking it to heart and the public. Could he leave, start a clean life? Everything was strange, undead and dented. He saw again, ghosting across his ceiling, a hundred thousand Guatemalan civilians murdered by US-backed troops. He'd confirmed this afterwards, but how could he have known it before the vision? He only watched CNN. In a strong convulsion of logic, Skychum sat up.

At that moment, the phone rang. A TV guy accusing him of dereliction of banality—laughing that he had a chance to redeem himself and trumpet some bull for the masses. Skychum agreed, too inspired to protest.

It was called *The Crackpot Arena* and it gathered the cream of the foil hat crowd to shoot the rarefied breeze in the hours leading up to the turn. This interlocking perdition of pan-moronic pundits and macabre gripers was helped and hindered by forgotten medication and the pencil-breaking perfectionism of the director. One nutter would be crowned King of the Freaks at the top hour. The criteria were extremity and zero shame at the lectern. Be ridiculed or dubbed the royal target of ridicule—Skychum marvelled at the custom joinery of this conceit. And he was probably in with a chance. In the bizarre stakes, what could be more improbable than justice?

The host's eyes were like raisins and existed to generously blockade his brainlobes. As each guest surfaced from the cracker-barrel he fielded them with a patronising show of interest.

A man holding a twig spoke of the turn. 'All I can reveal,' he said, meting out his words like a bait trail, 'is that it will be discouraging. And very, very costly.'

'For me?' asked the host, and the audience roared.

'For me,' said the man, and they were in the aisles.

'Make a habit of monkey antics,' declared another guest. 'Pleasure employs muscles of enlightenment.' Then he led in a screaming chimp, assured everyone its name was Ramone, pushed it down a slide and said 'There you go.' Skychum told him he was playing a dangerous game.

A sag-eyed old man pronounced his judgment. 'The dawn of the beard was the dawn of modern civilisation.'

'In what way.'

'In that time spent growing a beard is time wasted. Now curb this strange melancholy—let us burn our legs with these matches and shout loud.'

'I . . . I'm sorry . . . what . . .'

And the codger was dancing a strange jig on the table, cackling from a dry throat.

'One conk on the head and he'll stop dancing,' whispered someone behind the cameras.

Another suspect was the ringmaster of the Lobster Circus, who lashed at a wagon-ring of these unresponsive creatures as though at the advancing spawn of the devil. 'The time will come,' he announced, 'when these mothers will be silent.' And at that he laid the whip into a lobster positioned side-on to him, breaking it in half.

A little girl read a poem:

behind answers are hoverflies
properly modest,
but they will do anything
for me

One guy made the stone-faced assertion that belching was an actual language. Another displayed a fossilised eightball of mammoth dung and said it was 'simply biding its time'. Another stated merely that he had within his chest a 'flaming heart' and expected this to settle or negate all other concerns.

Then it was straight in with Skychum, known to the host as a heavy-hitter among those who rolled up with their lies at a moment's notice. The host's face was an emulsioned wall as he listened to the older man describe some grandiose reckoning. 'Nobody's free until everyone is, right?' was the standard he reached for in reply.

'Until *someone* is.'

STEVE AYLETT | 239

'Airless Martians still gasping in a town of smashed geodesics,' he stated, and gave no clue as to his question. After wringing the laughs out of Skychum's perplexed silence, he continued. 'These Martians—what do they have against us?'

'Not Martians—metaversal beings in a hyperspace we are using as a skeleton cupboard. Horror past its sell-by date is dismissed with the claim that a lesson is learnt, and the sell-by interval is shortening to minutes.'

'I don't understand,' said the host with a kind of defiance.

'The media believe in resolution at all costs, and this is only human.' Once again Skychum's sepulchral style was doing the trick—there was a lot of sniggering as he scowled like a chef. 'Dismissal's easier than learning.'

'So you're calling down this evangelical carnage.'

'I'm not—'

'In simple terms, for the layman'—the eyebrows of irony flipped to such a blur they vanished—'how could all these bodies be floating out in "hyper" space?'

'Every form which has contained life has its equivalent echo in the super-etheric—if forced back into the physical, these etheric echoes will assume physical shape.'

'Woh!' shouted the host, delighted, and the audience exploded with applause—this was exactly the kind of wacko bullshit they'd come to hear. 'And why should they arrive at this particular time?'

'They have become synchronised to our culture, those who took on the task—it is appropriate, poetic!'

The audience whooped, flushed with the nut's sincerity.

'The great thing about being ignored is that you can speak the truth with impunity.'

'But I call you a fraud, Dr Skychum. These verbal manipulations cause a hairline agony in the honest man. Expressions of the grave should rival the public? I don't think so. Where's the light and shade?'

Skychum leant forward, shaking with emotion. 'You slur me for one who is bitter and raging at the world. But you mustn't kick a man when he's down, and so I regard the world.' Then Ramone the chimp sprang on to his head, shrieking and flailing.

'Dr Skychum,' said the host. 'If you're right, *I'm* a monkey.'

The ringmaster of the Lobster Circus was declared the winner. The man with the flaming heart died of a coronary and the man with the dung fossil threw it into the audience and stormed off. A throne shaped like the halfshells of a giant nut was set up for the crowning ceremony. Skychum felt light, relieved. He had acquitted himself with honour. He enjoyed the jelly and ice cream feast set up for the contestants backstage. Even the chimp's food-flinging antics made him smile. He approached the winner with goodwill. 'Congratulations sir. Those lobsters of yours are a brutal threat to mankind.'

The winner looked mournfully up at him. 'I love them,' he whispered, and was swept away backwards by the make-up crew.

At the moment of the turn, Skychum left the studio building by a side entrance, hands deep in his coatpockets. Under a slouch hat which obscured his sky, he moved off down a narrow street roofed completely by the landscape of a spacecraft's undercarriage.

During the last hour, as dullards were press-ganged onto ferris wheels and true celebrants arrested in amplified streets, hundreds of multidimensional ships had hoved near, denial-allow shields up. Uncloaking, they had appeared in the upper atmosphere like new moons. Now they hove into position over every capital city in the world, impossible to evade. Fifteen miles wide, these immense overshadow machines rumbled across the sky like a coffin lid drawing slowly shut. New York was being blotted out by a floating city whose petalled geometry was only suggested by sections visible above the canyon streets. Grey hieroglyphics on the underside were actually spires, bulkheads and structures of skyscraping size. Its central eye, a mile-wide concavity deep in shadow, settled over uptown as the hovering landscape thundered to a stop and others took up position over London, Beijing, Berlin, Nairobi, Los Angeles, Kabul, Paris, Zurich, Baghdad, Moscow, Tokyo and every other conurbation with cause to be a little edgy. One nestled low over the White House like an inverted cathedral. In the early light they were silent, unchanging fixtures. Solid and subject to the sun.

The President, hair like a dirty iceberg, slapped on a middling smile and talked about caution and opportunity. Everywhere nerves were clouded around with awe and high suspension. Traffic stopped. Fanatics partied. The old man's name was remembered if not his line—a woman held a sign aloft saying I'M A SKY CHUM. Cities waited under dumb, heavy air.

Over the White House, a screeching noise erupted. The central eye of the ship was opening. Striations like silver insect wings cracked, massive steel doors grinding downward.

The same was happening throughout the world, a silver flower opening down over Parliament, Whitehall and the dead Thames; over the Reichstag building, the World Bank, the Beijing Politburo.

The DC saucer eye was open, the bellow of its mechanism echoing away. Onlookers craned to see up inside.

For the space of two heartbeats, everything stopped. Then a tiny tear dropped out of the eye, splashing on the White House roof.

And then another, falling like a light fleck of snow.

These were corpses, these two—human corpses, followed by more in a shower which grew heavier by the moment, some crashing now through the roof, some rolling to land in the drive, bouncing to hit the lawn, bursting to paint the porticoes. And then the eye began gushing.

Everywhere the eyes were gushing. With a strange, continuous, multiphonic squall, the ragged dead rained from the sky.

Sixty-eight forgotten pensioners buried in a mass grave in 1995 were dumped over the Chicago social services. Hundreds of blacks murdered in police cells hit the roof of Scotland Yard. Thousands of slaughtered East Timorese were dumped over the Assembly buildings in Jakarta. Thousands killed in the test bombings at Hiroshima and Nagasaki began raining over the Pentagon. Thousands tortured to death showered Abuja.

Thousands of Sudanese slaves were dumped over Khartoum. The border-dwelling Khmer Rouge found themselves cemented into a mile-high gut slurry of three million Cambodians. Thousands of hill tribesmen were dropped over the Bangladeshi parliament and the World Bank, the latter now swamped irretrievably under corpses of every hue.

Berlin was almost instantly clotted, its streets packed wall to wall with victims. Beijing was swamped with tank fodder and girl babies.

The Pentagon well filled quickly to overflowing, blowing the building outward as surely as a terrorist bomb. Pearl Harbor dupes fell on Tokyo and Washington in equal share. The streets of America flooded with Japanese, Greeks, Koreans, Vietnamese, Cambodians, Indonesians, Dominicans, Libyans, Timorese, Central Americans and Americans, all beclouded in a pink mist of Dresden blood.

London was a flowing sewer—then the bodies started falling. Parliament splintered like a matchstick model. In the Strand the living ran from a rolling wall of the dead. A king tide of hole-eyed German, Indian, African, Irish and English civilians surged over and against buildings which boomed flat under the pressure. Cars were batted along, flipped and submerged. The Thames flooded its banks, displaced by cadavers.

No longer preserved by denial, they started to sludge. Carpet-bombing gore spattered the suburbs, followed by human slurry tumbling down the streets like lava. Cheap human fallout from pain ignored and war extended for profit. The first wave. So far only sixty years' worth—yet, tilling like bulldozed trash, it spread across the map like red inkblots destined to touch and merge.

Skychum had taken the 8:20 Amtrak north from Grand Central—it had a policy of not stopping for bodies. Grim, he viewed the raining horizon—dust motes in a shaft of light—and presently, quietly, he spoke. 'Many happy returns.'

THE END OF THE FUTURE

Colette Phair

I HADN'T KNOWN what time it was in two years. It was hard to wait when you didn't know how long you had. In a weird way I felt like I was on vacation. But there was work to be done.

Each of us was getting ready, adding in baby bottle drips to our modest stockpile. Plenty to look at, at least. Hooks to hold up all scraps we found, flowers and wires growing through the floor, holes pasted over with anything, metal turning into deep blue. A dull pastel as you came in, worn tile on the wall, ripped plastic shower curtain stuck to the window with army tape. And through it a calm ocean, eternity of restraint. You wouldn't have suspected the world was so close to ruin.

Two figures stood before a missing wall, real working shutters on the ground and "Pour le rêve" written in the dust. Broken glass popping underfoot, walking over busted doors to get to the real one. Shovels set up for a shelter but all we had to bury ourselves in was sand. Despite some sporadic precautions, everyone knew this place wasn't going to do us much good once the end hit. So what were they doing here? Japanese on the walls and Spanish on the ceilings, communication breaking down. Jule appearing for the occasion. She only spoke English when she had to.

"You come for end of world?"

She could tell they were cool or she wouldn't be talking to them.

Green in the head and on their clothes. They looked like twins, but only because everything on them matched, like twins who were still children. They were new.

"Welcome," Jule said. Why was she trusting them just because they looked interesting? It was the worst practice. I glared at them just to even things out.

The girl came up and made some hand signs, using them to say "We - trust - you - by - God - we - seek - we - feel - you." Then with her voice she said "Got lost."

"What your names?"

"Maria and Z."

"And where you come from?"

Z was standing with her now too. Watching like he got something useful out of everybody. He tossed his green dreads and laughed. "A sad childhood, like everyone." They were in.

JULE TOOK THEM in to the torture room. It was called the torture room because Calc practiced his drums in there. She gave them some scraps and the grand tour . . . down the wide-open barriers, the brief mouse maze. Rooms unused, rooms we'd forgotten about. Some rooms devoted to nothing but trash, our own landfill we had to live with. She led them through a human-sized hole in the wall that they had to lift their legs up to get through and stopped just on the other side to point out a walled honeycomb of tiny glass cells making up a larger cabinet framed in light pink plastic like a toy box. Inside each cell was a different supply: a compass, a condom . . . And then, through a cardboard tunnel and up the stair, turn right, you'd find the lab.

The lab . . . blue science, makeshift medicine . . . converted from a storage room into pink walls—whoever'd found it before us. Tools we didn't know the use for, parts saved from hospital Dumpsters and biohazard bins. A hammer like a bird's beak, stringy gauze like a spider web, malformed metals, shape and sharpness hinting at their use. Magnetic tubing coiling upward on a ternary coat rack. A kid's chemistry set, pretend solutions, surgical texts forming tables. A safety station had been set up next door, long abandoned. We'd already taken what we could use from it, but the place was uninhabitable, even by our standards.

I stood, idle notebook in my grasp, looking out on the station. Airplane trails showed through the window, heading up and down, and below me doors that were all French and shattered like breaking out of a mold. I imagined former tenants smashing through them in their escape. How much better it must feel to run outside to safety than in.

Calc sat on the floor below, arranging a few of his personal items. Matches, medical packaging, a surgeon's knife. It took awhile watching him to realize what he was preparing was a meal. Among historical newspapers turning into toilet paper, headlines illegible through slang. Food wrapping, half-used everything, garbage or what was becoming garbage. Light was reflected through dirt in the tile. Looked like it'd be so easy to clean it, but who was going to? He washed the knife in toothpaste, then set it back down on the floor.

"Calc, what's 286 divided by 13?" I asked.

He told me and I wrote it down. "Calories," I said. "What's the square root of pi minus 9?"

"Minus 7.2275461490945. Why?"

I smiled. "Just wanted to see if you could do it."

"Fuck you."

Jule was washing in the ocean. I could see her through the safe window. When she came in she sat down before us and said "My teeth hurt."

"Might be time to invest in a toothbrush," I told her.

"I do, it's not enough," she whined.

I motioned at her with the notebook. "It's all this sugar you've been picking up. We're not going to be going to any dentist. Stop with the sugar. We can't afford sugar."

"Sugar's all we have," she said.

*

I HAD AN idea it was evening when sun no longer hit the interior walls and the others had come in. Outside it was getting cold and inside it was getting colder. We gathered in the east stairwell. Z spoke biblically. Calc came in like sleepwalking and started a fire.

"You don't really think the world's going to end . . ."

Outside people were living in houses, like normal. They were doing what they always did. In here shelves housed KFMs and KAPs, potassium iodide and medicine droppers. We were better prepared for the worst.

Jule was talking now. "It's paranoia."

Calc held fire on a stick. He said that it was happening already. That the kids would be the first to go, like miners' canaries. They'd see. Everything familiar lost to the big machine in tear gas crowds.

"Why are my eyes watering?" he asked, it seemed of Jule.

"Maybe you're crying."

Calc put the fire down. "Am I crying?" he asked no one, his voice only now beginning to tremble.

Before sleep I crept down to the cupboards, and only as I came up upon the empty shelves was I able to admit how hungry I was. I'd wanted the orange but Maria had gotten to it first. Garbage was empty and world was dark. There wouldn't be anything new till tomorrow. For some reason this felt much worse than it was, so that I sat down and just couldn't get up. Then I wished I could starve for weeks, grieved that this was not even the sort of tragedy that could be profound, that you got something out of suffering through. It was just a night.

In the morning I settle down into a nest of wires braided into dysfunction, on a floor sprinkled with shards of glass. Jule is walking around barefoot. I feel like I should tell her not to, but I know she won't listen to me. I tell her anyway. She doesn't listen. She curls up in the corner of the room and starts reading intently the nutrition information on one piece of trash after another. She's as good as asleep to us, so that Z and I are the only ones in the room.

"Puzzle's almost done," I say. "They just need to make a piece that will fit with something so twisted." Z's decoding a scrap of Styrofoam. I realize this is the first time I've spoken to him.

"Did you do that?" he says in distinct syllables, each one stressed as much as the other.

I look behind me to where he's looking, at a graffiti mural bursting open with metal flowers on a giant egg, cracks in the walls betraying its two dimensions. Why he should assume it was me, when there are others living here, and many more before us . . .

"No," I say, turning back to him. "I'm not an artist."

"Ah," he sighs. "Me neither. But it's an important job. We need more beautiful pictures."

"Pictures? The world's about to end. We have more practical matters to worry about."

"What are your worries?" he asks, looking me up and down. I notice I haven't done anything all day.

"I'm not that worried," I say.

We both think of something for me to do.

"Maybe you should be an artist."

"No." He's looking for some explanation so I give him one. "Why strive for any great goal when we all might die soon anyway?"

"We all always might."

"Oh that's really some consolation," I tell him.

He's still decoding and smiling as though the speculations of this conversation couldn't interrupt any of his normal routines of action. "This stuff was invented by the dinosaurs. Their innovations getting dusty. When the old tech is finally set off . . ." he says, then pauses so long I almost don't care what he's going to finish with. ". . . Kind of an anticlimax."

We'd been hearing the forecasts since before I'd been born. As a kid I'd hoped that when the world blew up it would be when I was doing homework, or about to give a speech in class. Now I wished for it more and more of the time.

"Goodnight," Calc said coming in, dragging a loose mattress in from the other room. He dropped it with a bounce on top of some clutter and went back into the other room for a moment.

As he left Jule got up without looking down, as if the two were hooked up remotely. She looked determined moving forward, paused to maneuver around me, and stepped barefoot on the glass. I cannot replicate the sound she made, but I can imitate it. It was something like "Aaaeeeerrgmmm-mmm," and she landed softly on the mattress Calc had moved there.

"Shit," Z and I said in unison, though his was more one of concern while mine was just shock.

But she didn't even pause, just made the sound as she kept walking, and then she was silent, trying to make us think nothing could get to her. And maybe nothing could.

I TRY TO busy myself with cooking, but I can't get the fire started. The next day I take up interior decoration, but when I ask no one can tell anything's been changed. There must be a use for me here. Can't I do anything?

"Need help?" I'm asking Z while he works trying to build some machine I don't know the use for. I can tell this is going to turn out to be the kind of help that makes everything take much longer and the finished product not as good.

Instead I bring myself outside. I do the dishes in the sea and afterward go for a walk. At first just scaling the long government fence that surrounds our home. White picket in better times. Then once it ends I keep following where I think it would have gone. A straight line through other buildings—other objects that used to work, everything broken and impotent now. Nothing doing any good.

I come back in through the first room and Maria is in there. All she does is silently prepare, stacking crates of army paste and sewing protective costumes from material she goes out and gets during the days. I'm nonsensically comforted by the sound of the thread running through the crinkly fabric, to sleep almost.

I haven't seen Jule in a while. Actually a week, I think. The building isn't very big—I don't know where she could be.

Her voice was in my head, so it's what I expected to hear when Z came in and said, "Get the blood up from the reservoir."

I laughed at the contrast. "You alright there?" he asked.

"Yeah, but it doesn't sound like she is . . ."

He had every right to be concerned. I'd been dreaming up, computer-generating ways I could finish myself before the end struck. But at that moment my preoccupation turned stale. I'd figured it out. It didn't make sense why I should have to feel good. It didn't matter to the world, didn't change reality.

And now I did hear Jule, crying out from the other room, panicked voices consoling her. She was telling us something about pain. She said she didn't trust them. That there was nothing they could do for her. Then for the first time since I'd been here, we were making a trip to the hospital.

WAITING ROOM UPON waiting room . . . None of us knew where to go. I felt like I was killing her with my stupidity. We carried her, each of us taking a side. I had my arm around her back with Calc so I could feel how skinny she really was.

When we found it we put her on the table. She crumpled the paper beneath her like fresh grass. I imagined us all somewhere far away. When the doctor came in, she reached down and revealed her leg.

The doctor didn't have any reaction, but the rest of us hadn't seen anything like this yet.

"Oh, Jule," I murmured.

But then I wished I hadn't said anything cause she looked ashamed, like what had happened to her was her fault. I remembered the glass.

Doctor inspected her silently for a moment, keeping in her opinion which we all desperately wanted to know. She held her leg like a golf club. Then she said, "I'm afraid we're very late with this one."

"I don't understand," Maria said, looking at Jule.

"Just say what you mean," she said.

"We're going to have to remove your leg."

Jule made a new expression that seemed to change the whole shape of her face, like just by the doctor's words she had become a different kind of person.

Maria's face changed too, but slower. "No way," she said once she got it. "No way, we get you out of here."

"You're in the best hands with us," the doctor scolded. She got louder as we left the room. "This is serious!" her voice echoed down the hall.

We were bringing Jule back across thin carpet, maneuvering through dying crowds, shoving our way into the elevator . . . and before we even made it down, I had a thought that felt forbidden. Why should she care about her leg when we're all going to die soon anyway?

WE'RE ALL UP there, in the lab. Jule stretched out on a thin shelf, Calc and Maria cleaning her, among horseshoes and broken mirrors, a comforting bucket of stolen medicines. Everything looked so dirty, Maria's green dreads reminded me of mold just then, even though she looked pretty. Jule lay like an ancient statue, or a model for one, moving as little as possible. The others brought up the leg and a syringe. Then they said to her, "You do it." She injected herself with something green, then ate some pills that looked metal. Then they all sat around and told her how great they thought she was.

"Jule, you a beautiful woman. You deserve great life and you will once get."

"The goddess of the apocalypse . . ."

"We love you, Julia," Calc said easily.

They looked at me.

"Yeah, what they said," I told her from the doorway. The smile I gave her felt physically painful, and her expression didn't change.

I left as soon as they started burning leaves and dancing around her.

Heading down the crooked hall I could see it was almost dark out. In a room I claimed as mine I sobbed alone, watching the sunny day end and not being able to do a thing about it.

FOR A LONG time she stayed anchored to the lab, gazing at the glass-covered sea and crying out when she wanted something. And sometimes she just cried, animal wails we could not comprehend. But mostly she was silent and concentrative, as if working on something inside herself that no one else could reach. She got instructions on how to breathe. We brought her food and things to do. Two more trips to the medical warehouse went by. And after we let her leave her place on the shelf she still stayed, huddled like a worm under the mildew ceiling, till the others brought her out and only then did she realize that she could walk.

No one was in agreement on whether the leaves had anything to do with it, but before the season's change her malady had begun to evaporate. The mark divided into spots that resembled old bruises. We assailed her with science and religion, so like reverse gunfire her wounds cleared up; the colors on her leg went white. For the first time in my life I didn't hate technology. We could all see what the doctor said, that she was going to be alright. She would die intact.

PAST A YELLOW sunrise up from the coast, almost too far away to see a black castle-factory, from miniature abandoned cities, our own ghost town became visible again. The day was silent so far, like allowing for whatever needed to happen.

I was taking care of Jule today, not that she needed taking care of, but she didn't need not to be so I brought her in some pills and oranges, sat with her through far-away test blasts, each of us barely making out the benign puffs that beat like an awkward drum as I cleaned her and wrapped her back up.

"Thanks," she said in a way that made it seem true even though it wasn't an opinion. Then she asked, "What time is it?"

I smiled and said I didn't know.

Only when I left to gather more supplies did it occur to me how far away the future was. No matter the time, it just didn't exist. For me and Jule, we prepared for it, working constantly to prevent another infection with whatever moments we had left. And I knew that I'd been wrong. That it did matter what happened to her, just today, or any day. Everything mattered as long as it was still happening. I gathered the iodine and gauze among the mess, and an empty Easter basket and an old valentine just for the hell of it. I didn't want to let go of anything.

THAT NIGHT I'M on a mattress in the torture room, but I can't sleep so I get up, shuffling through complete darkness into the next few rooms. I stop and stand in each of them, smiling at the cool breeze that finds its way in through poorly covered windows. I feel like I'm somewhere far away, and yet this is my home. This is where I should be. I come to the last room on the floor and stop before I go inside.

Jule is inside masturbating. I hear her facing the other way, jerking and whimpering, crying almost, like she has more on her mind than her body again. She sounds so lonely I wonder if I should go in there, if she would want me to. I think about when I would have wanted someone to, just about anyone at the time so maybe she could accept me, but then there were also times when I just needed to be alone, to where I wouldn't even have acknowledged anyone's presence if they tried. I listen some more and decide that she doesn't want me to, but that I want to so much that I'm going to go in there anyway, despite what she wants. That I don't care what she wants, and how I could convince her that I'm what she wants and how happy we'd be together, until I realize she's not alone after all. There is Calc now too, making noise, probably impregnating someone I should be loving like a sister if at all. And it's better this way, I know. There's nothing I want enough to take it from someone else. Not because it's wrong, because I really don't care enough, about anything. And I think it's fitting then, that I'll die.

THAT MORNING I didn't even have a chance to wake up. I was already sleep-running through the rooms, looking for the others. I must have fallen asleep about five minutes ago.

When I get downstairs Z is there, looking straight up. When he sees me he runs over. He grabs me by the shoulders and shouts.

"They're exploding bombs in the sky!"

I run outside to look up and see but I've already heard the blasts right above us, so that I'm having trouble hearing anything else. It doesn't sound like the recordings, or my nightmares. People everywhere must be surprised. But we saw it coming from miles away.

I'M WORRIED ABOUT Jule, can't find her now. I'm standing on the gray shoreline, bent under an orange sky. Calc is crouched at the very edge, facing the horizon. I want to call out to him but it's too loud. I want to ask him what he's going to do. Instead I watch him stand Olympic with his arms outstretched, hesitating one moment. In that moment he looks back at me, smiling as he dives forward into still water and starts to swim.

CROSSING INTO CAMBODIA
Michael Moorcock

1

I APPROACHED AND Savitsky, Commander of the Sixth Division, got up. As usual I was impressed by his gigantic, perfect body. Yet he seemed unconscious either of his power or of his elegance. Although not obliged to do so, I almost saluted him. He stretched an arm towards me. I put the papers into his gloved hand. 'These were the last messages we received,' I said. The loose sleeve of his Cossack cherkesska slipped back to reveal a battle-strengthened forearm, brown and glowing. I compared his skin to my own. For all that I had ridden with the Sixth for five months, I was still pale; still possessed, I thought, of an intellectual's hands. Evening light fell through the jungle foliage and a few parrots shrieked their last goodnight. Mosquitoes were gathering in the shadows, whirling in tight-woven patterns, like a frightened mob. The jungle smelled of rot. Yakovlev, somewhere, began to play a sad accordion tune.

The Vietnamese spy we had caught spoke calmly from the other side of Savitsky's camp table. 'I think I should like to be away from here before nightfall. Will you keep your word, sir, if I tell you what I know?'

Savitsky looked back and I saw the prisoner for the first time (though his presence was of course well known to the camp). His wrists and ankles were pinned to the ground with bayonets but he was otherwise unhurt.

Savitsky drew in his breath and continued to study the documents I had brought him. Our radio was now useless. 'He seems to be confirming what these say.' He tapped the second sheet. 'An attack tonight.'

The temple on the other side of the clearing came to life within. Pale light rippled on greenish, half-ruined stonework. Some of our men must have lit a fire there. I heard noises of delight and some complaints from the women who had been with the spy. One began to shout in that peculiar, irritating high-pitched half-wail they all use when they are trying to appeal to us. For a moment Savitsky and I had a bond in our disgust. I felt flattered. Savitsky made an impatient gesture as if of embarrassment. He turned his handsome face and looked gravely down at the peasant. 'Does it matter to you? You've lost a great deal of blood.'

'I do not think I am dying.'

Savitsky nodded. He was economical in everything, even his cruelties. He had been prepared to tear the man apart with horses, but he knew that he would tire two already over-worked beasts. He picked up his cap from the camp table and put it thoughtfully on his head. From the deserted huts came the smell of our horses as the wind reversed its direction. I drew my borrowed burka about me. I was the only one in our unit to bother to wear it, for I felt the cold as soon as the sun was down.

'Will you show me on the map where they intend to ambush us?'

'Yes,' said the peasant. 'Then you can send a man to spy on their camp. He will confirm what I say.'

I stood to one side while these two professionals conducted their business. Savitsky strode over to the spy and very quickly, like a man plucking a hen, drew the bayonets out and threw them on the ground. With some gentleness, he helped the peasant to his feet and sat him down in the leather campaign chair he had carried with him on our long ride from Danang, where we had disembarked off the troop-ship which had brought us from Vladivostock.

'I'll get some rags to stop him bleeding,' I said.

'Good idea,' confirmed Savitsky. 'We don't want the stuff all over the maps. You'd better be in on this, anyway.'

As the liaison officer, it was my duty to know what was happening. That is why I am able to tell this story. My whole inclination was to return to my billet where two miserable ancients cowered and sang at me whenever I entered or left but where at least I had a small barrier between me and the casual day-to-day terrors of the campaign. But, illiterate and obtuse though these horsemen were, they had accurate instincts and could tell immediately if I betrayed any sign of fear. Perhaps, I thought, it is because they are all so used to disguising their own fears. Yet bravery was a habit with them and I yearned to catch it. I had ridden with them in more than a dozen encounters, helping to drive the Cambodians back into their own country. Each time I had seen men and horses blown to pieces, torn apart, burned alive. I had come to exist on the smell of blood and gun-powder as if it were a substitute for air and food—I identified it with the smell of Life itself—yet I had still failed to achieve that strangely passive sense of inner calm my comrades all, to a greater or lesser degree, displayed. Only in action did they seem possessed in any way by the outer world, although they still worked with efficient ferocity, killing as quickly as possible with lance, sabre or carbine and, with ghastly humanity, never leaving a wounded man of their own or the enemy's without his throat cut or a bullet in his brain. I was thankful that these, my traditional foes, were now allies for I could not have resisted them had they turned against me.

I bound the peasant's slender wrists and ankles. He was like a child. He said: 'I knew there were no arteries cut.' I nodded at him. 'You're the political officer, aren't you?' He spoke almost sympathetically.

'Liaison,' I said.

He was satisfied by my reply, as if I had confirmed his opinion. He added: 'I suppose it's the leather coat. Almost a uniform.'

I smiled. 'A sign of class difference, you think?'

His eyes were suddenly drowned with pain and he staggered, but recovered to finish what he had evidently planned to say: 'You Russians are natural bourgeoisie. It's not your fault. It's your turn.'

Savitsky was too tired to respond with anything more than a small smile. I felt that he agreed with the peasant and that these two excluded me, felt superior to me. I knew anger, then. Tightening the last rag on his left wrist, I made the spy wince. Satisfied that my honour was avenged I cast an eye over the map. 'Here we are,' I said. We were on the very edge of Cambodia. A small river, easily forded, formed the border. We had heard it just before we had entered this village. Scouts confirmed that it lay no more than half a verst to the west. The stream on the far side of the village, behind the temple, was a tributary.

'You give your word you won't kill me,' said the Vietnamese.

'Yes,' said Savitsky. He was beyond joking. We all were. It had been ages since any of us had been anything but direct with one another, save for the conventional jests which were merely part of the general noise of the squadron, like the jangling of harness. And he was beyond lying, except where it was absolutely necessary. His threats were as unqualified as his promises.

'They are here.' The spy indicated a town. He began to shiver. He was wearing only torn shorts. 'And some of them are here, because they think you might use the bridge rather than the ford.'

'And the attacking force for tonight?'

'Based here.' A point on our side of the river.

Savitsky shouted. 'Pavlichenko.'

From the Division Commander's own tent, young Pavlichenko, capless, with ruffled fair hair and a look of restrained disappointment, emerged. 'Comrade?'

'Get a horse and ride with this man for half-an-hour the way we came today. Ride as fast as you can, then leave him and return to camp.'

Pavlichenko ran towards the huts where the horses were stabled. Savitsky had believed the spy and was not bothering to check his information. 'We can't attack them,' he murmured. 'We'll have to wait until they come to us. It's better.' The flap of Savitsky's tent was now open. I glanced through and to my surprise saw a Eurasian girl of about fourteen. She had her feet in a bucket of water. She smiled at me. I looked away.

Savitsky said: 'He's washing her for me. Pavlichenko's an expert.'

'My wife and daughters?' said the spy.

'They'll have to remain now. What can I do?' Savitsky shrugged in the direction of the temple. 'You should have spoken earlier.'

The Vietnamese accepted this and, when Pavlichenko returned with the horse, leading it and running as if he wished to get the job over with in the fastest possible time, he allowed the young Cossack to lift him onto the saddle.

'Take your rifle,' Savitsky told Pavlichenko. 'We're expecting an attack.'

Pavlichenko dashed for his own tent, the small one close to Savitsky's. The horse, as thoroughly trained as the men who rode him, stood awkwardly but quietly beneath his nervous load. The spy clutched the saddle pommel, the mane, his bare feet angled towards the mount's neck. He stared ahead of him into the night. His wife and daughter had stopped their appalling wailing but I thought I could hear the occasional feminine grunt from the temple. The flames had become more animated. His other daughter, her feet still in the bucket, held her arms tightly under her chest and her curious eyes looked without rancour at her father, then at the Division Commander, then, finally, at me. Savitsky spoke. 'You're the intellectual. She doesn't know Russian. Tell her that her father will be safe. She can join him tomorrow.'

'My Vietnamese might not be up to that.'

'Use English or French, then.' He began to tidy his maps, calling over Kreshenko, who was in charge of the guard.

I entered the tent and was shocked by her little smile. She had a peculiar smell to her—like old tea and cooked rice. I knew my Vietnamese was too limited so I asked her if she spoke French. She was of the wrong generation. 'Amerikanski,' she told me. I relayed Savitsky's message. She said: 'So I am the price of the old bastard's freedom.'

'Not at all.' I reassured her. 'He told us what we wanted. It was just bad luck for you that he used you three for cover.'

She laughed. 'Nuts! It was me got him to do it. With my sister. Tao's boyfriend works for the Cambodians.' She added: 'They seemed to be winning at the time.'

Savitsky entered the tent and zipped it up from the bottom. He used a single, graceful movement. For all that he was bone-weary, he moved with the unconscious fluidity of an acrobat. He lit one of his foul-smelling papyrosi and sat heavily on the camp bed beside the girl.

'She speaks English,' I said. 'She's a half-caste. Look.'

He loosened his collar. 'Could you ask her if she's clean, comrade?'

'I doubt it,' I said. I repeated what she had told me.

He nodded. 'Well, ask her if she'll be a good girl and use her mouth. I just want to get on with it. I expect she does, too.'

I relayed the D.C.'s message.

'I'll bite his cock off if I get the chance,' said the girl.

Outside in the night the horse began to move away. I explained what she had said.

'I wonder, comrade,' Savitsky said, 'if you would oblige me by holding the lady's head.' He began to undo the belt of his trousers, pulling up his elaborately embroidered shirt.

The girl's feet became noisy in the water and the bucket overturned. In my leather jacket, my burka, with my automatic pistol at her right ear, I restrained the girl until Savitsky had finished with her. He began to take off his boots. 'Would you care for her, yourself?'

I shook my head and escorted the girl from the tent. She was walking in that familiar stiff way women have after they have been raped. I asked her if she was hungry. She agreed that she was. I took her to my billet. The old couple found some more rice and I watched her eat it.

Later that night she moved towards me from where she had been lying more or less at my feet. I thought I was being attacked and shot her in the stomach. Knowing what my comrades would think of me if I tried to keep her alive (it would be a matter of hours) I shot her in the head to put her out of her misery. As luck would have it, these shots woke the camp and when the Khmer soldiers attacked a few moments later we were ready for them and killed a great many before the rest ran back into the jungle. Most of these soldiers were younger than the girl.

In the morning, to save any embarrassment, the remaining women were chased out of the camp in the direction taken by the patriarch. The old couple had disappeared and I assumed that they would not return or, if they did, that they would bury the girl, so I left her where I had shot her. A silver ring she wore would compensate them for their trouble. There was very little food remaining in the village, but what there was we ate for our breakfast or packed into our saddle-bags. Then, mounting up, we followed the almost preternaturally handsome Savitsky back into the jungle, heading for the river.

2

WHEN OUR SCOUT did not return after we had heard a long burst of machine-gun fire, we guessed that he had found at least part of the enemy ambush and that the spy had not lied to us, so we decided to cross the river at a less convenient spot where, with luck, no enemy would be waiting.

The river was swift but had none of the force of Russian rivers and Pavlichenko was sent across with a rope which he tied to a tree-trunk. Then we entered the water and began to swim our horses across. Those who had lost the canvas covers for their carbines kept them high in the air, holding the rope with one hand and guiding their horses with legs and with reins which they gripped in their teeth. I was more or less in the middle, with half the division behind me and half beginning to assemble on dry land on the other side, when Cambodian aircraft sighted us and began an attack dive. The aircraft were in poor repair, borrowed from half-a-dozen other countries, and their guns, aiming equipment and, I suspect, their pilots, were in worse condition, but they killed seven of our men as we let go of the ropes, slipped out of our saddles, and swam beside our horses, making for the far bank, while those still on dry land behind us went to cover where they could. A couple of machine-gun carts were turned on the attacking planes, but these were of little use. The peculiar assortment of weapons used against us—tracers, two rockets, a few napalm canisters which struck the water and sank (only one opened and burned but the mixture was quickly carried off by the current) and then they were flying back to base somewhere in Cambodia's interior—indicated that they had very little conventional armament left. This was true of most of the participants at this stage, which is why our cavalry had proved so effective. But they had bought some time for their ground-troops who were now coming in.

In virtual silence, any shouts drowned by the rushing of the river, we crossed to the enemy bank and set up a defensive position, using the machine-gun carts which were last to come across on ropes. The Cambodians hit us from two sides—moving in from their original ambush positions—but we were able to return their fire effectively, even using the anti-tank weapons and the mortar which, hitherto, we had tended to consider useless weight. They used arrows, blow-darts, automatic rifles, pistols and a flame-thrower which only worked for a few seconds and did us no harm. The Cossacks were not happy with this sort of warfare and as soon as there was a lull we had mounted up, packed the gear in the carts, and with sabres drawn were howling into the Khmer Stalinists (as we had been instructed to term them). Leaving them scattered and useless, we found a bit of concrete road along which we could gallop for a while. We slowed to a trot and then to a walk. The pavement was potholed and only slightly less dangerous than the jungle floor. The jungle was behind us now and seemed to have been a screen hiding the devastation ahead. The landscape was virtually flat, as if it had been bombed clean of contours, with a few broken buildings, the occasional blackened tree, and ash drifted across the road, coming sometimes up to our horses' knees. The ash was stirred by a light wind. We had witnessed scenes like it before, but never on such a scale. The almost colourless nature of the landscape was emphasised by the unrelieved brilliance of the blue sky overhead. The sun had become very hot.

Once we saw two tanks on the horizon, but they did not challenge us. We continued until early afternoon when we came to the remains of some sort of modern power installation and we made camp in the shelter of its walls. The ash got into our food and we drank more of our water than was sensible. We were all covered in the grey stuff by this time.

'We're like corpses,' said Savitsky. He resembled an heroic statue of the sort which used to be in almost every public square in the Soviet Union. 'Where are we going to find anything to eat in this?

'It's like the end of the world,' I said.

'Have you tried the radio again?'

I shook my head. 'It isn't worth it. Napalm eats through wiring faster than it eats through you.'

He accepted this and with a naked finger began to clean off the inner rims of the goggles he (like most of us) wore as protection against sun, rain and dust. 'I could do with some orders,' he said.

'We were instructed to move into the enemy's territory. That's what we're doing.'

'Where, we were told, we would link up with American and Australian mounted units. Those fools can't ride. I don't know why they ever thought of putting them on horses. Cowboys!'

I saw no point in repeating an already stale argument. It was true, however, that the Western cavalry divisions found it hard to match our efficient savagery. I had been amused, too, when they had married us briefly with a couple of Mongolian squadrons. The Mongols had not ridden to war in decades and had become something of a laughing stock with their ancient enemies, the Cossacks. Savitsky believed that we were the last great horsemen. Actually, he did not include me; for I was a very poor rider and not a Cossack, anyway. He thought it was our destiny to survive the War and begin a new and braver civilisation: 'Free from the influence of women and Jews'. He recalled the great days of the Zaporozhian Sech, from which women had been forbidden. Even amongst the Sixth he was regarded as something of a conservative. He continued to be admired more than his opinions.

When the men had watered our horses and replaced the water bags in the cart, Savitsky and I spread the map on a piece of concrete and found our position with the help of the compass and sextant (there were no signs or landmarks). 'I wonder what has happened to Angkor,' I said. It was where we were supposed to meet other units, including the Canadians to whom, in the months to come, I was to be attached (I was to discover later that they had been in our rear all along).

'You think it's like this?' Savitsky gestured. His noble eyes began to frown. 'I mean, comrade, would you say it was worth our while making for Angkor now?'

'We have our orders,' I said. 'We've no choice. We're expected.'

Savitsky blew dust from his mouth and scratched his head. 'There's about half our division left. We could do with reinforcements. Mind you, I'm glad we can see a bit of sky at last.' We had all felt claustrophobic in the jungle.

'What is it, anyway, this Angkor? Their capital?' he asked me.

'Their Stalingrad, maybe.'

Savitsky understood. 'Oh, it has an importance to their morale. It's not strategic?'

'I haven't been told about its strategic value.'

Savitsky, as usual, withdrew into his diplomatic silence, indicating that he did not believe me and thought that I had been instructed to secrecy. 'We'd best push on,' he said. 'We've a long way to go, eh?'

After we had mounted up, Savitsky and I rode side by side for a while, along the remains of the concrete road. We were some way ahead of the long column, with its riders, its baggage-wagons, and its Makhno-style machine-gun carts. We were sitting targets for any planes and, because there was no cover, Savitsky and his men casually ignored the danger. I had learned not to show my nervousness but I was not at that moment sure how well hidden it was.

'We are the only vital force in Cambodia,' said the Division Commander with a beatific smile. 'Everything else is dead. How these yellow bastards must hate one another.' He was impressed, perhaps admiring.

'Who's to say?' I ventured. 'We don't know who else has been fighting. There isn't a nation now that's not in the War.'

'And not one that's not on its last legs. Even Switzerland.' Savitsky gave a superior snort. 'But what an inheritance for us!'

I became convinced that, quietly, he was going insane.

3

WE CAME ACROSS an armoured car in a hollow, just off the road. One of our scouts had heard the crew's moans. As Savitsky and I rode up, the scout was covering the uniformed Khmers with his carbine, but they were too far gone to offer us any harm.

264 | CROSSING INTO CAMBODIA

'What's wrong with 'em?' Savitsky asked the scout.

The scout did not know. 'Disease,' he said. 'Or starvation. They're not wounded.'

We got off our horses and slid down into the crater. The car was undamaged. It appeared to have rolled gently into the dust and become stuck. I slipped into the driving seat and tried to start the engine, but it was dead. Savitsky had kicked one of the wriggling Khmers in the genitals but the man did not seem to notice the pain much, though he clutched himself, almost as if he entered into the spirit of a ritual. Savitsky was saying 'Soldiers. Soldiers', over and over again. It was one of the few Vietnamese words he knew. He pointed in different directions, looking with disgust on the worn-out men. 'You'd better question them,' he said to me.

They understood my English, but refused to speak it. I tried them in French. 'What happened to your machine?'

The man Savitsky had kicked continued to lie on his face, his arms stretched along the ashy ground towards us. I felt he wanted to touch us: to steal our vitality. I felt sick as I put the heel of my boot on his hand. One of his comrades said: 'There's no secret to it. We ran out of essence.' He pointed to the armoured car. 'We ran out of essence.'

'You're a long way from your base.'

'Our base is gone. There's no essence anywhere.'

I believed him and told Savitsky who was only too ready to accept this simple explanation.

As usual, I was expected to dispatch the prisoners. I reached for my holster, but Savitsky, with rare sympathy, stayed my movement. 'Go and see what's in that can,' he said, pointing. As I waded towards the punctured metal, three shots came from the Division Commander's revolver. I wondered at his mercy. Continuing with this small farce, I looked at the can, held it up, shook it, and threw it back into the dust. 'Empty,' I said.

Savitsky was climbing the crater towards his horse. As I scrambled behind him he said: 'It's the Devil's world. Do you think we should give ourselves up to Him?'

I was astonished by this unusual cynicism.

He got into his saddle. Unconsciously, he assumed the pose, often seen in films and pictures, of the noble revolutionary horseman—his head lifted, his palm shielding his eyes as he peered towards the West.

'We seem to have wound up killing Tatars again,' he said with a smile as I got clumsily onto my horse. 'Do you believe in all this history, comrade?'

'I've always considered the theory of precedent absolutely infantile,' I said.

'What's that?'

I began to explain, but he was already spurring forward, shouting to his men.

4

ON THE THIRD day we had passed through the ash-desert and our horses could at last crop at some grass on the crest of a line of low hills which looked down on glinting, misty paddy-fields. Savitsky, his field-glasses to his eyes, was relieved. 'A village,' he said. 'Thank god. We'll be able to get some provisions.'

'And some exercise,' said Pavlichenko behind him. The boy laughed, pushing his cap back on his head and wiping grimey sweat from his brow. 'Shall I go down there, comrade?'

Savitsky agreed, telling Pavlichenko to take two others with him. We watched the Cossacks ride down the hill and begin cautiously to wade their horses through the young rice. The sky possessed a greenish tinge here, as if it reflected the fields. It looked like the Black Sea lagoons at midsummer. A smell of foliage, almost shocking in its unfamiliarity, floated up to us. Savitsky was intent on watching the movements of his men, who had unslung their carbines and dismounted as they reached the village. With reins looped on their arms they moved slowly in, firing a few experimental rounds at the huts. One of them took a dummy grenade from his saddle-bag and threw it into a nearby doorway. Peasants, already starving to the point of death it seemed, ran out. The young Cossacks ignored them, looking for soldiers. When they were satisfied that the village was clear of traps, they waved us in. The peasants began to gather together at the centre of the village. Evidently they were used to this sort of operation.

While our men made their thorough search I was again called upon to perform my duty and question the inhabitants. These, it emerged, were almost all intellectuals, part of an old Khmer Rouge re-education programme (virtually a sentence of death by forced labour). It was easier to speak to them but harder to understand their complicated answers. In the end I gave up and, made impatient by the whining appeals of the wretches, ignored them. They knew nothing of use to us. Our men were disappointed in their expectations. There were only old people in the village. In the end they took the least aged of the women off and had them in what had once been some sort of administration hut. I wondered at their energy. It occurred to me that this was something they expected of one another and that they would lose face if they did not perform the necessary actions. Eventually, when we had eaten what we could find, I returned to questioning two of the old men. They were at least antagonistic to the Cambodian troops and were glad to tell us anything they could. However, it seemed there had been no large movements in the area. The occasional plane or helicopter had gone over a few days earlier. These were probably part of the flight which had attacked us at the river. I asked if they had any news of Angkor, but there was no radio here and they expected us to know more than they did. I pointed towards the purple hills on the other side of the valley. 'What's over there?'

They told me that as far as they knew it was another valley, similar to this but larger. The hills looked steeper and were wooded. It would be a difficult climb for us unless there was a road. I got out the map. There was a road indicated. I pointed to it. One of the old men nodded. Yes, he thought that road was still there, for it led, eventually, to this village. He showed me where the path was. It was rutted where, some time earlier, heavy vehicles had been driven along it. It disappeared into dark, green, twittering jungle. All the jungle meant to me now was mosquitoes and a certain amount of cover from attacking planes.

Careless of leeches and insects, the best part of the division was taking the chance of a bath in the stream which fed the paddy-fields. I could not bring myself to strip in the company of these healthy men. I decided to remain dirty until I had the chance of some sort of privacy.

'I want the men to rest,' said Savitsky. 'Have you any objection to our camping here for the rest of today and tonight?'

'It's a good idea,' I said. I sought out a hut, evicted the occupants, and went almost immediately to sleep.

In the morning I was awakened by a trooper who brought me a metal mug full of the most delicately scented tea. I was astonished and accepted it with some amusement. 'There's loads of it here,' he said. 'It's all they've got!'

I sipped the tea. I was still in my uniform, with the burka on the ground beneath me and my leather jacket folded for a pillow. The hut was completely bare. I was used to noticing a few personal possessions and began to wonder if they had hidden their stuff when they had seen us coming. Then I remembered that they were from the towns and had been brought here forcibly. Perhaps now, I thought, the war would pass them by and they would know peace, even happiness, for a bit. I was scratching my ear and stretching when Savitsky came in, looking grim. 'We've found a damned burial ground,' he said. 'Hundreds of bodies in a pit. I think they must be the original inhabitants. And one or two soldiers—at least, they were in uniform.'

'You want me to ask what they are?'

'No! I just want to get away. God knows what they've been doing to one another. They're a filthy race. All grovelling and secret killing. They've no guts.'

'No soldiers, either,' I said. 'Not really. They've been preyed on by bandits for centuries. Bandits are pretty nearly the only sort of soldiers they've ever known. So the ones who want to be soldiers emulate them. Those who don't want to be soldiers treat the ones who do as they've always treated bandits. They are conciliatory until they get a chance to turn the tables.'

He was impressed by this. He rubbed at a freshly-shaven chin. He looked years younger, though he still had the monumental appearance of a god. 'Thieves, you mean. They have the mentality of thieves, their soldiers?'

'Aren't the Cossacks thieves?'

'That's foraging.' He was not angry. Very little I said could ever anger him because he had no respect for my opinions. I was the necessary political officer, his only link with the higher, distant authority of the Kremlin, but he did not have to respect my ideas any more than he respected those which came to him from Moscow. What he respected there was the power and the fact that in some way Russia was mystically represented in our leaders. 'We leave in ten minutes,' he said.

I noticed that Pavlichenko had polished his boots for him.

BY THAT AFTERNOON, after we had crossed the entire valley on an excellent dirt road through the jungle and had reached the top of the next range of hills, I had a pain in my stomach. Savitsky noticed me holding my hands against my groin and said laconically, 'I wish the doctor hadn't been killed. Do you think it's typhus?' Naturally, it was what I had suspected.

'I think it's just the tea and the rice and the other stuff. Maybe mixing with all the dust we've swallowed.' He looked paler than usual. 'I've got it, too. So have half the others. Oh, shit!'

It was hard to tell, in that jungle at that time of day, if you had a fever. I decided to put the problem out of my mind as much as possible until sunset when it would become cooler.

The road began to show signs of damage and by the time we were over the hill and looking down on the other side we were confronting scenery if anything more desolate than that which we had passed through on the previous three days. It was a grey desert, scarred by the broken road and bomb-craters. Beyond this and coming towards us was a wall of dark dust; unmistakably an army on the move. Savitsky automatically relaxed in his saddle and turned back to see our men moving slowly up the wooded hill. 'I think they must be heading this way.' Savitsky cocked his head to one side. 'What's that?'

It was a distant shriek. Then a whole squadron of planes was coming in low. We could see their crudely-painted Khmer Rouge markings, their battered fuselages. The men began to scatter off the road, but the planes ignored us. They went zooming by, seeming to be fleeing rather than attacking. I looked at the sky, but nothing followed them.

We took our field-glasses from their cases and adjusted them. In the dust I saw a mass of barefoot infantry bearing rifles with fixed bayonets.

There were also trucks, a few tanks, some private cars, bicycles, motor-bikes, ox-carts, hand-carts, civilians with bundles. It was an orgy of defeated soldiers and refugees.

'I think we've missed the action.' Savitsky was furious. 'We were beaten to it, eh? And by Australians, probably!'

My impulse to shrug was checked. 'Damn!' I said a little weakly.

This caused Savitsky to laugh at me. 'You're relieved. Admit it!'

I knew that I dare not share his laughter, lest it become hysterical and turn to tears, so I missed a moment of possible comradeship. 'What shall we do?' I asked. 'Go round them?'

'It would be easy enough to go through them. Finish them off. It would stop them destroying this valley, at least.' He did not, by his tone, much care.

The men were assembling behind us. Savitsky informed them of the nature of the rabble ahead of us. He put his field-glasses to his eyes again and said to me: 'Infantry, too. Quite a lot. Coming on faster.'

I looked. The barefoot soldiers were apparently pushing their way through the refugees to get ahead of them.

'Maybe the planes radioed back,' said Savitsky. 'Well, it's something to fight.'

'I think we should go round,' I said. 'We should save our strength. We don't know what's waiting for us at Angkor.'

'It's miles away yet.'

'Our instructions were to avoid any conflict we could,' I reminded him.

He sighed. 'This is Satan's own country.' He was about to give the order which would comply with my suggestion when, from the direction of Angkor Wat, the sky burst into white fire. The horses reared and whin-neyed. Some of our men yelled and flung their arms over their eyes. We were all temporarily blinded. Then the dust below seemed to grow denser and denser. We watched in fascination as the dark wall became taller, rush-ing upon us and howling like a million dying voices. We were struck by the ash and forced onto our knees, then onto our bellies, yanking our frightened horses down with us as best we could. The stuff stung my face and hands and even those parts of my body protected by heavy clothing. Larger pieces of stone rattled against my goggles.

When the wind had passed and we began to stand erect, the sky was still very bright. I was astonished that my field glasses were intact. I put them up to my burning eyes and peered through swirling ash at the Cambodians. The army was running along the road towards us, as terrified animals flee a forest-fire. I knew now what the planes had been escaping. Our Cossacks were in some confusion, but were already regrouping, shouting amongst themselves. A number of horses were still shying and whickering but by and large we were all calm again.

'Well, comrade,' said Savitsky with a sort of mad satisfaction, 'what do we do now? Wasn't that Angkor Wat, where we're supposed to meet our allies?'

I was silent. The mushroom cloud on the horizon was growing. It had the hazy outlines of a gigantic, spreading cedar tree, as if all at once that wasteland of ash had become promiscuously fertile. An aura of bloody red seemed to surround it, like a silhouette in the sunset. The strong, artificial wind was still blowing in our direction. I wiped dust from my goggles and lowered them back over my eyes. Savitsky gave the order for our men to mount. 'Those bastards down there are in our way,' he said. 'We're going to charge them.'

'What?' I could not believe him.

'When in doubt,' he told me, 'attack.'

'You're not scared of the enemy,' I said, 'but there's the radiation.'

'I don't know anything about radiation.' He turned in his saddle to watch his men. When they were ready he drew his sabre. They imitated him. I had no sabre to draw.

I was horrified. I pulled my horse away from the road. 'Division Commander Savitsky, we're duty-bound to conserve . . .'

'We're duty-bound to make for Angkor,' he said. 'And that's what we're doing.' His perfect body poised itself in the saddle. He raised his sabre.

'It's not like ordinary dying,' I began. But he gave the order to trot forward. There was a rictus of terrifying glee on each mouth. The light from the sky was reflected in every eye.

I moved with them. I had become used to the security of numbers and I could not face their disapproval. But gradually they went ahead of me until I was in the rear. By this time we were almost at the bottom of the hill and cantering towards the mushroom cloud which was now shot through with all kinds of dark, swirling colours. It had become like a threatening hand, while the wind-borne ash stung our bodies and drew blood on the flanks of our mounts.

Yakovlev, just ahead of me, unstrapped his accordion and began to play some familiar Cossack battle-song. Soon they were all singing. Their pace gradually increased. The noise of the accordion died but their song was so loud now it seemed to fill the whole world. They reached full gallop, charging upon that appalling outline, the quintessential symbol of our doom, as their ancestors might have charged the very gates of Hell. They were swift, dark shapes in the dust. The song became a savage, defiant roar.

My first impulse was to charge with them. But then I had turned my horse and was trotting back towards the valley and the border, praying that, if I ever got to safety, I would not be too badly contaminated.

(In homage to Isaac Babel, 1894–1941?)
Ladbroke Grove, 1978

'80s LILIES
Terese Svoboda

THE CALLA LILIES in New Zealand say we are dead, just step off the jade-strewn, rimed high-tide line here and a wave will rise up like Trigger, like some silent movie stallion, and suck us under, suck us beneath a continental shelf stuck out so far the waves whiten before they break. So too the calla lilies, all white and wild like that, all about to break in the greeny drizzle that the wind whips, all these wild calla lilies that will bear us away.

I see the lilies and I say Let's get off the bus. Then the bus' burring keeps on without us as we stand at the upper ridge of lilies, before they spill off the grave mounds corralled by wooden fences and multiply right on onto the waves. Lilies from old settlers' tombs, I say into the silencing wind with you tucking the baby onto my back and as far as we can see, green drizzle, jade beaches, white cups in clumps flattened by wind.

Mind the waves, she says. They will jump the beach and pull you in.

She comes abreast of us, nearly green-skinned in the green mist with a small-sized boy just as green, tugging at the end of her arm. Does she mean for us to mind those waves—or him, the green monkey among the lilies?

I hold up a rock. Jade? Really jade? I ask.

Tourists, she says in a tone that can't be confused. Tourists don't come here, she says.

Really? They skip this bit? I thumb toward all that various beauty. Those terrible tourists.

She laughs and my husband and I say all the little things against the wind that makes her lean toward us down the length of the beach until we are at her car that she unlocks and leaves in, waving. We wave back, a few more little things on our lips.

The baby takes away our wonder at the place and its people, the baby has his wants. At the end of the road the woman has driven away from sits a pub, curiously free of all the lilies, as if bulldozed free. We order pints there, and then we ask after rooms since the green mist can only give way to dark.

They have rooms.

We remark on the sheep smell of these rooms, and the drizzle-colored pub interior, its darts bent and broken, the dark growlings and the stares from the pub fiends, two steamy gold miners, silent and filthy in their mining gear, flakes of dirt green not gold falling from them onto their table, and we order another pint.

Going to the ladies, with the baby asleep, milk lip aquiver, I trip over huge bones in the corridor, vastly gnarled, prehistoric big grey bones that must be the source of the sheep stink. The dog that gnaws at such bones, as terrible an animal as he must be, thumps and growls from inside some further door when I shut mine, but he's quiet when I emerge, as if he has plans.

I haven't. I haven't said Yes yet to the room or to another pint. I just want to talk about those bones but at our seat there's no one to note my near miss with the bone-guarding dog, no man nor child.

One of the two miners nods to the window, Out there. She has them in her car.

Where else would you be putting up but here? she shouts over new pellmell rain. I have tea, she says.

WE RODE THE ferry that sinks, the ferry with a crèche where the children are roped to rockers through the big waves that slap the island apart, the ferry that, however, did not sink when we crossed but allowed us, vomitus, to board that bus.

That ferry's no problem, she says. Look in the phonebook.

I open the phonebook and the first page lists all the calamities: tidal wave, earthquake, floods, volcanic eruptions, and numbers to call. Such a safe place, I say they say, so safe for children.

We are fleeing, we explain, to some safe place. We're sure this time they'll drop it. We thought, Here's a place we'll be safe and gave the airlines our gold card.

They don't laugh, she and her husband. Just the way she doesn't laugh at the green rock I pull out of my bag, the rock, I say, that must be worth money. Their house is full of toys my baby knows and toys my husband can feel the remote of, and books I have read and admired. Her husband has my husband's charm and why not? They do nothing similar for work but charm makes the men match.

The baby inspects all the toys their boy brings so I can talk while she cooks because cooking is the point of visiting, isn't it, she says, a place where everyone meets. Then you can go back, if you like. After tea.

I look out into the pellmell greeny rain and even in the looking, smell sheep, and hear that growl. When real night falls about two drinks after tea—what is surely dinner—when the rain isn't seen but felt, they won't let us go, they make up beds.

Their boy bounces a ball off the baby's head and the baby smiles.

WE VISIT A gold mine in the morning, their idea.

Maybe they wanted to have sex, I whisper to my husband as he settles a hard hat onto his head.

A little late, he says.

We walk deep into the mines posted Do Not Enter and they say, Don't mind the signs, the baby is fine.

This is where we're going when it happens, says her husband. And he explains what he heard on TV yesterday, how it will blow ash all over the globe in ways nobody knew. Everywhere will be caught in the grip of its terrible winter.

Winter—you are obsessed with having seasons that don't match ours, I say. I look at my husband. So here is not safe either says my glance.

We walk along in the dark.

I expect a room of gold all aglitter at the end, jutting ore burnished to a sun's strength. What we get to is a small cave lit with mirrors which leave little flashes of faraway light on the dull rock.

Our faces facing the mirrors are just one grey ball, then another.

Their boy drops a rock down a shaft and it doesn't hit bottom. While we wait, the baby wakes as if the rock hits hard, and his wails echo all down the tunnel. We walk back through his wails, it's that physical.

WE STAY ONE more night. We stay up late and my husband says, Maybe the threat will blow over.

Blow over. We all laugh, drinking the wine from the grapes that grow among the lilies. Then we talk movies, all the same ones we have seen as if together.

We really came to see you, I say. Does it matter if we flee if you are here?

IN THE MORNING they tell us they do not write, they will not. No letters.

Consider them written, says my husband.

We take the next bus, a dark cave filled with more miners abandoning mines. The settlers we leave behind, such settlers as they are, wearing our clothes nearly exactly, franchise for franchise, who wave as our bus burrs off past the lilies, the big waves behind them lapping and reaching.

THESE ZOMBIES ARE NOT
A METAPHOR

Jeff Goldberg

WHEN THE FULL-SCALE zombie outbreak finally occurred I was the only one prepared. I don't mean with supplies and weapons and secure shelter—though, yes, that is a part of what I mean—but, more importantly, I had the proper mental fortification.

Baxter said to me, "These zombies are a metaphorical scourge upon the Earth. They represent all that is evil in humankind." Then he went outside, got bitten, and turned into one of them.

I held a meeting with the rest of my housemates. "Let's be very clear," I said. "These zombies are not a metaphorical scourge upon the Earth. These zombies are an actual scourge upon the Earth." I pointed out the window. We could see the hordes of walking dead in the streets, tearing into the flesh of the living. "These zombies do not represent all that is evil in humankind. They do not represent anything except zombies."

Yes, yes, Manny and Jeannine nodded at me, blank affirmative stares, eager for leadership in the uncertainty of the world's end.

A half-decayed, blood-smeared face smashed itself up against my metal-barred bulletproof glass window. I flipped a switch and activated the electric current. "Not an allegory, an analogy, or an allusion," I said. "This is not the foreshadowing of the downfall of man. This is the downfall itself."

Yes, yes, my housemates all nodded. But they didn't understand. With the apocalypse upon us, the human race appeared unequipped to process the bad news. So these few survivors were both my wards and my prisoners. I couldn't let them out of my sight for a moment or they'd shut down the defenses, wander outside.

I turned my back to work on the water purification system and Jeannine started fumbling with the locks on the front door. As I pulled her away she said she just wanted to pop out for some Starbucks. "Starbucks is gone," I said to her, "There is no more Starbucks."

She lowered her head. "Reliance on foreign investors puts American corporations at risk in the global marketplace."

That was when I started locking them in the basement.

I'd go down to give them meals and sometimes play a round or two of bridge. It got boring single-handedly holding off the zombie multitude.

Zombie Baxter turned up a few days later. His gray, withered skin; his barren, pus-filled eyes; the shreds of human flesh in his teeth: good old Baxter. I wouldn't have recognized him except he started banging on the front door and shouting "It's me, Zombie Baxter!" I eyed him through the peephole, one hand poised on the switch to activate the electric current.

"I didn't know zombies could talk," I said through the safety of my steel-reinforced door.

"What's there to say, really?"

"I'm not letting you in," I said.

"Come on, I want to eat your brains."

"No."

"What about Jeannine?"

"No."

"Manny?"

I said, "No," but he sensed my hesitation.

"Just give me Manny," he said, "Please."

"I'm going to activate the electric perimeter now."

"Go ahead," Baxter said, "We've built up a resistance to electricity."

"Really?" I asked.

"No," he admitted, "But our best zombie scientists are working on it. It's only a matter of time."

I flipped the switch and Baxter jolted away from the front door, then lurched off down the street. Either he flipped me the bird or his pointer and ring fingers were missing.

He was right: it was only a matter of time. But that was the point. I didn't expect to survive; I just wanted to hold out as long as possible.

Down in the basement Manny and Jeannine had managed to use their teeth and nails to pry the wooden boards away from the one small window. Now the room was crawling with zombies. I couldn't tell if the moaning, undead horde staggering around the former rec room included my housemates. No one seemed to be in a talking mood.

I ran a hose from the kitchen sink, stuck it under the door and started filling the basement with water.

THE RAPID ADVANCE
OF SORROW

Theodora Goss

I SIT IN one of the cafés in Szent Endre, writing this letter to you,
István, not knowing if I will be alive tomorrow, not knowing if this café
will be here, with its circular green chairs and cups of espresso. By the
Danube, children are playing, their knees bare below school uniforms.
Widows are knitting shapeless sweaters. A cat sleeps beside a geranium in
the café window.

If you see her, will you tell me? I still remember how she appeared at the
University, just off the train from Debrecen, a country girl with badly-cut
hair and clothes sewn by her mother. That year, I was smoking French cigarettes and reading forbidden literature. "Have you read D.H. Lawrence?"
I asked her. "He is the only modern writer who convincingly expresses the
desires of the human body." She blushed and turned away. She probably still
had her Young Pioneers badge, hidden among her underwear.

"Ilona is a beautiful name," I said. "It is the most beautiful name in our
language." I saw her smile, although she was trying to avoid me. Her face
was plump from country sausage and egg bread, and dimples formed at
the corners of her mouth, two on each side.

She had dimples on her buttocks, as I found out later. I remember
them, like craters on two moons, above the tops of her stockings.

SORROW: A FEELING of grief or melancholy. A mythical city generally located in northern Siberia, said to have been visited by Marco Polo. From Sorrow, he took back to Italy the secret of making ice.

THAT AUTUMN, INTELLECTUAL apathy was in fashion. I berated her for reading her textbooks, preparing for her examinations. "Don't you know the grades are predetermined?" I said. "The peasants receive ones, the bourgeoisie receive twos, the aristocrats, if they have been admitted under a special dispensation, always receive threes."

She persisted, telling me that she had discovered art, that she wanted to become cultured.

"You are a peasant," I said, slapping her rump. She looked at me with tears in her eyes.

THE PRINCIPAL EXPORT of Sorrow is the fur of the arctic fox, which is manufactured into cloaks, hats, the cuffs on gloves and boots. These foxes, which live on the tundra in family groups, are hunted with falcons. The falcons of Sorrow, relatives of the kestrel, are trained to obey a series of commands blown on whistles carved of human bone.

SHE BEGAN GOING to museums. She spent hours at the Vármuzeum, in the galleries of art. Afterward, she would go to cafés, drink espressos, smoke cigarettes. Her weight dropped, and she became as lean as a wolfhound. She developed a look of perpetual hunger.

When winter came and ice floated on the Danube, I started to worry. Snow had been falling for days, and Budapest was trapped in a white silence. The air was cleaner than it had been for months, because the Trabants could not make it through the snow. It was very cold.

She entered the apartment carrying her textbooks. She was wearing a hat of white fur that I had never seen before. She threw it on the sofa.

"Communism is irrelevant," she said, lighting a cigarette.

"Where have you been?" I asked. "I made a paprikás. I stood in line for two hours to buy the chicken."

"There is to be a new manifesto." Ash dropped on the carpet. "It will not resemble the old manifesto. We are no longer interested in political and economic movements. All movements from now on will be purely aesthetic. Our actions will be beautiful and irrelevant."

"The paprikás has congealed," I said.

She looked at me for the first time since she had entered the apartment and shrugged. "You are not a poet."

THE POETRY OF Sorrow may confuse anyone not accustomed to its intricacies. In Sorrow, poems are constructed on the principle of the maze. Once the reader enters the poem, he must find his way out by observing a series of clues. Readers failing to solve a poem have been known to go mad. Those who can appreciate its beauties say that the poetry of Sorrow is impersonal and ecstatic, and that it invariably speaks of death.

SHE BEGAN BRINGING home white flowers: crocuses, hyacinths, narcissi. I did not know where she found them, in the city, in winter. I eventually realized they were the emblems of her organization, worn at what passed for rallies, silent meetings where communication occurred with the touch of a hand, a glance from the corner of an eye. Such meetings took place in secret all over the city. Students would sit in the pews of the Mátyás Church, saying nothing, planning insurrection.

At this time we no longer made love. Her skin had grown cold, and when I touched it for too long, my fingers began to ache.

We seldom spoke. Her language had become impossibly complex, referential. I could no longer understand her subtle intricacies.

She painted the word ENTROPY on the wall of the apartment. The wall was white, the paint was white. I saw it only because soot had stained the wall to a dull gray, against which the word appeared like a ghost.

One morning I saw that her hair on the pillow had turned white. I called her name, desperate with panic. She looked at me and I saw that her eyes were the color of milk, like the eyes of the blind.

IT IS INSUFFICIENT to point out that the inhabitants of Sorrow are pale. Their skin has a particular translucence, like a layer of nacre. Their nails and hair are iridescent, as though unable to capture and hold light. Their eyes are, at best, disconcerting. Travelers who have stared at them too long have reported hallucinations, like mountaineers who have stared at fields of ice.

I EXPECTED TANKS. Tanks are required for all sensible invasions. But spring came, and the insurrection did nothing discernible.

Then flowers appeared in the public gardens: crocuses, hyacinths, narcissi, all white. The black branches of the trees began to sprout leaves of a delicate pallor. White pigeons strutted in the public squares, and soon they outnumbered the ordinary gray ones. Shops began to close: first the stores selling Russian electronics, then clothing stores with sweaters from Bulgaria, then pharmacies. Only stores selling food remained open, although the potatoes looked waxen and the pork acquired a peculiar transparency.

I had stopped going to classes. It was depressing, watching a classroom full of students, with their white hair and milky eyes, saying nothing. Many professors joined the insurrection, and they would stand at the front of the lecture hall, the word ENTROPY written on the board behind them, communicating in silent gestures.

She rarely came to the apartment, but once she brought me poppy seed strudel in a paper bag. She said, "Péter, you should eat." She rested her fingertips on the back of my hand. They were like ice. "You have not joined us," she said. "Those who have not joined us will be eliminated."

I caught her by the wrist. "Why?" I asked.

She said, "Beauty demands symmetry, uniformity."

My fingers began to ache with cold. I released her wrist. I could see her veins flowing through them, like strands of aquamarine.

SORROW IS RULED by the absolute will of its Empress, who is chosen for her position at the age of three and reigns until the age of thirteen. The Empress is chosen by the Brotherhood of the Cowl, a quasi-religious sect whose members hide their faces under hoods of white wool to maintain their anonymity. By tradition, the Empress never speaks in public. She delivers her commands in private audiences with the Brotherhood. The consistency of these commands, from one Empress to another, has been taken to prove the sanctity of the Imperial line. After their reigns, all Empresses retire to the Abbey of St. Alba, where they live in seclusion for the remainder of their lives, studying astronomy, mathematics, and the seven-stringed zither. During the history of Sorrow, remarkable observations, theorems, and musical arrangements have emerged from this Abbey.

NO TANKS CAME, but one day, when the sun shone with a vague luminescence through the clouds that perpetually covered the city, the Empress of Sorrow rode along Váci Street on a white elephant. She was surrounded by courtiers, some in cloaks of white fox, some in jesters' uniforms sewn from white patches, some, principally unmarried women, in transparent gauze through which one could see their hairless flesh. The eyes of the elephant were outlined with henna, its feet were stained with henna. In its trunk it carried a silver bell, whose ringing was the only sound as the procession made its way to the Danube and across Erzsébet Bridge.

Crowds of people had come to greet the Empress: students waving white crocuses and hyacinths and narcissi, mothers holding the hands of children who failed to clap when the elephant strode by, nuns in ashen gray. Cowled figures moved among the crowd. I watched one standing ahead of me and recognized the set of her shoulders, narrower than they had been, still slightly crooked.

I sidled up to her and whispered, "Ilona."

She turned. The cowl was drawn down and I could not see her face, but her mouth was visible, too thin now for dimples.

"Péter," she said, in a voice like snow falling. "We have done what is necessary."

She touched my cheek with her fingers. A shudder went through me, as though I had been touched by something electric.

TRAVELERS HAVE ATTEMPTED to characterize the city of Sorrow. Some have said it is a place of confusion, with impossible pinnacles rising to stars that cannot be seen from any observatory. Some have called it a place of beauty, where the winds, playing through the high buildings, produce a celestial music. Some have called it a place of death, and have said that the city, examined from above, exhibits the contours of a skull.

Some have said that the city of Sorrow does not exist. Some have insisted that it exists everywhere: that we are perpetually surrounded by its streets, which are covered by a thin layer of ice; by its gardens, in which albino peacocks wander; by its inhabitants, who pass us without attention or interest.

I BELIEVE NEITHER of these theories. I believe that Sorrow is an insurrection waged by a small cabal, with its signs and secrets; that it is run on purely aesthetic principles; that its goal is entropy, a perpetual stillness of the soul. But I could be mistaken. My conclusions could be tainted by the confusion that spreads with the rapid advance of Sorrow.

So I have left Budapest, carrying only the mark of three fingertips on my left cheek. I sit here every morning, in a café in Szent Endre, not knowing how long I have to live, not knowing how long I can remain here, on a circular green chair drinking espresso.

Soon, the knees of the children will become as smooth and fragile as glass. The widows' knitting needles will click like bone, and geranium leaves will fall beside the blanched cat. The coffee will fade to the color of milk. I do not know what will happen to the chair. I do not know if I will be eliminated, or given another chance to join the faction of silence. But I am sending you this letter, István, so you can remember me when the snows come.

THE CONVERSATION OF EIROS AND CHARMION

Edgar Allan Poe

I will bring fire to thee.
—EURIPIDES—*Androm.*

EIROS. Why do you call me Eiros?

CHARMION. So henceforth will you always be called. You must forget, too, my earthly name, and speak to me as Charmion.

EIROS. This is indeed no dream!

CHARMION. Dreams are with us no more; but of these mysteries anon. I rejoice to see you looking like-life and rational. The film of the shadow has already passed from off your eyes. Be of heart and fear nothing. Your allotted days of stupor have expired; and, to-morrow, I will myself induct you into the full joys and wonders of your novel existence.

EIROS. True, I feel no stupor, none at all. The wild sickness and the terrible darkness have left me, and I hear no longer that mad, rushing, horrible sound, like the "voice of many waters." Yet my senses are bewildered, Charmion, with the keenness of their perception of the new.

CHARMION. A few days will remove all this—but I fully understand you, and feel for you. It is now ten earthly years since I underwent what you undergo, yet the remembrance of it hangs by me still. You have now suffered all of pain, however, which you will suffer in Aidenn.

EIROS. In Aidenn?

CHARMION. In Aidenn.

EIROS. Oh, God!—pity me, Charmion!—I am overburdened with the majesty of all things—of the unknown now known—of the speculative Future merged in the august and certain Present.

CHARMION. Grapple not now with such thoughts. Tomorrow we will speak of this. Your mind wavers, and its agitation will find relief in the exercise of simple memories. Look not around, nor forward—but back. I am burning with anxiety to hear the details of that stupendous event which threw you among us. Tell me of it. Let us converse of familiar things, in the old familiar language of the world which has so fearfully perished.

EIROS. Most fearfully, fearfully!—this is indeed no dream.

CHARMION. Dreams are no more. Was I much mourned, my Eiros?

EIROS. Mourned, Charmion?—oh deeply. To that last hour of all, there hung a cloud of intense gloom and devout sorrow over your household.

CHARMION. And that last hour—speak of it. Remember that, beyond the naked fact of the catastrophe itself, I know nothing. When, coming out from among mankind, I passed into Night through the Grave—at that period, if I remember aright, the calamity which overwhelmed you was utterly unanticipated. But, indeed, I knew little of the speculative philosophy of the day.

EIROS. The individual calamity was, as you say, entirely unanticipated; but analogous misfortunes had been long a subject of discussion with astronomers. I need scarce tell you, my friend, that, even when you left us, men had agreed to understand those passages in the most holy writings which speak of the final destruction of all things by fire, as having reference to the orb of the earth alone. But in regard to the immediate agency of the ruin, speculation had been at fault from that epoch in astronomical knowledge in which the comets were divested of the terrors of flame. The very moderate density of these bodies had been well established. They had been observed to pass among the satellites of Jupiter, without bringing about any sensible alteration either in the masses or in the orbits of these secondary planets. We had long regarded the wanderers as vapory creations of inconceivable tenuity, and as altogether incapable of doing injury to our substantial globe, even in the event of contact. But contact was not in any degree dreaded; for the elements of all the comets were accurately known. That among them we should look for the agency of the threatened fiery destruction had been for many years considered an inadmissible idea. But wonders and wild fancies had been, of late days, strangely rife among mankind; and although it was only with a few of the ignorant that actual apprehension prevailed, upon the announcement by astronomers of a new comet, yet this announcement was generally received with I know not what agitation and mistrust.

The elements of the strange orb were immediately calculated, and it was at once conceded by all observers, that its path, at perihelion, would bring it into very close proximity with the earth. There were two or three astronomers, of secondary note, who resolutely maintained that a contact was inevitable. I cannot very well express to you the effect of this intelligence upon the people. For a few short days they would not believe an assertion which their intellect, so long employed among worldly considerations, could not in any manner grasp. But the truth of a vitally important fact soon makes its way into the understanding of even the most stolid. Finally, all men saw that astronomical knowledge lied not, and they awaited the comet. Its approach was not, at first, seemingly rapid; nor was its appearance of very unusual character. It was of a dull red, and had little perceptible train. For seven or eight days we saw no material increase in its apparent diameter, and but a partial alteration in its color. Meantime the ordinary affairs of men were discarded, and all interests absorbed in a growing discussion, instituted by the philosophic, in respect to the cometary nature. Even the grossly ignorant aroused their sluggish capacities to such considerations. The learned now gave their intellect—their soul—to no such points as the allaying of fear, or to the sustenance of loved theory. They sought—they panted for right views. They groaned for perfected knowledge. Truth arose in the purity of her strength and exceeding majesty, and the wise bowed down and adored.

That material injury to our globe or to its inhabitants would result from the apprehended contact, was an opinion which hourly lost ground among the wise; and the wise were now freely permitted to rule the reason and the fancy of the crowd. It was demonstrated, that the density of the comet's nucleus was far less than that of our rarest gas; and the harmless passage of a similar visitor among the satellites of Jupiter was a point strongly insisted upon, and which served greatly to allay terror. Theologists, with an earnestness fear-enkindled, dwelt upon the biblical prophecies, and expounded them to the people with a directness and simplicity of which no previous instance had been known. That the final destruction of the earth must be brought about by the agency of fire, was urged with a spirit that enforced everywhere conviction; and that the comets were of no fiery nature (as all men now knew) was a truth which relieved all, in a great measure, from the apprehension of the great calamity foretold. It is noticeable that the popular prejudices and vulgar errors in regard to pestilences and wars—errors which were wont to prevail upon every appearance of a comet—were now altogether unknown. As if by some sudden convulsive exertion, reason had at once hurled superstition from her throne. The feeblest intellect had derived vigor from excessive interest.

What minor evils might arise from the contact were points of elaborate question. The learned spoke of slight geological disturbances, of probable alterations in climate, and consequently in vegetation; of possible magnetic and electric influences. Many held that no visible or perceptible effect would in any manner be produced. While such discussions were going on, their subject gradually approached, growing larger in apparent diameter, and of a more brilliant lustre. Mankind grew paler as it came. All human operations were suspended. There was an epoch in the course of the general sentiment when the comet had attained, at length, a size surpassing that of any previously recorded visitation. The people now, dismissing any lingering hope that the astronomers were wrong, experienced all the certainty of evil. The chimerical aspect of their terror was gone. The hearts of the stoutest of our race beat violently within their bosoms. A very few days sufficed, however, to merge even such feelings in sentiments more unendurable. We could no longer apply to the strange orb any accustomed thoughts. Its historical attributes had disappeared. It oppressed us with a hideous novelty of emotion. We saw it not as an astronomical phenomenon in the heavens, but as an incubus upon our hearts, and a shadow upon our brains. It had taken, with inconceivable rapidity, the character of a gigantic mantle of rare flame, extending from horizon to horizon.

Yet a day, and men breathed with greater freedom. It was clear that we were already within the influence of the comet; yet we lived. We even felt an unusual elasticity of frame and vivacity of mind. The exceeding tenuity of the object of our dread was apparent; for all heavenly objects were plainly visible through it. Meantime, our vegetation had perceptibly altered; and we gained faith, from this predicted circumstance, in the foresight of the wise. A wild luxuriance of foliage, utterly unknown before, burst out upon every vegetable thing.

Yet another day—and the evil was not altogether upon us. It was now evident that its nucleus would first reach us. A wild change had come over all men; and the first sense of pain was the wild signal for general lamentation and horror. This first sense of pain lay in a rigorous constriction of the breast and lungs, and an insufferable dryness of the skin. It could not be denied that our atmosphere was radically affected; the conformation of this atmosphere and the possible modifications to which it might be subjected, were now the topics of discussion. The result of investigation sent an electric thrill of the intensest terror through the universal heart of man.

It had been long known that the air which encircled us was a compound of oxygen and nitrogen gases, in the proportion of twenty-one measures of oxygen, and seventy-nine of nitrogen, in every one hundred of the atmosphere. Oxygen, which was the principle of combustion, and the vehicle of heat, was absolutely necessary to the support of animal life, and was the most powerful and energetic agent in nature. Nitrogen, on the contrary, was incapable of supporting either animal life or flame. An unnatural excess of oxygen would result, it had been ascertained, in just such an elevation of the animal spirits as we had latterly experienced. It was the pursuit, the extension of the idea, which had engendered awe. What would be the result of a total extraction of the nitrogen? A combustion irresistible, all-devouring, omni-prevalent, immediate; the entire fulfillment, in all their minute and terrible details, of the fiery and horror-inspiring denunciations of the prophecies of the Holy Book.

Why need I paint, Charmion, the now disenchained frenzy of mankind? That tenuity in the comet which had previously inspired us with hope, was now the source of the bitterness of despair. In its impalpable gaseous character we clearly perceived the consummation of Fate. Meantime a day again passed, bearing away with it the last shadow of Hope. We gasped in the rapid modification of the air. The red blood bounded tumultuously through its strict channels. A furious delirium possessed all men; and, with arms rigidly outstretched toward the threatening heavens, they trembled and shrieked aloud. But the nucleus of the destroyer was now upon us; even here in Aidenn, I shudder while I speak. Let me be brief—brief as the ruin that overwhelmed. For a moment there was a wild lurid light alone, visiting and penetrating all things. Then—let us bow down, Charmion, before the excessive majesty of the great God!—then, there came a shouting and pervading sound, as if from the mouth itself of HIM; while the whole incumbent mass of ether in which we existed, burst at once into a species of intense flame, for whose surpassing brilliancy and all-fervid heat even the angels in the high Heaven of pure knowledge have no name. Thus ended all.

APOCA CA LYP SE:
A DIP TYCH

Joy ce Car ol O a te s

Identifying dismembered body parts
is particularly difficult when the
parts have been scattered. This
is often the result of animal
activity over a period of time.
Of course, it sometimes happens
that the perpetrator of the crime,
having dismembered the body, will
scatter the parts himself. Where
decomposition is rapid, owing to
warm weather, moist earth and
other physical conditions, the
identification of such parts poses
a challenge to forensic scientists.

I could not move my leg!
I could "feel" my leg attached
to my body yet I could not move
my leg. When I commanded my
leg to move, by an exertion of

will, there was a sympathetic twitch of nerves as if an electric current had shot through the tissue; a tightening, an <u>expectation</u> of movement; yet finally there was no movement. And I saw that I'd been mistaken, that is my eyes had been mistaken seeing what they had been conditioned to see. The fact was, <u>my</u> <u>leg</u> <u>was</u> <u>no</u> <u>longer</u> <u>attached</u> <u>to</u> <u>my</u> <u>body</u>.

Let me demonstrate: this action of a <u>paring</u> <u>knife</u> against bone. (In fact this is an actual human bone, a femur. Lent by the dissection lab downstairs.) When you scrape the blade against bone, the thinness (of the blade) causes it to "chatter"; that is, to scrape unevenly, jumping just perceptibly and irregularly, as you can see. This will leave identifiable marks so that you can determine that a paring knife was used to dismember.

The horror of this realization filled me slowly . . . as a sponge slowly absorbs water by a curious action of its multiple cells. (Is the sponge a "single" organism? If "dismembered," am I, or was I, a "single" organism?)

My leg would not move. It would
not move because it was no longer
attached physically to my body.
The leg would not move because
it was no longer "my" leg. It
was merely "the" leg. It was . . .
"a" leg.

By contrast, this hunting knife
with the heavier blade. When
you scrape it against bone, it
moves smoothly, producing a different effect on the bone. The
distinction between <u>paring knife</u>
and <u>hunting knife</u> can be crucial.

As with my leg, so with my arms.
And my hands. And my torso. And
my pelvic region. And my head . . ,
This head no longer attached to
a body, nor even to the hacked
remains of a body, but kicked
approximately four feet away
where, rolling like a malformed
soccer ball, it came to rest
in marshy soil buzzing with
bright-winged insects. You
might envision the blank-eyed
dignity of a Roman bust except
the head was not sculpted from
inviolate marble but was com-
prised of mere organic matter.
I could not move my eyes! I
could not blink, I could not

cease seeing. Where in life I
had towered over such wildflowers
as loosestrife (that erect, ver-
tical spiky purple flower that
grows in profusion in wet mea-
dows and roadside ditches) now
in this new state (which I am
reluctant to call "death") this
wildflower towers over me.
Bees cluster close by. Gnats,
mosquitoes. Dragonflies, horse-
flies. And butterflies--so many !

The language of bones. For bones
speak. Types of sprains, frac-
tures, breaks . Clean breaks and
not-so clean. Splintered bone.
The shearing of joints by the
action of an ax. A bone can
become porous with time. A bone
can decay. Only slowly, relative
to flesh. You must put your faith
in bones, of which teeth may be
said to be a type. Identification
through dental records is very
helpful. A filling may outlive a
tooth. A ring may outlive the
finger it has adorned. Baling wire
wound tight around wrists and ankles
of the victim may outlive the victim.

God erupted in a swarm of
iridescent-glinting wings.
Never had I gazed upon such

Beauty. Amid the tall
marsh grasses and loosestrife
dreamy clouds of wings.
Cobalt-blue, red-orange,
sandy-brown, pale golde,
deep crimson, luminous
twilit ivory. God in a swarm
of butterflies . . .
I opened my mouth to scream
and I could not.

A confession in itself is not
sufficient. Confessions must be
corroborated with evidence. To
prove murder, you must have a
corpse and evidence linking the
corpse to the suspect. Even then,
you may not be able to prove
murder.

And in that instant my terror
became ecstasy. I was transformed into beauty as the
butterflies--dozens, hundreds--
eagerly covered my eyes, and
penetrated my mouth, nose and
ears and covered my head. A
seething roiling ball of butter-
flies--so many Seeing me, so
transformed, you smile; for
beauty alone redeems us.

The Salvation of the Grass
A Parable

IN THE DISTANCE, viewed through a telescope, the D___ family was sitting down to supper. You could see them clearly through the window of their one-storey woodframe ranch house at 33 Sycamore Lane. You would guess it's a fairly ordinary weekday supper and you'd be correct. The D___ family of four seated at the Maplewood table in the dining room, a rectangular table that can open up to seat as many as ten for such special occasions as Thanksgiving and Christmas. But this evening in midsummer is just an ordinary evening. We sit down for supper at 6 o'clock sharp when it's still bright as noon. There are pink plastic placemats beneath our plates, the kind that can be sponged off easily, and paper napkins, Mom's meatloaf baked with a thick catsup crust. Mashed potatoes are being passed in a heavy bowl. Dad at the head of the table smiling. Bis Sis to Dad's right and Toby to Dad's left. The chairs are positioned just so. And Mom facing Dad across the table.

No one is speaking. There's just silence. It isn't an easy, relaxed silence. Like if you struck it with a fork, the silence would shatter and fall into pieces.

At this short distance, our family features are obvious! They would cause you to smile. It isn't just that Big Sis and I resemble our Dad and Mom, as if we'd been shaken up into a molecular mix and poured out into molds to bake, but Dad and Mom resemble each other, too. Our eyes shifting in their deep sockets, our naked ears that look as if they'd been pinched to sharp points, the oily glisten of our skins and the pale-waxy parts in our hair that look like cracks in a shellacked surface. Our smiles are identical smiles though Dad's and Mom's teeth are larger than Big Sis's and Toby's.

Big Sis is eleven years old and she is big for her age. I am seven years old and a runt. I am watching Dad out of the corner of my eye. Dad is watching me directly, smiling. And Mom is watching Dad watching me. No one has spoken. Yet the bowl of potatoes is being passed. Mom won't pass it to me but will spoon a serving onto my plate. As she has positioned a piece of meatloaf on my plate.

I remember Toby. I don't remember being Toby.

At this moment, viewed through the telescope, there is silence as Toby reaches for his milk glass. The glass is a former jam glass, three-quarters filled with very white milk. Homogenized vitamin-fortified whole milk. As Toby reaches for the glass, Dad watches. For Toby always spills his milk—or almost always. Poor Toby! It isn't clear whether Toby is sub-normal in intelligence or possibly he's dyslexic or has some motor coordination problem that may erupt one day into multiple sclerosis or paranoid schizophrenia. Mom is anxiously watching Dad who's smiling grimly and Big Sis is watching, too, biting her lower lip in anticipation of the usual milk-spill and Dad's fury which will explode in a nimble backhanded blow propelling Toby backward in his chair and his pugnose blossoming in blood. Except—

A sound in the street. Voices, a truck's engine. A police siren. "What the hell—?" Dad exclaims, throwing down his napkin.

Up from the table! Dad in the lead! The D___ family runs out onto the asphalt driveway to see what's going on.

In Sycamore Street, a narrow suburban street, grass is growing!

A sprinkler is lazily sending arcs of sparkling water onto the vivid green tufted grass!

Our neighbors Edith and Ed Covenski are standing in their driveway, too. Looking puzzled, but smiling. Edith in baggy white shorts and Ed in khakis and a striped sports shirt swelling at his gut. Earlier we'd heard them shouting at each other but now you'd never know it, Edith has twined her fattish arm through Ed's.

There's Mr. McMichael two doors down, standing by his mailbox. A little suspicious, that's McMichael's way, already he's had two heart attacks in his early fifties but he's intrigued, he's smiling. And his daughter Junie the cheerleader at Eastern High, in tight-tight jeans and T-shirt and her red hair in a bouncy ponytail. Next door there's Bob Smith, a lanky kid of eighteen dropped out of school to work with his dad at Brewster's, staring and grinning, scratching his chest.

Myra Flynn across the street who's been sick, coming down the front steps with her aluminum walker. She sees Mom, and they wave to each other. Mom's a good neighbor.

Up and down Sycamore, our neighbors came out. We were all staring at the lush, new grass. We seemed not to see that it was a "sod carpet" laid on the pavement, approximately two inches deep. Stretching maybe fifty yards along the street. Who had placed the grass there, and why, we would not know and would not wish to know.

It's enough to know your life has been saved. Not once but many times.

AFTER ALL

Carol Emshwiller

IT'S ONE OF those days, rainy and dull, when you remember all the times
you said or did the wrong thing, or somebody else said the wrong thing
to you, or insulted you, or you insulted them, or they forgot you altogether, or you forgot them when you should have remembered. One of
those days when everything you say is misunderstood. Everything you pick
up you drop. You knock things over. You slip and fall. And your nose is
running, your throat is sore. *And* it's your birthday. You're a whole 'nother
year older. At your age, one more year makes a big difference.

At least I'm alone. No need to bother anyone else with myself, and my
temper, my moods, my dithering and doubts, my yackety-yacking when
others want to keep quiet.

And my voice is too loud. I laugh when nothing's funny.

Having had a night of nightmares about what might have happened
if this or if that bad thing had come about. (Good no one's here, because
I would be telling them the whole dream detail by detail.) Stop me if I
go nattering on. I talk and talk even when I mean to keep quiet. *Especially*
when I mean to be quiet.

There ought to be something else to talk about that wouldn't be my
long, long dream or the weather, where the sunshine, gruesome and gar-
ish, causes spots before my eyes.

It's time to go somewhere. Anyplace else is better than here. It will be a makeshift journey. No purpose except to get away. I didn't pack. I didn't plan. I won't bring a map. I can't depend on strangers because of my beady eyes. I have a mean smile.

YOU SEE, THIS evening I was sitting in the window of my cottage looking out at my piece of desert with squawking quail in it. (Tobacco! Tobacco!) I was thinking to write a story about somebody who needs to change (the best sort of character to write about), and all of a sudden I knew it was *me* who had to change. Always had been, and I didn't realize it until that very minute. So I have to be the one to go on a journey, either of discovery or in order to avoid myself.

I won't pack a lunch. I won't bring a bottle of water. I know I don't look my best but I don't even want to. My hair . . . I don't want to think about it.

If you crawl out the hole in the back fence, right away you're on the road to town.

"A pointless coming and going," they'll say, and I'll say, "That's exactly what I'm after."

I've lived all this time a different kind of pointless coming and going: Concerts and plays and then reading all the books one *should* read—that everybody else was reading, so how could you not read them? But this will be a different kind of pointless. I don't care what they think.

THEY!

Why can't they just take me for granted like most children do? Being chased by your own children. How could that happen? Being followed and watched.

I suppose to catch me out, *non compos mentis. Mentos?* If that's what it's called. *Mentis sanos?* If I can remember the words for it, how can it be true? Except I don't remember.

THEY'LL SEE ME if I leave in the daytime.

IT'S ONE OF those nights with a fingernail moon. It's one of those nights with a cold wind. Who'd expect Grandma to be out in this weather and at this hour? Who'd expect Grandma to be walking down the road to town, leaning against the wind. (It's been a long time since I was allowed to drive.)

That's my son behind the arborvitae. My middle daughter by the carport. (Carport without a car.) I see her shadow. My oldest? I don't know where she is.

"Mama, you're not as young as you think you are." (I *am*. I *am*. Exactly as young as I think I am. I'm maybe even a little more so.)

I'll be set upon by this and that. Snarling dogs let free to roam at night. Maybe there's other snarling people like myself out here. Hard rain or hail. Smells that sting the nose. Sky, a preposterous overdose of stars. If I fall asleep behind a creosote bush, what will come get me?

I suppose I ought to trust in some sort of god or other. There's one under every bush. At least I hope so. Feats of faith. I can do that.

Here I am, gone. Forever. So far, forever. I regret my books. The children will keep all the wrong ones. The good ones will get thrown in the garbage. My best scarf—they'll think it's just any old scarf. They don't know I got it from my own grandma. I told them, but they forget.

WHAT I'VE DONE for them! It was endless! Of course that was a long time ago.

But after that, what I've done for my art! If that is art. I don't know what to call it. I could call it leisure time. My hard-working leisure time. Most of it spent looking out the window.

But art is . . . *was* my life. I mean looking out the window so as to think about it was.

I always had plenty of ideas. I didn't exactly *have* them. They grew—
little by little, a half an idea at a time. First, part of a phrase and then a
person to go with it. After a person, then a little corner of a place for the
person to be in.

CAN I MAKE it through town before morning? It's six miles to the other
end of it. If I do, I might be able to get my usual nap. I could rest in the
ditch by the side of the road.

I've disguised myself. Big floppy hat, sand-colored bathrobe. . . . (I forgot not to wear my slippers.) I had a hard time deciding how I could be
unobtrusive and yet not be like myself, because I've always tried to look
unobtrusive. There's those earth colors which I always wear anyway.

I already stay in the corners and the shadows. I already never look people in the eye. I already hunch over. Now I'm shuffling because my slippers keep falling off.

I hear footsteps. When I stop to listen, they stop, too. I knew one of
them would follow. I wonder which it is? You can't get rid of your children.

"I'm laughing at you . . . whoever you are. Ha, ha, ha. Hear that?"

Well, I can't keep stopping and listening and laughing all the time. I'd
never get anywhere. I have to keep going if I want to get somewhere or other
in time for anything at all. It's bad enough when your slippers won't stay on.

IF I HAD A diary, I'd write: Next Day, or, Day Two. (I'd have to write the
days that way because I don't know the date, I hardly even know if spring
or summer, but that's not a sign of *non compose* . . . whatever . . . because
I never did pay attention to things like that.)

I'd write: Had a nice nap by the side of the road, and that I don't know
if long or short, but a nice one. (With my sand-colored bathrobe I'll bet
I looked like a pinkish/tan rock.) I'd write how I *must* begin working on
myself. They say writing things down is a good way to begin, so I'll do
that. Or will when I get the diary.

If I'd brought money I could have bought one in town. Except I went through town at about dawn and the stores were closed. (If I'd brought a watch I'd know when.)

WHOEVER IS FOLLOWING me has not made themselves known except in rustlings and snappings and scuffling sounds. I have to admit I'm a little bit scared.

LIVING IN A clearing in a forest might be nice. A mountain pass would be nice, too. I'd like a view. A view can make you happy. And with a view you'd be able to see who's creeping up on you.

I've decided. I turn, sharp left, leave the road, and start straight up. It's hard going in these slippers but I have a purpose. I'm taking charge of my own life. I know exactly what I'm doing, and when, and how much and why, and the time, which is right now.

IT'S A CUTE . . . you could call it a cute pass, up there where I'm heading. The cliff walls on each side hug a marshy spot. There's an overhang to sleep under. Old icy snow to chew on. Though it's high, it's sheltered enough for there to be fairly large trees. The ground glitters all over as if with tiny chunks of gold. (If it was gold, it would be gone.) There's things to eat. I'll nibble lambs quarters and purslane. Do they grow up there? I'm probably thinking of the olden days back East. Anyway, there's wild rose hips, so small I wonder that I've ever bothered eating them but I always do.

EVEN FROM HERE, well below that pass, you can see fairly far. I study the landscape. The orange lichen that dots the boulders looks like something left in the refrigerator too long. The sky looks as if it's got the measles.

I see movement on the hillside below me. For sure there's something down there. I catch glimpses from the corner of my eye.

It's inevitable, your children will track you down. There they are. I didn't actually see them, but something is out there, I'm sure of it, creeping up on me. What do they want? What do they have in store for me? *If* they can catch me. Of course it *is* my birthday—or was, a couple of days ago. Perhaps they want to have a surprise party. Perhaps their arms are full of presents, paper hats, tape recorders for the music for dancing. . . . What if they're bringing champagne? What a lot to carry! No wonder they haven't been able to catch me.

If they bring me sweets, they'll have forgotten I can't eat chocolate. If blouses, they'll be too big. (A mother is supposed to be bigger than the children, but they forget I'm the smallest now.) If paper hats, I suppose I'll have to put one on. If horns, I suppose I'll have to blow one.

Maybe, if I can get far enough ahead, they'll give up. I try to hurry but it's getting steeper. At least, if they're carrying all those things, they're having a hard time, too. The champagne will be the heaviest. I suppose they'll have those plastic champagne glasses you have to put together, and I suppose they think that'll be a good job for Grandma. I won't do it. They can't make me.

If I *DID* have a diary, and if I *did* write anything in it, it would be misunderstood anyway, just like everything I say is, so the first thing I'd write (page one, January first) should be: *That isn't what I mean at all.*

But I'd rather write about how my feet hurt and how it looks like rain.

ONCE I GET up there, I may have to stay forever. I might not be able to climb down. A long time ago when I was still spry, I came up to that very spot to die, but I didn't die after all. I waited and waited but nothing happened except I had my usual dizzy spell. I had to climb back down, though I had to wait until the spell passed. Good I hadn't told anybody.

THIS TIME I haven't thought (even at my age!) about what would be the best way to die. I know I should, but, after I didn't die back then at the top of my favorite pass, thinking about it began to seem a waste of valuable time. I was contemplating art. That seemed the important thing to do.

But, from now on, what to hope for out of life (and art)? Or is it the art part that's done with? I'm still full of longing . . . so much longing . . . for. . . . I don't know what, but I'm breathless with it.

I lie down with a rock for a pillow. I rest a long time. When I wake up, I think: Day two or day three or day four? Even if I had a diary I'd be all mixed up already.

BUT NOW I'M THINKING perhaps my own attic is the best place to disappear into. I could go down to the kitchen any time I wanted. I could get clean underwear. They say, "East or West, home is best."

I start back. It'll be easier going down because I won't keep stepping out of my slippers all the time.

SOMETHING STREAKS BY. Lights up the whole sky. Dizzying, dazzling even in the daytime. (Talk about spots in front of your eyes!) Well now, *there's* something beautiful. One nice thing is happening on my birthday. (If it still is my birthday.)

The ground shakes. Boulders come bounding down—whole sides of mountains. . . .

Who would have thought it, the end of the world as if just for me. Right on time, too, before my slippers give out entirely. We're all going together, the whole world and me. Isn't that nice! Best of all, I'm in at the end. I won't have to miss all the funny things that might have happened later had the world lasted beyond me. So, not such a bad birthday after all.

SAVE ME FROM THE PIOUS
AND THE VENGEFUL

Lynne Tillman

for Joe Wood 1965–1999

OUT OF NOTHING comes language and out of language comes nothing
and everything. Everything challenges the tenuous world order. Every
emotion derails every other one. One rut is disrupted by the emergence
of another. I like red wine, but began drinking white, with a sudden thirst,
and now demand it at 6 P.M., exactly, as if my life depended upon it. That
was a while ago.

What does a life depend upon? And from whom do I beg forgiveness
so quietly I'm never heard? With its remarkable colors and aftertastes, the
wine, dry as wit, urges me to forgive myself. I try.

Life's aim, Freud thought, was death. I can't know this, but maybe it's
death I want, since living comes with its own exigencies, like terror. In
dreams, nothing dies, but birth can't be trusted, either. I remember terrible dreams and not just my own. Memory is what everyone talks about
these days. Will we remember, and what will we remember, who will be
written out, ignored, or obliterated. Someone could say: They never
existed. It's a singular terror.

The names of the dead have to be repeated daily. To forget them has a
meaning no one understands, but there comes a time when the fierce pain
of their absence dulls and their voices become so faint they can't be heard.

And then what do the living mean by being alive, how dare we? The year changes, the millennium, and from one day to the next, something must have been discarded, or neglected, something was abandoned, left to wither or ruin. You didn't decide to forget. People make lists, take vitamins, and they exercise. I bend over, over and over.

I'm not good at being a pawn of history.

The news reports that brain cells don't die. I never believed they did. The tenaciousness of memory, its viciousness really—witness the desire over history for revenge—has forever been a sign that the brain recovers. But it's unclear what it recovers.

Try to hang on to what you can. It's all really going. So am I. Someone else's biography seems like my life. I read it and confuse it with my own. I watch a movie, convinced it happened to me. I suppose it did happen to me. I don't know what I think anymore. I don't know what I don't think. I'm someone who tells things.

Once, I wanted to locate movie footage of tidal waves. They occurred in typical dreams. But an oceanographer told me that a tidal wave was a tsunami, it moved under the ocean and couldn't be seen. This bothered me for a long time. I wondered what it was that destroyed whole villages, just washed them away. In dreams, I'm forced to rescue myself. This morning's decision: let life rush over me. The recurring tidal wave is not about sexual thralldom, not the spectacular orgasm, not the threat of dissolution and loss of control through sex—that, too—but a wish to be overcome by life rather than to run it. To be overrun.

I don't believe any response, like invention, is sad. The world is made up of imagining. I imagine this, too. Things circle, all is flutter. Things fall down and rise up. Hope and remorse, beauty and viciousness, and imagination, wherever it doggedly hides, unveil petulant realities. I live in my own mind, and I don't. There's scant privacy for bitterness or farting or the inexpressible; historically, there was an illusion of privacy. Illusions are necessary. The wretched inherit what no one wants.

What separates me from the world? Secret thoughts?

What Americans fear is the inability to have a world different from their fathers' and mothers'. That's why we move so much, to escape history.

Margaret Fuller said: I accept the universe. I try to embrace it. But I leave it to others to imagine the world in ways I can't.

I leave it to others.

Out of nothing comes language and out of language comes nothing and everything. I know there will be stories. Certainly, there will always be stories.

CONTRIBUTORS

GRACE AGUILAR (1816–1847) was the author of *The Spirit of Judaism*, *The Women of Israel*, and several other books of fiction and nonfiction, as well as poetry. Her novella *The Perez Family* was the first book about British Jews written by a Jew. "The Escape" was first published in the collection *Records of Israel* (1844).

STEVE AYLETT is the author of *Lint*, *Slaughtermatic*, and a dozen other books. Though effectively about 9/11, "Gigantic" was first published in 1998.

ROBERT BRADLEY is writing a novel in stories titled *Invisible World*. "Square of the Sun" is from this collection. He teaches the Alexander technique on Long Island and in NYC and works nights in a psych ward.

DENNIS COOPER is the author of the novels *God Jr.* (Grove Press, 2005), *The Sluts* (Carroll & Graf, 2005), *My Loose Thread* (Canongate, 2002), and The George Miles Cycle, an interconnected sequence of five novels that comprises *Closer* (1989), *Frisk* (1991), *Try* (1994), *Guide* (1997), and *Period* (2000), all published by Grove Press. His books have been translated into sixteen languages. He's the editor of Little House on the Bowery, an imprint of Akashic Press. He currently lives in Paris and Los Angeles.

LUCY CORIN's novel *Everyday Psychokillers: A History for Girls* was published by FC2 in 2004. Her stories appear in such publications as

Ploughshares, Southern Review, Conjunctions, as *Fiction International.* She teaches fiction at the University of California, Davis.

ELLIOTT DAVID is a writer and artist; he lives in New York. Contact: elliottwdavid@gmail.com.

MATTHEW DERBY is the author of *Super Flat Times.* He lives in Pawtucket, Rhode Island.

CAROL EMSHWILLER's new novel, *The Secret City,* will be out in April 2007. Another short story collection will appear shortly after that.

BRIAN EVENSON is the author of seven books of fiction, most recently *The Open Curtain.*

NEIL GAIMAN is the critically acclaimed and award-winning creator of the Sandman series of graphic novels, and the author of several novels and children's books, the most recent of which include *Anansi Boys* and the short-story collection *Fragile Things.* Originally from England, Gaiman now lives in the United States.

JEFF GOLDBERG is former vice president of a Fortune 500 insurance company. He lives in New York City. Contact: jeff@mixedmetaphors.net.

THEODORA GOSS was born in Hungary. Although she grew up on the classics of English literature, her writing has been influenced by an Eastern European literary tradition in which the boundaries between the real and the fantastic are often ambiguous. She is currently completing a PhD in English literature at Boston University. Her first short-story collection, *In the Forest of Forgetting,* was published in 2006 by Wildside Press. Visit her at www.theodoragoss.com.

NATHANIEL HAWTHORNE (1804–1864) was the author of *The Scarlet Letter, The House of the Seven Gables,* and other classic works of

312 | CONTRIBUTORS

American literature. "Earth's Holocaust" was first published in 1844 and then collected in *Mosses from an Old Manse* (1846).

JARED HOHL was born and raised in southeastern Iowa. "Fraise, Menthe, et Poivre 1978" is his first published story.

SHELLEY JACKSON is the author of *Half Life*, *The Melancholy of Anatomy*, hypertexts including the classic *Patchwork Girl*, several children's books, and "Skin," a story published in tattoos on the skin of 2,095 volunteers. She is cofounder of the Interstitial Library and headmistress of the Shelley Jackson Vocational School for Ghost Speakers and Hearing-Mouth Children. She lives in Brooklyn and at www.ineradicablestain.com.

URSULA K. LE GUIN is the internationally acclaimed author of twenty novels, ten collections of short stories, six volumes of poetry, four volumes of translation, thirteen books for children, and four collections of essays. She has three children and three grandchildren and lives in Oregon.

STACEY LEVINE's books include *My Horse and Other Stories* and *Dra—*; her novel *Frances Johnson* was published last year by Clear Cut Press. She also wrote a libretto for a puppet opera about the Quileute tribes of Washington State. Formerly a creative writing instructor, she is now working on another book.

TAO LIN is the author of the poetry collection *you are a little bit happier than i am* (Action Books, 2006) and the story collection *Today the Sky Is Blue and White with Bright Blue Spots and a Small Pale Moon and I Will Destroy Our Relationship Today* (Bear Parade, 2006). He earned an MFA in hamsters from The Pessoa Institute. His web site is http://reader-of-depressing-books.blogspot.com/.

KELLY LINK is the author of two collections, *Stranger Things Happen* and *Magic for Beginners*. With her husband, Gavin J. Grant, she edits the fantasy half of *The Year's Best Fantasy and Horror*.

H. P. LOVECRAFT (1890–1937) was the author of *At the Mountains of Madness*, *The Dream-Quest of Unknown Kadath*, and many other works of horror fiction, as well as *Supernatural Horror in Literature*, a nonfiction study of the genre. "Nyarlathotep" was first published in the November 1920 issue of the *United Amateur*.

GARY LUTZ is the author of *Stories in the Worst Way* and *I Looked Alive*.

RICK MOODY is the author of the novels *Garden State*, which won the Pushcart Press Editors' Book Award, *The Ice Storm*, and *Purple America*; two collections of stories, *The Ring of Brightest Angels Around Heaven* and *Demonology*; and a memoir, *The Black Veil*, winner of the PEN/Martha Albrand Award. He has also received the Addison Metcalf Award, the Paris Review's Aga Khan Prize, and a Guggenheim Fellowship. He lives in Brooklyn, New York.

MICHAEL MOORCOCK published *Outlaws Own* magazine, at the age of nine (in 1949) and made his first professional appearance in print at the age of sixteen. A professional editor at seventeen, he became editor of *New Worlds* in 1964 with policies creating what became known as the New Wave. He has won many literary awards and lives in Texas and France.

ADAM NEMETT is the writer/director of the narrative feature film *The Instrument* (Magister Productions, 2005).He received a BA from Princeton University (Religion, Creative Writing) and an MFA from California College of the Arts. He lives in San Francisco, where he's working on his first novel.

JOSIP NOVAKOVICH was born in Croatia and moved to the United States at the age of twenty. He has published a novel (*April Fool's Day*, HarperCollins), three story collections (*Infidelities: Stories of War and Lust*, *Yolk*, and *Salvation and Other Disasters*), two collections of narrative essays (*Plum Brandy: Croatian Journeys* and *Apricots from Chernobyl*), and was anthologized in Best American Poetry, Pushcart Prize, and O. Henry Prize

Stories. His work has been published in translation in a dozen countries. He teaches in the MFA program at Pennsylvania State University.

JOYCE CAROL OATES is the author, most recently, of *Black Girl / White Girl* (Ecco HarperCollins).

COLETTE PHAIR used to think that people would just keep getting taller—that mom and grandma would be giants by the time she grew up, till she figured out that people die. Her book *Nightmare in Silicon*, winner of the Chiasmus Press First Book Competition, is about a woman who gets turned into a robot, and will be published this year. Photographs to accompany "The End of the Future" can be found at her Web site, Apocolis.com.

EDGAR ALLAN POE (1809–1849) was the author of numerous poems, including "Annabel Lee" and "The Raven," short stories, including "The Fall of the House of Usher" and "The Masque of the Red Death," and the novel *The Narrative of Arthur Gordon Pym of Nantucket*.

TERESE SVOBODA has published nine books of prose and poetry, including *Tin God* (University of Nebraska Press, 2006). Geoffry O'Brien named her *Cannibal* one of the best books in print. She won an O. Henry Prize for this short story, grants from the New York State Council on the Arts and the New York Foundation for the Arts, and the Bobst Prize.

JUSTIN TAYLOR is a graduate of the University of Florida and The New School. He lives in Brooklyn, New York. http://www.justindtaylor.net/.

LYNNE TILLMAN is a novelist, short-story writer, and essayist. Her fifth novel, *American Genius, A Comedy*, was published by Soft Skull Press in October 2006.

DEB OLIN UNFERTH's fiction has appeared in *Harper's, Conjunctions, Fence, Noon,* and the Pushcart Prize anthologies. Her first book is forthcoming from McSweeney's.

H. G. WELLS (1866–1946) was the author of *The War of the Worlds*, and other novels, as well as the science fiction classics "The Time Machine" and "The Invisible Man." "The Star" was first published in *The Graphic* (1897).

ALLISON WHITTENBERG is the author of *Sweet Thang* (Random House, 2006) and *Life Is Fine* (Random House, 2007). She is a native of Philadelphia.

DIANE WILLIAMS is the author of five books of fiction. A new book—*It Was Like My Trying to Have a Tender-Hearted Nature*—is due out from FC2 in the fall of 2007. She is the founding editor of *Noon*.

PERMISSIONS

Time, and Fate (Grove Weidenfeld, 1990) and then in *Excitability: Selected Stories* (Dalkey Archive Press, 1998).

"The Escape—A Tale of 1755" by Grace Aguilar, "Earth's Holocaust" by Nathaniel Hawthorne, "The Conversation of Eiros and Charmion" by Edgar Allan Poe, and "The Star" by H. G. Wells are all works in the public domain.